HARD FEELINGS

HARD

DON BREDES

FEELINGS

NEW YORK   1977   ATHENEUM

Library of Congress Cataloging in Publication Data
Bredes, Don.
    Hard feelings
    I. Title.
PZ4.B8294Har   [PS3552.R363]   813'.5'4   76-42213
ISBN 0-689-10745-5

Published simultaneously in Canada by
McClelland and Stewart Ltd.
Manufactured in the United States of America by
The Book Press, Brattleboro, Vermont
Designed by Kathleen Carey
First Edition

To my mother and father

HARD FEELINGS

LEE AND I CADDY at the Crescent Club. Though it's a fancy place, we hardly make anything, maybe ten bucks a week, and the job is frankly a pain in the ass. But it is money. We actually don't go that much, say once a week after school and on weekends. The weekends are when you make the money.

Today we're on the bench half-asleep at 7:00 A.M. just for show really, because Hawkins, the caddymaster, can never see his way through to us until ten or eleven—if we get lucky. We sit slumped on the bleachers under the elms behind the clubhouse, watching the white ball-washers on the first tee come into focus through the mist. Hawkins, wearing those seersucker Bermudas and thin maroon kneesocks, comes out of his office by the kitchen with the list of parties and reservations. He's like some coach, only we don't feel like part of the team, Lee and I, since he never flaps his liver-lips at us. He might call up later down at the caddy house, but he never talks to us then either, even if he wants one of us sent up.

There can be about forty caddies in the bleachers, and he looks around quick and says, "Eagle, Finster, Houghton, and X-ray, and Michaels, and Crossley . . ." He'll pick ten, fifteen of us on a busy day. Some guys like Eagle and X-ray are older, in their thirties, and they live on this, poor bastards—except they make good money, in tournaments especially. They smoke constantly and shoot lit matches at each other, yukking like kids. They always get out. It's their livelihood. You figure the other guys that get picked must suck up to Hawkins, the way he knows all their names and wrinkles his eyes when they answer, "Saddle me up," and other insanities. Then, to the rest of us who he never glances at (he's usually walking away when he says it), he calls out, "Well, that's all for now, boys, and I'm real sorry. Run on down to the playhouse. We'll give a ring-a-ling." At this, Lee throws him his patented royal finger, swinging his whole arm up from below his hip like a punch. It is a gesture of frustration for all of us who got up so early for nothing, which is about the same crew every week.

The caddy house is just a two-room cabin with chairs in it down back of the tennis pro's shop, sort of hidden in the trees. An old geezer named Roscoe runs the place. He smokes Camels and coughs up clams into a hanky which he keeps in his pocket, and he's always talking about mashies and niblicks with the guys that suck up to *him* (I could care less about golf), as if that would help—all Roscoe does is answer the phone. Also, in one room he sells candy and poppy seed rolls out of a glass case. In the other room, some Negro guys pitch nickels or play some advanced form of mumblety-peg with their knives. Today, as soon as we get down here, Lee goes outside to take a nap in a heap of pine needles. It's warm out for April. I read Roscoe's *National Enquirer*. "Boy Cuts Up Grandmother, Feeds to Goldfish" is about this kid in England, Thomas Fewkes, really young too, like nine, who stabs the old woman in her sleep, then drags her downstairs and out into the backyard, where he whacks her into pieces with a hatchet. The goldfish are huge, not the indoor type.

Then I go bounce a golf ball off the stoop in back, and I think about Lee. He said last night he got a finger in Helen Bundy. Maybe he did. He said I could've smelled his finger, and I told him I wouldn't want to smell his finger or anything else, and that was that, but Helen Bundy worries me. Lee and I have this ten-dollar bet on who'll get the first I.I., which stands for Insert the Instrument, a saying we got from his parents' marriage manual, where they can't stop referring to your bone as the instrument. All along I've somehow figured to win the ten bucks, not that I've got any hot prospects lined up, but I just can't imagine Lee's little bent dink doing the damage. Well, I do have one prospect I should mention: Leslie Wolstein. How hot it is I don't know, but she did invite me over to where she's babysitting tonight, and I have heard from her best friend that she may even want to do it, but as they say, you don't count your chickens. Unlike Helen Bundy, Leslie is a virgin, so you can see why Helen Bundy could be trouble. Her old boyfriend was Sal Anunziato, a greasy all-conference guard for South Huntington. Sal is the type who could pave the way. I mean, you figure Sal almost had to get it in, not that he's so handsome, but she's so ugly. Not that ugly, really, but just plain as a brick for a cheerleader. At least she *was* a cheerleader until this fall when she and some other girls got caught painting HOMOS in huge letters across the front of Hobbes High where you go into the auditorium. It's still there. They'll have to sandblast it before graduation.

I once got some tit off Helen Bundy while we were on a Thespian field trip to New York City to see a play called *Trojan Women*. She got to go along because she'd helped with make-up during the one-act play competition. We were in the driver's ed Rambler station wagon, which has one of those seats that face backwards. That's where we sat. Of course, normally I would sit with Barbara, my girlfriend, and we would probably make out some, too, but she had the flu, and she missed the field trip. Helen's mouth tasted kind of like bad milk, so I nuzzled her neck mostly and stuck my tongue in her ear—something new for me—but she turned her head. I couldn't unhook her bra, but I managed to get the back of my thumb down inside, and I wiggled it against her nipple. I told Lee it was my whole hand. He always wants the details. I said that nipple got hot and hard like a jujube you suck in the movies and wouldn't he like a bite. I mean, who knows what deeps I could've sounded on a real date, but Sal Anunziato popped into her life about then, and besides I felt a little sick for a while afterwards, you know, when I thought of Helen breathing hard, her smell, and her oily forehead. Also, I had Barbara to consider. She luckily never did find out about me and Helen Bundy, but only because it was nighttime, and nobody in the Rambler could get a good glimpse of what we were doing back there. I'm thinking all this over, holding the golf ball in my hand, when Lee comes around the corner.

He says, "What are you hiding back here for?"

"Just throwing a golf ball."

"Oh, yeah?"

"Yeah. And I was thinking of you and hot Helen Bundy," I admit, knowing this will flatter him, not that he needs it.

Lee smiles. "Huh!"

"Did you really get a finger in her?" I don't know why I should doubt his word, except he's only been out with her twice, and Helen still proudly wears Sal's fat Class of '63 ring on a chain around her neck.

"You're damn straight I got a finger in her. Shit, she was ripe for it. She was hot. I probably could've plugged her right there, but I can wait. The I.I. is next, I swear. There was just enough smell to beat off with this morning."

"You didn't beat off this morning," I say. Who would get up at six to beat off?

"Hell I didn't. This morning, last night . . . what do you care anyway?"

I don't say anything. Lee crouches on the stoop, yawning, and I throw the golf ball at him. He catches it. I'm not sure if he's more of a man because he's got so much juice or whether I am because I control it better. In junior high when I would sleep over Lee's house we would have races, beating off and shooting for distance, not that they proved anything, even when I won. Also, I remember in Boy Scouts, camping in somebody's tent lit by a Coleman on the ground, we would have hard-on contests. You would see how much of your uniform you could hang on your bone like a clothes-peg until it gave up. Geoffrey Mumford once hung both his shoes on there, tied together by the laces. But that didn't prove anything either, except that camp was pretty boring. Nobody ever beat off then, as far as I know. We were eleven, twelve, so young. It seems stupid when I think back on it now. And it's stupid to talk about beating off all the time the way Lee does. I mean, now everybody does it, so why talk about it?

I'm sitting next to Lee on the stoop. Some brown bird, a sparrow, is scratching in the pine needles. He is hungry, like me. Birds eat one hell of a lot of food every day, in spite of what you hear. Lee throws the ball at it, but the bird hops into the air when his arm jerks up. I can hear the Negro guys hooting in the other room.

"What do you say we hit the road?" says Lee. "We get out now, it won't be till after lunch. That pecker hasn't called down once yet."

I don't really care what we do. A few bucks would be nice, but Lee's right. If we get tapped for a loop at all, we'll be dragging bags all afternoon for the ladies' foursomes, and only because the big-time caddies can't be bothered, not that I blame them. Those ladies'll hook a ball into the woods, and you'll hear the damn thing ricochet off five or six tree trunks, and then they'll stand gabbing in the shade for half an hour while you hunt through the prickers for it. You can't bring out a ball you've been saving in your pocket either, because all their balls have little gold monograms stenciled on. To tell you the truth, I have no love for caddying. Lee got me into it, telling me it was easy money, but even when you get out it's not easy. For example, on the long fourteenth you have to stand on a rise fifty yards ahead of the tee so you can see where the ball goes. Lose a ball on the fairway and you can lose your tip, too. Once I was on the fourteenth waiting on the rise with Weisner, a squirty 105-pound guy who was a wrestler. We were leaning in the bags, looking out toward where the first drive had bounced. Then a Dunlop smashed about a hundred miles an hour by some pharmacist with long sideburns bulleted into Weisner's thigh. For as much as it must've hurt (especially considering there would've been one less squirty guy around if he'd been beaned), he took it all right, not exactly crying, just gulping there on the ground like a fish. But you could tell the pharmacist had decided Weisner had got in the way of his best drive all afternoon, even though poor Weisner probably saved it from the damn trees. They're all like that. Blow their concentration on one shot, and you've blown a whole round that was headed for the low eighties. Golf is absurd, a game for lazy people. But it's better that way, I guess.

Otherwise, they might want to carry their own clubs.

So Lee and I angle down through the trees by the grass tennis courts, where a few old bags are taking a lesson, swatting every other ball over the fence. That's my game, tennis, though I've never had a chance to play on grass. Last year as a sophomore, I made the varsity, by beating Lee in fact. We've grown up playing together, and since he knows I'm better, I don't think he felt bad about it. I mean, he felt bad enough (nobody wants to be stuck on the dippy J.V.), but he understood. Anyway, this spring we made the varsity together, paired up in the first doubles slot. Our high school hasn't lost a match in seven years, so it's sort of a big deal.

We follow a dirt utility road that winds through the woods past a police department shooting range they don't use any more and out the back gate (just a chain between posts) to the paved road. In these woods there are raccoons, rabbits, and some black squirrels we hunted once with bows and arrows to no avail. There used to be deer also, but New York City slinks its way out along the island, pushing the suburbs and the deer out to Sag Harbor, the Hamptons, and all, where the woods are flat and scrubby. They're pretty thick out there now, the poor, dumb animals. If you ask me, the woods they're left with are hardly woods at all, but what can you do? In the twenties, Long Island was a popular place for the slick and wealthy. Now it's a popular place for just about everybody, which is the way those things go.

That's how we came to live here, in fact. My father's in construction, and when I was five he moved us here from Maryland so he could work on some big project, the Brookhaven atom-smasher. My mother found this cottage she talked the old man into buying, and we've been in it ever since, though now my mother hates it with a passion. It was small even then, and Jane, the youngest of my three sisters, wasn't born yet. I don't know, I guess some decisions you make are more important than you realize at the time you make them, more far-reaching, anyway, which is the same thing. We were only going to stay a year, and now it's been eleven.

Lee and I are kicking a soda can from side to side so it rings over the asphalt and holding our thumbs out half-heartedly for rides, but nobody stops. Actually, we don't have that far to walk, about three miles through a couple housing developments. Suddenly, something thunks onto the road in front of us.

I say, "Hey, somebody's chucking things at us."

Another cracks onto the road ahead. You can't tell where they're coming from, so, not taking any chances, we zigzag across the pavement and duck behind a thick hedge at the foot of some lawn. Another rips through the hedge leaves.

Lee shouts, "Hey, you! Cut the shit!"

"Don't yell, you'll rile him up," I say.

"It's rocks," Lee says. "*Rocks.*"

"Just keep low," I say. "He can't see us."

"You could get *killed* by a rock."

One thuds hard into the ground behind us. They must be coming from the hillside across the street, up above the grove of dogwoods. Now I remember whose house is up there, past the dogwoods, at the end of a sweeping driveway.

I say, "It's Richard Linwood. That fuckhead."

"How do you know?"

We're both crouching close in against the hedge stalks. "Because that's his father's house up there, I think. He visits him on weekends. He used to." Richard lives with just his mother.

"That asshole. He's got toys in his attic." Lee jumps up and shouts, "Hey, asshole, looks like the factory forgot more than two hands." He squats again. A rock thuds behind us.

"You idiot," I say. Lee can be very reckless. "You want him to come down after us, or what?"

"What do you want to do? Sit here and shiver? He's after us already."

Richard Linwood was born with one arm that ends in a stump. It's got fingers on the end like pencil erasers. He's quite crazy, but not because of his stump. I mean, I know other deformed people who aren't crazy like Richard. I was friends with him in fifth grade and through one summer, though he is older. In those days Richard's mother worked nights as a nurse, and in the daytime she would mostly sleep in her room downstairs with the air-conditioner humming, so at his house we could do whatever we felt like. He had a magnifying glass big as a plate that he would use in the sun to burn ants with. They would pop. He sizzled the heads off of plastic cowboys, saying they were Mr. Carcanno, his teacher. He also would burn me when I wasn't looking. He once put a hole through my sneaker and sock. He laughed about everything, and I thought it was funny, too, I guess, except when it was supposed to be my sneaker. He was smart then in school, but now he gets in trouble all the time, and he's absent often, and he has a collection of German army stuff in his room, helmets, flags, seals, shirts, bayonets, which he buys in these special sales they have, like conventions in New York. It's a club. I wouldn't mind having one real swastika, but I wouldn't *collect* that junk. It's too symbolic.

"I know he's after us," I say, "but you shouldn't antagonize him."

"Jesus, what did *I* do?"

"You made fun of him."

"So what? The prick is throwing rocks at us."

"That's what I mean. He's dangerous."

"So? You think he scares me?" Lee squints fiercely out through the hedge.

Of course I think Lee is scared. When some maniac that you can't see is chucking these potato-size rocks at you, you're scared. It's that simple. But I can't tell Lee that. He gets mad when I start sounding logical. More rocks keep landing, but they don't get much closer. We slip down along the hedge. At the end of it, we break off down the street and around a bend, then up into the woods to follow a shortcut we know. We're both a little shaky when we start walking again.

Lee says, "Jesus, you know, I hate it when I act like a chicken. Because I'm not a chicken. We should've done something. We should've charged him. We should've gone up there and shoved those rocks up the fucker's ass, you know? But shit, we can still do something. We can plan some night raid, like for tomorrow night. You wanna?"

"You're nuts," I say. Even in sports that's the way Lee is, passionate and full of rage. He'll slam his racket into the fence if he misses an overhead, and he'll hit balls at you if he thinks you made a bad call. I'm not that way. I'm sort of the opposite, seemingly thoughtful, not overaggressive. Three years ago, Richard Linwood walked up to me on the beach and shot a glob of spit into my face. The reason he did it was, at the time, I was on the bus safety patrol. I got to wear a white sash and a badge. It's something I expected I would love, and it turned out to be a miserable responsibility. Anyway, I had given Richard a summons for something, kicking somebody or running in the aisle, and when he met me a week later on the beach, he spat on my cheek and eye. My father was right there, too, lying on his towel, but I just couldn't react. I was paralyzed. Right now I think I should've bitten Richard's nose off and stomped on it. His arm, though, is like a club. He can hit things much harder with it than with a regular hand. My father was furious. Later he said to me, "You got to hit the bastard. Belt him with a stick. Knee him in the colyoons. You're gonna hate yourself if you don't. I *mean* it. You can't worry about a busted tooth or a split lip. It's your mental attitude you got to protect. You stick up for yourself, understand? Or you amount to zero. *Zero.*" The old man's right, of course. But when an episode like that happens, you don't think about your old man's advice, you just do what you do. I can't change that, no matter how much he thinks I should—which doesn't mean I'm a zero. That is, I have to find other methods of sticking up for myself, methods you could call sly.

Lee is saying, "OK? How about it? Tomorrow night. You know where he lives?"

"I'm busy tomorrow night," I say.

"Busy? Like how?"

"Like with Leslie, remember?" I explained all this to him once. He knows I'm meeting her at the Hendrickses' house, and he also knows I may have a shot at his ten bucks.

He says, "Oh, right. Here, I got it. Why don't you tell her you're tied up. You got other very serious plans."

"Yeah, you wish. Listen, I just hope you're saving up those nickels. Tomorrow night is *the* night. The hairy instrument takes the big dive." I raise my eyebrows and pat my fly.

"Huh! You're so full of shit. All right, so next week we plan something for Linwood. We'll figure something, don't worry."

Lee's the one who's full of shit. He enjoys inventing plots of harsh, complicated revenge, but that's about as far as he gets. True, I go along with him when I feel like it. I have a few evil qualities, I have to admit. But really there are sinister things about everybody—unless you're very religious. They give you a complete personality. Two summers ago our honeysuckle woods was torn up by machines. Lee and I had a fort in there that we painstakingly constructed in the brick foundation of some long-gone house. The fort had a roof and a lantern and rugs and tables inside, even a kind of fireplace. We pulled vines and leaves and dirt down over the top so you could hardly see it unless you were looking for it. But someone wanted the land all scraped off to build houses on. At night they would leave the bulldozer and truck in the woods. We knocked the gas cap off the bulldozer with a crowbar and poured a box of sugar into the tank. Lee said it would destroy the engine. I guess it did because the police came house-to-house with a notepad asking for information. Maybe a few kids suspected us, but nobody said so. It was too serious. And my mother probably missed the sugar, but she didn't say anything either. Now on that lot there are three houses, the Gallaghers', the Nicholses', and the Roerles'.

At Lee's place we see his mother's Valiant is gone. Right away Lee wants to go upstairs and take out the marriage manual so we can read the ring part again. To arouse her husband, who is somehow a dud in this section, the wife is supposed to put her wedding ring up inside her, then get all dressed and ask her husband to hunt it out. I don't know why that should work, even if to us it's very intriguing. I mean, a dud's a dud. Why should he care about her ring? Maybe he would be glad she lost it. I tell Lee, forget it, I'm going home for lunch, and I'll call him later. He calls me a pansy. He can be surprisingly irritable.

We live a half mile apart, less if you cut through the woodlots and backyards. We have made our own little path over the years. Walking along it, I always wonder how many millions of times our soft feet had to keep slapping down so that the undergrowth would give us our own narrow, brown stretch of territory. And how fast will it come swarming in again when we leave? Overhead, a jet tears through the air. It sounds like a blowtorch. As I approach our house, I hear Zekey, my Dalmatian, barking. He's whining and pushing at the door of his pen with his foot. I reach over the fence to pet him. We can't let him out too much because he's bitten a few people, I don't know why. He's very friendly. But kids relentlessly tease him and throw things into his pen. They do that because our family is secretly resented around here, I suppose. Our neighborhood is quite ritzy, right on the water and all, with no Jews or Negroes or anything. My mother can't stand the ignorance and selfishness of most of the people who live around us, and she doesn't mind telling them either. So we haven't joined their private beach club, and my parents don't go to the barbecues or the dances, not that they would if things were different anyway. Of course, everybody is very kind, especially to us happy kids, but they would never stop in for a visit, and underneath, they would really like to get rid of us. Our house is sort of an eyesore, with the shutters falling off, the shingles cracked, the bushes growing every which way, and the cesspool overflowing into a smelly pool in the backyard. That's strange, I know, when you consider my father is in construction and has these two beautiful, varnished tool boxes downstairs full of saws and planes and mallets and levels, but people are the way they are, and I don't know the answer. So kids take out these feelings of hate on our house by throwing eggs at it on Halloween, and they tease poor Zekey. He has a disease of the intestines that gives him the continual runs. There are dry pancakes of shit all around the pen. Every week or so I climb in there and shovel them into a bag. It's an awful job.

Down by the front of the house my father is leaning into the engine of our white Buick working on something. I know he would like me to be fascinated by mechanics the way he was as a boy growing up in Brooklyn, but I'm just not, and I can't help it. For Christmas one year he bought me a radio kit with all these tiny colored parts and a book of instructions with diagrams like mazes, but I couldn't work myself up over it. It was hopeless. Finally he put the thing together with me silently watching. I felt guilty and incompetent, you know, standing in the basement by his work desk, fetching the solder and asking little questions. He turned the thing into a genuine radio, though, and it was fun for the next few days tuning in the old man down at Lee's. He would say, "This is Station WFAH"—his initials—"with a wonderful selection of your musical favorites," and he would let my sister Claudia sing for five seconds, and then he would break in to tell a joke. Now that radio is stuck in a box up in the attic. It gives me a twinge just to see it.

"Don't fuss now," I say to Zekey. "Later we'll go down for a run on the beach." He loves that. He'll gallop along looking for stimulating things to sniff. But now he keeps whining and gazing sadly up at me. "You ignorant old dog," I say.

I cross the driveway to get out of sight behind the back of the house before my father spots me because I'm afraid he'll want me down there aiming a flashlight at some black mechanism of the car, and the plain fact is at the moment I am starving. I ease the screen door shut behind me. It's quiet. Nobody's around, I guess because it's too nice a day to be home inside, seventy-four degrees, says the thermometer outside the window. A lot of dirty glasses and pots and pans are piled next to the sink. From the refrigerator I take a fat, nubbly cucumber, some American cheese, an onion, a tomato, and the mustard, and I carefully build this sandwich that's too thick to bite. The ingredients keep sliding out like they're trying to escape.

Then I wander into the livingroom and plop myself onto the couch. Little dust bits swirl up through the sunbeams. There's this U.N. report I'm supposed to be writing for history, but I am not motivated in the least. I feel like a piece of furniture. Some soft whirring noise is coming out of the background, I realize. I look around, and it's the record player going without a record on it. I stretch across the arm of the couch to reach the knob, but I don't switch it off. Instead, after a few seconds, I set my father's big can of Sir Walter Raleigh tobacco on there. The record player keeps revolving, but slower, like it's hypnotizing me. It goes, "Les-lie. Les-lie. Les-lie." Ever since she invited me to Hendricks's for tonight, the girl has been buzzing behind all my thoughts like a big fly in your room. Like yesterday I was supposed to phone Barbara the way I promised her on Friday, but the day wore on, and I just couldn't bring myself to do it because, shit, there I would've been, joking and talking gentle and using our private expressions with her like I would normally do—only my whole thought pattern would've been concentrated on Leslie and on how I was madly hoping to nail her with the old salami the next evening. I had a dream about Leslie last night, too, but I can't remember how it went.

The back door squeaks open. It's my sister, one of them, I can't see who. I sit up. I hear her rummaging through the refrigerator, for some fruit probably. Then she bangs out the door again. I look over at Sir Walter etched black on the orange can. He's still going round and round, slowly, with his flat eye fastened on me like he is the most patient man that ever lived.

CHAPTER 2

SO, WHAT DO YOU KNOW, here I am at the Hendrickses' fancy house, with one foot on their rhododendron and one on the electric meter, just high enough off the ground to see through the filmy curtains. And Leslie's in there all right, crosslegged on a hassock, looking at the TV. Since the kid's not in sight, I figure he must be in the sack, but you can't count on sneaky little peckers like him, I know from experience. My foot's killing me. I've got it jammed in the fork of this overgrown bush with no socks under my sneakers. I work my foot loose and drop silently into the dead leaves. It's hard to know what to do, not feeling really sure about the kid, though she did say nine, nine thirty.

From her shoulders up the TV was in the way, but she had on that tight red French ski sweater which I'm familiar with from seeing it a few times in school. I pad around from the side of the house to the front porch, where there's a light on over the door. Then I stand off to the side to think about this because, actually, being honest, what I've done up to now with Leslie hasn't been all that hot. I must say *she's* been hot, which is part of the problem.

Like last month we were on the beach in this boat locker. How we got there was at school, during lunch, the French club had been having a brownie sale for our trip to a big French restaurant. I had coq au vin, which in reality was chicken and very good, though you might not think so. It was strong-flavored. Leslie and I were selling on the same lunch period and making jokes about brownies and turds, not very sophisticated, but kind of sexy if you know what I mean. Leslie lives not far from Nathan Hale Rock, a monument they put up where Nathan Hale supposedly landed on the beach before the British caught him and hanged him as a spy in New York City. So I asked her if she ever went for walks down by the rock, and she said sure, and I said so did I but I never saw her down there, and she said she never saw me either. When did I usually go, she asked me. About four on Fridays, I said, which wasn't true. I hardly ever go down there. She probably doesn't either.

Anyway, that Friday was our first date. It was March and very cold and windy at the beach. I had gloves on and a hat, and I never wear a hat. Walking down there, I started thinking she wouldn't show up, it was so cold. I had a blanket I took from the house, though, just in case. I was edging along the seawall, looking down at the sand and the water out to where Connecticut was a blue line across the Sound. Seaweed and sand and ice were knotted into clumps along the tideline. The sky was gray. The bay hardly ever freezes over, being salt, but it can if it's cold long enough. It was solid once when I was about ten. I remember because Lee and Louie Baum and I were down there smacking rocks across the ice with sticks like hockey players, except the ice was too rough really, and at the same time we all saw a box, or a corner of it, sticking out of the ice. It was a Campbell's soup carton tied with string. We went crazy trying to hack it out with our sticks and shouting who had dibs on what was inside and who saw it first and so on. I don't remember what we thought was in there. What it was was a few drowned puppies, mutts that looked stuffed, with no hair.

I was thinking about that box and looking out from the seawall when Leslie said, loud, "*Well*. What a surprise meeting you here."

I looked around. "Oh, hi," I said. "Don't I know you from somewhere? You look familiar."

"It's possible," she said.

"Wait, it's coming to me. Could we have met in the cafeteria this past Tuesday?"

"It's possible," she said. "Brownies?"

"Is that what they were?" Big joke, I know, but she laughed. Actually, we'd known each other, sort of, since sixth grade. Her father's a Jewish doctor. Her whole family's Jewish. She was wearing one of those green loden coats with a hood and loops instead of buttonholes. She had her hands in the pockets. The hood wasn't up and her brown hair fell into it. A hairband held it off her face, which always, it seems to me, has a slightly yellow tone to it. The rest of her skin does too, I found out later. The cold made her eyes look bright.

Looking back on it, I guess it was obvious what we'd made the date for. Without ever having done much more with a girl than make out (plus that one feel I got in on Helen Bundy), I can tell somehow when a girl wants it. I could tell at the brownie sale that Leslie wanted it, and I'd never even held hands with her.

So we sat there in the cold talking about Nathan Hale, what it would be like to be hanged, and Puerto Ricans. Set into the rock, on three sides of it, you can see rectangular blanks as big as table tops. The blanks are where the bronze plaques about Nathan Hale used to be. His story and famous last words were on them. A couple years ago Puerto Ricans from South Huntington came down here drunk, tore off the plaques, and threw them in the bay. Also, one morning once, my father was driving my mother, my sisters, and me to the Green Stamp Redemption Center through the housing projects. I was getting a bat. Suddenly, my father said, "Lock your doors! Lock your doors! Press down your buttons!" We were stopped for a light, and, in the street behind us, running alongside the cars, was a Puerto Rican. Other Puerto Ricans were after him. He tried to open my door while we were moving, picking up speed. He looked right in at me through the glass, but he wasn't seeing me. He was terrified as hell.

Well, by the time our conversation dwindled down to the subject of the weather, I had my arm around her, and she was leaning against me. We had the blanket over our legs, but I was freezing and trying not to show it. Every time I let out a shiver she would say, "Are you cold?" And I'd say, "Nah, I'm all right."

It went on like that a little while, me trying to think up interesting or amusing things to say, shivering in between, until finally, with my hand under her chin, I got her to tilt up her head, and I sort of dropped my mouth onto hers, and we were kissing.

Leslie is a hot one, as I said. She went right away to French kissing, putting her hands on my neck to draw me in close. I got my hand inside the loden coat, but my glove was still on. "Wait, wait, Bernie," she said. "Let's find someplace out of the wind."

We jumped down into the sand where I thought it would be better in the lee of the wall, but she wanted to go someplace else. So we pulled each other along the beach until we came to a row of boat lockers. Most had rusted locks on them. We dug the hard sand away from in front of one without a lock so the door would come open. I pulled it out just enough for us to squeeze in. It was empty except for some chain and soda cans on the floor. I slid the chain to the corner so I could spread out the blanket. Lying down, we could just barely fit together if we didn't stretch out.

The most exciting thing then was she just opened her coat, even though it wasn't any warmer in the boat locker. We were making out again, and I had my one leg between hers with my boner against her thigh and my hipbone against her crotch. I knew she could feel it. I worked my hand up under her sweatshirt onto her bra, and she has *jugs* for a junior. All the while we were kissing. I tried my tongue in her ear. It didn't bother her the way it bothered Helen Bundy. Then she started to moan, and she made little grunts, and she moved against me.

I got my hand around back to undo her bra, and I started to moan back at her, something I never do. I don't get emotional enough to seriously moan. She leaned on an elbow to let me undo the clasp. When I got my hand around front, I was almost afraid to touch her naked jug. I didn't want to seem too horny or anxious, so I rubbed her stomach, and eased my way up slowly. I could actually see the bottom of it almost to the nipple. I closed in on it, and what do you think—she worked *her* hand down to my bone and started stroking it. I realized it was like a reciprocal trade agreement. I mean, you hold her hand, she can hold back. You put an arm around her, she can lean into you. Then maybe you can kiss her. If she Frenches, maybe you can try for tit. If you can get some tit on the outside, you can maybe lie on her. If you can get some tit on the *in*side, the way I had, she can grab your bone on the outside. Before I could find out what would happen if I went for her crotch, I just shot my wad all in my jeans. That was that. I mean suddenly her spidery hand was right there. I had hardly any warning before it was all over. The trouble was Leslie had just got going. Her hips—her whole pelvic region—was reaching up for me, and her mouth was swarming all over my face. Then what she did (when I think of this now, I grow faint), she took her hand away from squeezing my pecker, which was just beginning to fade, and the other hand away from the back of my neck, and she undid her buckle and unbuttoned her pants. The way I felt then I could have been a priest, and with her doing *that*. All along, of course, I was nuzzling and snorting into her neck, trying not to let on how my sex drive had zeroed out into a wet spot near my pocket. If you can believe it, while she was undoing her belt, I simply rolled off her. I was afraid her hand would come after my dong again, which was as limp as a noodle. I'm thinking now who would want anything more than to get some fingers in those pants, but right then, I'm saying it disgusted me, her raw desire. I felt sour, and I was freezing.

As soon as I was off her, bent into the corner with the chain, she gave me a look of fear, like she thought her quick move to her pants scared me off, or I had a seizure. So I fiercely went back to kissing her, making sure to keep my crotch out of reach. She moved toward me, moaning again. Her idea of what was going on and my idea were totally opposite. There she was, sunk in grubby passion, and I was above it. We stopped kissing, and she whispered, "What's wrong?"

"Nothing," I said, "nothing," really sincere.

She didn't say anything. Her sweatshirt was half-up, and I looked at her skin, kind of yellow. I could see the bottoms of her jugs, how they drooped down to the sides. It was strange.

Then she started saying, with her eyes closed, "I'm the

enchanted princess locked in this cold castle. In an enchanted slumber. My slumber can only be broken by a kiss from the hotshot prince." She was trying to stimulate me. "That's you," she said. Jesus.

"Aren't you cold?" I said. I was really freezing. I bent over to kiss her, and she opened her eyes, looking up. I kept kissing, but she knew it was over. I don't know if she figured it out or not, about shooting my wad. She wasn't very experienced, if you could tell anything from the way she went after my bone, so maybe she didn't figure it out. Anyway, you can see the problem. I explained it to Lee, and he said, "Some problem," but it really is. He's jealous and dense. I've talked to Leslie a couple times since then in school. And Joe Redfield had a party where everybody was making out with the lights on because of his parents. They kept walking in. I think maybe I might have made out with Leslie in the dark, like with Helen Bundy in the Rambler, since Barbara wasn't there, and in the dark Leslie and I could've slipped off somewhere, but it was hopeless.

Three days ago, when she phoned me about this baby-sitting thing, what I began to fear is that I will, as my mother says, flub the dub before I really get started, because of Leslie and her greedy hands. What also scares me is I found out she really wants to have sex.

Pam Sokel let that out the day before yesterday while we were riding through Smitty's Carwash in her mother's Oldsmobile. After school I had to stay for a tennis team meeting. Because Lee had a dentist's appointment, I was hitching alone, and Pam picked me up. When I slid onto the seat, she said to me, "Where to, you big hunk of he-man?"

I said, "When did *you* get a license?" Pam is Leslie's best friend, but you couldn't tell to look at her. Pretty all right, but no shape.

"What do you mean by that?" she said. Pam is sensitive.

"What I mean is, when the cops pull you over, do you have something to show them so we don't get arrested?"

"Look, smartass, do you want to pilot this bomb, is that it?"

I can't drive and she knows that, the little witch. "I could give it a try," I said.

"Ho, ho, ho, said Santa. It so happens I got my license today."

"Congrats."

"Thank you. My mother said to put some gas in it, but if you're good maybe I'll buzz you into town."

That got me, "if you're good." Like a little mother. She steered with both hands, and I noticed she had this cushion under her, to peer out over the hood.

"How kind of you," I said. "In town you can get a fill-up at Smitty's and they give you a free carwash."

"That's wonderful," she breathed, looking sideways at me. "Say, Leslie's babysitting Sunday at Hendricks's."

"I know."

"I know you know. She says you're going over there, on your bicycle or something. Are you?"

"It's not that far from my house."

"So I hear. Does that mean you don't have to pedal?"

"It means it'll be no trouble to stop over, if I feel like it."

"From what I hear, loverboy, you feel like it already. That's according to Leslie anyway. You *are* a loverboy, right?" Pam is quite smart in school, but on the outside there's not much sign of that. She tends to be annoying, like a snappy chihuahua. Her boyfriend is Rodney Lippett, a senior who quit the track team because they would only let him run relays. He's always walking around the halls with a Polaroid, taking pictures of you at your locker for the yearbook. But Pam is so icy, I wonder what a guy like Rodney can be getting off her.

"Oh, I'm a loverboy all right," I said. "By the way, where'd you stash old Rodney? The trunk?"

"How'd you know?" she said. "He's taking a time exposure of the spare tire."

I chuckled, looking out the window. I didn't want to give her too much for that, but it was good. She pulled into Smitty's and rolled down the window. The guy, a Negro, came out, and she said, "Fill it the whole way up." He stuck the nozzle in, just like a dick, I thought. We watched him check the oil.

Driving around back to the carwash entrance, she asked, "Say, how's things with you and Barb?"

Now I've been off and on with Barbara since eighth grade and everybody knows it. She's the first girl I ever kissed, not that that's so special, but it gives you a certain idea. She's an actress and always qualifies for the big roles in the school plays. She's why I'm in the Thespian Society. She's a redhead. I teach her how to play tennis, and her father teaches me chess strategy, at which he is a master. I make out with her, but I wouldn't try anything that might scare her or offend her, because, I'll admit, we're in love. In a way. "Good," I said. "Why do you ask?"

We lurched forward, and the chain belt began clinking us into the spray. Pam looked straight at me. "Look, Bernie," she said, "I just . . . I want to know what's up. So does Leslie."

"So she'll ask me then, won't she? Where do you come in? I don't have to outline my life for you."

"I'll tell you where I come in. Look, if you haven't guessed, Leslie *likes* you. She wouldn't be thinking about going all the way with you if she didn't."

That was it, and it made me nervous, but also proud or brave. It's hard to explain. There was an edge to her voice so I'd hear her over the carwash noises. Right at the collar button she wore a gold circle pin. Looking at that, I said, "So what? What's that supposed to mean?"

"It means she *likes* you, you clod, though I can't imagine why. But she does. And because Leslie's my friend, I have a right to look after her."

"Well, I like her, too," I said. I do like Leslie.

"*And* Barbara?"

"That's right."

"Well, ho, ho, ho—"

"—said Santa," I threw in. "You have a ho-ho-ho complex."

"Said *Barbara* when she heard all about Nathan Hale Rock."

"Are you really that piggy?"

"I might ask you the same question," she said. "Or, how's this: When you go over there to make out and do whatever else you're going to do, if Leslie asks to wear your sweater to school, will you let her?"

"I'll wait till she asks me," I said. I could never give Leslie my sweater. I'm not sure I want Barbara to wear my sweater. I don't feel that way about girls, to claim them like that. It's not healthy.

"You're a bastard," she said. "On the make and on the take."

We emerged from the carwash, and the Negro guy came around wiping off windows, polishing that stupid hood rocket. "Well, I'm glad that's not Leslie's opinion."

"Give her time," she said.

I got out. "Thanks for the ride, ma'am," I said.

"Sure, Bernie, it's been vivid."

Out of all she said, it was her sighing my name like that right at the end that gave me a twinge. Of what, I don't know.

I've moved around to the side of the house again to make double-sure the kid's not around, and now I'm thinking, what the hell does Pam Sokel know about Leslie's true feelings or about what's going to happen tonight. She's not witch enough to predict who's about to lose whose virginity and who's going to hate who because of it. Inside on the TV I can hear the Four Seasons singing "Walk Like a Man," so, instead of climbing back up the rhododendron, I shuffle through the leaves to the front of the house, feeling determined enough to rap on the door. Just as I do, I hear a car behind me in the street. I'm ready to run, but for God's sake, what's so wrong about standing on a porch?

"Who is it?" I hear Leslie say. She doesn't open the door.

"Me." This feels like a movie.

"Bernie?" A half whisper.

"No, Dracula."

She opens the door. "Oh, come in. For a second I thought you were Bernie Hergruter. I've been expecting him for a half hour."

"Je-*sus*! What happened to you?" It's her hair. One ball of curls all over. It used to be regular, you know. Just hanging down simple, not conspicuous.

"How do you like it?" She tilts her head. It's huge.

"What did you do it for?"

"It's a permanent."

"Yeah, but . . . you look like you're in a bathing cap. I almost thought you had a wig, or—"

"It's a *permanent*."

"I—"

"And you hate it, don't you?"

"I *don't* hate it. It's brand new." She is mad. I hope the kid's a heavy sleeper. "It's a shock is all. You never told me about it, when you called. You didn't tell me you were getting it."

"So?"

"So, I have to get used to it. It looks good. I think it looks good."

"You think *bull*. Why should I care what you think?"

"Shhhh," I go. She's almost yelling.

"Shush you, you moron."

We're in the hallway. It has a rubber plant in a clay pot and a mirror which Leslie is now looking into. Under that hair her neck is like a stick. In the livingroom I can see a maroon couch and a bamboo chair next to a table with a lamp that's made out of a barrel. A commercial is on the TV. The Hendrickses are wealthy people. There are plants all over. An enormous painting of the stormy sea hangs right here in the hallway.

"Seriously, Leslie, you just surprised me. I think your hair is fine, really."

"Something's wrong with the top," she says to the mirror. "It's all—it stands *up*. God, I knew it wouldn't come out. I knew it wouldn't. It cost twenty-five *dol*lars."

"Twenty-five dollars?" Wow.

"And everybody said they liked it. 'It looks great, Leslie.' Great, great, great. Great, bull-oney."

"You know, I think you'll have to get used to it like everybody else. Really. I mean, you look like a new person."

"Well, I don't care. I wanted to do it, and I did it. That's it."

"My honest opinion, though, Leslie, is I like it." By now I do like it. I can accept it.

She turns and gives me an even look. " 'Gunsmoke' is on in five minutes," she says.

I say OK, and we walk into the livingroom. "Hey, I hope the kid's not a light sleeper," I whisper, tiptoeing into the room as a joke. "Wouldn't want to wake the little devil."

"He never wakes up, and so what if he does," she says, dropping into a chair.

I sit on the couch alone. It's strange to have someone else talking while you're whispering. Things look bleak all of a sudden, so I say, "Here you go. Does a light sleeper sleep lighter with a light on, or does a hard sleeper sleep harder with a hard-on?" Lee made that up last summer.

"What?" She gives me a look.

I say it again anyway, in a raspy voice like a gangster.

"That's pretty crude," she says, aiming her face at the TV.

Naturally, it's crude, but Leslie usually gets a laugh out of crude things. Maybe it's her hair, but I'm not going to tell her it makes her look like Miss Rheingold. She wouldn't want that anyway. Not that I'm claiming to know what she does want.

Now we see the two guys who burned down the farmhouse, a young guy and a grizzled old guy, squatting around a fire, eating. They don't know the woman never got out of the farmhouse. Back in Dodge, even though he somehow suspects foul play, Doc has no way to reach Marshal Dillon because he's away fishing. It's promising to be a long show. Leslie is locked right in. I get up to head for the kitchen, but she doesn't say anything.

The kitchen is huge. Without flicking on the light, I open the refrigerator, which turns out to be packed. My mother listens to Carleton Fredericks on the radio. He's a health buff and would get along very well with my mother. She's a fanatic about nutrition, so we never have white bread or candy or Coke around. And no cornflakes or anything like that. She smokes like a locomotive, though. Usually, I feel so deprived I grab a soda whenever one comes into view, but there's beer in here, too, which we also never have. I've had two or three beers before so I know what it's like. Miller High Life. There's an opener stuck by a magnet to the door of the refrigerator.

I sit on the couch away from the TV. Leslie glances at me. "Help yourself, why don't you."

"Oh, what a gracious hostess," I reply. If you've ever drunk it, you know what beer tastes like. I can get it down when I'm thirsty. Now all I'm trying to do is make an impression, "walk like a man." Most liquor is made from fruits or grains while they ferment, or in common language, rot. The man who discovered liquor had to drink the juice from rotting fruits or grains until he got used to it enough to like it. Then he had to prove to his friends he wasn't crazy so he could get them to do it. I don't know how it caught on. My father, who is a Moose, gets bombed at the Moose bar. My mother can't drive, so she sends out for six-packs of wine which she stores under the sink. Both my parents are miserable alcoholics, but I'm not really bothered by it. You can't blame them for being the way they are—it's a very complicated problem. I won't explain why, but I learned all about it for a research speech I gave this fall in English. It's never the fault of just one person, and it's much worse in places like Germany and France, where kids don't drink milk and five-year-olds get loaded on wine for lunch. It's hereditary, too, which is what worries me. I'm bucking bad odds, especially with a beer in my hand when I don't even enjoy it. So, between swallows, I begin pouring a few glugs into this big plant, another rubber tree, that's growing out of a pot on the floor.

"You idiot," says Leslie, out of nowhere. "What do you think you're doing?"

"Who me?"

"Do you think that's good for a rubber plant?"

I lean over to put my arm around the leaves. "Why not? It won't hurt him. Just don't let him drive home."

"You're an idiot, Bernie. If you think you're funny, you're not."

"Well, you're not such a joy yourself."

She stands straight up. "Oh, you're just great," she says. She marches by me into the hall and stops in front of the mirror. "If I'd thought you were going to be this way to me I wouldn't even have asked you over." A commercial has given her a break so she can inspect her hair-do.

"What way?" I feel like getting out before the roof falls in.

"The way you are. Heartless. You should appreciate me more."

"I'm heartless?" In a way I am pretty heartless.

"Not really heartless, but, like when you see me you're not glad. You just make fun of me."

Putting down the beer can, I get up. "I *did*n't make fun of you. And I had just about a second to be glad. After that I was surprised. I was surprised *and* glad. I like your hair, too. I said I liked it."

"If you liked it, you'd say it right away."

"I said it as soon as I could."

She pouts for a few seconds in the hallway. I'm about to ask how much Pam Sokel has to do with this cheery attitude, but my good sense seals my lips. Anyway, I think I know. I'm just standing by the coffee table looking down at a lumpy glass ashtray. By the sound, Leslie can tell "Gunsmoke" has returned to her life, so she moves by me to the TV while I thumb through a Horizon book I've picked up. Just as I begin to say, "This is ridiculous," she sits on the couch instead of a chair, so what the hell, I do too. I don't say anything. Somehow on the show a girl has got involved with the men who burned down the farmhouse. She's leading a mule up to where they wait at the mouth of a cave or a mine. They know now they killed the farm woman. The grizzled old guy is sick. The young guy is figuring how many miles they've still got to go.

The smell of Leslie's permanent swims over to me. It's like coming into a room where they've just had Chem lab. But it's a reek you want to keep sniffing, like gasoline. I put my arms up along the back of the couch. My armpits don't look wet because I've got this sweater on, so this is a sensible first move. My wrist is about even with her shoulder, and, as I flex it, I can watch the neat little muscles move in my forearm because I've got the sleeves pulled up to the elbow.

With her eyes still on the marshal clinking slowly through the cave, Leslie suddenly reaches behind her neck, takes my hand, and snakes it along her back to her other shoulder. I slide over, also while looking at the TV. Damn it, I've got to make my own moves. It's almost eleven o'clock, and there's school tomorrow. My mother thinks I'm out playing Ping-Pong. So I twist Leslie's head toward me, trying to be casual, and I drop toward her mouth. She keeps her eyes open, but I kiss her anyway. Sometimes people do kiss with their eyes open. When I inhale I get her permanent, and when I exhale I taste her mouth, sort of oniony. Bullets start crashing around inside the cave. I look at her eyes so she closes them. I close my eyes and then open them again, and she has hers open. She's watching the end of the show. I pull back from her a little to ask her if she wants to watch it. I'm starting to get a boner.

"No, no," she says. "I don't care. I know, let's go upstairs."

"What for?"

"They have a big bed up there," she says.

"They do?"

"Yes, a double bed."

"What about the kid?"

"I told you he never wakes up," she says.

"Whose bed is it?" I don't feel like messing up somebody's bed.

"*Their* bed, who do you think?"

"When are they coming back?"

"They said late," she says, tugging my arm. "Are you coming or what?"

Sometimes I don't know why I am the way I am. For example, yesterday I was thinking I felt hot as Seymour Zimmerman must have been two years ago when he got caught putting it to Denise Block in the janitor's storage area. Mr. Russo was principal then, and he suspended them for the year. Last spring Denise Block married a Death Rider, Will Bowes, who I worked with last summer at the highway department. He has a heavy equipment license.

So, with Leslie in the lead, we hurry up the stairs. I want to do it all right, but something about the bed of someone I don't even know makes me feel brutal, like a robber or something. I wonder if I've got a below-normal sex drive. But then, I can't compare myself to Seymour Zimmerman, who was nuts.

"In there," says Leslie, pointing to a dark doorway.

"What about you?" I whisper.

"Go ahead," she says. "I'll be back in a minute." She shoves my shoulder toward the room and runs down the stairs again.

I go in and turn on a light. There's a big wooden bureau with pictures on it, a make-up stand with bottles and jars, and the bed with a white bedspread. My house has two double beds. In the basement is the one my mother and sister Claudia sleep in, and in the back bedroom upstairs is the one my other two sisters sleep in. My father and I sleep in the front bedroom, which has twin beds. I must point out that it's not as depressing as it may sound, living with parents who have to be that way, though the basement is pretty dingy.

The sliding closet door is open, so I look in. Suits, shoes, and, up on a shelf, a *rifle*, with the bolt in it. God.

In comes Leslie.

"There's a *rifle* in here," I whispered.

"So?"

"What for, do you think?"

"How do I know? It's not against the law, is it?"

Then the light goes off, just as I realize my father has a rifle in *his* closet, only in a canvas case.

"Bernie?"

"Where are you?" I say. It's completely dark.

"Over here on the bed."

"Did you take off your sneakers? The bedspread's white." I'm very nervous.

"Yes, Bernie," she whispers. "What's *wrong*?"

"Nothing," I whisper back, and I slip out of my sneakers. I can hear the TV still on downstairs. Walking over, I see Leslie like a shadow on the bed. I kneel next to her, and she pulls me down. I start passionately making out with her, getting my hand right away under her sweater, and Jesus, she has her bra unsnapped already. She pulls up my sweater and shirt and rubs my back hard. She's moaning and moving her hips. I squeeze her jugs. She responds with, "Oh, oh," from the back of her throat. She lifts up her sweater so our chests can touch. I slide down so I can lick her nipples. They feel softer than it says in the books. She's really moving and pressing on my head, smothering me almost. I'm worried she'll go after my pecker again, so I keep it against the bed. I slip my hand along her belly to her belt, and she helps me undo it. A zip, and I'm down there. Hair. It's wet. I've never *felt* this before. She's shuddering. I put my finger in, and it's like there's something in there. Bumps.

"Bernie," she says, "put your *penis* in me. I want you to do it."

Amazing. The I.I. I'm going to get it. I take my hand out to unbuckle my pants. My heart's pounding.

"Here," she says, "use this."

"What?"

"A contraceptive," she says. "Put it on."

A *rubber*. She hands it to me. It's in a foil package. I pull my pants off, and she pulls off her pants while I open the rubber. It's lubricated! I've seen these only a couple of times in my life. Suddenly, she grabs my bone.

"Wait," I say. "I'll do it." She lets go, and I figure out how the thing goes on. It unrolls. It slips over my bone. I'm about to shoot. Jesus. I get between her legs. Again she grabs, and wham, I shoot into the rubber. I put it in anyway. In, I'm *in*. Leslie moans and squeezes me. This is really it. I move in and out a few times. Then, a flash of light through the window. A *car*.

"Listen!" I whisper.

She stops. We hear gravel crunch in the driveway.

"Oh, God, they're *home*," says Leslie.

"Jesus *Christ*," I say.

We scramble into our pants. I fumble on the rug for my sneakers. "Hurry," says Leslie. "Go out the back and over the back fence."

"How?"

"The kitchen."

So I whip down the stairs in my bare feet. My undone buckle jingles. I duck into the kitchen. It's dark. I feel my way along the cupboards, the stove, the sink, the window. They're coming into the hallway. Oh, God. No door. I've missed it. I go back along the windows. No door.

"Leslie?" Mr. Hendricks.

I stand dead still. The TV is still on.

"Oh, hi," says Leslie, coming down the stairs. "You just woke me up. I was taking a nap."

"A nap, eh? A nap's a good idea," says Mr. Hendricks. "Mrs. Hendricks would rather have had a snooze than go watch that excuse for art, or whatever."

"Really?" says Mrs. Hendricks.

"Was it bad?" says Leslie.

"Oh, I don't know," says Mrs. Hendricks. "There were parts I liked, I think."

"She *thinks*," says Mr. Hendricks.

This is crazy. I'm trapped, frozen, a goner. I can hear my heart hammering. There must be a *door*. Leslie, you . . . Why am I standing here? I can't go out there, that's why. I have to stand here. They'll find me. They'll come in here, and I'll be here, right here, standing, holding my sneakers. The curtains are slightly parted. Against the sky, behind branches, I see a searchlight pass like a finger. I am a fugitive. Or a lowly animal, with weasly blips for eyes, panting in the dark. I'm shivering. And I have to take a wicked whiz. Holy God, the rubber is still on me, stuck to my leg. I reach in, peel it off, stuff it in my pocket. Then I kneel to slip on my sneakers, tucking the laces inside. My legs feel like Jell-O. They're still chattering away out there, Leslie saying they've given her more than she's earned, Mr. Hendricks telling Mrs. Hendricks he'll be back in fifteen after he buzzes Leslie home, Mrs. Hendricks asking Leslie to say hello to her parents. "I will," she says.

After Mrs. Hendricks calls, "Goodbye, Leslie, and thank you," the front door closes. I've sidled over to the refrigerator, where I think I can squeeze out of sight between it and the cupboards, but there's a trash bag here already. The news is on the TV. She must be watching it—I can't hear anything else. I lift the trash bag and work myself in sideways against the refrigerator and the wall. I set the bag in front of me. This is stupid. I couldn't be more hemmed-in. What if the woman heard me? What if she's out there *think*ing she heard me? What happens when her husband gets back? "Honey, I'm so glad you're here. I think I heard something in the kitchen." "And what did you *think* you heard in the kitchen?" "Well, it sounded like . . . breathing, or else the trash bag moving." "Breathing, eh?" "Yes, do you want your rifle?" Lord. I should give up right now. Walk out there. Surprise. What if they want a midnight snack? There's all this food in here.

"Well, I don't care to *hear* his analysis." I almost jump against the wall. She's talking to the TV. At once it's off, and, she's walking. To the stairs. No, *here*. I should say something. What? I could snarl. She'd cover her eyes, and I'd run. Footsteps on the linoleum. My eyes close. I open them. There she is! Into the trash, she drops my beer can. She turns. Footsteps. And gone. Up the stairs. I push out the trash bag and take long, soft steps to the kitchen door-way. No one. Long steps across the bright room to the hall-way. Quietly, I twist the knob, ease the door. I'm out. I rip across the lawn, almost losing both my sneakers. I didn't even close the door.

I'm so pent up I can't stop running until I reach the little piece of woods across the wide yard in front of our neighbor's house. I duck into the trees to catch my breath. Whoosh. It steams. I can hardly stand, my legs are so shaky. Am I lucky, or what? I mean, she was right *there*. Of course, if she'd seen me, she would've dropped her drawers. I sit down on a root. This woods used to be gigantic, full of raspberry patches. Now, down into the gully and up the slopes, it's Marble Hills Homes. Right in front of me is the sump with a chain-link fence around it. I stand up to whiz on the fence. A few hundred yards away I can see some houses still have their lights on. Must be near to midnight. Old Leslie is hitting the hay without any idea how close she came to losing her ass. Boy.

I think one of those lights is Freddie Umphenour's house, or his house before he moved to Florida. I slept there once, and for dinner we had this special meat that I hated. His father made me sit there, made me take little bites until I almost threw up. In his room later, Freddie gave me a metal Canadian Mountie.

Fortunately, I remember the rubber in my pocket. It's possible my mother would find it there. I'm not saying she'd pass out at the sight, but she wouldn't get any chuckles either, so I throw it into the sump. I feel kind of serene and not that tired. It'll catch up with me in the morning, though.

CHAPTER 3

You know, I'm sitting here in French thinking about drinking that beer last night, and what it reminds me of is when I was young, about seven or eight, and my mother and father used to watch the news together. We put our TV downstairs then where my mother tried to set up a kind of den area in the basement. With a spray-paint bottle you operated by a trigger, she lightened the cinderblock walls to a thin khaki color, and she taped up photographs of peaks in the Alps. My father's drafting table and his desk, with a thick plate of glass on it, the double bed, some cupboards with games and coloring books, and the TV were all down there. It was always pretty much the basement, though. The ceiling was just the underside of the kitchen floor with white insulated pipes running along to the radiators. By the head of the bed, which was the best place to sit for the TV, the big drain for the kitchen sink came down. It was a long, sweating tube, with splotches of rust, like a giraffe's neck. What gets me is I'd sit there and actually watch the news. I hated the news. I thought it was doing something for me though. By sitting through all the film clips of faces, of men getting out of cars and walking up steps, of maps and cities, and by listening to the careful, droning newsman, I figured I was gaining on my future. Somehow I guess I thought if I could stand the news, I was burning off my childhood instead of letting the years wear it away. During the news, I could sort of feel how hard it was to be an adult. Sure, I was a crazy kid then, but what just dawned on me, sitting here at this carved-up desk, is drinking that beer at Hendricks's last night was the same kind of situation. I mean, something about having my fingers around that open beer can was making me solemn and sad and full of complications like my father.

The lights just went out, and behind me a movie projector is clattering. A long hair is making a shadow crooked as a coastline wiggle on the screen. It's a black-and-white film about a peasant family. The narration is real French, and they jabber so fast I can pick up only a few words, though this is my third year.

Outside, I see between the blinds, silvery rain slants down into the parking lot. I could fall asleep very easily. Leslie did not show up at her locker before homeroom, so I guess for some unknown reason she didn't come to school.

This is my first day as a whole man, because I put it in the hole. I've been thinking that all day. I said that phrase to Lee at the bus stop this morning, but he knew I'd done it as soon as he saw me. He started laughing before I opened my mouth. I don't think he was really very jealous either. What could he do, anyway? He expected it. I doubt I'll get the ten bucks out of him, though. I'm not sure I'd have come up with it myself.

On the bus I related the story, leaving out nothing. He said, "Fan-fucking-tastic!" over and over. Then he told me I should have stuck around to put it to Mrs. Hendricks. He thought that was hilarious.

For some strange reason, I just now remembered Wendy Morton, who was a fat-legged, buck-toothed girl I knew in the seventh grade. On the class picnic at some park a few of us were holding a sex discussion, not that we had much to discuss, but it was a form of enjoyment, even then. And Wendy Morton whispered to me, "I'd let you sleep with me anytime, Bernie." Of course, I was too young and too timid to take advantage of it, and that summer she moved to Hauppauge. For months afterward I kept her invitation in the back of my mind. I even got her new address from telephone information. This was the year Rockefeller was urging everyone to build fall-out shelters in the backyard so we could ride out World War III. Although my mother insisted it was all crap and that we'd all be cooked in our shelters like baked potatoes, she stored a few cans of tuna, some blankets, and flashlights in the furnace room downstairs. But my biggest worry then wasn't survival, it was sex. I couldn't stand the thought of dying without ever having done it. So, while the air-raid sirens howled and the black bombers droned over Canada, I figured I'd be on my bike headed for Hauppauge and manhood. Or else I'd call Wendy and have her meet me somewhere in between to save time. I had quite a few fantasies like that. In fact, I still have them, of all kinds. Being a whole man makes no difference. Not that I think it should.

Lunch today is pizza patties, canned green beans, and white bread, a truly wretched meal, but at noon I'm faint with hunger, and I have to eat it. Coming out with my tray, I scan the rows of eaters for friendly faces. This school is so huge there are two cafeterias and four lunch periods. Over with the bunch I usually eat with, Pam Sokel is pretending she hasn't seen me. Somehow I don't want to join those idiots anyway, so I sit near the windows with three freshmen who have finished their pizza patties and are sucking up pudding with their straws and playing blow-gun. I bang down my tray. "Look," I say. "I'm gonna *eat* my lunch here. You guys can go finger-paint or something." They glare at me to show how tough they are, but they move out finally, screeching their chairs.

Far out over the puddled athletic field is a shopping center where a Chevron sign is turning on a pole. Some cars in the parking lot have their lights on, the sky is so dark. I'm forcing down the last of my beans and trying to remember the difference between meiosis and mitosis without looking it up in my notes, when behind me I hear, "Hey, you want your ginger cake?"

"Yeah, I want it," I answer, though really I wasn't going to eat it. I'd just spooned the whipped cream off the top. I twist my head, and standing there, his arms folded in his peculiar, sickening way, is Richard Linwood. It's a shock.

"You sure?" he says.

"Yeah. Why, you want a hand-out?"

His flat face looks colorless in the light from the window. His mouth is tense. "I'm only asking because I like cake," he says slowly. "What makes you such a wise-ass, anyway?" He pulls out the chair next to me and drops into it.

"Do you mind?" I say. "I'm having a peaceful lunch."

"Oh. Well, keep chewing then. Don't let me piss on your picnic."

"Thanks," I say. "I'm finished."

"Yeah? Then I'll have your ginger cake." Already his hand is on the dish, but I snatch off the cake with my fingers. "I said I *wanted* it," I shout. "I'm saving it for my dog."

He stares at me. "I oughta kick you into next week just for being so selfish," he says. Like a crane dropping a piece of junk, his hand lets go of the cake dish a foot above the table. It clanks against the Formica. Heads at the tables around us turn our way. Upside down, the dish is rattling. Suddenly, Richard's stump lashes out from behind his good arm, and *wham*, he pins the dish to the table. I flinch. The thing is like a pink blackjack attached to his elbow. On the end are those five nubs like a row of warts. Years ago, during that one summer we were friends, Richard made me hold his stump and squeeze it a few times. We were in a hammock his mother strung up behind his garage. I tried to pretend it didn't bother me, but it was like licking a toad on a dollar bet. It may seem strange, but I suppose we must have hated each other a little even then.

All at once I notice I am very nervous. It's like hundreds of spiders are crawling through my crewcut, and my stomach is queasy. Richard draws in his stump and lays it across his good arm. "You know," he says, "there's something about your selfish attitude that makes me want to puke."

My attitude? I can't understand what he's getting at. No one complains about my attitude except my mother and Mr. Kirk, the French teacher. "So puke," I say. "It won't bother me." People nearby have stopped talking. It crosses my mind to mention the rocks Lee and I ducked on Saturday, but he wouldn't react well to that.

"No," he says, quickly jumping out of his chair and making me jump slightly. "This isn't the place for it."

"What a pity. I'm sure you're a talented puker." I'm about to stand up when suddenly he jams his stump hard into the back of my neck. My head snaps back. I stiffen. He forces my face down toward my plate. Some beans are still on it.

"You little fuckhead. I oughta hang you from some tree by your itsy-bitsy dick."

An attack from behind by a Class A bastard like Richard Linwood will have a terrifying and weakening effect on you, I can guarantee. I am hunched into the table in shock with this thing like a gun at the base of my skull. I can't move. Then he gives an extra jab and stands back, wondering probably whether he should puke on me after all, but instead he just lets out a sort of snort and turns away. I spin around, and, as viciously as you can do a thing like this, I throw the cake at him. It smacks him in the ear. He whirls and jumps at me, but I'm up, and I ram my chair into his legs. I'm breathing hard. All I can see is Richard, at the end of a tunnel. Luckily I'm very quick by nature, and in a flash I have the table between us. There's no way he can catch me. Then I see Mr. Fitch has Richard by the shoulder, and I feel someone's grip on my arms. "All right, all right, all right," Mr. Fitch is saying.

"He hit me with his goddamn cake," yells Richard. He tries to shake off Mr. Fitch, but not seriously. I twist my head to see who's got me. It's a couple of guys I don't know. My throat is tight. I have the shivers. They let me go, and I slip into a chair. I'm holding back tears that have rushed into my eyes out of fear and sheer relief. Mr. Fitch has led Richard to a corner by the American flag. He still has him by the shoulder. I'm holding my head down and trembling. This lunch is over. I see the legs and shoes of everyone going by me with their trays. A squeaky voice says, "You shoulda broke off his other arm, Bernie," but I don't look up. I know my face is red. All this tension is rising to my head like steam. Christ, am I a coward. The least I could've done was stab the bastard with my fork. The bell rings.

Mr. Fitch teaches history and international relations. In fact, he is the department chairman. Everyone respects him, even though, to look at, he's a bit clownish. He's fat and wears baggy pants. I'm sitting now in his office, which, actually, is the history book room. There are rows and rows of books arranged around me like sets of encyclopedia. Mr. Fitch is at his desk, drawing on a Winston, and pointing his round face out the little window by his coatrack. It looks out past the flagpole to the senior courtyard. I suppose because of the rain the janitor did not raise the flag today. Once last winter some numbnuts from another high school hoisted a half-rotten dolphin up the flagpole. That's our school symbol, the dolphins. The teachers were horrified, though it turned out the dolphin had washed up on a beach and was dead when they found it. I mean, no one had killed it. But many people were outraged. Parents whipped off letters to our local paper, *The Long Islander*, like it was a contest or something. Finally, when I got tired of expressions like "demented delinquents" and "sanctity of nature" I wrote a letter myself, which they printed. In it I admitted it was not funny and an insult to wildlife, but I said people with truly understanding minds would chalk these things up to "the whims of youth." It was important to say that because hundreds of kids, me included, would probably consider a prank like that if they fell over a dead dolphin on the beach, and a lot of us might even do it. And we're not all demented. A boy who feeds his grandmother to the goldfish is demented.

Mr. Fitch is saying, "I think I don't have to tell you that Richard must have—he thinks he has—reasons for taking his anger out on you."

I say, "I bet he does have reasons."

"That is, he's not just *after* you. There's something behind it." He puts out his cigarette.

"Yeah. He hates me."

"All right, why does he hate you?"

Well, there's no honest, no accurate way to answer a question like that, and I figure Mr. Fitch doesn't really expect one, so I don't say anything. As a sort of game, many teachers are in the habit of asking these questions when they get you one-on-one, but Mr. Fitch isn't one of them. Anyway, my guess is Richard's reasons for hating me and for being after me (in Mr. Fitch's words) are no doubt of a deep, psychological nature and therefore hard to fathom. Of course, you have to reckon with his stump, but that's only the beginning, anyone can see.

Mr. Fitch is rubbing his yellow-stained thumb and forefinger together and gazing at his desk blotter as if sunk in thought. He keeps rubbing. He is very absorbed. The longer I stay in here, the more chemistry I miss, so I'm happy. For all I care, he can wear his fingers away. At last he looks up. "Well, Bernie," he says, "my only advice to you is that you stay out of Richard's way for a while. Avoid him. I know that must seem easy to say, but, if it's any comfort to you, you know that we all have our run-ins with bullies. We *have* had them. The more you challenge these bullies, the more determined they get."

"Who's challenging him? I was only eating my lunch. You think I should switch lunch periods?"

"That's a thought."

"You know, Mr. Fitch, Richard has this Italian switchblade a foot long, not that he'd use it, but he's got it. Who knows? He *might* use it."

"Well, tell Mr. Devoe, and he'll confiscate it, if you ever see him with it in school."

"Thanks, but I hope I never get the chance."

"All right. I'll take care of that. I'll see Richard after school. You'd better get to your Chem class."

He writes a pass, I thank him for everything, and I'm gone. By the drinking fountain I stop to look at the pass, a green piece of paper. It says, in ink, "Conference, 12:15," and "A.F.," his initials. With my own pen I change 12:15 to

12:45, which is six minutes before the end of chemistry. It looks perfect. Now I can relax a while, maybe sneak into the library. I bend for a drink, though the water here tastes like metal. The chrome drain says, "Halsey Taylor Warren, Ohio," which must be the drinking fountain capital of the world. My mother has a rich uncle in Warren, Ohio, who used to send me sporting goods every Christmas. I've never met him. He's so old he can't walk any more, my mother says. He's eighty. Maybe he's the drinking fountain king.

Not until my last class of the day, English, do I finally catch sight of Barbara. It's the only class we have together, but usually at the beginning of the day I have time to drift over to the science wing, where she always gabs with friends in the hall before homeroom. We joke around some (she's very witty), and I get to see what she's wearing. Because it's so early, her eyes are small and sleepy-looking, her make-up is a little stark, and her wavy, red-gold hair is very neat. I didn't go over there today, though. I mean, after last night with Leslie, I was somehow afraid. When I think of Barbara, there's this balloon of guilt inside my chest. It pumped right up again when I finally caught Barbara's eye. She's wearing a plaid, kilt-type skirt, mostly green, and a white sweater with the sleeves pushed up on her forearms in a sexy way. As I passed into the room and by her desk, her face flashed up at me without a smile, without any expression at all, then down to concentrate on some drawing she's still doing on the cover of her notebook. "Hi," she said. She's in the habit of keeping me in doubt and feeling insecure, but now, after last night, all I feel is this guilt that makes me wince inside. But, hell, it's crazy to react like this because I have never promised Barbara a damn thing. Going by, I glanced down at her hair, which in the sun is like orange cotton candy, but I didn't say anything. I wove back through the rows to my chair by the window and I slumped into it. Around me everyone's buzzing, and outside the rain is still pattering. I smell chalk dust and Verna Silbert's fruity perfume. In grade school Verna used to think she was a ballerina. I guess she still does, but she knows better than to show off solo in weird talent shows. She would dance and then sit on a stool and sing "Hang Down Your Head, Tom Dooley." Verna has terrible eyesight. She was always very comical spinning around up there in thick glasses and a blue tutu. I used to be master of ceremonies.

Imagining that Barbara has somehow found out about Leslie and me sends a chill down my backbone to my asshole. But I know not even Pam Sokel would spill it. She has no reason. No, it would have to come from me, and it never will. Barbara gets fiercely jealous. Naturally, so do I, and I feel terrible because if she ever did to me what I did to her, I'd probably blast her in the mouth. My affair with Barbara is quite intense in many ways, especially when you consider how unusual it is. I mean nobody else I know has a girlfriend in the true meaning of the word. Socially, they are all cavemen, even Lee. An example of what I mean just happened two seats in front of me. Mr. Parizzi has not shown up yet, and in the middle of all the jabbering and confusion, Harlan Glick sort of shifted up on one cheek and cut the cheese. At the sound, the guys all shoved their seats away with expressions of horror. Jake Rifkin, who you might think of as quite mature since he works in his father's pharmacy, is a football star and very smart, just yelled, "Jesus, Harlan. Harlan let fly." And now Harlan slides around in his seat and gives a little bow. With a half smile on her face, Barbara looks back his way too, but she avoids my eyes. She is a very cool type of person, Barbara, always controlled and full of poise. Usually I think I'm that way too, but when I'm around her, the things I say don't come out right, and my actions become sort of ragged, as if I were thoughtless or impulsive. And the thing is I'm not, you see. I'm mature. But somehow with Barbara I don't feel as much confidence as I do with, say, Helen Bundy, or even Leslie. So if this whole I.I. business ever came to light, well, it could be very painful.

Actually, I know it's a shame that relationships seem to always work this way, under a black cloud of jealousy. When I was a kid, I had this fantasy that I would conjure up at night before I slipped into sleep. I would be having a summer party with all my friends on the beach when suddenly, looking out over the Sound to Connecticut, we would see them coming, the Russian version of the B-52's (bombers again, I know, but I was packed full of fear of them), huge, howling squadrons, with bombs raining down like turds. So, immediately, I would take charge, leading all my friends on the run down the beach to Nathan Hale Rock, and there I would flick a hidden switch, and one of the plaques would slide back (this was before the Puerto Ricans), and we would all hop down this long chute into an enormous, very well equipped fall-out shelter. It was sort of an underwater paradise, you know, with lots of food, weapons, bowling alleys, tennis courts, go-carts, everything unlimited. For a whole year I worked on this fantasy every night. It began the same way until we got down there. Then I would go off on one tangent or other. First there were war aspects. Wearing special protective suits, we would sneak out at night to shoot the Russians. Then sex took over. Of course, all the beautiful girls I knew were at the party, so they wound up in the shelter. Guys I knew were there, too, but there was no jealousy. We all had a good time. There was the mud room, the feathers room, the rubber room, the grass room, even the shit room. We would go to these rooms and fuck, you know, but as the leader, I decreed that all serious attachments were forbidden. Anyone who did not obey would be banished to the upper world, where the Russians were in control of everything. True, I was nuts to be so wrapped up in my imagination, but the point is, I had the right idea, about relationships, I mean. Of course, people can't really live that way—they're too weak. It's a shame, as I said.

Mr. Parizzi is an outstanding teacher, but by the end of the day I'm bored with school in general, even though English is a subject I enjoy. The discussion is about Penelope's wait. She put off dozens of suitors for years until Odysseus returned from his business trip. That's classic loyalty, another impossible ideal. The rain has let up.

After the last bell, I'm rummaging through my locker for a piece of plastic to cover my books with when I hear Barbara say in a teasing way, "I hear you had a fight with Richard Linwood." When English ended, she bolted out of the room. It disturbed me, but I wasn't going to run after her. Now she's on one foot, her shoulders and other foot pressed back against the wall next to my locker. She has her raincoat on, and she's hugging her books to her chest.

"Oh, that," I say into my locker. "Just gossip."

"*Did* you?"

"No, he wanted my ginger cake, so I hit him in the head with it." I clang shut my locker.

"Really?"

"Really."

"Well," she says, "Marjorie's story somehow had more to it than that."

"Oh, you know Marjorie," I say. Here I am, acting against my own best interests again. I swear I don't know why conversations progress the way they do. They just aren't logical. The emotions behind them are very complicated. What I *want* to do is tell Barbara all about it and have her spill out the sympathy. But I guess I can't really want to do that because that's not what I do. Once, walking back to Barbara's from playing tennis, she skipped over a fence into somebody's yard to pick a red flower for me. She curtsied—a thing that's not easy for most girls to pull off without looking stupid—and she presented it to me. For some unknown reason, I ate it. I chewed it and swallowed it. It almost made me sick.

"I know Marjorie," says Barbara, pushing herself off the wall. "According to her, Richard hit you with his crippled arm, and you hit him with a chair. Is that close to it?"

I relent. "Yeah, that's close."

"How close?"

"But really," I say, "I don't feel like talking about it. I don't want it spread around. As it is, Richard will probably pull out his switchblade tomorrow and slit my weasand." Phrases like that appeal to me. It's the only reason I use them.

"Well," she says, "do you deserve it?"

I purse my lips and look straight down the hall. I know Barbara's head is cocked at me in her sort of amused and uncaring way, and so I don't want to even glance at her. Ordinarily, I'd be staying for tennis practice and Barbara would be walking me down toward the gym, but because of the rain we're both headed for the noisy lobby where everyone waits for buses out of the wet. I've got one eye peeled for Richard, in case Mr. Fitch forgot his promise. I turn away from her to a locked display case full of some art class's horse drawings. They're quite stylized. One has three tails. I run a finger along the glass. I'm thinking there really isn't much to say about Richard Linwood anyway.

"Ignore me, then," says Barbara. "I thought of inviting you over for dinner, but I've changed my mind. You'd probably just twiddle your fork in the mashed potatoes." She turns right around and goes off the other way.

I call out, "Barbara!" Not that I expect her to stop, she's such a hothead.

She spins around. "Yes?"

I enjoy going to Barbara's for dinner, and I know it means making out in the garage before dinner and in the TV room after dinner, but when she barks that *yes* at me, I can only answer, "I'd like lilies for my casket," quite a cold remark, which I could kick myself for making.

"Lilies," she says, turning again. "I'll make a note of it."

Hell, I'll have to call her on the phone to smooth things out. I talk more sensibly when I can concentrate on just talking.

Lee is not on the bus. He's stayed for chess club, which he can go to only when there's no tennis practice, so I sit alone near the front watching the gray houses and gray stores go by. At times like this, life can be pretty depressing. It shouldn't be, you tell yourself. You're headed home for Graham crackers and milk. You're very healthy and young. You know a little about what sex is like now. You have friends who give you respect and enemies who keep you alert. And what else can you expect out of life, anyway? You are lucky. If you were a lowly peasant in India or Brazil, life would be so miserable you might as well take poison and die. You tell yourself you're too selfish and moody. You're an ungrateful bastard. But it doesn't help.

We chug by many lawns where the forsythia is blooming, standing out like yellow hands. Most of all I feel hungry. Just that is enough to make me unhappy. People are pretty simple that way, like any animal.

Zekey is barking at me as I climb the little hill by his pen, but I'm thinking food, so I ignore him. I don't even look at him, which is terrible of me. All he wants is affection. The wet grass has made my sneakers soggy.

On the kitchen table I see two glasses with rings of milk in the bottoms and the blue Graham cracker box. It's empty. My sisters are pigs. They get home before me and they have I slap my hand down onto the box, and some crumbs fly out.

no consideration. Under the milk carton is a typed note from my mother. On Monday afternoons she walks to Mrs. Carruthers's house for some kind of philosophy discussion and cocktails.

> *Dear Ones:*
>
> If your shoes are muddy, take them off here, please. Girls, there's only one packet of crackers left, so save some for your brother. He has no tennis practice today. There are saltines, too. You can make do with those. Please do not bother me at Carruthers's unless there's a blood-curdling emergency.
>
> Bernie, please, please attend to the garbage that you forgot yesterday and Saturday before you go anywhere. Thank you.
>
> Love,
> *Mom*

My sisters get away with almost anything because I can't retaliate without opening myself up for serious punishment. Once a few years ago I spent the whole day putting together the U.S.S. *Arizona* from very complex instructions, and that night, for some unknown reason, Claudia wormed her way into my room and snapped off all the cannon barrels with her fingers, quite a vicious act. Whatever the old man did to her for that, it wasn't enough.

Just plain, without soup or anything, saltines are rotten, so, even though the milk is warm from being left out, I fill a bowl with Wheaties. Wheaties are no better for you than any other cereal, in spite of what the name might make you think, but my mother buys them if I promise to eat them with wheat germ and without sugar. I complain about fanatical attitudes like that (after all, we buy Graham crackers, which are shit), but, to tell you the truth, I like Wheaties with wheat germ and maybe some raisins. The milk is too warm. I eat as much as I can and then, as evidence of how mad I am, I leave the rest soaking on the table.

After dumping the bags of garbage, I give in and let Zeke out, he's whining so much. He tears around the yard in circles for a while to see if he can arouse me, but when my mood comes across to him he ambles off into the Ferrises' yard, sniffing the ground. When you think about it, with his empty, empty life, old Zeke is like some peasant. It's quite sad to me. One day when I was in the third grade shuffling through the snow in the woods down to the bus, it dawned on me how every day I hated to leave Zeke shivering in that little house inside his pen, day after day, while I went to a warm school. He would come out of his little house when the back door slammed, and he would watch me march by with his nose stuck like a bird's beak through the hole in the bottom of the fence. Then he would go back inside. Somehow this one day I couldn't stand it, so I circled back through the trees, climbed into Zekey's pen, and crawled right into his doghouse. I was planning to stay there all day, curled up on his dog blanket. But Zeke went crazy, wriggling around with joy and licking me. I was cramped in there in the dark, and he was squirming and slapping me with his tail. It smelled awful. I couldn't see anything. In a few minutes I was crawling out again. I was nauseated. I told my mother some big kids pushed me down in the snow and made me miss the bus. Whether she believed me or not didn't matter much. She never forces us to go to school if we don't feel like it. But I always go. I haven't missed one day since that one. I just never get sick, it's that simple. Every year I get an attendance certificate. Looking now at the opening in Zeke's house, I find it amazing to think I was ever small enough to crawl through it.

Now that my chore is done, my mind is a real blank. I

have nothing to do but read or study. I feel suddenly like digging out my old slingshot and shooting at trees, but it's buried somewhere in the attic. I could go up there and unlock my father's navy trunk which has packets of three-cent-stamp love-letters in it from girls named Katsie and Rachel. The phone is ringing. I run to the door, but Claudia's answered it before I get there. It was so quiet while I was eating my Wheaties that I thought everybody was gone.

Claudia shoves the phone at me. "For you. Leslie."

I take it and put my hand over the mouthpiece. "What did you hog all the Graham crackers for?" I say. "Can't you read?"

"I didn't."

"How come they're gone then?"

"Don't ask me," she says. "I only had about *one*."

"One my ass. I'd like to X-ray your fat gut." Then in the hallway I see Lucy Kane, Claudia's best friend, staring at us, a little butterball with round eyes. She has pale, pale skin and hair that's so blond it's white. "Well, if it wasn't you, it was Large Lucy," I say. "If she ran out of food for ten minutes, she'd eat her tongue." Lucy turns right around like a soldier and heads for the bathroom.

Claudia screams, "You big fucker! She didn't even have *one*," and she runs out of the room.

Into the phone I say, "Did you hear that?"

"What?" says Leslie. She sounds irritated.

"My sister, swearing at me."

"I was lighting a cigarette," she says.

"Are you out at the phone booth?" In her house she would never dare smoke. She must be at the fire station, which she would walk to only for a very serious call.

"What do *you* think?" she says.

"I think you are because you're lighting a cigarette."

"Swift, very swift," she says.

What's wrong, I wonder. Suddenly, my predicament of last night, sweating it out in Hendricks's kitchen (it seems like a week ago) all comes back to me, and I blurt out, "Hey, you know, goddamn it, I was stuck there last night. There's no door in that kitchen. After you left, Mrs. Hendricks walked in there, right up to me, right *up* to me, but she didn't see me. I was very lucky. W*e* were very lucky."

"So what?" says Leslie.

"What do you mean so what? It was your damn fault." Now I know there's trouble.

"I mean you left that Trojan wrapper right up there on the bed and they found it."

"They did?"

"Well, what do you think, they'd just throw it away? They called up my mother—*she* did, and she went on and on about how she trusted me and liked me—" Leslie's voice breaks, and all at once she's crying. "And now my mother just went and locked herself in her *bed*room."

"Why?"

"She didn't know what *else* to do, that's why," Leslie shrieks into the phone. "I'll tell you what I want to know. Why are you such a dumb shit, such a dumb shit that you can act like—"

"I hardly even knew the thing *had* a wrapper," I say.

"You act like you don't even care. You probably wanted them to find it."

"Are you kidding? Listen, I was trapped in the goddamn kitchen for fifteen minutes because *you* said there was a door in there. But I got away. I escaped. And it was no damn thanks to you, either."

"Well, what difference did it make, if you left the Trojan wrapper right on the bed anyway?"

Obviously, Leslie cannot appreciate my dramatic story. Mentally, she is quite shaken up, and I can see why. She is very close to her mother, after all. But hell, I'm not to blame, not really. I hardly noticed it had a wrapper. Actually, she's more at fault than I am, being the last one out of the room. She's crying again. "Well, Leslie," I say. "I'm truly sorry. That doesn't help, I know, but—"

"Big shit."

"Well, what am I supposed to do? Go to Hendricks and ask to have my wrapper back please? Tell her I forgot it? Tell her I got a wrapper collection and I dropped one?"

"You are heartless. A heartless, heartless bastard. I wish I never met you."

At this moment, something sails in at me from the hallway and lands on the floor. It's a Graham cracker. Claudia's head is sticking out around the door frame. "Go ahead, hog," she says. "Eat it! Eat it!" She slams the door.

"Leslie," I say, "all I can do is tell you I'm sorry. I mean, I was very nervous last night. I didn't leave it on purpose. I don't know what you expect from me, anyway."

"Ex*pect*? Boy, if I don't know by now I shouldn't expect one damn thing from you, I guess I'll never learn."

"Well, what did you call for, then?"

She sighs. She isn't crying any more. "I really don't know. Maybe to warn you. They found out it was you, you know. I told my mother. I know your mother will find out."

"That's all right. But just do me one favor, and don't let it out to Pam Sokel." If my mother finds out, she finds out, she can handle it. She knows how mature I am. But Pam wouldn't hold back on this one, and it would get to Barbara, which would be curtains.

"For your information, Pam knows all about it. I called her before I called you."

"Are you serious?"

"Yes, I'm serious."

"You're crazy. You might as well put it in skywriting."

"She's my best *friend*."

"Jesus. You told Pam Sokel."

"You're worried about Barbara, aren't you?"

"What?" This surprises me. "No, why should I?"

"I knew it. You're worried about that snot, Barbara Holland. Oh, you are a *bastard*." Then she screams, "I *hate* you!" and she hangs up.

I'm stunned. I look down at the pieces of Graham cracker on the floor, holding the phone like you hold a sandwich you've just found a hair in. Maybe I'll call her back later, try to calm her down.

Outside in the yard I see Zeke sniffing up the ass of Beauty, the Holmeses' boxer. She stands still, like a person waiting for a bus. Looking out this same window once, I actually saw Zeke dicking some mutt over by the spruce tree. So did my mother. She was so upset she ran out with a pot of cold water, which she dumped on them. They went into a panic, the poor dogs. They got twisted around facing opposite ways stuck together like paper dolls. My mother just stood on the stoop with her hands over her mouth.

I don't know what to do now. I could call Barbara and intercept the news. But what would I say? Who knows, Pam might clam up for some reason or get hit by a train. You can hope.

Then I hear the front door open. I guess it's one of my sisters, so I sit still on the stool, thinking. But it's my mother.

"You're home early," I say when she comes into the kitchen. That's what she always says to me, no matter when I show up.

"Yeah," she says. "Hey, what's for dinner?" which is what I always say.

"Steak and fries. You better wash up, though, right away."

She laughs.

"Hey, what is for dinner?" I say.

"Spare ribs. Peas and salad. Are the girls around?"

"Claudia is. She's been throwing crackers at me, the ones she and Lucy didn't eat."

"Please don't start in now," she says. "I've had a tolerable afternoon. I don't want squabbling or reports of squabbling."

As you can imagine, my mind is not on squabbling anyway. I say, "Got it," and I spin around and push open the storm door to the outside. It's chilly, and the sky is turning pink down behind the trees where the clouds seem to be thinner. Usually I enjoy evening. Everything eases up, calms down. The word *evening* has a definite meaning, you know. The night begins to sort of balance the day. The winds die out. Everything is subdued, it seems, and *even*. It can be so relaxing. Just for example, right now, sitting here on the rubber footmat, I can hear our oven door creaking open, pots clunking, Claudia chuckling in her room, a dog yipping somewhere far off. From somewhere the smell of onions cooking floats to me. This would all be quite soothing to my normal self, I know. But all I feel right now is my brain turning all my fears over and over like a cement mixer.

It's dark now, and I'm on the couch trying to read the comics. The TV is on in the basement. It's a variety show I left when the dancers came on, the ones that lie on the stage and make shapes like a kaleidoscope with their legs. I get bored with that. At the end of dinner my father came home from work and a few drinks at the Moose Club. My mother started in with, "Oh, the ogre's rolled in. The ogre's home to fill his gut."

He just pulled a plate down from the cupboard and dished himself some food from the stove. Taunting does not get to him very easily. But watch out when it does. My mother immediately got up to clear our places. She said, "We don't want to watch the monster slurp and slobber, do we?"

"Lay off, lay off, lay off," said my father.

"Oh, we're blotto tonight, aren't we," said my mother. Then she went downstairs to iron the girls' clothes for tomorrow. To the tune of an old song, she was singing, "Blotto tonight, blotto tonight."

When he drinks a lot, it isn't very obvious unless you know him. I mean, he walks and talks all right. His face may get red, but that's all. Lizzie and Jane got up complaining that there wasn't any dessert. I brought up the Graham crackers conflict again, and they loudly denied they had any at all. My father shouted, "Don't *fight*," through the meat in his mouth. The girls all went downstairs. My father asked me to dig out the pan of biscuits from behind the towel racks where my mother had hidden them from him. Then I went down to the TV for a little while.

That's the usual kind of madness that goes on in this house. I'm used to it. It only becomes terribly upsetting when they start clobbering each other and breaking plates. That's very, very rare. Then everybody cries but me. I just go lie down on my bed, feeling almost like the mattress. Because they're young and female, the girls always side with my mother in any battle, but I can't, the problem is much too enormous and complicated. When I stay neutral, it enrages my mother, of course. After things die down, she'll start analyzing my father for me. "You see how sick he is?" she says. I listen, but I never discuss it with her. I would get nowhere, I know.

I haven't called Barbara yet. I know I shouldn't somehow. You have to trust fate in circumstances like this. Fiddling will only make your predicament worse. However, you can get in fate's way a little, as I did before dinner when Mrs. Hendricks called. She asked for my mother, who was right next to me, peeling a cucumber, but I said, no, she was away at a meeting, could I take a message. She said, thank you, she'd call tomorrow. I told my mother I was just joking around with a wrong number. Somebody wanted Penelope. She believed me, since we often do that. We don't respect the phone very much. My father always answers it in a different accent. That bitch Mrs. Hendricks has a lot of nerve, I must admit. Just think of what she wants to say to my mother. It's rotten and low. I wonder how she's going to put it. Maybe it's a good idea to go over there and snip her phone wires. Lee would enjoy being in on that. But, hell, if my mother finds out, she finds out. I won't be in for a spanking.

I'm now lying here on my bed in the dark with my heart going like a ten-foot woodpecker. There was scratching in my sleep, and a hard tapping. I opened my eyes wide, and without even thinking, I turned to the window. Outside, two feet from the head of my bed, was a *knife*. And a hand holding it. I just sort of said, "Hehh," and I ducked for the bed. I just stared into the black of the sheet. Then I got up on my knees again. The knife was gone. A dark figure jumped out of the bushes by the window and darted away. Now I can only lie here shuddering. You have to tell yourself a thing like this is only a joke, but you know it is an evil joke. In fact, it's almost not a joke. On the other side of the room my father is snoring in a regular pattern. I strip the blankets from my bed and carry them out to the livingroom couch. I tiptoe through the kitchen to lock the back door. The room still has the greasy smell of cooked meat in it, and that reassures me somehow. It could only have been Richard Linwood, because Lee wouldn't do it. That's logic. Or it could have been someone I don't even know, someone from another planet or a mental ward. Would Richard come all this way in the middle of the night just to terrify me with his switchblade? He's crazy enough. But what did I ever do to him? What?

As soon as I wake up I see it's a sparkling day. Faint green maple buds are jiggling in the breeze past the livingroom window. My father is standing in his neat gray suit next to the coffee table. He asks why I moved to the livingroom, and I say I just couldn't sleep in the other room. He knows his snoring wakes me up sometimes. It's early. My bus comes after my sisters' buses, and they're not up yet. So I just sit here with the blankets over me. I can't get up yet anyway because somehow I got this fat hard-on. I must have been having a good dream—or else it was a bad dream, depending on how you look at it.

Lizzie just got up, looked sleepily in here at me, then shut herself in the bathroom. My father's Buick rumbled off down the road a minute ago. It's a very familiar sound.

My mother used to get up early to cook eggs and bacon and pancakes for us, but now she stays up so late reading and listening to Jean Shepherd on the radio that I never see her before I leave in the morning, not that I think I'm deprived, though, since I admit I'm a very talented egg cook. I've just scrambled six eggs, which I am eating with a few pieces of toast and juice. I'm a hearty eater. Lizzie and Jane don't like my cooking so they eat shredded wheat. Every morning it's Shredded Wheat. Without eating or saying goodbye to anybody, Claudia tromps out the back door, clomp clomp clomp, bam.

I'm at the sink rinsing out my milk glass when suddenly the door flies open, and Claudia bursts in again, crying. She screams, "Zekey's *dead!* Zekey's *dead!*"

I stare at her. She gives us all a wild look. She runs down into the basement where my mother is. Jane starts to cry and follows Claudia down the stairs. Lizzie looks into her bowl of milk. She turns her head up to me, and we just look at each other. I peer out the window toward the pen, but I can't see anything, so I push open the door and walk out into the yard. My brain feels empty. Zeke is dead. I can believe it without seeing it, but I want to see it, too. Birds are tweeting all around.

Zekey is lying on his side with his eyes open. His tongue sticks out about an inch, and I'm thinking this is it, this is it, this is what Zeke was always going to look like dead. This is exactly the spot he was always going to be in, and this is exactly the way he would be shaped. I imagine myself climbing into the pen and outlining his body in the dirt with a twig the way the police do with chalk on TV. I know it's crazy to think this way. So I'm sort of looking around in me for the right feeling to use. But all I can feel is the sun on the back of my neck and the breeze brushing through my hair. Suddenly I know that it's terrible to be alive because terrible things are always happening that you don't expect and aren't prepared for. You can't react.

I feel my mother put her arms around me from behind. She is crying. This is the first time I realize that I'm as tall as she is. Then I start to cry too.

CHAPTER 4

EVEN WITH THE WHEELS SAYING, "Don't think back, don't think back," I tell myself I ought to get out in Cold Spring Harbor, walk right to where Richard is now, no matter where, and kill him, like a showdown. I would need spurs to clink with every step. *Ha.* I don't know why I think I should do that. For Zekey maybe, since I never did much for him while he was wasting away in that pen, as my mother would say. What I'm doing actually is just the opposite. I'm making a getaway, on the commuter train to the city.

With her elbows locked straight and her hands balled up in the pockets of her aqua robe, my mother stood there in the kitchen telling us Zeke had died in his sleep. I don't think she believed that, but the girls did. They snuffled for a while, and then my mother called a cab to come take them to school, because their buses were gone.

After they left I was sitting at my desk in my room

knocking marbles into each other on the blotter, and from the other side of the door my mother said, "Bernie?"

I didn't answer.

The door has no lock, so if she'd wanted to, she could've come right in, but my mother is quite sensitive about privacy, though one afternoon years ago when my parents shared that bedroom my father went into it and shoved the dresser against the door so he could be alone there. My mother was so furious that she went downstairs into my father's tool chest and got a hatchet and hammers and chisels. She plain *smashed* a big hole right through the door. When she broke in after all the racket and yelling, my father was there just lying on his back across the bed with his hands behind his neck looking at her. Now there's white-painted cardboard my mother taped over the hole, but you can still see chop marks in the door.

"Bernie," she said, "are you going to school?"

Again I didn't answer, not because I felt miserable, but because I felt blank, sort of like you do when your kite disappears after the string breaks, and so I acted blank. My mother stood outside for a few minutes, listening I guess, and then I heard her walk into the kitchen.

There were little jagged patches of sunlight slipping across my blotter when a breeze passed through the new leaves outside the window. When I looked up my heart jumped. Right outside the screen on a branch of the dogwood a cardinal sat. I could see his black-and-yellow eye like a jewel tilted up at me. It's amazing to me that any animal could be that red without being plastic. The way he was sizing me up he was probably wondering how real I was. His tail feathers were twitching or else the wind jiggled them. Then, like an idiot, I had to say, "Well, howdy, Mr. Red." That terrified him. He took off, dipping through the air like a rollercoaster and was gone. I started thinking

I must have a pretty twisted personality to speak out loud to simple birds like that when I know they're not interested in my remarks. Cartoons and children's books do that to you. Somewhere in your mind you develop the idea that all birds think like people and that chipmunks and woodchucks and mice have little beds and rugs and read little newspapers. It's such a comfortable idea that it wears off very slowly. In fact, you can almost believe that, say, a raccoon has a life with no bad troubles. You might even want to *be* a raccoon if you could.

Anyway, with my jumbled brain giving in to thoughts like that, I knew I had to get away. Hell, standing there in the sun by Zekey's pen, I knew it. This is it, I told myself. This is all I need. Now I can go. I can cut out for good. It seemed like there was nothing in my life I wanted any more, not Barbara, not Leslie, not my family, not the neighborhood or the high school, not even happy-go-lucky Lee. I was falling into two pieces: the pathetic, troubled me of the past and the wonderful carefree me of the future. What was I waiting for? I had what it took, my two feet and a few dollars to light the fuse.

So I shoved back in my chair to dig into my bottom drawer for my strongbox, which I use for valuables. I keep old coins in there and my silver birth cup with my initials on it. From the plastic billfold with my $2.00 bills in it, I slipped out the $25.00 savings bond I won years ago in a Boy Scout lightbulb-selling contest. I went door-to-door for days telling people you could always use a few more lightbulbs. So I got this $25.00 savings bond, which was really worth, when I cashed it at the bank this morning, $17.45. When I think of how I spent all my spare time for two weeks wandering around housing developments peddling lightbulbs, it seems crazy. I sold $212.00 worth, and I got $17.45. Of course, afterward I had to deliver all those bulbs, too, which was a pain in the ass.

I pocketed the savings bond, and with two fingers I fished into my birth cup for my 1803 Large Cent. It's as big as a fifty-cent piece and has a profile of Liberty on it. Liberty is a woman, like the statue. They used to put her on many coins until they decided to use real people. I personally like coins that don't try to glorify figures of history, or, say, buildings, for Christ's sake. Like, I appreciate the Buffalo nickel, the Indian-head cent, and the Mercury dime, which all stand for America and ideals and everything, but in a romantic way. So, for good luck I took my 1803 Large Cent, shut up my box, and walked into the hallway.

I heard water running and dishes clinking in the kitchen, but I couldn't just sneak out the front door. If I was leaving I had to do it straight out. When I walked by the sink, my mother looked up and said, "So you are going, then?" Smoke from her cigarette curled around her hair.

"Yeah," I said.

"Well, before you go, I want to ask one thing of you."

I stopped with my hand on the door handle, but I didn't turn around. I gazed out through the screen at the clothes-pins fastened to the line like rickety fence posts. She must have figured it was strange I didn't have my books with me.

"The sun's out, and you've got to cover him up with something, a piece of canvas, if you can't pull him into the shade. Please do that much," she said.

I let the door slam behind me and walked over the slates, through the hedge, and across the Ferrises' yard into the trees. I wanted to be done with everything and gone, but I paused there, with the bluejays making angry, creaking noises around me, and I imagined my mother gripping her dish towel there at the sink as I went out of sight, and that made me turn back.

I didn't look toward the house or Zekey's pen. I just

yanked open the garage door and started rummaging for the old boat cover I once found washed up by a hurricane. You couldn't fit a car in that garage, there's so much crap in it. The canvas was draped over a stack of shutters my father and I spent many days four years ago building to replace the ones that were rotting off the house. They're all good, new wood, sanded and primed, all the screws are countersunk in their own little craters. I first thought I should leave them hidden under the canvas, but it was the only shroud for Zeke. Then I thought if he saw them there, my father might finish the job and put them up. One of the livingroom shutters came loose this spring, hung by a screw for a week, and fell into the pachysandra.

There were flies zipping around old Zeke already. That made me mad at first. I mean, I thought they should be damn satisfied with all the shit in there that I never did get to with my shovel. But then, I've always figured flies are typical of all the brainless, inconsiderate, simple animals. They're too selfish to be selfish, if you know what I mean. You just let them buzz and buzz and when they bother you, you kill them, and it doesn't matter to them or anybody else. Zeke's belly was swollen. I hadn't noticed that before. Probably he was poisoned, I decided, and that sent a pang through me. I gritted my teeth. His fur was dirty, not white like a Dalmatian's should be. For a second I thought I might wash him, a really crazy idea, and then I wondered what his fleas were going to do. I felt sick. I leaned over the fence and blanketed him with the canvas, for all the good that would do.

I ran off fast, over the lawns, down through the woods, past Lee's house, and up the paved road. When you're running through woods, that's really all you can think about, so you don't fall down.

The bank where I do my business used to be my father's

bank, but he moved to the new branch when it opened closer to home. I stuck with the old one because up on the wall over the tellers' counter is this huge painting. In the foreground is a bluff with trees where there's a handsome Indian looking anxiously out over the water. Another Indian is beckoning to a few more to come have a look. Far out on the water between two necks of land that makes it look just like Huntington Bay, a square-rigged ship is approaching, and a second one is following behind. The painting gives me a feeling of tragedy. Right now, looking out this smudged-up window at the rows of old cheesebox houses, the blowing scraps of paper, the wrecked cars, the wires going on and on, the stingy little lots where the kids have to go to throw the ball around, I wish to hell that the whole place could be the way it was in that painting, innocent, you know, and pure. I can be too romantic when it comes to Indians. Of course I know if we'd left the land to the red man, I wouldn't be here. I'd probably be a Lithuanian thistle-farmer. And there'd be no tennis, or television, or school, or anything, not that they are wonderful advancements, but life without them would be very, very dull—though, come to think of it, I'd never know the difference. I suppose, leading that dull kind of life, if you had an enemy like Richard Linwood, you could put a bloody end to him and nobody would blink. But, on the other hand, if your enemy was vicious like Richard Linwood, he would shove a spear through your throat before you saw it coming. Such a brutal life would have all kinds of drawbacks, and when you start to idealize the past you have to remind yourself of that.

I would have taken the twenty bucks plus interest out of my savings account when I turned in the bond, but I forgot my book, so all I've got now, after the train ticket, is fifteen. It ought to be enough to get me somewhere if I'm careful with it, don't ask me where. Maybe Florida. It's quite peaceful in Florida.

We just switched trains at Jamaica. I'm stuck now with a seat that faces backward, and the buildings and neighborhoods are all whipping by and shrinking in the distance like the exercise you have to do in art when you're learning perspective, with everything slanting off to the vanishing point. That suits me. My whole past could vanish, and I wouldn't complain.

They're going to be worrying something fierce in a few hours. My mother will call Barb to ask what she knows, and Lee, and it will move from there. Even Richard will know I'm gone. I should send him a letter that says, "Beware," in it so he could worry too. I wonder how he'd open it.

Maybe I should head west and get a job in a lumber camp or on a road crew and save my money and take judo lessons. Then in a few years I'd come back and turn Richard into piss and jelly. By then, I'd be quite a worldly person, though, so I probably wouldn't come back at all, except to see if my initials were still in the maple tree by the golf course.

When I jump off the train and start weaving through all the sluggish people so I can hurry up the stairs to the information booth, I realize I am truly running away, escaping. Why else am I hustling along through the crowds like a purse-snatcher? It's ridiculous. I mean suddenly my whole life is out ahead of me empty as the goddamn desert, and I'm running like I'm late for a final exam. So I take the escalator, gliding up with everybody else like I really belong in this hole of a train station. In a way, of course, I do belong here. I mean, where else on this churning planet should I be? This is a lowly, public place, and I'm not a bit conspicuous. Nobody looks twice at me, just as if today is an ordinary day in my hectic life like it is for all these dull-eyed city people. But in fact what I am doing, I know, is I'm fulfilling every kid's dream. Shit, I'm off to seek my fortune. My fortune is something I have wanted to seek ever since I began reading stories about the boy who would go off full of hope and determination, shuffling his boots in the road dust and carrying a gold sovereign and some bread and cheese in a leather pouch while his mother stood in the cottage doorway with chickens all around, sniffling and waving goodbye. He always wound up with a princess, some treasure, and at least half a kingdom, after taking in some excitement, too, on the side.

I ask, "Can you tell me how much it would cost to take a cheap train to Tallahassee?" Then I add, "And some idea when it would leave?" Tallahassee just popped into my head. It's a smooth name, and it's the capital, so there's probably a lot going on in it.

Hunched down behind the metal slats, the information man says in a gruff voice like the troll under the bridge, "We don't got that information here. Try Grand Central."

"Well," I say, "I don't much care when it pulls out, but I would like a rough idea of how much the ticket is."

"Try Grand Central," the man says.

"How about a very rough idea?"

"Look, sonny, will you try Grand Central? They got all the ideas you want."

"Don't whine and don't lose your temper," I say. And he shoots me this tight-lipped look like if I stood there another second he'd flick the trap-door switch and I'd drop into the sewer with the alligators, so I say thanks and walk away to buy me a Nedick's and a hot dog.

It's almost noon, but only a few people are eating. One Negro man in overalls with his forehead pressed down on the edge of the bar is sending a string of spit down between his legs. He sucks it in and sends it down again like a yo-yo.

The truth is I hate the city. It's a goddamn ant-hill, and when I'm here I never know where I am, or what I'm doing here, or what it's all good for, or anything. I don't know where Grand Central is, either, and any moron knows that. Then, using my noggin, I decide to just spend a dime and call them up.

When I finally get through to a man with information, standing here against the glass of this piss-stinking phone booth, I learn I'd have to sell my whole coin collection to ride the train to Florida. The man says the bus is not much cheaper, so I tell him, book me a suite on the ten o'clock train to the Gulf, and he says I'll have to call the proper railroad, so I say forget it and hang up. I'll have to thumb it.

My ninth grade civics teacher used to tell us if the world had a capital it would be New York. The place is enormous, just miles and miles of stone and asphalt. You couldn't hitch out of it if you were Jayne Mansfield. So what I wind up doing is walking to the Port Authority Bus Terminal, which turns out to be close by.

Here they give out information in a sensible way. On the wall is a map of the U.S.A. with the bus routes crisscrossing all over it and the cities dotted and printed in. Underneath the map is a wall of blue telephones without dials or numbers. You pick one up and somebody is right there to give you the answer. They're quite polite. My question is what cities can you go to for less than $10.00. This is of course an odd question, but the woman gives me a straight reply. She must have a list right there handy. I decide on Williamsport, Pennsylvania, because it sounds small, and on the map it looks like once you got there you could go anywhere, it's right in the middle. And it only costs $8.70.

My mother is a lover of Broadway musical shows. Sometimes she goes to them, but mostly she listens to the records.

She bought our hi-fi on time and signed up for this mail club that fires out new records every week. By now she has enough for her own radio show. What I'm getting at is I'm quite familiar myself with show tunes, since my mother got sucked into this hobby, and in a show called *Guys and Dolls* there's this song called "My Time of Day" which has always appealed to me. Some very tough guy is singing about his time of day, "a couple of hours before dawn, when the streets belong to the cops, and the janitors with the mops, and the grocery clerks are all gone." And it's about the "smell of the rain-washed pavement" coming up "clean and fresh and cold, and the lamplight gleam fills the gutter with gold." I don't know why, but to me that's a very moving song. Partly, it means this guy is a lone wolf, very independent, you know, since he can be out so late with no place to skulk off to. He's just there, very casual, sniffing the pavement and gazing into the gutter, nodding at the patrolman, glancing into dark store windows. He doesn't care if he never gets to bed, and nobody else does either. It really *is* his time of day. I mean anyone he sees has a reason to be there, like a job, but he's wandering around for the joy of it. But he sings the song to his new girlfriend, who in slang is his doll, telling her he wants to share it with her. That ruins it for me. She would never appreciate it, even though for him she might pretend to. Years later she would complain he was always going out at 3:00 A.M., and he would only shrug and be sad. Anyway, because of that song, I don't mind that my bus will pull in to Williamsport at 2:40 A.M. I'm not saying that's *my* time of day, though you don't really know until you try it, but it appeals to me. When I imagine walking around the streets of Williamsport, I sort of narrow my eyes and set my jaw tight and feel like a lone wolf. Actually, I guess my time of day, if you have to have one, is eight or nine in the morning. The sun's bright but not hot yet, the slates in front of the house are still cool under your bare feet, and you have the whole day to fill with whatever you want. If that's your time of day, though, you're no lone wolf, that's for sure.

Before my bus leaves this godforsaken city, I've got a few hours to kill. True, there are earlier buses heading out for cheaper towns, but now that I've got Williamsport planted in my head I can't go back on it.

In the stationery store behind a revolving rack of combs and toothbrushes, I find another rack with a sign, Cards for All Occasions, which has a lousy selection, especially for New York City. But, then you can't expect card categories like "To Your Parents When You Run Away" or "For the Killer of Your Pet," and anyway, when you think about it, the card I pick doesn't matter much. So I very quickly decide on one with a little boy on the front laughing and holding a beachball. It says, "Now you are FIVE." On the inside the beachball is way up in the air, and it has a 5 on it, and "Happy Birthday." I pick out another one that has white and silver flowers on a lavender background and says, "Our Deepest Sympathies . . ." and on the inside ". . . in your time of loss." The clerk in the store, a bald man, doesn't say a word when I pay for the cards, and when I ask to borrow his pen, he just hands it over.

I write, in the beachball card, "Dear Folks and Sisters, Please don't worry about me. I'm off to seek my fortune. I'll phone when I can. Bernie." I close it, feeling better, almost like they got it already, but then, looking at the cover again I suddenly realize you *could* think "Now you are FIVE" means now our family only has five people in it. Probably nobody would think that, nobody except me, but if somebody *did* read it that way, it would seem like a very harsh message. But I can't help that now. I seal it up and address it and wander out into the crowds looking for a machine that sells stamps.

There's no point in sending the sympathy card to Richard, I see now, because for one thing he might even enjoy knowing he stimulated me into buying it. It's crazy, but I think he gets a thrill out of being hated. It gives him all the reason he needs to strike. He's quite sick, that bastard, and anyway I don't know his address.

Back in the stationery store the bald man says nothing when I tell him I don't want the sympathy card any more. With his quick fingers he zips my change out of the cash register. I hold my hand out for it, but he slaps the coins down on the counter.

I say, "That's good of you, kind sir. For the likes of me, every penny counts."

He just keeps eyeing me, sort of like that cardinal outside my window. Maybe he is a mute.

Everybody waits for the buses in a long, sloping tunnel that has rows of plastic chairs strung out down the middle. There's baggage all over, kids screaming and chasing each other, old men asleep with their heads bent onto their shoulders and their mouths open, some Puerto Ricans in a bunch all jabbering in Spanish. A tall woman just accidentally clobbered me in the leg with a water ski, and I got mad. I'm tired and on edge. The bus leaves in a few minutes. Only about ten other people, all Negroes, are waiting with me at Gate 28. Our driver just sidled through us and the suitcases out into the smelly cave where all the buses are rumbling and roaring. Now he gives us the signal, wiggling his hand like he's our daddy, and we trudge out alongside the Greyhound. They all have bags to put down below, so I get on first, and I pick a seat near the back, but far enough from the bathroom so its fumes won't seep out at me. The last time I rode on one of these was on our ninth grade field trip to Washington, D.C. We sang songs the whole way, and we stayed in a hotel and threw water bombs out the window. Of course we saw all the sights. It was very enjoyable. Now, though, I'm friendless and alone. And also, looking out at the long line of buses angled into the curb and feeling the dull thumping and scraping as the baggage slides into the compartment below me, I wonder what the hell I'm doing this for. I am a dumb shit of a kid. By now everyone is very worried about me, probably crying, phoning the police and all. I try to tell myself there are monumental, significant adventures waiting ahead, and that after sixteen years my life is finally gathering steam. But, you know, here I am running away through the gloomy city, with a ticket to no place special, making decisions, pretending I'm in control of things, when actually I don't control shit, I mean *zero*. I mean this bus could roll off a cliff or Khrushchev could press the button, or anything. This whole fortune-seeking business is a joke. What kind of say in your future can you really have? Actually, you stumble along through your life waiting for your fortune to jump you from some alleyway, and wham, there's your adventure, your excitement. Life seems too chancy and miserable to me right now, especially as I study the empty, somber expressions of everybody around me. Who's happy in this world, if anybody?

Seated in front of me is this huge Negro who looks like Hank, the driver of our highway department crew truck last summer. Hank was six-foot-six and weighed 300 pounds. He once played tackle in semipro football. He was so good with that dump truck that he could steer and read the *Daily News* at the same time. He kept the paper propped against the wheel. My last day on the job he asked me what I had for future plans. I really couldn't think of any. He never talked much, so for him to ask me that was a surprise. Finally, what I said was, "College, I guess. Something that will lead me to success." We had just pulled into the truck yard, and I was anxious to wash up, grab my paycheck, and head out of that place for good. I had my shirt off, and my back slid in sweat along the seat vinyl. He looked at me from deep in his shiny head with big, dull, brown eyes, and he made me nervous.

He said, "You gon' be a success?"

"I hope," I said.

"Well, listen to me. Don't you forget Hank, now. You a success, you need a bodyguard, you know? You need some protection when you get all you money, you come to me."

"I will," I said.

"You remember," he said, and he smiled at me in a self-conscious sort of way like he felt embarrassed, which he probably was.

"I'll remember," I said, slipping down out of the cab.

"Hank Johnson," he said loud. "I got seven children."

All at once I'm somehow pumped full of this insane hope that the man in front of me *is* Hank, following me around for my protection. He would be my sidekick. But before the lights flicker and go out, he removes his hat, one of those Tyrolean jobs with the little feather, and I can see he's not Hank. He's not as big.

When I wake up the driver is saying, "Scranton. Scranton." We stop outside a restaurant with a sign flashing *Babe's* in orange, and everybody gets out. I wake up again when the motor starts up. My eyes feel like I've been swimming all day in a pool. Looking around, I realize I'm now the only passenger. What's the attraction of Scranton, a very dismal town, for all the others to go disappearing into it like beetles when you lift a rock? So it's my bus, a long, empty box. I imagine I'm balanced cross-legged on the last seat of a bicycle-built-for-thirty with twenty-eight vacant saddles and twenty-eight sets of free-spinning pedals, and I'm all alone except for the driver up there sweating in his brown uniform and pumping away like a madman, and we're sailing along through the dark so fast and smooth that I can't feel the gritty road under me, and I can't think of names for the shadows that shoot by, and in the rush I don't have any time to remember what I left behind me or where I want to go.

It's 6:00 A.M. and getting light outside along the tops of the buildings. I'm in Williamsport, in a silvery diner, on a stool, eating a doughnut. I have a cup of coffee here which is a strange drink, very watery. From just looking at it, I always expected coffee to feel thicker in your mouth, like cocoa. To be honest, it's horrible, and I can't drink it. A waitress came by with a pot and said, "Fresh coffee?"

"Never tried it," I said.

"You kidding? Here, then, live it up." And she poured me some. I admit it smells wonderful, but that's all. There are six waitresses in this place and only one customer, me. They all trooped in at five thirty to relieve the two night waitresses, who I liked better. They were friendly enough without trying to get too familiar with me. Now that the new ones have wiped off the salt and pepper shakers and filled the sugar bottles, they have nothing to do but cluster around me like geese in the park, squawking questions and dumb advice. They act like I'm twelve. "You need a raincoat. It rains in these hills, you know." "I hope you're not making your parents suffer." "You think that's enough money to get you anyplace?" "There's dangerous murderers and weirdos on the highways. The world ain't roses."

"Look, I know what the world is and isn't," I say. "I can read the newspapers." I feel like telling them I got weirdos and murderers in my own backyard, but that would really set them off, so I gulp my doughnut and walk off toward the men's room, where I can find peace.

Usually I'm talented at taking big bites of things, like toast, which my sisters pretend to be disgusted at, but this dry half-a-doughnut is now wadded in my throat like cotton, and I'm about to choke. Staring into the water fountain and swallowing, I read again what you always read (Halsey Taylor Warren, Ohio) and I suddenly know where I'm going.

I'm going to Cleveland or Warren or near there to find my rich Uncle Ike. I'll get a job pumping gas or else polishing porcelain at the water fountain factory, and I'll gradually get to know my uncle better and better so that he will realize I deserve to inherit his fortune. Of course, I'm nuts to have such a fantasy, but if you have to seek your fortune, you should go where you know there is one. And maybe he has a beautiful granddaughter sunbathing naked in the apple orchard. Don't I wish. Hell, I don't really know what I wish. I could take the next bus to New York and make the waitresses happy, or I could still head for Florida and get a job at some tennis courts or maybe be a lifeguard or something.

When you come right down to it, though, making decisions is a waste of energy. It's hard to explain, but it seems to me if I go south everything will either turn out terrific or it won't. The same if I go north. It's almost like you're helpless. You just do what you do, and what happens happens. So out of my pocket I pull my 1803 Large Cent. I'm standing smack in the middle of this glary, green-tiled men's room with a row of pisspots on one side and shit-pots on the other, saying, "Heads it's north, tails it's south." I flip the coin, catch it, slap it over onto my left hand, and there's Liberty, staring into space. I'm relieved. I really didn't want to go all the way to Florida. Summer there can be awful. You have to have air-conditioning.

It's quite light out now, I can see through the grainy window over the radiator, and the tension has gone out of me enough to set my bodily processes moving. I have to drop a tear, as my father says. Sitting on the toilet, I realize how quiet things are at 6:00 A.M. Water is gurgling in the pipes. Faraway trucks rumble outside. I've still got the Large Cent in my hand. You know, in 1803 the old U.S.A. didn't even extend to the Mississippi River. Thomas Jefferson was in charge then, as only the third president in history, and in 1803 he made the Louisiana Purchase. But don't think Louisiana was all there was to it. In fact, Napoleon of France sold us this huge chunk of land, all the way up to Illinois and beyond, for three million dollars, which was a great deal, even then. Fortunately, we had the bucks handy because otherwise we might still have a piece of France running right up the middle of the country. And we might never have found out about California and Oregon and all until too late. Spain would have them, or even Russia. This whole continent would be carved into pieces like Europe. So, in a symbolic way that I can appreciate, this worn piece of money has American wisdom behind it, and if it decides I'm going to Ohio, that's where I'm going, no buts about it. I've got myself excited now. I'm getting my ass out of this place, spitting fire.

My father, who is a worrier, is dead against hitch-hiking. "Hitch-hikers take their life into their hands," he says. "In the paper they get knocked off every day of the week." True, it's a chancy way to get around, but that's the joy of it, and the challenge. You can't go through life protected from all danger anyway, even if you got Hank Johnson tagging along. I mean, your doom is out there, black and unstoppable as the night. You can even be in your own bed and it won't make any difference. In fact two summers ago when I was asleep downstairs in the basement bed for some reason I forget, this gigantic *Ka-BOOM!* woke me up. At the top of the stairs my father was yelling, "Bernie! Bernie!" It was all over, I knew it. The bombs were dropping, the fireballs were spreading out to sizzle us like lumps of bacon fat, and my father was getting the family together to pray, or something. Doom. I felt it. But it was just a powerful thunderstorm. Strong winds swept rain against the house like a hose. My father wanted me to be sure the basement windows were latched tight. I got pretty wet shutting the windows, but what I felt was sheer relief, like heaven, you know. I swear I thought I was a goner. So the way I see it anything you do is about as safe as anything else, and if you worry about your doom all the time like my father, you won't be any safer. You'll be miserable.

Well, those waitresses were no help with directions, but when the Texaco man came in to buy a paper he told me where to stand to catch the outbound traffic, and he even took me to his gas station for a good map. "Lotsa luck to you," he said.

Now I'm settled into the back seat of a car with two fishermen up front. They both wear pulled-down sailor hats with hooks stuck in them. They're drinking coffee out of a Thermos. You can't get away from coffee. They were the second car to go by my spot and very friendly, asking me my name and age and everything, laughing, and telling me a boy can't become a man until he's run away from home a few times.

We've put Williamsport behind us, which I regret a little, because I never did get to walk the streets any. I was so exhausted when we rolled into that diner that all I could do was sit slumped at the counter. Out on the street, stumbling around half-asleep in my wrinkled clothes, I probably would've been arrested.

But now I feel wonderful. The day is beautiful. My mother would say exquisite. I'm listening to the laughing fishermen talk about their wives. They are both sure the wives went back to bed after cooking up the eggs, packing the lunches, and waving them out the door. In a joking way, they act put-out by such laziness, but they'll allow it. I just can't imagine wives who perform those duties like mothers or even slaves. My mother usually makes dinners and pushes the vacuum around, you know, but she's not about to get up to make breakfast for anybody, especially my father. Of course, these men are not as old as my father, and they probably have young wives who try hard, but still. . . . Lee's mother doesn't operate like that either. Of course, she is a very troubled person. I don't really know the details, but she is. She drinks. When Lee gets up early, he cranks the electric burner way up until it's fiery orange. Then he throws a pan with butter and an egg in it onto the heat and lets it crackle for a few minutes. He loves eggs like that. He calls them rubber eggs.

After a while, just to remind them I'm back here, I ask, "What are you fishing for?"

Trout, they tell me. It's the first day of the season. This is new to me. I've done my share of fishing, but in salt water only, after porgies and flounder and snappers. There isn't any season. You just row out and drop your line in. I like fishing, but not that much. It's quite a messy pastime. Like, sometimes a sea robin or an eel will swallow your hook and so you have to dig into him with your knife while he's flopping around in the boat.

When they let me out near a town called Lock Haven, I imagine I'm some kind of fish myself, thrown back into the sea for being too little or too bony. Walking along the roadside gravel, I feel full of freedom. I can go anywhere and do anything because nobody is expecting me anywhere and nobody is after me to get something done. Far up ahead is a pale yellow farmhouse with white sheets and dark clothes strung out on a line behind it and swaying. Next to me down the bank are thick weeds and a barbed-wire fence. A whole herd of cows, all-brown cows, is ambling out this way from the farm.

I hook my thumb out for a pick-up that I see a lady is driving. She zooms by, and I shout, "Wa-HOO!" I know I'm a bit carried-away, but there's nothing wrong with that. It feels like I have more possibilities ahead of me than leaves on a tree. But at home they must be in bad shape by now. All I can hope for is that maybe it will somehow help pull the family together a little. Once years ago, my parents were deeply in love, I know from letters I found and from other evidence like the photos in our family album. One picture shows them standing beside our old De Soto, kissing. Only their lips touch. In the border of the picture my mother inked in, "Oh, you darling cad! November, 1948." She has on a suit with built-up shoulders, and my father's wearing his Golden Gloves jacket with the leather sleeves and golf shoes. The letters are from when he was working up in Buffalo and would be gone for days and days. I was five or six then. They are from my father and quite startling to me because of their sexual nature, not bold and outright, but suggestive. Like he will describe how when he gets back they'll go to bed early with a bottle of champagne, but they won't shut their eyes until daybreak. Now they get along about as well as two people on the subway, and I can hardly find in my memory more than maybe two times I've seen them smooch.

There are no cars on this road. Crunching along in my sneakers, I pass the farmhouse and head up the gradual slope of a hill covered on top with pines. Birds flit by in the high grass. I hear farm machinery somewhere. This is a perfect moment, I know. You get these probably only a hundred times in your entire life, if that. With the sun warm in my face, looking back down the highway curling through the hills like a ribbon, I could care less about school, my family, Richard, Leslie, tennis, even old Zeke. A cool, piney breeze just wafted out at me from the woods, like the land is touching me, you know, and telling me it likes me. It's enough to make you sing.

I am now stuck high up in the cab of this semi which the fat driver just jammed to a stop right in the highway and jumped down out of with the motor running and a machete in his hand. I am shot through with fear, but I'm calming down.

What happened was I stood in those pines for an hour's worth of being ignored by a car or two and many trucks. I was relaxed though, not at all impatient. Then this huge truck saying Fremeau Bros., Harrisburg, on the door beeped its horn and braked next to me, sending up billows of road dust. I climbed inside, and before I could thank him, the driver said, "God*damn*, you're young. You're *young*, ain't you?"

I was insulted. I think of myself as young, I guess, but I didn't like the way he made it seem like a drawback to my whole existence. "I'm sixteen," I said. Very true. I'll be seventeen on June twenty-first, the first day of summer, the solstice.

"Well, that's young," he said. "You look young. It's in your face."

His face was red and round with two big eyes magnified behind his glasses, and he had a T-shirt stretched over his stomach like a full sail.

"Nothing wrong with being young," I said in a quiet voice, not looking his way, but just casually inspecting the cab, all the dials and levers.

"Nope, nothing wrong with being young," he said. Then

he added, "That a little aging wouldn't make right." I felt him glance at me. A wise guy. He revved up and started us rolling.

Probably he *could* see it in my face. Big deal. I can't say I shave yet, not that I'm all hot to start. It's just another dull duty to perform on yourself over and over. Then, not for any reason, except I was feeling heady, I threw in a saying of my mother's: "Youth is strength." My mother misses her younger years.

"Wanna wrestle?" he said, eyeing me in a menacing way that I thought he figured was funny. He's fat all right, but not a bag of guts. He has these thick arms with hair and freckles. Wrestling disgusts me. It's a worse sport than golf. All you do is roll around on a sweaty mat in a hot, smelly room, getting pinched, scraped, bent, and crushed. When it comes around in gym, I can usually find a way out, like a note from my mother saying I've got a skin infection. Then Coach Fergusen sends me to the library.

"I'll pass," I said. "Muscles aren't everything."

"Well, you little hardass," he said. He thumped the steering wheel with his hand. "Where you headed, anyway, this fine morning?"

"Cleveland."

"Cleveland, hell," he said. "Ain't nothin' for you in Cleveland but bad air. Nome, Alaska's, the place to set your sights on. They got country up there. You know what I got this truck full of?"

"Bad air," I said, not looking at him.

"Well, you little son-of-a-bitch. You're wrong. I'm freighting Eskimo spearheads. Harpoon heads. Sharp as razors and a foot long. Forty crates to Nome, Alaska. It's a drive of two goddamn weeks."

Of course I knew the blowhard wasn't serious. When Lee hears somebody talking that way, he always asks, "Are you serious, or delirious?" I would get nowhere with that remark. He probably has mattresses back there, or old newspapers, but I wasn't going to call him on it. It was obvious he's streaked with mean, who knows how deep? "Spearheads?" I said.

"Harpoon heads. Solid American steel a foot long. Nome ain't the end of it. Once we roll in there we got ten more days by dogsled over the ice. Interest you?"

"It might. But I'm already going to visit my rich uncle."

"The hell with your rich uncle. Christ, how many times you get a chance like this? Huh?"

"None," I said. I knew he was jerking me around, but craziness in people is a thing you learn to tolerate, like bad breath, unless it goes too far. He laughed.

Outside, the pines streamed by the window, and slants of sunlight flashed through the cab as we roared along. All at once, I was very sleepy. My eyelids felt thick like quilts and kept trying to settle shut. Mostly to stay alert, I asked him, "Where are you really going?"

But at that sudden moment, he wrenched the wheel over hard, and we swerved like a carnival ride. I slid into the door. "*Gotcha!*" he yelled. The whole truck screeched to a standstill in the middle of the highway. There were no other cars out there, nothing at all, and the driver turned to me with this wild grin and said, "Want a souvenir?" He plunged his hand down between the seats and came up slashing the air with this huge, rusty machete. I was stiff with terror. My hand was on the door handle, but I swear to God I couldn't move it. Then he threw his door open and clanged down out of the truck, clutching the machete like a torch.

In fact, my fingers are still hooked through the door handle, which is vibrating with the rest of the truck, and I'm pointing my eyes down the highway, not really seeing anything, just trying to breathe slower. For a second, I thought it was all over. There was no escape.

In the side mirror I can see him now trotting his big body back alongside the truck. He climbs in, wheezing fiercely, and he jams the machete into the slot between the seats. "*Hooo,*" he says. He has little sweat drops all over his forehead, like the tiny sequins on my mother's old purse that Claudia plays dress-up with. "I got here a present for your uncle's trophy case," he says through his breath, and he tosses me this thing that I catch and then drop on the seat when I recognize what it is. It's a rattlesnake rattle. "That's nine buttons," he says.

"Jesus," I say. I pick it back up.

He says, "This rig, this goddamn thing don't stop for shit. It was half a mile before I could choke her off. Wasn't it? At least half a mile. When we get back from Nome, I'm firing a fart right to the top, and with you for a witness. This baby got the brakes of a scooter. There's doughnuts in that sack there, if you're interested."

"Well, thanks," I say, actually meaning thanks for the snaketail, not the doughnuts, which give me a sort of clogged feeling behind my Adam's apple when I think about them.

"Help yourself. No, I can see why Nome, Alaska, wouldn't tickle you. To be frank, it don't tickle me." He pauses, like he might take this chance to level with me. He rubs the back of his hand under his chin and stares out past the bug splats on the windshield. "OK," he says, "you tell me when you want out, and I'll shove you right out. On your ass or on your feet. You be ready."

I unfold my map and trace my finger along the route I want to follow so I'll know if he turns off it. Reaching behind to get the map back into my pocket, all at once I catch a whiff of myself, a sour, but not exactly ugly, smell. I like it, sort of. It's me, a new me. Only a few years ago, before puberty overtook me, I didn't give off much B.O., but my smells were always interesting to me, especially my asshole. It's crude, but in bed I would stick my finger in there and sniff it. I would smell my turds, too, sunk in the green toilet water like logs. Turds are fascinating because they're the only solid thing your body makes. When you think about it, we're all just turd factories. But hell, you could do worse.

The hotel across the street looks like one giant bicycle reflector, with the low, gold sun glancing off all its windows. In a way, the sun is almost caught there, in a glass-and-steel frame, dimming and dying, you know, but without any power, like a plate. This is Cleveland. It's getting chilly, and, sitting in this phone booth, I'm sort of trapped in glass myself, with my wits slipping away like the light. I was just dumped here by a weird homo who it turned out was very friendly. He would have driven me to my uncle's, but I said I had to call first. Only I just realized I can't call because I don't know my uncle's last name. I tried Schultz, my mother's maiden name, but what if Uncle Ike was her mother's brother? That's probably it. I'm stuck. Her mother died of pneumonia when my mother was four, and so she was brought up mostly by her father's sisters. They still live around here, but they're all married, and I don't know their last names either. Christ. And I left my snaketail in the homo's car, gone for good. Shit, shit. My only choice now is to call home. I mean, I could jump from some bridge into Lake Erie and gurgle to the bottom, sliding down past the fish like an empty soda bottle, but what the hell, you have to go through with everything. You can't give up. I admit I do think about suicide, about ways to do it, but I never would. My mother once took all the pills in the medicine chest, every last one, and we had ten or twenty jars. Then she walked out and told my father. He threw down his paper and called an ambulance with my mother trying to grab the phone away. At the hospital they pumped her stomach and she was OK. Well, life can be awful. And you have to wonder if all the awful times you'll go through in your life will be balanced by all the good, joyful times. Who knows? You gamble, I guess.

So I phone home collect, and my father answers. The operator says, "I have a collect call for anyone from Bernie. Will you accept the charges?"

"Yes, yes," my father says. "Where in the hell are you?"

"Cleveland."

"Cleveland! What the hell are you doing in Cleveland?"

He's angry, and I'm glad he is. I'd hate to have him cry, which he might do if he didn't make himself angry. He can can be quite emotional, like me, but we both hide it. Behind his voice I hear the girls babbling, "Bernie! It's Bernie! Let me talk. Where is he? Let *me* talk." And my father telling them to shut up.

"Sitting in a phone booth outside Lundgren's Cigar Shop," I say, sounding cheerful as I can.

"How the hell did you get there? Don't you know what you've thrown us into? Goddamn it, we've had a twenty-eight-state alarm out for you for two goddamn days. The FBI's dredging the rivers for you. You're a missing person."

"I hitched," I say. His mood is weakening, he's so relieved to know I'm safe.

"Well, goddamn it, what are you going to do now?"

"I don't know. Don't we have some relatives here? That I could stay with?"

He heaves a big sigh. "Here," he says, "talk to your mother."

"*Bernie*," she says, like someone on television. "Do you have any idea how worried we've all been over you?"

"Yeah."

"I don't think so. You wouldn't have done it if you knew.

To us, and to your sisters. They—"

"Well, I sent you all a card. Did you get it?" Of course I know they didn't get it. I just mailed it yesterday, though it seems like last week.

My mother rattles on about the pain I've caused, you know, everybody staying up all night, being questioned by the police, my sisters getting hysterical, Lee calling up every couple of hours acting nonchalant like he would, and Barbara so upset she couldn't go to school thinking how it had to be her fault, even with my mother insisting it wasn't, it was much more than that, it was Zekey, the family, so many things, though my mother doesn't mention Leslie. I wonder whether Mrs. Hendricks has got to my mother yet, or worse, whether Pam Sokel's dropped the bomb on Barbara. On second thought, I actually don't much give a shit. I feel like my life's come apart from all of theirs. They're going on doing whatever they're all supposed to do like citizens or machines or something, and I'm off no place doing anything or nothing, like the one Easter egg you don't find until August. My mother asks if I've got money. "Yeah, a little," I say, and she says they'll wire me fifty dollars, which is more money than I've ever been given, just free.

"Well, what will you do then?" she asks. "Are you ready to come home?"

This is a shock to me. I have no desire to go home. "No, Mom, I just got here a half hour ago."

So she explains I should stay right here at Lundgren's and she'll call her Aunt Joanna and arrange everything. She says they all love me and not to worry. I give her my pay phone number and hang up.

Along the upper floors the hotel windows are dull pink now, washing to shadowy, gray tones as you move your eyes to street level. There's a jumble of cars screeking, honking viciously at each other, blowing milky exhaust into the air.

Cities suck, that's all I can say. You can't even see the sky. My shivering is all that keeps me from falling asleep right here in this smeary glass box. I have to flex my legs to ward off cramps. In the homo's big Chrysler I had to bite my lip to stay awake, and even then my head kept falling sideways against the window like a melon rolling off a table. I'd jerk up straight and there would be all these furrowed fields going by forever, and before I knew it my head was clunking into the door again. I was too scared to sleep. I mean, this guy wanted to seduce me, you know, with his actual dick. Of that I'm positive. He picked me up on the interstate ramp. When he got up some speed, he didn't just throw me some questions like most people, he wanted a conversation, and he had this very soothing voice. At first I didn't suspect him, though I've run up against homosexual guys before and I've heard about them, because with his clean face and black-rimmed glasses he reminded me of Mr. Langley, my ninth grade earth science teacher, who died of throat cancer. He looked exactly like him, and Mr. Langley was a wonderful person, full of jokes. So that put me off. But then the first time I nodded off, without seeing it happen, I realized his hand was resting on my arm and thigh. My eyes sprang open, and there it was like a tarantula. My arm shook it off, and I slid to the door.

He turned his calm face at me. "Don't you like to be touched?" he said.

"Sometimes," I said.

"Do you mean by some people?"

"Yeah, all kinds of people," I said. "There's hardly anybody I let just go and touch me." I was very nervous, trying not to rile him. I didn't know what was going on behind his plain smile. I mean, maniacs escape all the time, and you never know you've crossed one until it's too late. Of course, the odds are way against getting raped by a maniac, not that you ever consider the odds when some guy starts acting like a maniac. Hell, I thought the truck driver was a maniac, and when I left his truck he said, "Good luck to you, and I mean it. Good luck." I wish to God I still had that snaketail. Also, as I mentioned, the homosexual guy turned out very nice, too, but you never know. So I tell him how I don't even enjoy my mother touching me unless I'm sick and all, and he said, "That's really a shame." Then, with that sneaky hand he began rummaging in his glove compartment, and what it came out with was this Kleenex box full of these amazing pictures, which he set in my lap. "Here," he said. Well, you probably think pictures like these, taken with a camera and everything, would be pretty disgusting, pictures of men kissing naked, a young, foreign-looking boy with his jaws around somebody's hairy bone, close-inspection angles of wet bones going into assholes, but it honestly didn't bother me, I don't know why. When I saw them, they seemed just like any pictures, like a landscape, just shapes. They were only black-and-white, though. Color might have been another story. But anyway, they got me worried, very worried. I figured I was as big as he was, in weight, and I knew I was quicker, and so I could just grab the flashlight attached to his dashboard by a magnet and whap him with it if he got funny. I sat there for a minute and looked at the pictures, and then I shoved the Kleenex box to the middle of the seat.

He said, "Well?"

"They're amazing," I said.

"Oh, they're amazing, all right," he said. He shut the pictures back up in the glove compartment and didn't say another word. The radio was playing a sportscaster's report on the baseball trades. With an eye on him sideways in case he tried a quick one, I concentrated on the sports to stay awake, but it was no use. I kept fading out. He was a perfect gentleman, though. He was going to Illinois.

Now I'm feeling about as fat as this toad of a chair I'm in because I just jammed down three Big Boy Burgers, fries, cole slaw, onion rings, cherry pie, and milk, which Aunt Joanna and her son Newton bought for me on the way over. The last time Aunt Joanna saw me I was seven, and now she can't get over how big I grew. I don't know what she expected. Friends of your parents who visit from far away always tell you you've expanded to an astounding size, like the blob from outer space or something.

This room is full of antiques, glass lamps and ceramics, lacy doilies, ticking clocks, and polished wood tables all over. In fact, Aunt Joanna sells antiques in a shop attached to the house called Age Renewed—Antiques and Curios. She's upstairs "making a place" for me, and Newton is explaining how I can find the park tomorrow if I want to, but I can't listen.

"You got all that?" he says. "It's really not far."

"Oh yeah," I say. Newton is about thirty and a speech therapist. My mother used to babysit him years ago. He once visited us on Long Island, which nobody ever does, we hardly have any room. He slept in the livingroom, and one afternoon he taught my mother the cha cha, dancing next to the ironing board. They drank and listened to musicals on the record player and laughed and everything. But my father didn't like it. He considers Newton a jerk. Here over the mantel is this bluish photograph of Judy Garland, who Newton adores, leaning into a microphone with her eyes shut and her mouth in a tiny O. Newton took it himself, right off the TV, in color, and he paid twenty dollars to have it enlarged. It looks odd in here with all these antiques.

Aunt Joanna just came down the stairs saying she could

kick herself for not remembering to buy a toothbrush for me because she thought of it talking to my mother on the phone, and she thought of it when we stopped at Big Boy. "I'm getting *old*," she says, winking at me.

"Positively ancient," says Newton.

"That's OK," I say. "My teeth won't fall out overnight."

She smiles, but she doesn't look happy. "Let's hope not. You sleep well, now, Bernie. And as late as you want."

I'm heading up the stairs. "Yeah, I will," I say.

"Nighty-night," says Newton.

Jesus, poor Aunt Joanna. I know she must be wondering what to make of a wildass teenage jerk like me. While I was down there gobbling the burgers, Newton sat back in his soft chair with a glass of whisky, and Aunt Joanna wandered to and fro over the carpet, sort of touching the knick-knacks she has set out here and there, getting herself primed to converse with me. Finally, she asked how was my hitch-hiking experience, and I said it was pretty enjoyable. Then she said, "Well, I know you're probably a little frayed at the edges after a long day on the road, and we can surely talk more in the morning, but I've promised your mother I'll call back when I find out your plans, just for the next few days, that is. And I told Jean that you are invited to stay here with us just as long as you want, to rest, or even live here awhile if you have that desire."

Right then my desires weren't aimed much beyond my jelly-glazed cherry pie, and so I was stunned. *Live* here. Christ. "Oh, don't worry about that, Aunt Joanna," I said. "I won't be staying more than just a few days. I mean, I'll be glad to stay a few days. A week, maybe."

"Well, we'll be happy to have you, Bernie, as I said to Jean. And so you'll be going home, then, in a few days?"

"Yeah, I could go home. Or, I don't know, I could just move on, too, I guess."

When I said that, I knew it was a mistake. It scared Aunt Joanna. "Move on?" she said. "Move on where?"

The thing was, I still had Uncle Ike and the water fountain factory on my mind, you know, even though I was beginning to realize I will never hook up with the old guy now. Blowing in free and on-the-loose from Long Island would've been one thing, but if I stay here a few days and then tool up to his mansion in a taxi or something, forget it. A move like that would have no style, no impact. Besides, I'd have to get his address from Aunt Joanna. So I sat there, munching the pie, and mentally it felt like my fortune was slipping through my fingers.

"Move on where?" Aunt Joanna repeated.

I glanced up at her. "Oh, home, probably," I said. "I really haven't thought that much about it."

Then Newton sat up in his chair, his ice cubes tinkling. He said, "Say, what made you come all the way here to Cleveland in the first place?"

"Well, see, first I was going to drop in on my Uncle Ike, because years ago—"

"*Ike?*" said Newton. "Oh, Lord. I'd give you about ten minutes over there. That would be it."

Aunt Joanna shook her head. "You know, Ike is Newton's uncle, actually. He's your *great*uncle."

"Isaac the Great," said Newton, and he laughed his high laugh.

"I know," I said. "He used to send me presents."

Newton said, "What I meant was why did you run away from home in the first place? What was your *raison d'être?*"

I looked down at my burger wrappers for a few seconds, trying to come up with the right phrase, and Aunt Joanna said, "Newton, the boy hasn't been here an hour. Let's give him a chance to recover himself."

Newton sighed and looked up at the ceiling.

When Aunt Joanna left the room to call back my mother, I told Newton it was just that my loyal dog died and I couldn't take it, so I hit the road, putting my sorrows behind me.

"You mean the Dalmatian?" he said.

"Yeah. Zekey," I said.

"Sure, I remember Zekey," said Newton. "He lived out there behind the house."

Then Aunt Joanna called down, "Bernie, your mother would like to talk with you."

"OK," I said. I got up, and Newton put the rim of his glass up to his forehead, sort of like a salute.

All my mother had to say was she would send me a package of clothes and my Jack Kramer, if I wanted it, as soon as she could. She warned me to be a help, not a bother, and to make my bed and rinse off my dishes—the same crap she hands me when I'm home. And she urged me to drop them a postcard when I felt ready to head back east, if not sooner. Then she asked me if I had any messages I would like her to pass on to anyone special. "Oh, no, no," I said. "Just give 'em my address, anybody that calls. You know, tell 'em I'm fine—a little crazed, but fine. OK?"

"Count on me," she said.

I laughed. "I would talk to the girls, though," I said. "Are they up?"

"Oh, no, they're long gone to dreamland," she said. "We were awake all night, you know. Did you know that?"

"Yeah, yeah," I said. "OK, 'bye."

"Sleep tight, now, Bernie," she said, and we hung up.

From this feathery bed, which I'm now sunk into like a big rock, I can see the stars, part of the Big Dipper, in fact. An exchange student we had once from England called it the Great Saucepan. It's strange, but somehow I'm not sleepy. Far off I hear the metal drumming of a train. It lets

96) Raison d'être : means simply reason for being.

out a low hoot-hoooot, hoot-hoooooot. Suddenly, I wish I was on it, and I wish I had my snaketail, and I wish I had enough money to buy a house for all my friends and my family in some warm, green place, like a farm. I can almost trace it in stars. The Great Farmhouse. With a long, long drive winding up to it and fluffy, blowing trees all around. You could string up a hammock and lie there forever. Someone in a long dress would bring you Big Boy Burgers and milk on a red tray. That would be wonderful. She would read to you, and you wouldn't want to have anything else.

CHAPTER 5

THE BEST TREE to climb is an oak. They are big and very solid and secure with good, thick branches perfect for sitting or building on, whatever you want. The bark is rough, but not really brittle like hickory, and it will take a nail. Most trees as old as the one I'm up in now (which must have been here since before Ohio was Ohio) you can't get around in because the branches are too far apart, like elms, which are lousy. In this wind all the tiny new reddish-green leaves are fluttering and the small branches are weaving and tossing, but the tree trunk doesn't budge. If you work your way up, say, a maple as high as this, you sway like crazy in breezes that would barely hold up a kite. Oak limbs have knobs and elbows to them, which make them valuable for shipbuilding, I don't know why, and they grow very slowly, the big ones maybe an inch a year, or less. It makes them dense and heavy.

Well, I can see plenty from here: downtown Cleveland, a good patch of the lake, stores close-by, strings of houses all the same size like Monopoly pieces, a hill with a radio tower on it, and a lot of the park, which is where this tree grows. It's at the far end of the baseball diamond's right-field foul line on the edge of a small woods with asphalt paths running through it.

A Negro boy went by just now on a bike, and I missed him. It's almost impossible to hit anything on the ground from this far up because of all the branches you have to shoot through and the wind. It's pretty windy. After three days here (this is called Lakewood, actually a suburb of Cleveland), I am crazed with boredom. So yesterday, when I found this tree, and today, I've climbed up here with a baloney sandwich, the library book, *Genghis Khan and the Mongol Hordes*, and a pearl-colored pea-shooter, with which I am talented at close range. I bought it with my leftover travel money.

Shit, a wasp is on me walking up my arm, sniffing and twitching with its legs. You can't kill them on you like a yellowjacket, because they'll jab you before they croak. They're tough. He's off, humming. He dives down through the lower branches. Once I was stung on the thumb four times by wasps and it swelled up like a cucumber. I had to have shots.

The mail is slow as a one-legged turtle. On Thursday my mother must have sent off those clothes and my tennis racket, and they aren't here yet. It's Saturday. If I was only a branch of this four-hundred-year-old oak tree, Saturday wouldn't mean a thing. All I could do would be to *be* here, plain and simple, which isn't really *do*ing at all. I would just soak up sun and water, and I would have no worries and no choices. I know I'm nuts. Who would want to go through life as a tree? The trouble is, if you're a person, your existence sometimes gets so complicated and painful that you would rather be absorbed by something, a wave, a cloud, it doesn't matter, than to go on with it. Other ways-to-be can attract you by looking so peaceful, like, for example, just sitting high up in a tree. But it's impossible, I swear. If you think a guy like me up here with a tasty sandwich and a book feels serene and all, you're wrong. My mind is tossing my thoughts around and around like a clothes-drier.

I think Newton is a homo. This friend of his named Brian, who Aunt Joanna hates, lives above the antique shop and does small carpentry jobs. He's forty or so with tattoos all over him from the navy. He was on a sub-chaser in World War II. Newton's over there all the time, and they are quite affectionate with each other for men, you know, patting and touching and stuff like that, which is perfectly OK with me, I mean not disgusting or anything, just odd. Newton slaves over this very elaborate garden of flowers in the backyard, though now only a few are blooming. He has over sixty kinds, and in the evening when I help him water them all Brian comes around and the two of them compliment me on my muscles. They're joking with me, but they're sort of serious, too. It's a little embarrassing. I know they would never try anything funny with me, not even like the homo driver from Illinois did, and so I get along all right with them. They may even think I'm too immature to understand what's going on with them, I don't know. It doesn't bother me, though, I know that.

Bits of my bread crust sail down through the branches like the pennies you throw into a well. On the paths two squirrels are waiting for them. They chew them like my sisters eating corn-on-the-cob, with their heads cocked up at me. Maybe they think it's funny that I'm in the tree and they're on the sidewalk. I sort of like squirrels, they're quick and perky, but I sort of dislike them too, because they're mean and angry like rats almost, which they are related to. This vantage point of me up here and them below reminds me of when I was real young, about five, and we lived in Maryland. From the outside of our apartment, a lot of steep cement stairs lead down to the cellar, where my mother did the laundry. A drain for water was at the botttom of those stairs, and all kinds of mice lived in it. I would wait at the top for them to come out of the drain, and I would try to bash them with red bricks like a bomber. I thought I was a bomber.

The bat whips around—*crack*, and the ball is at me on a line. My glove goes up over my shoulder. The ball smacks in. My palm stings through the leather. I didn't have much time to warm up. My hands are cold, but they still can nab the old apple. I toss the ball to short, and my eyes follow it to third, to first, and back to the mound. "*Yeah*," the pitcher says. First I think they skipped the catcher, but then I realize he's on their team, not ours. You supply your own.

"B! B!" yells the left fielder. They're calling me B, they decided, because they already know somebody named Bernie, though he's not playing. I look out his way to smile at him, but really that wasn't a hard play. I'm worried I'll get one on the ground. I haven't even looked at a grounder since last summer. That was the second out. The third guy up is this tall, big-shouldered Negro guy in a T-shirt with the sleeves ripped off, black pants, and pointed black shoes. "*Bust* dat tater, Latham. Go on," a woman yells. About five fans are in the bleachers, and she's one. He takes a couple of mean cuts and steps to the plate.

This game was starting up when I got down from the tree, and these guys, who mostly are Negroes except for two Italian guys who are brothers, asked me to play. I told them infield, and just like that they stuck me here at second. I hardly had a chance to feel the ball. In Little League I was always pretty decent. I played short and had a good bat my first season, but in my second I somehow got ball-shy, and I didn't hit much. My average tailed off about 300 points.

Out in left I see our guy trotting backwards about ten yards like you go back for a lob in tennis. Latham lets the first pitch by. Looked like a low strike, but we don't have an ump, so what's the difference. If I knew these guys, I'd yell, "Looked good, looked good," or something, but I feel like a real stranger, and besides I never played with Negroes before. I don't know their style. Our pitcher is Vinnie, one of the Italian brothers, who are short, kind of pudgy, and have duck's-ass haircuts. They're ugly guys, if you want to know. Vinnie hangs the next one, and Latham swings late but he wrists it very hard high over my head and out toward our right fielder, who runs fast for a few yards to the foul line, then stops, waiting like a stargazer. It was really hammered, that ball, for it to stay up there so long, even in this wind. Suddenly, the fielder runs in a few steps. The ball glances off his glove and lands in front of him. I'm out on the grass for the cut-off, and I know Latham is behind me toward and maybe past second, I heard him pound by. The play's at third, but the throw's over my head, and the pitcher has to pick it off. Big Latham's breathing hard on third, but he doesn't look proud of his hit. He's there stone-faced, knocking the dust out of his pants. His team's yelling and hooting, though, mostly to dig at our right fielder, who's lying on his back in the grass on a straight line between me and the oak tree. Now he stands up, looking at nobody. The woman in the stands is going, "Whoooo, whoooo, whoooo," and shaking her fat arms in the air. The next guy up is little and wears glasses, but he sends a chill through me cause he's a lefty. I would definitely have to make the play or give up a run. I'm nervous. The guy takes three pitches, and I'm hoping maybe he'll pop up. Then he taps one at me. It bounces twice, I catch it and flip to first. I'm full of relief, trotting off the field.

They beat us, 9 to 6, in a good game for pick-up, and afterwards with the sky clouding over, most of the guys sit in the grass smoking cigarettes. A bell nearby clangs four times, and I decide I ought to head out for Aunt Joanna's before she starts to worry that I've taken off for New Zealand or someplace. The guy, Neil or Eel, who was our right fielder, a real card with a slick joke for every occasion, calls while I'm walking up the bank, "B! You ain't half-bad . . . for a cat with them horseshoe legs." He's referring to my sort of bowlegs and also to the last catch I didn't make, when the ball shot between my ankles out into right. I never touched it. In general I played all right, though. I had one good hit and one crummy hit, and my glove was pretty steady. I know he said what he did to be friendly and just to have something to say because he sees me walking away without comment.

So I say, "Oh, thanks. You got an eye for talent." A couple guys laugh. Far out past left field I see big Latham walking in a bunch of other guys, Vinnie and his brother, and also the best hitter on our team, a skinny, light-colored guy named T.J., and they're headed toward a duck pond I saw from the oak tree, though from here it's out of view. When I turn to leave again, Neil or what's-his-name says, "Hey, tonight's a party at Randy's. Can you make it?"

His high and fast voice grabs your attention. I look back at him blowing smoke out his nostrils. I don't remember which one's Randy, and, being honest, I'm not all that interested in a party, even though after-supper TV at Joanna's isn't what I call lively. "What kind of party?" I say.

"What *kind*?" Neil turns to the other guys sprawled

around him. "The cat wants to know what *kind* of party. Don't raise up doubts and questions, man," he says to me. "Just you be there, you hear?"

Well, at that I know I won't be there. I'm not going to ask where Randy's is, and anyway, parties are no fun if you don't know a soul. I say, "If I can make it, I'll be there."

At the top of the bank, I can hear them all cackling away, joking and smoking. I angle up through the park, past the tennis courts, where nobody is playing, and past this bare patch with brick paths going through it and like a court-yard in the middle, which is a rose garden, but I see only a few buds. Maybe they're sick, though it is early. A lot of gardeners were poking around here yesterday.

When I finally leave between the granite pillars and walk a block down toward Aunt Joanna's, I realize, shit, I forgot *Genghis Khan* and my pearl pea-shooter. I left the book on the ground by first base with the pea-shooter shoved inside like a bookmark. It's only a library book, which they could never stick me for, but I'm only half-finished, and also it was a fifty-cent pea-shooter.

I take a lazy run back through the park. It's not cold yet, but the sun is now completely gone behind gray clouds that are like the flannel pajamas I had as a kid. They had feet with plastic bottoms, and I used to wish they were the kind of clothes people always wore, they were so simple and comfortable.

When I get to the diamond, the book is missing. It's not where I left it—by a clump of dandelions so I'd remember where it was—and nobody threw it over by the bleachers. Hands on my hips, I stand there, staring down at home plate. I hate being scatter-brained. I don't think of myself as scatter-brained, but when this happens to you, well, you're not as *aware* as you ought to be.

When I look up from digging my sneaker toe in the dust,

there down the third base line I see this tall Negro girl ambling and kind of swaying with every step like she's really dancing more than walking, and it looks like in one hand she has *Genghis Khan*. I scoot up the bank to get behind a row of pines so I can move up on her without her noticing. I don't want to come clumping up behind her like some madman. What if she swung around and slugged me and it wasn't even my book? But I see now it is my book. I recognize the plastic library cover and my pea-shooter sticking out. I'm suddenly mad. Why would a girl just walking along like that pick up somebody else's book? She's almost to the break in the hedge, which I think must open out on the path to the duck pond. I step out from the pines. "*Hey*," I yell. "You got my book."

She stops and faces me. She has a lot of black hair hanging down.

"That's my book," I yell.

"No it ain't," she yells back, and she ducks through the hedge.

For a second I'm stunned. What would she want with that book? Maybe all she wants is my pea-shooter. I take off after her, down the bank, slapping across the asphalt path, and into the hedge. I guess because my sisters are always so easy to catch, the way they gallop along almost tripping over their own feet and screaming, I think this girl could be no rabbit either, but when I pop through the hedge, I see she's already fifty yards ahead of me along the shore of the pond and *flying*, with her hair waving and everything. So off I zoom myself. I am truly the fastest person I know, except for Geoffrey Mumford, and he moved away years ago. If there's enough running room, nobody gets away from me. Speed is sort of my best natural resource. So I'm not worried, even though this is probably her territory, her turf, as the hoods say. But, Jesus, she can really move her feet. She's now around the bend on the far side of the duck pond (which is much bigger than it looked from the oak tree). In her blue shorts her legs are going like crazy, but I'm gradually closing the gap. White ducks squawk and ruffle away as I go by.

I'm only ten yards back. She's slowing. All at once the book flutters on an arc over her head like a bird you surprise in the woods. Splash, it drops into the pond. I dig into the grass and skid down on one knee right where the book landed. It's not quite sunk. I yank it out. Water from under the cover streams onto my sneakers. The pages are wet, but not really soaked.

"Now look what you done," I hear the girl shout.

I whip around and she's standing there behind a green-painted bench a short way off. She's got her head bent forward between her shoulders, panting. "*What?*" I shout back.

"What you mean '*what*'? Don't you act like the blame don't come onto you. That's a *li*-brary book, and you know it. You gonna *pay* for it."

"You can eat shit. This is *my* library book which you robbed from *me* and threw in this swamp. If anybody pays, it's you."

"You can't mouth me like that, toilet-face. I din't rob from nobody. It was only layin' there in the grass, and there is *rain* comin'. And I work at that *li*-brary, and I was takin' it back to where it wants to be, not layin' in the wet."

"Well, you're real smart. You don't want it to get ruined, so you fling it in the pond."

"I threw it 'cause the hounds was on my tail, and I din't mean for it to flop in the water. *You* made me throw it. You can set your mind to pay for it."

I tromp up toward her, shaking out the pages, but she backs away from the bench like a shy horse. Her eyes shine.

I stop. "I'm not paying one goddamn penny for this lousy book. I'd rather let the frogs have it. I want to read it, and that's why I fished it out."

"You crazy," she says.

"Besides, I left it back there on purpose. And I was coming back to pick it up, but you robbed it."

"Whyn't you say it, then, instead of chasin' me down like some crazyman or worse?"

"If you would've given me half a chance, I would. You just took off with it. And, hey, where's the pea-shooter that was stuck in here?" I realize just now it's missing. I don't see it on the ground anywhere, or floating in the water.

"*What?*" Her voice is quite squealy, like everything annoys her.

I drop down onto the bench, and she backs off a little more. "My pea-shooter. You can pay me fifty cents for that. I don't give two shits about the book."

"It's a *li*-brary book," she says, like I can't remember that.

"*Or* the *li*-brary." It was actually not too bad a library, with comfortable chairs all around, and sunlight washing in over the racks of magazines and newspapers. I know probably I'll find my pea-shooter along the path somewhere, unless some jerk finds it first, not that I can't pick up another one, but, you know, you get attached to tools that you own, and if they get lost, you feel sorry for them sort of, as if they're attached to *you*, which is stupid. I mean, I know it's only this plastic tube, but that's sentimental value for you, what can you do? I'll have to hunt for it.

Actually, considering it was underwater, *Genghis Khan* is not in such bad shape. Somehow about half the pages stayed almost dry, but because it landed like a tent, the middle half got it bad. The book will fatten up with ripples like they do after they fall in the tub. I've done that before, but only with paperbacks.

"What's your name anyway?" says the girl in her high-toned way. She's around the side of the bench, not afraid of me, I guess, now that I'm settled, drying the book page by page on my shirt front.

"Why? You want to turn me in to the librarian? Go ahead. I'm Phil McCracken." That's one of Lee's names. He's got a bunch of them, Hugh Chardon, Anita Lay.

"No, I honestly don't fuss with him *or* the *li*-brary. I put away books is all. But leavin' that book in the rain ain't right, I know that."

"Yeah, and neither's throwing it in the pond."

"I din't mean it."

"And where's this rain, anyway?" I say, even though it probably will rain. The wind's dying.

"*Shit*," she says, sharp and loud, and she turns her back on me. Her sweatshirt is darker blue than her shorts. The writing on the back was just a blur while we were running. "WHOA—the Sound of Soul." A big, bare footprint is stamped on it, like Friday's in the sand. She has thin legs, coffee-with-milk color, but you can see muscles under the skin, tense and stringy, not like Barbara's legs or Leslie's, which are always smooth like a rubber doll's. Even Billie Jean Moffit, the tennis player, doesn't have muscles showing like that. Most women have this layer of fat over everything so they can be warm and soft. That's why ladies can ice skate in those little skirts. They don't get cold.

"Well, since you don't care about the library book either, the least you can do is help me hunt for my pea-shooter, seeing as how you lost it," I say.

With her back still to me, she sings, "You just open your zipper, my little man, and there it will be."

At that I let my mouth fall open, and I roll my tongue around inside. That's crude, pretty slutty, and more like the kind of thing you would hear Lee say. If he was *inspired*.

Maybe she doesn't know what a pea-shooter *is*. Maybe she's never seen one. "You got a mouth like a garbage barge," I say. "I'm talking about a bean-pipe, a blowgun let's say, that I just bought yesterday in a dime store and that *you* just lost trying to run away with it."

She whirls around laughing. It surprises me to see her suddenly so jolly and cheerful. "I swear I never did see you *pea*-shooter, or what you call it, and it can't be that I lost it, if I never knew what it even *was*."

This floors me really. How can anybody be a kid and not know what a pea-shooter is? You would expect a Negro to know, too, wouldn't you? After a while I say, "So, what's *your* name, then?"

"You tellin' the librarian? Well, go ahead. Winona Lockhart." She laughs. She thinks she's wise.

"Winona is your name?" I never heard that before.

"Winnie," she says.

"OK," I say. "It's a long, plastic tube like a straw, and it's pearl-colored. You shoot dry peas through it. I think you should help me find where it fell out. It's along here somewhere."

"No, thanks. I gotta be home right off."

"If you don't help me find it, I'm telling the librarian who threw this in the pond."

"You go and do that, then. The blame is all onto you, for chasing me down like the Klu Klux Klan."

"We'll see," I say. I put the book under my arm and stand up.

"Well, all right, I'm gonna help you find that thing. But you go right on and tell him anyway. It's Mr. Lewis. He got his name right on his desk."

"Forget it. We'll just walk back to where we started, you on the right, me on the left. Look in the leaves and all around." We only go about five feet, and I find it in a bush, right about where she let the book fly into the pond. "I got it," I say.

She gives a big smile. "The *pea*-shooter. Show me how you work it."

I take some peas from my pocket and spit a couple splashes into the pond. She holds out her hand, so I give it to her along with some peas. She looks at it for a minute. The skin on her face has not a single bump or line on it, and her round nose is like an ice cream scoop melted on, and her lips rise out just below like somebody about to smooch. She gets it right away and starts chinking them into a metal sign that says Pedestrians Only. At first, most girls, like my sisters, can only blow, and then the peas just roll out the end. "You're a real tomboy," I say.

She spins and stings my chest with a pea.

"All right, if you're getting wise, hand it over."

She twirls it in her fingers like a baton and flicks it at me. I catch it. "You got that at the five 'n' dime?" she asks, with her eyes open wide.

"Yup." I stick it in the book again. I know where she'll be off to as soon as she gets fifty pennies together. Droplets of rain start to nick my face and arms, making my skin twitch. Before it really opens up, I ought to scamper to my aunt's place, no doubt she's already worried. But instead I just stand there in the stillness, looking at the silver surface of the pond, which also is what Winnie's looking at. It's speckled in the rain. The ducks are cruising around like tugboats. Many trees, maples it looks like, that are barely green, form the park boundary out past the pond. On a pole above the trees a huge sign says Firestone. With the beads of rain collecting in it, Winnie's spread of hair looks glossy like a wig. We both just gaze, and I'm thinking the longer you go in silence the harder it gets to say anything. I stoop for a stone and whip it high, high up beyond the ducks.

Finally, it hits the water, *phhht*. Bubbles rise up through the hole it made. Ripples reach out around. I say, "You know, probably no one will touch that stone again ever. I am the last person in history to touch it."

Winnie turns her face to me. "Whoopee," she says, but her remark doesn't bother me.

"It's something to think about, that's all."

She says, "Hey, do you know Randy Cosgrove?"

"No, I'm not from around here."

"Whereabouts you from, then?"

"New York."

"Yeah? Well, what you doin' out here?"

"Just running away from some bad times."

"I know how that is," she says. "I lived in Harlem till I was twelve years old. Well, listen, Randy Cosgrove has this party on tonight. You go to Clement Avenue, to the big, brown house with the cars parked every place around it."

"Yeah," I say, "I'm already invited."

"Well, fine, then," she says, giving me her flashy smile. "See you there." She turns, and I watch her lope off along the path, a natural runner, graceful and springy. She could be a track star some day, I wouldn't be surprised.

When I clomp up the porch steps, shaking the water off my sneakers, and through the livingroom, where, if you don't walk quiet enough, all the glass objects in it sort of tinkle, I find out Aunt Joanna's not worried about me (at least she doesn't act it), and she's baked me a chocolate cake with marshmallow icing. You may be thinking, *yum*, but actually I don't like cakes, and I hate icing. I make out to be very enthusiastic, though, going, "Wow, thanks a lot, Aunt Joanna," and that makes her happy. I know I can manage to eat a piece or two.

"You'll have to restrain yourself until it's time for

dessert," she says. She lifts it with both hands to the top of the refrigerator.

Also, there's mail. No box from home, but *three* letters, from Claudia, Lee, and Barbara. I have never in my life had three letters at once, and I have always been very excited by the mail. In a way, when some message or some package —a thing you never expected, with your name right on it —appears at your door, it's magic. I wouldn't do it now, but when I was in eighth grade I wrote many letters to foreign governments to ask them for information about themselves, and they would send me large, official envelopes with a typed letter to me inside and maps, pamphlets, and photographs. The Soviet Union sent me this brown package tied with string that had my name in the Russian alphabet on it and that my mother had to sign at the front door for. It contained a thick book, *The Land of the Soviets,* which I couldn't read, it was so boring. It was wrapped in a Russian newspaper. There was a letter, too, and papers about the five-year plan and the seven-year plan and all the ways they were getting their country in shape, but the strange thing about it was the Russians sent me this used map. You always got a map, and the other countries always sent brand-new maps, but my Soviet Union map was a little creased and wrinkled, and it had a city circled in blue ink, *Kiev.* It could have been a secret message to me, I thought, but when you think about it, that didn't make sense. I guess they just ran out of new maps. Also, when I felt like it, I would throw bottles into the bay with messages inside that asked whoever discovered them to write to me. I waxed the corks tight, put a stamp in, and I put sand in the bottom for weight and everything. I was scientific. I got replies from interesting people in Nova Scotia and Martha's Vineyard, though most that I launched never got found and most that got found never made it past Connecticut.

I have my own room, too, for the first time in my life, which is where I am now with my letters in front of me on the bedspread, arranged in a row. I haven't opened them yet. Downstairs I hear Aunt Joanna clacking pots and kitchen utensils, making spaghetti. She interviewed me a couple days ago about what I like to eat. I'm not hard to please, really. I'll eat anything that tastes all right, even anchovies, but there isn't very much I *love* to eat. One thing I told her was spaghetti, so she's down there throwing some sauce together. She's a very kind person. It gives me a sudden pang to think of that cake. When my mother was being raised by Aunt Joanna, she got whatever she wanted to eat, chocolate milk, ice cream, strawberry jam, and all. In the old days nobody knew much about nutrition. When she was ten, my mother had to take a cab to the dentist to have eight teeth pulled. She came back in a cab, too, in the back seat all alone, holding a towel under her chin for the blood.

First I open Claudia's. I knew this letter was coming. Yesterday I got a short note from my mother, in which she mentioned that Claudia was in the kitchen, bent over a pad of yellow paper with her tongue sticking out between her lips, writing to her big brother. My mother sent me a fifty-dollar check. I'm supposed to save it for my bus ticket to New York.

> *Dear Big Brother Bernie,*
>
> All of us here were certainly worried when you didn't come home Tuesday night, but we got over it! So your all the way in Cleveland. We were all wondering what made you run away, but mommy said it was many things, and I know if I was a boy I might do the same thing. So I don't blame you, and I understand. We all miss you, daddy says to say.
>
> Daddy carried Zekey in an old beach towel behind the

garage and buried him with a rock over his grave. Mommy made a wood cross with a black ribbon and a white one wrapped around it that said Zeke. We said a prayer for him. And we all knew there is no more suffering for him.

She goes on about the weather, how warm it's been getting there, how she thinks she may plant some vegetables out back. That's sort of a depressing thought. The small backyard, where we used to have grass and swings and a sandbox, is now a lot of the time, when it rains especially, a sunken area of muck from our cesspool overflowing. The cesspool men have been there with their truck and hoses, but it does no good. We need a bigger cesspool. Ours just can't handle all the crap the family sends down the pipes. It really stinks, too, which upsets the neighbors. You can't blame them, not that they ever actually come complaining to us, but you can tell how they feel. They just don't understand it. I can't imagine sticking a garden in all that, but maybe she hopes it will work as a disguise, I don't know.

In his scratchy handwriting, Lee says,

Dear Dipshit, you sure had us fooled. I was hoping you committed hairy kary or something so I could read about it in the papers and tell everybody I knew you. But you never did have guts, just luck. So you get to miss all this school and tennis practise. Coach Nicely just about shit his pants till it filled his socks and covered up his saddle shoes when he heard you took off, and I'm serious. He is NOT glad. He wants you back for the start of the season against Northport next Wednesday. You think you can make it? Myself I'm not loosing sleep over it, but you got some people going in circles, not mentioning any names, but especially ARBBRAA. Just what you wanted, ha ha! Seriously, she was worried. She told Sue Jacobowitz she thought you left because she got mad at you. I told Sue BULLSHIT, it was because your dog died. But I didn't tell her about Rick the Prick who sucks the Dick and would probably give my Turds a Lick. Who would want that faggot cripple swearing revenge on them. Not me, you never know what he could do. He got suspended for a week on Monday for not giving Mr. Devoe his switchblade. I don't know if he had to give it then or not. Larry Bauer told me. Well I think you even shook up old Leslie too. Around me she pretended she didn't give two shits, but Pam Sokel was asking Sue J. for the whole story, where you went and that, so maybe she's still hot for your warty old cocktail frank, who knows?

Lee goes on, throwing in a description of the weather and how nice it is for tennis. He tells how on Wednesday, Burton Whitney Davies, who is fat as a hippo, fell down the stairs in the home ec wing. Everybody laughed and even kicked his books all over until they realized he broke his ankle. Lee went for the nurse, but they couldn't carry him on a stretcher, they had to wheel in a special bed. I know Lee is able to feel a little sympathy for people, but he hides it to the end. He says on the bed Burton had tears rolling out down the sides of his head into his ears. I can imagine it real well, and it seems very sad. Next Lee mentions he got a letter from Jennine Potter, which he will show me when I get back. He always likes to have something over you, that Lee.

Barbara has always written me short letters. The time I went to Boy Scout camp for a week she was sailing up with her family in Maine, and I was expecting a whole essay from her, you know, because she can really write, she's so smart, about the Atlantic, and the pine wilderness, and sleeping on the boat, with details and all, but what she wrote then was, "Dear Bernie, I am fine, Mommy is fine, Daddy is fine, George is fine, Ben is fine, Sassy is fine. We hope you are fine. How are you? Sincerely, Barb." George and Ben are her brothers. Sassy is her slobbery mutt of a dog.

This one goes,

> *Dear Phillippe Maurice,*
>
> Alack and alas, you are gone to the wars and I am left miserable and alone here in dreary Nambia Pambia. How dismal for me with no company but my bitter tears. I did not see you depart. Everyone said the last they saw of you you were gallopping into the setting sun on your faithful yak, Leslie, waving the banner of freedom and the colors of Hobbes High Castle. I hope you are taking good care of yourself and not letting the ugly Beast of Linwood get your goat. (He can have your yak). The castle halls are hollow without your ringing step. Please bring me a trophy. Awaiting you with sorrow, love, and impatience, I am your fiery beauty,
>
> > *Esmerelda,*
> > *luscious and true*

Love. My eyes fasten onto the word. It's the first time she's ever mentioned love directly. Well, in a way it's directly. You have to know Barbara to see that. I mean, even though the letter seems like a joke, it contains some serious emotions. *Leslie,* for instance. She knows about Leslie, but she doesn't seem disturbed by it. You never know, that could mean all kinds of things, Barbara's so unpredictable. But maybe she thinks going all the way is acceptable. Maybe now she wants to do it. These thoughts are always enough to give me a hard-on, if I really let myself go.

Normally, I will answer a letter as soon as I get it, but

here I have *three* letters, and besides, Aunt Joanna is calling me in a straining voice, "Spaghetti is ready. Spaghetti." So I'll wait to think up clever replies.

After the game, when Neil or Eel brought it up, the party idea really didn't intrigue me. That's because I think those guys were not actually *inviting* me to come, they were more like daring me. I didn't try to figure out what they might mean by that then, but now that I've decided to go it concerns me. Negroes are difficult to understand, but you can talk to them and get along with them, if you stay relaxed and natural, not like Puerto Ricans, who usually are much more difficult and unfathomable. Negroes didn't just come to this country because they felt like it, the way regular white people and even Puerto Ricans did. They were kidnapped in Africa by slave boats and then sold down south as cotton-pickers and servants for rich plantation families who would then laze around on the porch drinking iced tea with mint. The Negroes forgot all their African customs and got to be more and more like us, so that they dressed like us and ate like us and had to adopt Christianity, the English language, and everything else. When you really think about it, you realize what a setback it was for them. We had been doing all those American things right along, and so we were used to living that way, but they had to start all over, figuring everything out. They didn't get a hell of a lot of encouragement, either. No wonder so many people I know think they're inferior. To me they're not inferior, just confusing in the ways they act. True, when I'm around Lee or some other guys I know, *most* other guys actually, I use terms like *jigaboo, tootsie roll, coon, boon, spade,* and I feel a little guilty about it, because in fact I am not that prejudiced. I just talk that way to be ruthless and tough. I would get nowhere talking like a pansy. When my father uses the word *nigger*, my mother calls him a bigoted bohunk slob. He denies it. In Brooklyn he grew up with niggers, and the niggers he knew called each other niggers. That infuriates my mother, which is why he does it. Still, I think my father knows he is prejudiced. He just doesn't give a shit that he is. Come to think of it, almost everybody I know is prejudiced, everybody except my mother and, say, Barbara, whose whole family is for Negro rights and equality. Her parents are the only ones besides mine that I ever heard of who voted for Adlai Stevenson in 1956. On the playground back then all the kids had I like IKE buttons and viciously made fun of me because I was a Democrat. I was an outcast, but what could I do about it? I just didn't like Ike, and that was that. He was an empty-headed general. My best friend at the time was Arnold Tolley. Once at Arnold's house we were in the kitchen making ketchup sandwiches, which were his favorite, and he told me Adlai Stevenson was an agitator. I couldn't figure that out. The only agitator I knew was the one that once broke into pieces in our G.E. washer. So I told him Eisenhower was plain stupid and dull. His mother was in the diningroom polishing the silver things from the big glass cabinet, and when she heard that she got quite angry. She said the President deserved my respect even if I didn't agree with him. She made me apologize, and after that Arnold was a little embarrassed but cheerful, too, and I couldn't stand it, so I went home. Anyway, the first Negro I ever knew was Arnold's cleaning lady, Milly, who was fat and didn't smell good. She was very friendly, though, and she was a lively talker about baseball. She loved the Yankees and so did I, and she could rattle on about Bill Skowron or Yogi Berra with lots of knowledge and enthusiasm. Behind Milly's back Arnold and I would laugh and play tricks on her. Arnold would ask her if she was so poor she couldn't buy soap, and Milly would shake mop dust at him and call him a devil. Besides that, because of our exclusive neighborhood and everything, I never got to actually converse with any Negroes until last summer at the highway department when I met Hank, my future bodyguard—except for one I remember from the seventh grade. It was before the new junior high was finished, and we had to go to Rasmussen Junior High in South Huntington with a lot of Negroes. It was strange, but somehow I got to know a Negro guy they called Moon because his hair could only grow in weird patches on his head because of a fungus he had once, and so his head was like the moon, except the skin was of course brown. He was very tall, too. He was interested in me, and we would sometimes talk after school leaning up against the building in the sun listening to the band practice inside. He had to walk home, and my bus was always late in coming from taking the high school kids around. All we had in common was sisters, so that's all we really talked about, but I guess we somehow liked each other. I was going to go home sometime with him for supper, but that winter Moon knocked out the eye of Mr. Gormley, the assistant principal, with a snowball on the playground and got expelled and sent to reform school. After that, Mr. Gormley, who was big and an ex–marine hero in World War II, had this glass eye that never moved in his head.

But until today those three were honestly the only Negroes I was ever in contact with, the only ones with personalities that I had the slightest chance to figure out, not that I got anywhere. And now I have the chance to actually go into a Negro's house, foreign territory, you know, where I will be outnumbered and maybe in danger, who knows?

Of course Winnie is the reason I'm taking the chance, which, I can convince myself, is not much of a chance at all. I mean, these are all friendly guys who I played baseball with, and we got along OK in the park, and they all go to a school like Rasmussen, mixed like vanilla fudge.

So actually, walking along over the slick, gleaming sidewalks in the same clothes I've been wearing since Tuesday, I am in quite a joyful mood, the way you are before any party. I do wish I had my party duds, but these are at least clean. Aunt Joanna washed them yesterday while I was in the tub. In my stomach I've got a two-ton load of spaghetti, and I'm moving slow. Because of her weight problem, Aunt Joanna would eat only cottage cheese and apple slices, and Newton was suffering from an earache, Aunt Joanna said. He stayed up in his room watching television. So there I was, alone at the gray Formica table under the humming fluorescent light shoveling in the red, juicy spaghetti while Aunt Joanna stood by like a guard, looking satisfied and ready to pile on more if my plate got half-empty. It was very good, I admit. Then we both had cake, and Aunt Joanna made me promise I wouldn't tell Newton *or* Brian she ate any. When she started in reciting the night's great TV line-up and warning me about the choices we had to make because some good shows were on at the same time on different channels, I had to tell her about the party. Suddenly her face fell into a look of concern, just like I expected. To Aunt Joanna I know I seem a little wild. She can't stop worrying something will happen to me, and she'll be to blame. I told her it was a small party that would be made up of the baseball players I met in the park. She explained to me how to get to Clement Avenue, though she didn't much like the idea. She said, "I don't mind telling you that's a whole part of town been taken over by the colored. Ten years ago my cousins lived off Clement Avenue, and that neighborhood's turned black as ink since they moved to Gary." She said she had half a mind to forbid me from going, but I tensed up at that, and she realized she didn't really have the right.

Jesus, this must be the house, big and boxy with the Marvellettes filtering out the yellow windows, and cars all over, parked crooked on the lawn and across the sidewalk.

Because I don't like to rush into things and because outwardly I'm a thinker and a smooth-acting person, not many people know how nervous I can get, or rabbity, as Lee would say, in my social life especially. I mean, here I am, not making any move like you might expect, but just leaning my ass against the cold fender of this long car, which is, now that I look at it, a Cadillac. I'm rubbing my hand along my neck and down inside my shirt along my shoulder, feeling how tense I am. My muscles are hard as tire rubber. A shiver runs along my skin that I can feel jiggling all my little hairs everywhere. I wish I didn't have to go in there, though I'm not afraid of anything, or if I am I don't know what it is.

Suddenly, another car turns in off the street, swinging its headlights toward me. I duck behind the Cadillac. Peeking over the hood, I see the lights aiming for a spot just the other side of the car from where I'm crouching. They'll never glimpse me, I know. It's a very dark night. But as they edge alongside the Caddy and the smell of exhaust seeps around me, I realize this is not a good place to be if somehow they do glimpse me, so, bent over, I scuttle off between two other cars, heading for a tall hedge of bushes I can see faintly lit by the light from the house. I dart sideways into the hedge, and *thunk*, shit fuck suck dick, I clobber my shin into some big object. I fall onto my side, hugging my leg like a tree branch. Jesus *Christ*. I suck my lower lip. When I realize my eyes are clamped shut, I open them. In front of my face are a few hedge stalks. My side is pressed into the clammy ground. I sit up. Whooo-ee, it throbs. Through my pants I can feel a lump growing, but there's no blood. I twist my head, and there behind me I can make out this giant white thing, lying in the hedge-break. It's a round washing machine. Who the hell would dump a washing machine into the goddamn hedge? A Negro, that's who. It's the way they live, sort of haphazard.

I stand up, trying to see if I got my shirt dirty. I can't really tell. It's wet, though, along with one side of my pants. Shit. My shin really hurts. You can sometimes make yourself feel like a real idiot. If Lee saw me, he'd yuk it up, you know, and he'd say, "Hey, way to go, Ace." Suffering amuses him.

The door on the porch just swung open, letting light flash out over the closest cars and letting in the two who just got here in the car that shooed me into the washer, a tall guy and a tall girl, it looks like, but it could be two guys. The music sounds loud.

My shin feels like a second heart down there, pushing away. Shit. I sit on the washer. Another set of headlights curves into the yard and goes out. The doors open and bang shut. I hear Negroes laughing in their singsong way.

All at once this very weird thing happens. I'm just sitting here, I swear, not imagining sexy sights or anything, and my dick starts to twitch up into a boner. For all the control I have over it, it might as well be Roy Rogers's. Jesus, I mean, I'm in pain and all, but my magic twanger has a mind of its own. Hopping to my feet makes no difference. It keeps rising like one of those cobras the flute-players in India toot for, so determined that I'm tempted to drop my drawers right here and give it what it wants. But this really isn't the time for that, so all I do is jam it upright behind my belt to keep it from looking like a pocket full of cucumber. Since I gave up wearing underpants, my dick is more adjustable than it used to be. I used to hate having my jewels crammed in there, if you know what I mean. That bothered Aunt Joanna. I was handing my clothes out to her around the bathroom door, and she said, like I was a little kid, "Come on, Bernie, I'll have to do your underthings, too. No fuss, now, you won't embarrass me."

"I don't have any," I said.

"You don't?"

"Nope."

"Why not?"

"I hate 'em." I do. They're ugly, if you really take a good look at them. My father is the same way. Whenever he spots me pulling my pants on over my bare nates, he says, "When are you gonna get off this no-undies kick? It's not healthy to go around like that. What're you trying to do, advertise?" His big reason is you got to protect your pants, and I think he also believes good jockey shorts will trap your smells in there and make you more socially acceptable. I tell him to me it's just not worth it, they're too uncomfortable. "But you're not *civilized*," he says. Well, so what? He doesn't like me developing habits he doesn't have himself.

Now that I'm ignoring it, thank God, my bone is shrinking back to its normal self. I'm easing my way among the cars like a cat in an alley full of garbage cans, slinky and quiet. From high up in some tree a water drop splats down on my head, but the sky's clearing, I think. I can see a pale, glowing spot in the clouds where the moon must be hiding. My leg is OK. It hurts, all right, but I'm not limping on it, which is a good thing—I wouldn't want to have to explain it to everybody.

I spring up onto the porch over a rickety trellis, plant myself full of courage on the doormat, and jab my thumb into the black buzzer. Inside, all I hear is music and loud voices. I tell myself, hell, I was invited, wasn't I? I didn't walk all this way for nothing, did I? This is the way I like to think of myself—bold-acting, with a will of iron, like

Genghis Khan. An attitude like this can get you into a lot of trouble, though, especially if you're not used to it. You should never lose touch with your real personality.

I press the buzzer again, long and hard, but still nobody answers. A feeling of loneliness sweeps over me. My feet are icy, my clothes are wet on one side, my leg hurts, and who gives a shit? My life is so aimless. Helter-skelter, I run away from dangers and problems back on Long Island just to end up all alone in this hole called Lakewood, Ohio, standing outside the door of a party I'm scared to go to. When I remember my Uncle Ike and the reason I decided to travel to this location, I have to laugh. Jesus, I am a dumb turd, a dipshit, like Lee says. Just as I decide it could have been a real mistake not to head for Florida, which it's still not too late to do, I hear through the door, "No lie, babe. You is the homecoming queen." So, bam bam bam, I knock on the wood panel, and the door opens so fast I jump back. A big Negro guy in a purple cape is there holding a wine bottle.

"Hi," I say, but he's squinting back into the room where a bunch of people are dancing and moving around.

"Hey," he shouts. Then his big head swings to face me like it was on ball-bearings. His eyes are red and drunk-looking. He says, "You comin' in, or is you makin' a milk delivery?"

Well, I might try to slip in if he wasn't all bulging and swaying there like a grizzly bear, but I'm not about to tell him that, so I keep my mouth shut. He swoops the bottle up toward his mouth, but jerks it away again without tilting it for a swallow. In the light from over his head, his cape is shimmery, like silk. He stares at me a few seconds, making me more and more nervous, as you would expect. Then he says, "Is you a *ghost*?"

"No, I was invited to this party," I say, which I know is ridiculous, but I can't think of anything else. He is really loaded.

"So's everybody else, man," he says. He takes a step back and turns away with the back of his cape swirling, and I walk right in behind him and close the door. I keep going out of the bright hallway all the way into the big room, two rooms really, where they're all dancing. There's no furniture in here at all hardly, just mats along the wall, and the lamps are set low on the floor so you can see people's skittering feet better than anything else. It's mostly all Negroes around me, which feels pretty strange, though it didn't during the baseball game, I guess because it was outside. And they're gyrating like monkeys all over.

I don't see Winnie anywhere, but it's pretty thick in here. Next to the record player is a guy with glasses hooting on a harmonica to the music. In the game he was first base on the other team. On my first hit, after I rounded the bag and held up, he said, "Boy, you cracked it," which I thought was friendly to say. He's really going at it over there looking like he's making out with his hands. The record is just horns and pianos, a kind of jazz record, music I never hear, and it's very loud. There are people in one corner drinking and hugging, I can see now. I'm over against the table that has these paper cups and wine bottles all over it. The kind that grabs my eye is the stuff my mother often gets from the liquor store, Ripple, though I've only tried it once. I pour some into a cup to carry around with me like everybody else. It's bitter-tasting, not really how you would want it to taste if you never had any before, but, as my mother said that time in the kitchen when she gave me a sip of hers, you somehow get used to it, like coffee and beer or anything else. So, very casual, I start wandering through all the bunched and moving people to the other room. On one end of the room is a big box of what turns out to be shoes. I already noticed a lot of people not wearing shoes, and now I know they're in for real trouble getting their own back. Maybe they don't care.

Suddenly, I feel a slap on the sleeve of my shirt, and I hear, "B. There he *be*," and it's Neil, the guy who invited me. Now I realize that during the whole baseball game he had on sunglasses. That wouldn't seem strange, except in this dim room he still has them on. Then I realize my mother wears her sunglasses, wide and spreading like wings, at night quite often, but I never thought about it before.

"Hi," I say.

"Hey, you all right, man," he says. "Hey, you meet Randy? Randy's outside." His head doesn't stand still.

"Not yet," I say.

"Don' worry. He be back. Good you come down, man," he says, and he backs off and turns away. He moves like he's made out of rubber.

I'm thinking all I'm going to do is make one slow pass around, and if I don't glimpse Winnie, I'm ducking out the door. So that's what I start to do. The song ends. Suddenly, a guy beside me fiercely yells, "You *owe* me, motha, hear?"

"No, I don' hear nothin'," a low voice answers. I look around the shoulder of the first guy to see who he's mad at, but who I see first is Winnie. Amazing, she's right over there. Her mouth flies open. She shouts, *"Latham!"* An elbow lashes back into my face. My eye flares up like an explosion. On fire. Somebody shouts something. My hands cup my eye, my back hits the wall, I slide to the floor. A girl is screaming. My whole head is full of blazing, and I'm thinking Jesus Jesus Jesus, I want to see myself in the mirror. I hear scuffling and yelling and running. My cheeks are wet. The lid of my good eye lifts. There's nobody near me. They're clustered in the hallway. I've got an egg on my left cheekbone. It feels like the center of my body, a knot of red electricity. God*damn*.

Talking and laughing are going on again. The music cranks up. I slowly get back on my feet. Christ, when she sees this, Aunt Joanna will have a coronary attack. Where's the bathroom? I take a few short steps, trying to eye through the jumble of people for a door. A guy notices my face and says, "Shit, man, somethin' laid into you."

"No kiddin'," I reply.

"You OK? You feel OK?"

"Yeah, yeah. They got a bathroom around someplace?"

"Oh, yes, you got hooked. Whew, you got hooked." He's shaking his head.

"Where's the bathroom?" I ask again. All I want is a gander at how awful I look, and then I'm getting out.

He points to the bathroom and tells me I should buy a beefsteak to slap on my face. "Ain't nothin' can help that now but a fat old T-bone," he says.

"Thanks," I say, moving off with my hand over my eye.

It turns out the room he sent me to is the kitchen, and a bunch of people are there playing cards and drinking liquor. Just before I turn to leave, I'm shocked again by Winnie's face, which always is appearing out of nowhere. She rises from a seat at the table and shouts, "Hey!"

I just stop, holding my eye, not saying anything. A couple guys at the table glance up from their cards at me and then down again. Winnie goes over to switch on the fluorescent bulb over the sink. "Come over where I can see you," she says.

So I do.

"Who poked you like that?" She winces at me.

"Nobody. I caught an elbow."

"I'll say. *Man*." She gives it a close inspection. Her breathing smells a little winey. "You know, if you skin was the right color, it wouldn't show so bad. Wait, I'll get you a ice cube." She pulls a bowl of loose ice from the refrigerator, wraps a couple chunks in a dish towel, and holds it out to me. "Press it there, nice and soft," she says.

I press my eye, but it hurts.

She switches off the light. "Nobody wants you for scenery," she says, shooting me a grin. "Say, it wasn't Latham got you, was it? Or that Gabe Harper?"

"You were right on top of it when it happened. I didn't see anybody but you," I tell her, which is true. "Then this fat elbow came into view, and ka-blam, everything was stars."

"Man. Well, somebody got you, then, if you was standin' in the way of *that* ruckus."

"I can't deny that," I say in a grumbly voice.

"Nope, it swole up good, but, say, you don't look so bad to be moanin' like that. Gabe Harper by this time must look twice as bad as you, at *leas'*. Latham don't take it from nobody, I know that."

Suddenly I realize I'm afraid Latham is turning out to be Winnie's boyfriend—which makes me feel like a jerk, I mean, that I should want her sympathy and all. Why should I even care? It's like my feelings run ahead of me sometimes, and it takes me a while to catch up, you know, and get a grip on myself. For a minute there, I was even about to show her my shin so she'd ooo over that and ask who kicked me and put ice on it, but enough is enough. I don't want to be soothed, all I want to be is gone. But just as I open my mouth to tell her I'm leaving, she puts her fingers around my wrist. "C'mon out back," she says. "They bother easy in here."

I gaze down into the sink. It has lots of bottle caps in it. She's still touching me. "Well, actually, I'm hitting the road. I think this party's lost its spark, for some unknown reason." In fact, I don't know what to do. I can't go to my aunt's yet. She'll still be up, all ready to collapse when she lays eyes on me. What I really feel like doing is just curling up in a big heap of leaves, don't ask me why. Maybe it's an instinct.

She heads for the door. Back over her shoulder she asks, "You got a car?"

"A car?"

"Yeah, you know, a car."

"No." Shit, I wish I did. And a license.

"Just askin'. Just askin'." She squats down on the stoop.

I ease the door shut against the spring. Up above the raggedy black skyline of house tops some stars are glittering. I can't see where the moon's got to. "Look," I say, "stars."

"Yeah? You *still* seein' 'em?" She laughs. Her face looks very smooth in the dark.

We sit through a few minutes of quiet. The air is quite cool. The wooden steps under my buns vibrate from the dancing inside. A sour wine-smell keeps drifting up at me, and I keep thinking it's from her, sitting on the step below me with her chin in her hands and her hair hanging down to her shoulders in a thick fan, still as a rock, but when I look down I can make out on my blue shirt this splotch like a bib where my wine must have ended up. Finally, because I don't know what else to say, I ask her why she thinks I would have a car. Her head cocks up a bit. She says she was just asking is all, because Latham took off, and now she has to wait for T.J. to finish with the card game so she'll have a ride home.

"You mean he just left you?"

That's nothing new, she explains. Latham has sudden ways, sudden style. It makes their mama mad, but you can't change him. Latham's fixed and on his own.

He's her brother. Shit, I should have guessed it. His color is darker, but he's built long, I could tell in the game, with many muscles showing just like Winnie, and with that same round, melted-on nose. Making this connection all at once sends this wave of relief through me, and I want to get a look at her face again, but she isn't budging.

After a while, I really can't think of anything to say because my eye is going like an African tom-tom. I stand up and slip my feet very slowly from the edge of one step, dropping to the next to the next until I'm on the dirt. "Well, take it easy," I say. "See you maybe in the park."

"Yeah. Goodnight," she says to me.

I walk around front through the cars again, feeling the bomp bomp bomp of the music almost like it's in my eye. Aunt Joanna's probably asleep now. She won't see my eye until morning, and I can wash my shirt tonight in the sink. I bend over for a dim look at myself in an oval side-view mirror. Je-*sus*. Am I *ugly* or what? My eye is like swallowed in a big, fat plum. Old Winnie must have been disgusted. Shit. "See you in the park," I said, acting like everything was normal, like I took it for granted she'd still want my smashed face on display for her. I'm a jerk, I know, no matter how you cut it. I mean always when you look back on some way you acted socially, a remark you made or didn't make, you can think, well, I should have said this or I should have done that, but what good does it do? You're still a jerk, and actually you're a double jerk for trying to think you could have had it come out so you wouldn't look jerky. You can't change history.

Winona, Winona. I just realized she doesn't know my name.

"God almighty, where in blazes did you get that?" It's my Uncle Ike asking, with his eyes snapping out at me, and his wispy white hair gleaming like milkweed in the sun streaming through the window. Some of the upper panes are colored and thick, and they spread shades of blue and green and yellow over my lap like a quilt, like the quilt Uncle Ike has folded across his knees and draped over the footrest of his wheelchair to keep out drafts, Aunt Joanna said. He's her oldest brother, age eighty, a real, genuine geezer.

"It was an accident, Ike," says Aunt Joanna. "Somebody accidentally bumped into him."

"Hah! Bumped into him. Hah!"

"Ike, this is Jean's boy, Bernie, from Long Island. He's visiting."

"*Greta*," Uncle Ike shouts, "bring *tea*."

After I rolled out of bed this morning and got another load of my black eye, I knew I just couldn't walk down into the kitchen with it and let Aunt Joanna take it cold, you know. I knew I had to announce it was coming. So I called down the stairs to her that she better be ready because I was coming down there with a black eye. I felt fine, I said, but I had a black eye. Newton heard me, and he suddenly stepped out of his room into the hall in his pajamas. He said, "Wow," and he stared at me a second. I heard Aunt Joanna's slippers slapping up the stairway. Newton said to her, "Mom, it's all right. People don't grow up without at least one black eye in their boyhood." Aunt Joanna turned the corner. Her eyes flipped wide, and she said, "Oh," and her hand shot up to her hair like a spider just fell in it.

For breakfast I had scrambled eggs, rye toast, and sliced tomatoes. They drank their coffee, and I told them the whole true story of what happened (leaving out everything about Latham and Winnie), and they didn't say much except that I could not go to another party while I'm here, which I quickly agreed to. I wouldn't want to anyway. Aunt Joanna said a doctor should see me, but I chattered on like I didn't hear her, acting full of cheer, about my hitch-hiking experiences and how I wished my tennis racket would get here, and they finally got talking about how, since I came here to see Uncle Ike, we should all drive out to his fancy place so I could meet him. The two of them were feeling a little sorry for me, I could tell.

Years ago they would visit Ike every Sunday, Newton told me while we drove over in the Rambler, but he gradually got to be hard to talk to. He would sit and talk on and on, never listening to what anyone else had to say. Rubber was how he made his money, Newton said nobody knows how much, but *plen-tee*—as if that wasn't obvious from the neighborhood we were cruising through. Ritzy isn't the word for it. His house is white and gigantic like all the others, and it had a blue gravel driveway winding and winding up past fruit trees, hedges, and tidy gardens with a few Negroes puttering around in them. And the door, which usually is an ordinary thing that you hardly notice, was amazing. I mean, you could have a giraffe for a pet, and he wouldn't have to bend over going outside for a whiz. It was pulled slowly open by a skinny maid in a ruffled white apron, and she guided us along through these long, hollow halls with urns and statues and huge plants in them to the sitting room where Uncle Ike spends his mornings because it's sunny there, and it has a wide view of the lake, which is flat out to the horizon like an ocean.

"So, shouldn't you be in school?" Uncle Ike says into his teacup. He was softly slurping his tea, holding the saucer, not the cup handle, and Aunt Joanna was making some remarks about this beautiful day, since no one else was saying a word, but his boisterous question instantly shuts her up, and he raises his head to glare at me.

Newton says, "Uncle Ike, it's *Sun*day."

"For Christ's sake, I know it's Sunday. You think I can't keep track of days? It's Sunday, and tomorrow, by God, is Monday. What reason does the boy have to spill into this neck of the woods in the first place, and then catch that shiner in the second place, that's what I'm trying to find out. How old are you?"

"Almost seventeen."

"If you're sixteen, say *sixteen*."

"I'm sixteen." What an ornery fart.

"All right, what brings you to this neck of the woods? You a high school dropout?"

"No," I say. "I was leading a very boring life, and I was after adventure."

"From the looks of you, I'd say you found it. This boy should see a doctor, Joanna. The eyes are precious, very precious. I'm in my ninth decade—no great shakes there —but I have my sight, and I have all my teeth, every one, and do you know what I have to thank for that?"

"What?" says Aunt Joanna.

"Luck, sheer luck," he says. He's sloshing tea out of his cup. It splats to the floor and lies there shining. Behind him, with her hand resting on the pushbar of the tea wagon, Greta watches the little puddle creep along.

"Well, you're feeling downright chipper," says Aunt Joanna. "I'm glad to see that."

"Chipper? I accept that. I'm chipper, but not in the pink of health, by any means. I suffer, by Christ, just like anybody else. You know this home was mine once, and *only* mine. Now I'm forced to pay toadies and fools to keep it for me. But I keep my perspective. I'm thankful for that, by God. You go bananas if you don't keep your perspective." Greta snatches his cup from him, pours in more tea, and sets it on the arm of the chair. Through my bad eye, which is open just a slit, the steam from his tea looks like campfire smoke far away. "You know," he says with a deep sigh, "for months now I've had pain urinating in the morning. I endure such things. It's nothing. But last week I passed a stone, a tiny, jagged kidney stone, and it dropped in the crapper. Now God only knows why, but I desired to have that stone. It was mine. I shouted for Bruce to come fish it out for me, but he was out of earshot. Well, I'm stiff, you know, but I'm not buried yet, so I slipped down, put my hand in the water, and fished it out myself. I carried it in the palm of my hand to the breakfast table, and I set it there, while I ate, on a napkin. Before long, some item in the miserable newspaper caught my attention, and Greta began whisking away the table setting. At the same instant we grabbed for my napkin, and the kidney stone jumped off it to the floor. I shouted at her and called her a brainless Kraut, but because she *is* a brainless Kraut, it does no good to point it out. We looked for the lost stone, and she found it in a few seconds. I had Greta fetch a small ring box with a snap top, and I shut the stone inside there, safe. Well, some days later, I had a visit from a young Goodyear executive and his wife. We were sitting in the front room drinking the Scotch they brought—I'm permitted a ration of Scotch— and I had Greta bring out the ring box. They looked into the box, a slight bit timidly, you know, only to humor the old man. They think I'm an eccentric. And Greta handed it back to me, and I looked in, too. Nestled inside on the red velvet was an English muffin crumb. I laughed for half an hour."

We all think this is funny (I never heard of kidney stones, but they sound horrible), and we all laugh, even Greta, who mostly stands around looking like a constipated piano teacher. Her hand jiggles the tea wagon, which makes the faint lights reflecting off the teapot shiver along the wallpaper. Then in the middle of laughing Ike winks at me like we have a secret. His teeth are yellow, and the gums are sort of peeled back from them. He lets out a groan and leans back into his chair. Past his white head far out on the lake there is a white ship just barely moving.

Aunt Joanna puts her hand on her chest like she's feeling for her heart and says, "Ohhh." She tells Uncle Ike we really must run, Newton needs time in his garden.

"Get going, get going," says Uncle Ike.

It turns out his chair runs on a battery. He follows us down the hall to the door, with Greta trailing behind. "You're the bee's knees, Joanna," he says, "but that boy needs a doctor's attention. Remember what happened years ago to Wise Willy Waters."

Newton swings the giant door open, and we all say good-bye. All at once, when I look at him sitting there, bent and pale, as we go out into the sun, I feel this urge to touch the old man. I'll never see him again, I know. You may think, well, so what? But the feeling affects me, and I go up to him holding out my hand. The move surprises him a bit, but he grips my hand and pumps it and looks me hard in the face. His skin is soft and hot. "Uncle Ike," I say, "I just wanted to thank you for the Christmas presents you sent me every year when I was a kid, the Ping-Pong set, the softball bat, and everything."

His eyebrows go up. "Presents?"

"The basketball and the games and stuff."

"Yes, I hear you. Well, don't thank me. Mrs. Frances Barnes was responsible for those presents—my secretary. I only signed the checks. You could thank her, but she's under the sod. You just remember me to your pretty mother and get that eye looked at, that's all I want from you."

"OK," I say. We all say goodbye again, and Greta shuts the door solid behind us.

Newton throws his head back. "Well, thank *God*," he breathes. Aunt Joanna walks quickly ahead of us toward the car.

In the driveway I stop to pet an old yellow cat that's

stretched out in the sun on top of a huge bag of peat moss. He doesn't even open his eyes when I touch him.

Newton watches me. "That's Alexander," he says. "He's a eunuch, poor boy."

"Is he Uncle Ike's?"

"Are you kidding? Uncle'd just as soon roll his chair over him as look at him." Newton bends and roughs the cat's fur. "You're Greta's baby, aren't you, Al? Aren't you?"

Al stiffens out his legs and yawns wide. He's at peace with the world.

From the other side of the Rambler, across the roof, Aunt Joanna calls, "Newton?" Past her, the lake shines, and that white boat is much closer now. I can see lettering on it, on the stacks.

Newton looks up at her.

"Bernie's never been to Daly's," she says. "Let's go get us a cone."

"Why not?" says Newton.

As you would guess, Daly's turns out to be an ice cream place, where they make *real* ice cream, says Aunt Joanna, and she has me worked up for a crunchy pistachio cone, but when we get there Daly's is closed. A red sign hangs in the door. "How can *that* be?" Aunt Joanna says to herself. Newton's outside, peeking through the windows, trying to tell if they're still in business, or what. He and Aunt Joanna used to come over here in years past, after their Sunday visits to Ike, and it was always packed with ice cream lovers. Aunt Joanna says her secret reason to come into this part of town was always to have a strawberry double-dip at Daly's, not to visit with her crotchety brother. It's like she's apologizing to me for his gruff nature, but I think in fact she plain doesn't like the old buzzard because he makes her uneasy, and the same with Newton, I wish I knew why.

On the way to Daly's Newton asked me, "Well, Bernie,

you think Isaac the Terrible is your cup of tea?"

"He's OK," I said. Of course I knew that I had been stupid all along to imagine I could've been taken under the buzzard's wing when I had no dim idea what his personality was like, but still he seemed friendly to me beneath the surface, and he really was responsible for those presents. "He just needs some one to talk to," I said.

"*Bitch* to, you mean," said Newton. "In*ter*minably."

Aunt Joanna said, "It's mostly his frustration, and the limitation he has now of a wheelchair. He was such a do-things person."

"But maybe he'd hire you on as the bitch-boy," said Newton. "The official bitch-boy."

We are now at Howard Johnson's because the two of them took it for granted that I was very disappointed to miss out on a cone (*they* were disappointed, is more like it), and I just gave in my order for peach, I at last decided. Ike's tea has now fattened my bladder to whiz-level, so I tell Newton and Aunt Joanna I'm going to the bathroom. To get there, you have to go through the dining area, which is full of eaters gabbing and clinking silverware. When I turn the corner to walk by the rows of tables, I adopt a horrible-looking limp, like as a child I was stricken with a cruel disease that maimed me, and it sort of puts a little hitch in everybody's meal, you know, because they all have to slightly glance up at me, out of the sides of their eyes.

Thwack thud, thwack thud is the sound of me belting my tennis ball against the excuse for a backboard they've nailed up at one end of the park courts. It's really about ten planks stuck together so that when you hit a seam the ball comes off at weird angles, which sucks if you want to get up a rhythm. Still, just having my fist around the old Jack Kramer feels wonderful, and the bad hops keep me alert.

Jesus, it never fails. As soon as you tell yourself you're alert, *pow*, you send one six feet over the board and out into the bushes. After a couple of minutes I find it lying beside a Three Musketeers wrapper, but instead of returning to backboard drills, which, honestly, are boring, I flop down in the grass in a row of fancy magnolia trees. I have to admit that I really didn't come down to play tennis. I mean, I'd love to actually *play*, if anyone was around who could hit the ball back half the time, but tennis doesn't seem very popular around here, the courts are always empty.

The truth is I'm here to keep an eye out for Winnie. If she doesn't show up, I guess I'll head over to the library. I don't really want to do that, though. Because of my shiner I look pretty conspicuous. Even the faces of strangers shrivel up in pain when they see me, like I have leprosy. And it's better today, too, so that even Aunt Joanna agreed a doctor wouldn't be interested in me. The swelling's gone down some, and my eyesight is nearly normal, except for the purple lump always in the foreground.

English is where I'd be right now, gazing at the orangeish back of Barbara's head, most likely bored with the *Moby Dick* discussion, wondering whether it was going to be too windy for tennis practice to be worth it. But I'm not. I'm hundreds of miles away, feeling abandoned in a way, or maybe more like I abandoned a hectic, depressing routine that I now suddenly miss. It's like my regular old life was some tense, low-key war that I have retreated far back from, and now I'm finding out that without all those struggles and stimulations filling it up, my life is just shapeless and blank and drifting like the clouds overhead. I told Uncle Ike I was running away from boredom to adventure, but now I think it's just the opposite. Of course, Richard Linwood isn't the type to bring you the adventure you'll treasure the rest of your life. You have to remember that.

School's out. Group of carefree kids in their good clothes, carrying books, amble down the pathways heading home to their mamas. Their noisy joy makes me homesick, but also angry in a way that's hard to explain. They just ignore everything but their own little selves. They have no perspective.

I slide a shoot of grass out of its stalk to chew on. With the tip of my tongue I flip the slick, clean pieces of it out to where my racket is lying in the grass. Finally, by the time I almost forget what I'm waiting for, I spot a cluster of Negro girls yakking and moving in formation toward the circular bandstand in the little sort of meadow below the rose garden. The lanky one in yellow could be Winnie, but I'm too far away to tell for sure. They all hop up over the rail under the bandstand canopy. Their matches flare up like lightning bugs. Cigarettes are a thing I've never tried, and I'm not about to, either, I swear. Only morons smoke. If you have that habit, you're sick in some way, I don't care who you are. Last year, in the special ed class there was a kid named Mickey, who was quite retarded. He was a real cigarette addict. I guess, being such a cross-eyed retard, Mickey couldn't know any better, but other people can, at least you would think so. Now Lee calls anybody who smokes a Mickey Mental, and that includes both our mothers. They puff away all day long.

That *is* Winnie. She has on a yellow sweater. I casually angled my way down into the meadow to the side of the bandstand, and now I recognize her fan of hair and her square shoulders. The trouble is I can't come up with a reason to just plop myself down in the empty green here, where I guess she'd notice me sooner or later. All I can do is keep moving. I march up to the gravel road, twirling my racket in my hands to attract attention. From here I look back, and I know she hasn't picked me out because she's leaning over and laughing at what another girl is saying. Instead of walking on back to the courts, but closer this time to the bandstand, which I know will look suspicious, I just shout, "Hey, Winnie," and she turns to look at me. It's terrible to plain shout like that, I realize, but I didn't think of that fast enough to stop myself. She says something to the other girls and then comes trotting out toward me.

"Hi," I say.

"How's that eye?" she asks me in a puff of breath.

"Well, it's better. It's getting better."

"Yeah, it don't *look* as bad," she says. "You play tennis?"

"Yup."

"I never played it."

"Really?" I can believe it, though. Many people have never played tennis.

"Well, I *seen* lots of people playin' it. It's a slow game."

Slow? "What do you mean by slow?"

"Nobody's ever runnin'."

"You're nuts. If you can say that, you've never seen any real tennis." Nobody ever says tennis is *slow.* A guy named Noodles, who thinks he is a comedian, once said to me and Lee on the bus when we were carrying our rackets that if you played tennis you had soft balls. Lee said, "I'd rather have soft balls than no balls," and Noodles reached for his crotch and said, "Oooo, that hurt, that hurt," and everybody laughed at him, which is what he wanted. Sure, some jerks, football players maybe, will say tennis is for pansies, but who ever calls it slow?

Her girlfriends pretend they're ignoring us as we walk back by the bandstand up to the courts. She's hefting my racket and fingering the strings. "Not bad," she says, referring to what, I don't know.

I'm saying, "Bowling, that's slow. And golf is so slow it's like going on a picnic." I once caddied for a rich man who carried bread and beer and salami in his bag. Actually, of course, I carried it, and the bag had a four-foot thing of salami, I'm not kidding, and a long, white, insulated tube of beer cans. He would slice off salami and offer pieces to me. He was very friendly, I admit. I ate a lot of his salami.

I knock the ball into the backboard for a few minutes to give her the idea. She looks on from the side with her arms folded and showing no expression. I hit the ball from side to side, forehand to backhand, backhand to forehand to show her how, if you were playing anybody good, you would never really stop running unless you missed the ball. She says, "OK, let me try."

I show her how to hold the racket. The skin on her hands is very smooth, like legs in nylons, and her nails are short and even. I tell her everything she has to do to hit the ball right, in detail, and then she whops the first one ten feet over the board. "Shit," she says.

"All right," I say, "what did you do wrong?"

"Nothin'," she says.

She fetches the ball and smacks it a few more times, not improving very much. I'm squatting down with my tailbone against a net pole, trying not to give her any advice. She's frustrated enough, I can tell. Her jaw muscles are tense. Now and then, the ball soars over the fence, since she won't stop powdering it, and she has to hustle after it out through the clanging gate. You can see she has ball-sense, much more than Barbara, more than a lot of guys I know, in fact. She reacts well, and when the ball rebounds so she can't get the racket on it, she catches it. Her hands are quick. What she hasn't got is patience. Whenever she hits the ball wrong, she chitters at herself like a mad squirrel. I say, "Easy does it, easy does it," and she just grits her teeth. Finally, she lets the ball roll away into the leaves in the corner, and she tromps over, aiming the butt of the racket at me like a gun. "B, this game is damn stupid."

"Only because you're playing it stupid," I want to say, but I don't. She'd just flash her mad eyes at me. So I tell her you can't learn anything as complicated as tennis in five minutes, and she says, "It's like baseball, only you swing a fatter bat."

To that, all I can say is, "Oh, Jesus." I wish she could just see Ken Rosewall or Chuck McKinley or Pancho Gonzales or *me*, even, in an actual tennis match, so she'd get the true picture. So she could love tennis. I guess that's what I want.

I hold the fountain faucet on for her. The bandstand is empty now. Nobody's around except for a few kids playing Wiffle Ball down on the diamond. The sun is like an orange balloon, flattening low over the houses. Sitting around in these shorts, I realize I got chilly, and I'm hungry, in fact, starved. Also, I wonder why she hasn't said a word about my banged shin. She's ignoring it. Or else my eye is enough for her to think about.

We wander over to the bandstand, and Winnie asks me when I'm supposed to go home. I say, "No special time," but actually Aunt Joanna wanted me at five. It must be near that now.

"No," she says, "I mean home at New York, where you come from."

Just like that I look at her, at her face, with her eyes rounded and turned down in the corners all perfect and concerned like the face of a doll, and just like that I know she likes me, and I like her. My throat feels like it's swallowing a marshmallow. "I don't know," I say. "I haven't thought about it," which of course is a lie. I decided about half an hour ago I had to be back Friday or even sooner. As it is, I'll miss the opener against Northport, and even though Coach Nicely won't bounce me from the team, he'll think up some punishment. I'm glad I don't take Latin, which he teaches, or else I'd feel it in the classroom. He can hold a grudge, the old peckerhead. Besides that, my schoolwork was on its way to the dogs before I took off, and now, whenever I get back, it's going to be trouble. My U.N. report that I haven't even started was due today in history.

"Maybe you don't *want* to think about it," says Winnie. Her arms are hooked through the spindles of the bandstand railing.

I just look at her.

She tilts back her head. "Maybe you don't even want to go back there," she says. "Maybe those bad times you left ain't worth the bother."

"Maybe you're right. You know, I had Alaska on my mind when I first took off. Maybe I should keep traveling, roaming on."

"Maybe," she says. "It depends."

"On what?"

"On how bad those times were. I mean how do you finally know when you got farther enough away?"

"When you stop, that's it, you're far enough."

"You stop yet?"

"Yeah, to be honest, I think I miss everything, you know? I miss school and everything."

"Even those bad times?"

"I guess."

"Well, how long you stayin', then?"

"Maybe the end of the week."

We both look down at her sneakers, blue Keds. "Hanh," she says, through her nose. "If you miss it all so bad, why'd you run away?"

"You really want to know?"

"I'm askin', ain't I?"

"A guy wants to kill me."

She grimaces in a scornful way. "Shit, if anybody truly wanted to kill you, you be dead right now."

"The night before I took off he killed my dog and cut him up into little pieces. I *had* to run away."

"That the truth?"

"It's true, all right. Even if you don't believe it, it's true."

She shakes her head. "Listen, man," she says. "Right now I got to eat and go to work. But it's Latham you got to tell about your enemy. Enemies is what he got more of than anything except girls. Maybe they don't have a mind to kill him, but they like to hurt him bad, if he let 'em, but he don't let 'em, so it don't happen. At nine he gets me there at the *li*-brary. Want me to tell him you be comin' down?"

"OK," I say. And off she goes running, like a film clip of some graceful animal loping across the African prairies right through the Wiffle Ball game, over left field and into the hedgebreak.

The sun just flicked out, and the chill is sharpening. I trot up through the rose garden. All the bushes are dry and twisted, with green tags on them, barely alive, it looks like. Now, because I told Winnie I'm going back to Long Island soon, I guess I really am. Sometimes your true thoughts don't become clear until you put words around them. But sometimes, I guess, putting words around them can make your thoughts fuzzy, too. I mean, Jesus, do I *really* think Richard Linwood wants to kill me? Why would he want me dead? Then again, you have to ask, Why would he want Zekey dead? But shit, most of the time I can't understand what I want, and I'm not half as crazy as Richard Linwood, who is, after all, a maniac, a mysterious maniac. I don't even know why I would tell Winnie he wants me dead. Well, it enhances me, I can see that. If somebody wants to kill you, you're enhanced. You are, I know it sounds weird.

I'm getting drunk. We're riding slunk down in Latham's car getting drunk, going around corners fast with the radio so loud you have to shout and the windows open. He's a wildman, he really is. He bought us some bottles of this cheap wine called Thunderbird, which again is the same type my mother often orders from the liquor store. That's what I told Latham while we were idling out in the lot behind the trash cans with the neon sign making the air flash green around us, and he said, "Well, here's to you hip mama," and took a good glug.

Of course, to me it tastes awful, at least it did at first. But I keep thinking it's a means to an end, a means to an end, and now it slides down like warm lemonade. But it still isn't very delicious. More fancy and expensive wines must taste much better. I really don't know how they would, but they must.

When I got to the library, the old janitor didn't want to let me in. He stood jangling his keys in the vestibule, and told me just to drop my *Genghis Khan* through the slot because the library was closing. Actually, I was going to use the slot anyway, because the book looked suspicious, all swollen with wavy pages, and I didn't want the librarian, you know, scrutinizing me. So I did. I heard the book flop hollow down behind the wall. Then I explained I was supposed to meet Winona Lockhart, and the geez shot a frown at me, but he opened the glass door.

She was in there in a soft chair, not reading or anything, just leaning back and smiling, with the same yellow sweater on. She looked so relaxed, and, well, pretty there, you know, that I suddenly realized that I had never seen her when she didn't act jittery with her quick eyes and tense muscles. Now that I think back on her smooth face and how she gently said, "I saw you get embarrassed out there. Don't pay old Jerry no mind. He don't have no say around here," I realize in a rush that I wanted to touch her and even kiss her right there and take her with me to Long Island or else just stay with her inside the wall where all the books drop down. We would have pillows and lamps around in there and things to eat, and we would read the books that fell in around us, very comfortable and serene.

Latham just sang out, "Tomcats! Tomcats on the prowl." He's slowed way down. We're easing down the streets with our heads resting on the seat backs. Just before we got the Thunderbird, Latham dropped Winnie off at their place, which is a small white house. "You boys got to talk," she said, leveling her eyes at me, and then she said, "I'll come by the park tomorrow," and she shoved the car door shut. So it's the two of us drinking this stuff and not saying very much either, as a matter of fact. I'm watching him drive with his big arms stretched out to the crosspiece of the wheel like a water skier. I feel almost like I'm back hitch-hiking again, except now it's dark.

"You gotta go slow," Latham says over the radio racket, "so the *man* don't come down on you."

"The man with the badge," I say.

"Yeah, that's him," says Latham. "Say, you right on top of it, ain't you?"

I know he's teasing me. I only laugh, and he laughs along with me. He hands me the bottle. I wonder if he actually means that about going slow because, well, it's funny he would say that since just a few minutes ago we were going seventy along a main street, and people spun to watch us zoom by. He turns down a long hill that I can see leads to a lit-up asphalt lot by some piers on the lake. A bunch of ships are tied up there like in New York City, and cars are parked all over the place. We slowly cruise through an open gate.

"What're we after in here?" I ask.

"Privacy, man."

"Really?" It doesn't look very private in here, groups of men wandering around, lights, and noises.

"Yeah, man, be cool. My daddy was boss of this yard for a hundred years. Anybody you see around here I'm tight with. They know me."

We glide along to a corner of the lot that looks out over a pier wide as a highway. The lake smells like oil and also a little like something going bad in your refrigerator, old and stale. The workers passing by don't act like they recognize Latham. They ignore us, in fact. Latham switches off the engine and the lights. The radio dies. Quiet rushes in, carrying along with it a whole slew of little sounds from the lakefront—metal banging, men shouting far away, a motor running. Latham lights up a cigarette. He plinks his lighter shut over the flame. I keep waiting for him to say something, but he doesn't, and so neither do I. For twenty minutes, my mind has been going over ways to tell Latham about Richard Linwood in case he finally asks me about my enemy, but I can't come up with anything special to say, and now that I'm getting drunk it seems stupid to try. I mean, I'll say what I say. How Latham sees it is his business. He's over there puffing away, and I'm over here with my head fat and loose like one of those dolls that have springs for necks. The cigarette smoke drifts out flat across the hood of the car and disappears.

"You juiced?" he says, making me jump.

"Me? No. A little."

He reaches into the back for the second bottle. The bag rattles. He twists off the cap, swigs, and passes it to me.

"Damn, man," he says, "I guess I owe you an apology."

I say, "Really? I bet you don't," which I know is dumb, but, shit, my tongue is out on its own.

"Winona says it was me messed you up like that, or Gabe Harper. And, fuck it, I apologize for him, too."

"Oh, that's OK. I know it was an accident. You didn't mean it."

"Man, like I know I din't mean it. If I *meant* it, you be in the fuckin' hospital."

I laugh. "That's for sure."

"Yeah, and soon as you come outa the hospital, you be comin' after me, right? For revenge and that bullshit?"

"Well, not without three big friends."

He laughs and shakes his head. "At leas', man, at *leas'*. You talkin' to one bad cat, you know? I am bad. I am mean. And I get my respect, man, dig it. I get respect."

"I believe you," I say. I do, not that I'd say so if I didn't. I hand him the bottle. I can't really tell what Latham's trying to get at. People who brag do it because they feel insecure and they don't want anybody finding out. But Latham acts about as insecure as a police dog. Maybe he's just feeling his oats, working his way up to the subject at hand, which is why we're here after all, to discuss enemies. Now though, he's silent and, like, thoughtful, so that I'm almost wondering if Winnie could've left everything up to me. I'm also wondering what time it is. Aunt Joanna wanted me back at ten. "Sure," I told her, "ten o'clock," and when I said that, I honestly thought this would amount to a pep talk, you know, and not a binge. But things never turn out the way you expect, you'd think I'd learn, wouldn't you? Shit, if I could, I'd just stop expecting anything to be like anything. The future would just roll in point-blank, and I'd accept it. Nothing would disappoint me. It would all be wonderful. Jesus, I am a little juiced. I feel like jumping out of this car and going for a swim. My aunt can go piss up a rope. There's a whole lifetime of events out there waiting to happen to me, only me, and so I'm the only one who can be responsible for me. My life is all mine, and I'm running it. The trick is knowing *how* to run it, so you get your respect, so nobody thinks you're an asshole. And my aunt is not going to respect me when I blow in after midnight with a tankful of Thunderbird.

"Winona says you got sumpin' to talk to me about, B. That what you thinkin' about?"

This sudden comment surprises me. "She did?" I say, and I clear my throat.

"Yeah, man. That the truth?"

"I guess so. I didn't—I just wasn't sure she mentioned anything to you about it. What'd she say?"

"What she said is you got a problem, man, and I see you been thinkin', so like, what's on you mind?"

Respect, I think, so I say it. "Respect. I was thinking about getting respect and also having enemies."

"Well, what you thinkin' about, B, is *me*. I got respect, man, and I got enemies to go with it."

"I'm thinking about more than you, if you want to know the truth. I'm thinking about me."

He thinks this is very funny, and he laughs. He laughs loud, but in a nice, deep, and comical-sounding way. And I laugh, too. He says, "It's all bullshit, man, you know? Goddamn, but you a serious cat."

"You're not the life of the party yourself," I say.

"Yeah, man, I know that." He flicks his butt out the window. "I'm just sittin' an' waitin' an' wonderin' what you got to lay down. You feel like talkin', or you feel like givin' me lip?"

In his big, brown face, his eyes shine round and white like he has a little light back in his brain. He pushes the wine at me, and I sigh and take a swallow. The bottle tastes like a cigarette. "Well, shit," I say. "I guess we're talking about enemies."

"Enemies," says Latham.

"Yeah, how to handle your enemies."

"OK," he says.

So I start in explaining all about Richard Linwood, how dangerous and unpredictable he is, and how he's a cripple and a true maniac with a switchblade and everything. Latham listens, slouched in the seat with another cigarette hung out over his chin. I go through the whole history of me and Richard, as much as I can remember, and I end up with him slicing Zekey into pieces. I've got to exaggerate like this because it's what I told Winnie, but also I think a good, horrible detail is sure to give Latham the true picture, you know, even if the detail isn't true. Otherwise, Latham might not understand Richard is crazy, really crazy.

Latham takes a deep breath. "Man, that motherfucker means business."

"Yeah," I say, feeling glad that he's got the idea, "and it's me he wants to do his business *to*."

"But *why*, B? Listen, man, the mother is insane. All right? He is insane. But like, he still got to have reasons, man. Big reasons, you know?"

"I know. That's what everybody says. 'What's his motive?' 'What's his motive?' But you know what I think? I think he just wants me to suffer. That's what he wants. Pure suffering."

Latham twists to face me and leans back into the door. "Well, goddamn. That is strange."

"You don't have to tell me."

"The mother could kill you, man."

"Yeah, that's what scares me." Suddenly, I realize Richard actually could kill me. He *could*.

"Fuck it, man, you got to stop givin' the cat what he wants." Latham reaches for the bottle.

I gaze out at three tiny lights moving on the lake. I know what he means. My mother always used to give my sisters the same advice about me. Claudia would come crying to her saying, "Bernie keeps poking me and calling me a numskull," or something, and she'd say, "He only does those things for your reaction, honey. If you wouldn't react this way, there'd be no satisfaction in teasing you." It never worked, though. My sisters were always too sensitive, and I was too mean. And I know it won't work on Richard Linwood, either. He's meaner by a shitload than anybody I ever heard of. I explain this to Latham. All he does is shrug. Then he hiccups.

"Listen, B," he says after a while. "The mother got to you so bad you ran and come to Lakewood, here. Right?"

"Well, yeah. But it wasn't all him."

"Shit, you got more enemies?"

"No, just more problems."

"I know, man. But that's nothin'. If you fuckin' *alive*, you got problems. What I'm sayin' is you come here 'cause the cat is fuckin' you over, right?"

"Yeah."

"And now you goin' back. Well, B, you goin' back, but things got to change, man. He ain't gettin' one more chance to fuck with you, see? Man, this bullshit is *over*. The mother is gonna respect you, or he is gonna *bleed*, see? This the way it is, B. You got it?"

"Well, I hear what you're saying."

He pulls his cigarette out of his mouth and shakes his head. "Damn, B. Ain't you got *pride*, man? You tell me, you tell me now what you gonna do when you get back and that crazy motherfucker busts all the windows in you fuckin' house, man. It ain't over. You know it ain't over. What you gonna do, man, when he come up at night and slips that blade under you collar button? Huh? Tell me."

Latham's loud voice hangs in the dark air like his smoke. I wipe my hands on my chinos, and I let out my breath. "Well, to be honest, I guess I never thought about doing anything. I never considered it. So I don't know what I would do. Kick him or something."

"B," says Latham in a tired voice, "you is a whole lot dumber than you look."

Somehow, hearing Latham call me dumb is a relief. That's sort of how I feel, dumb. "Well, if I was smart I wouldn't be here getting advice from you. I wouldn't need it."

"Man, if you was smart, you be in New York kickin' the fucker's ass down the halls of you school." He drains the bottle and drops it back behind the seat. He hiccups again.

"Shit, he *would* kill me if I tried that."

"Yeah, man, maybe. But, dig it, at leas' he be killin' you for a *reason*." He looks hard at me, and then he chuckles. "See? You got to give the cat a reason, man."

"Well, Jesus, why the hell should I give him a reason?"

"Listen, B. You hear what I say now. You goin' back there, right? An' you know if you keep actin' simple and runnin' scared like you been doin', this bullshit is gonna get fuckin' worse, man. That crazy mother ain't gonna change, man. See? *You* got to change. Show him you got pride. Be cool. But, like, when he starts callin' you down and shit, that's all, man. You got to mess up his face, see?"

I know I could never do what Latham's telling me to do. He just doesn't know Richard, how vicious he is, and strong, and full of hate. "You really think I can go after that crazy-man? Shit, you don't know what he can do."

Latham sits back and closes his eyes like he's thinking. Then he says, "B, I don' know if you can whip that cat. I just know you got to do it. Ain't no other way, man. Long as the cat don' respect you, he gonna keep on fuckin' with you. That's it, man. Rule Number One."

"Well, OK," I say, "but you have to tell me how I'm going to do it. I mean, how would you do it, if he was after you?"

"Fuck it, man. How can I know what *I* would do? The cat'd respect me, man. Like, he would not run my bad ass outa town. Listen, soon as you get back, you call him down. Show him you a new man. Call him on the phone at like four o'clock in the morning, see, and you mouth him every way you know how. Let him talk, but tell the cat you done with the bullshit."

"OK, and then what? Do I just wait until he comes the next morning with his switchblade?"

"No, B, you through waitin'. You get a bedpost and you go after the mother and you beat his fuckin' legs off, man. You don't stop till he nothin' but jelly below the belt."

"Yeah, and when he's out of the hospital, he'll sneak up on me some day and carve out my Adam's apple."

"No, it don't work that way, B, 'cept on TV. Respect, man. The cat'll give you respect."

I start to shake my head, thinking how impossible it would be for me to be brutal like Latham. His advice is exciting to me, of course, and Jesus, I would love to club Richard to a pulp, but it's just too, like, animalistic to actually *do*.

The engine starts up, but Latham doesn't flip on the lights. He hits the accelerator a couple times and then lets it run. "You feel high?" he says. "You want some more wine?"

"I feel all right," I say. Tired is how I really feel, and dizzy. "I guess I should say thank you for your advice, but I wish there was something, you know, less brutal I could do to him, like shoot him." I laugh.

"Yeah, you could ice him good," says Latham. "You

could go to fuckin' reform school forever, too. Fuck it, B, you do what you want, man. But, like, face up to the mother, see? That's what I say, you know? That's all I'm sayin'." He backs the car hard and swings around without lights through the lot. Men walking with their lunchboxes watch us go by. Latham is still hiccuping. Hiccups always remind me of my eighth grade French teacher, Mr. Lacolle, from France. He had only two shirts, one pink and one blue with these buttoned flaps on the shoulders like a uniform, and sweat stains under the arms. He was shy and very small. He had tiny eyes and whiskery spots where he missed shaving, but he was kind, you know. He liked us, and he hated the shit the school made him do, so you could cut his class all the time if you wanted, and nobody would find out. What he somehow developed, though, after we had him a month, was hiccups, bad hiccups. For eight goddamn *months* he had these hiccups. First we laughed at him all the time, but then we started feeling real sorry for him because they just wouldn't go away. You'd go in there every day and hope to God that first hiccup wouldn't come, and you'd watch him, with his piece of chalk, and his back would be to you, and "hic," you'd see it. His shoulders would jig up. In the back of my notebook I always wrote the date and the number of hiccups. Some days were a lot more than others. We heard his diaphragm didn't work right. Mr. Lacolle never talked about his hiccups, though. He was too shy. In June he went into the hospital, and nobody ever saw him again. Could be he's still hic-ing.

Cruising by Aunt Joanna's, we see the lights on. She's waiting up. Christ. We go on up the street.

Latham says, "Shit, B, be cool. What she gonna do, man? Cut out you Adam's apple?" He pulls to the curb and shuts off the lights.

"No, it's just that she'll question me and all. And I got

wine on my breath."

"Fuck it, B, you can apologize. But like, you ain't been doing bad. You been out talkin'. That's all it is. With me, you friend."

When I look at him sitting there so relaxed in his black jacket, one hand resting on the wheel of his car, and smoking another cigarette, I realize I must seem like quite a nervous person. "I know you're right," I say. "I must be the type that worries about other people's feelings too much."

"But not enough about you own, man, dig it."

I say, "I guess so," but then I think, no, that's wrong. I probably worry about my own feelings too much, too. We sit for a few minutes with the engine running and the radio on, playing soul music. I'm hoping the lights will go off in my aunt's house, but they don't. "Well," I say, "I guess I'll see you around."

"Yeah, man, OK," he says.

"Where you gonna go now? You going home, too?"

"I got some business. It's early, man."

"Doesn't your mother care when you blow in?"

"Yeah, man, she cares. But she don' say nothin'. Nothin' she can do. Like, she don' want me movin' out, see? I'm just too young and too sweet, know what I mean?"

"But you got enemies. She knows you got enemies."

He shrugs.

"Latham, who you got for enemies, anyway? I mean, you know, who would want to get you?"

"Shit. Husbands, mostly."

"Husbands?"

"Yeah, man. I keep a lot of women happy."

I can see him smiling, and I can't tell if he's serious or not. "Well, I wouldn't want to keep you from business like that," I say.

"You right there, man."

I tell him thanks again for the advice. I'll have to think it over, I say.

And he says, "Be cool. You don't need no more fuckin' advice than that."

I slam the door and stand there while his taillights shrink away smaller and smaller and blend in with all the other moving lights at the end of the long street.

Aunt Joanna was stretched out in her big chair in her robe snoring away with a book going up and down on her stomach. I snuck by, changed into my pajamas, brushed my teeth, and came down to tell her she could turn in, I was safe. She yelled a bit in a high voice about how inconsiderate I am. All I said was I was very sorry I didn't call to tell her I'd be late, and she kept on about how I was her responsibility, what would my mother say, and all, and I just listened. Right then her face started to look so old and wrinkly and unhappy to me that I just felt a pang in my heart, and I had to hug her. She hugged me some, too, but I pulled back, and then we went up to bed. I flopped down onto the blankets, and I just looked out at the stars I could see. It felt like we were all rocking and floating, traveling in some huge boat, some ship, to a faraway place. I was hoping and hoping I wouldn't puke. I didn't, but it was close. I felt so terrible and lonely curled up on the bed that I started saying, like a crazyman, "Good ol' Lee, good ol' Barbara, good ol' Mom, good ol' Mr. Fitch, good ol' Dad, good ol' Coach Nicely," and so on and on, good ol' anybody-I-could-think-of. I knew then I was getting my ass back to Long Island the next day if I could.

So now I'm on a bus again, barreling down the flat black countryside, going home, and Christ, wouldn't you know it, the whole idea of my former life looming ahead is plain scary and depressing as ever. Florida, Florida, I say to myself. The thought of it warm and open down there keeps gnawing at me. Even the shape of it. It's like the dick of America, dangling into those soft seas. I ask myself, why not?—I have money now, and clothes, and my tennis racket. Florida wouldn't have relatives to pamper me and hound me. I could swim and swim, bake my skin brown like Winnie's, live in a clammer's shack behind a sand dune ... why not? Well, I don't really know why not. All I know is I'm going home, and I don't really know why I'm doing that.

Partly, anyway, I'm escaping Cleveland. At breakfast the morning after my night with Latham, I told my aunt and Newton right off that I was getting out. I didn't expect them to be as shocked as they acted. Newton said he thought I would at least stay the week like I said when I first arrived. I think they realized they couldn't give me what I wanted, that they somehow didn't make it as friends for me, and they felt sorry for me, who was to them just a lonely boy with a black eye. So what they did that afternoon was Aunt Joanna stuck up her closed sign, and Newton came home at lunch, and we all went to this Wild West museum, even Brian. They kept saying wasn't it terrific, wasn't it wonderful, and I kept saying it sure was, but it wasn't. It didn't suck, it was OK, you know, but it wasn't any Museum of Natural History. Brian took my picture standing next to a tall wax cowboy, and we looked at some Indian relics, which I enjoyed, though all in all I had a miserable time. My mind was on Winona. I had to intercept her on her way home through the park. I had to tell her I was leaving the next day and ask her if Latham said anything to her I should know about. I wanted to give her my address and get hers, and basically, I wanted to see her.

So I acted quite enthusiastic about all the crap in the museum, and I rushed us along to make sure we'd be out by three. It worked, but it was late by the time I ran down to the park, and I would've missed her if she hadn't waited, sitting in the grass up by the backboard, eating barbecue potato chips.

We joked around about tennis, because I had my racket with me, and about my eye, which is still very colorful. Then we walked to the scrubby rose garden, moving slow and close together so we bumped shoulders going along. We sat on a bench, and I touched her arm a few times, but I just couldn't slip my arm around her. Now I think she probably wanted me to. Hell, I could even have kissed her, but I was too nervous. She was too, I guess. She said she never had a chance to talk with Latham. He didn't come home that night, and she was in school all day. She asked if he showed me his piece. I knew she didn't mean his dick, but I couldn't figure out what else it might be. I wasn't thinking about him then, anyway. It turned out all along, in his glove compartment he had a gun, a .22-caliber gun, new and shiny. That stunned me. All that time it was two feet in front of me. I asked her if he ever shot anybody with it, and she said she didn't think so, not with that gun, but four years ago he did shoot a guy with another gun, right in the stomach. And for that he ended up in Wiltwyck, a school for boys outside of New York City, where he spent years. That was why her family moved out of Harlem, to get Latham out of trouble. About then Winnie had to take off for home so she wouldn't be late to the library. I said I wanted her address, but neither of us had a pencil or paper, so she said she'd see me off at the bus station the next day, and I said I hoped she would. I worried the whole day about having Newton and Aunt Joanna and Winnie and maybe Latham all there together saying goodbye, but actually it went fine, or about as fine as you would expect something tense and emotional like that to go. Latham showed up, and he stood with Winnie over by the phone booths, smoking. I hugged Aunt Joanna, and she kissed me, and I shook Newton's hand. Then I went over to give Winnie my address all written down on a card. She forgot hers, she said. I told her she could send it to me. I was going to stick out my hand to shake with Latham, but I couldn't, he looked so fierce, without a smile on his face. I said, "Well, thanks and so long. You two are my only friends in Ohio." I said it backing away. I wanted to touch them, but it was too late. They both laughed and stayed around to wave at me on the bus. It was weird to have a pair of white people and a pair of Negroes on opposite ends of the bus platform both cheerfully focusing on me, on my bus window, and flat-out ignoring each other. Latham and Winnie followed the bus a ways in his car, tooting.

Across from me a man has a *Sports Illustrated*, which he just stopped reading. I noticed it has a tennis player on the cover so now I lean over to ask if I can borrow it. Certainly, he says. Last year Ollie Griggs, the captain of our tennis team, had his picture in the Faces in the Crowd section at the end of the magazine, and it told about how he was undefeated in over fifty straight matches and how our tennis team hadn't lost in seven years. But when the man hands it across the aisle to me I see it's not a tennis player on the cover. It's some pole vaulter, a Russian pole vaulter.

CHAPTER

YOU CAN DENY all kinds of things. You can deny you're prejudiced, like my father, and you can deny you're plain scared of what's going to happen to you in the future, which helps you imagine you're courageous, and you can deny you love a person, and you can even deny somebody's opinion that it's a lovely day or a rotten day, but what you can't deny is the way everything changes. For one thing, everything's constantly getting older, all the little molecules in everything. They're ageing, whatever that is, and so, if you know what I mean, everything is always new to you, even if you don't realize it.

That was the longest I've ever been away from home, ten days, and now that I'm back I can tell it's all different, and I'm different too, of course, which is partly why everything else is different. I mean, if you think in a different way about something, it's going to *be* different. And what I'm thinking is I don't *want* it to be different, I want it to be back like it was before I took off, and before Zekey died and everything, which is insane, because the way it was sucked most of the time. I know that, but when I think on it, it doesn't seem that way. It seems so rosy. I just want to slip into my old life like nothing's happened. It's how I feel, I can't help it.

Like outside my window the dogwood where I saw the cardinal is quite a bit leafier. That's fine. But God, my room is suddenly something out of *Boys' Life*, with matching blue bedspreads and yellow, green, and red throw pillows all over, and it's been painted. When I left, it was just wallpaper, mostly tan with berries and things on it. There was a long brown spot where my father once spat on the wall one night drunk. But now it's all a light, fresh green, like cream of celery soup, and old army air corps recruiting posters are tacked up on the new walls. Even my tennis trophy, Most Improved Player, is now on a shelf instead of boxed away in my closet. It's a gold cup on a wood base with a guy in the middle of serving standing on top. In the awards assembly when Coach Nicely presented it to me, the plaque on it said, Most Improved Player—Bob Hergruter. The old peckerhead sent my name in wrong. A month later I got a new plaque in the mail. They slide in and out. I saved "Bob Hergruter," though. It was actually pretty funny.

My mother and sisters all had to hustle to finish my room in time, when they heard I was coming back early. They stayed up real late working on it—"on your surprise," my father said, driving out from the city. He took the day off to meet the bus at the Port Authority, and my mother stayed home to put on the finishing touches.

I was flabbergasted when I walked in there. It was like a scene for a movie that would star the all-American boy. My mother came in behind me, all eager, holding her hands together. I said, "Wow, this is great—amazing," but I was really thinking it was pathetic, and later I felt sad to be thinking that way. Why couldn't I just appreciate it? All that work, just for me. But, you know, I couldn't help thinking the redecorating and rejuvenating was supposed to make home better for me so I wouldn't cut out again, and I couldn't stand that. It gave me a trapped feeling.

I had to go through the black-eye story twice, first for my father in the car, and then for my mother when I came through the door. My mother was very shocked by it. I guess old Aunt Joanna couldn't work up to breaking it to her on the phone, even after she promised she would.

I chatted with them for a few minutes to show them I was happy to be back, and then I had to get out into the sun, it was such a terrific day, warm and clear. I also couldn't say another word about how Cleveland was, how my trip was, how Aunt Joanna and Newton were and all, when really I didn't even want to think about the whole episode any more. They were there, my father in his green chair with his feet up, and my mother standing by the book case, and I told them I'd take a run down to the beach, something I remembered with a jolt that I always did with Zeke. My mother said, "Yes, it's been very warm while you were gone—spring!" and my father asked me if I wanted company. I sang, "No, no," and I went into the kitchen, grabbed two apples, and zipped out the back door. No garden had been dug out there yet, it was the same old swamp. Then what hurt was the sight of Zekey's pen with nothing in it but dust and shit. I wanted to say, well, he's better off dead, but no dog is better off poisoned. Then I scuffed over the crabgrass to the road, avoiding the place where they stuck his grave.

I wondered what Latham would think of me poisoning Richard Linwood, if I could come up with a foolproof method. It took a minute for me to figure that was a dumb-ass idea. Would I put arsenic drops in his high school cafeteria tuna-pea casserole? I am still in his lunch period, but I'm not about to get anywhere near his food. No, I didn't want to think about Richard any more until I absolutely had to. The bastard had been right in the foreground of my thoughts all the way from Cleveland anyway, and where did it get me?

In the pavement of the road to the beach if you knew where to look you used to be able to find a very old, worn, shiny belt buckle, brass with crossed cannons, embedded there like a nut in a cake. But a few years ago they repaved the road, and now it's gone from view. When I walk over the spot, I always think of it, and it makes me sad. Yesterday was no different. I pressed my foot down over where I knew it was buried in black tar a couple inches down like a fossil, and I thought what a terrible waste of a beautiful belt buckle. Somebody could make up a story about that buckle for kids, and it would be quite moving.

All the houses looked so calm, with everybody at work or in school, and it hit me that the neighborhood was that way day after day, with the shrubs and flowers around the neat, low houses growing and blooming and the sky so blue and nobody enjoying it, like it was the village under the curse of Sleeping Beauty. Of course I realized there had to be a few housewives rattling around inside, loading up dishwashers and watching "I Love Lucy," and stuff, but nobody was out and around. It was weird and depressing. Then in her front yard I spotted Mrs. Scattergood pouring a bucket of water into her birdbath. I stopped still by a telephone pole until she went inside.

The last house before the beach is a large, wood-shingled place with screened porches and wide windows that overlook the water. It's Melissa Powell's house. I have loved Melissa Powell from afar since the first grade, and the reason for that is she's so beautiful, I mean really beautiful, perfect.

She has long, shimmery blond hair and blue-blue almond-shaped eyes, a few freckles, a small nose with a sort of careful flare to it around the nostrils, white even teeth, and two lips like tulips, ha ha. Her body is just right, too. You wouldn't want to change a thing on her, not even her feet, which on most girls you just ignore. Her toes are so round and pretty that when you see them you feel like drawing little faces on them, or something.

She was the first girl I had sex feelings about, though I didn't understand that at the time. I just knew I wanted to carry her into the woods and take off all her clothes. I drew a big blank about what would come next. I had no idea, being only about eight, but I was sure moving in the right direction.

For most of my childhood she lived miles away in a big development they built on the old golf course, but then her father, who is a pilot, finally got rich and bought the old Shaw place and fixed it all up. I was amazed when she actually moved in right down the street from me. It was like somebody giving you a wonderful present for no reason. They hung a sign out that said Baycrest Nest, which is dumb, people naming their houses, but of course I could forgive them.

Now I would see her every day on the bus. This was around sixth grade. Melissa hadn't been in the same class with me since the second grade when we had wonderful, dark-eyed Mrs. McCullough. She was Miss Olsen at the beginning of the year, and by the end of the year her stomach was swelling out under her smocks. I remember how right before we left every day Mrs. McCullough used to gather us around her in our little chairs for joke time. Anyone who wanted could tell a joke. One day Melissa sang a rhyme that ended, "Match in the gas tank—boom boom," that I'd heard before. It wasn't very funny to me, but I loved hearing Melissa sing it. The thing was, though, was that when

Mrs. McCullough heard it, she went nuts. She fell back in her chair, laughing and laughing and laughing until she had tears on her cheeks. We were all amazed. The bell rang for the end of school, but she was a hopeless case, like she was being madly tickled. Her head nodded back and forth, and when it went back, I could see the roof of her mouth, I was so close to her. Since then I have tried hard to figure out what hit her as so powerfully amusing, but I can't. It's a real mystery.

My next strong memory of Melissa is, strangely enough, of a time when she was telling another joke. It was in summer a few years later, and I was visiting Wayne Kirsch, a guy who lived in her development. We met up with Melissa and her friend named Judy, and we threw crabapples at each other a while, not hard, and then we all sat under the crabapple tree together and told dirty jokes. Hers was about a boy named Johnny Fuckerfaster who somehow lured a little girl up to his room for a lollipop. The joke went on and on about how she wouldn't go up there and wouldn't go up there until finally she did. The kid got her to pull off her panties and then he stuck in his thing. His mother started calling from downstairs, "John-ny," over and over, but he wouldn't answer until she yelled, "*Johnny Fuckerfaster*," and he said, "That's what I'm trying to do." The joke was lousy, but hearing her say those words and actually talk about sexual activity—*fuck*ing—like she knew all about it, well, that really stunned me. I grew a bone right on the spot. Later that same day while we all walked up to Tubb's store to buy some of those little wax bottles that you bit open for the syrup inside, Melissa hung back with me for a minute, and then she said, "You love me, don't you?" "No," I said, with my face tingling. Then when she just chuckled to herself I knew she would never love me back.

Still, when she moved right down the damn street from

A **gerund** is a word that ends in -ing and acts as a noun in a sentence. The **gerund phrase** is a unit and can be used anyplace a noun can. For example Talking on the phone at midnight was not a good idea. The **gerund phrase** here is talking on the phone.

http://answers.ask.com/Reference/Dictionaries/what_is_a...

What is a gerund phrase?

gerund phrases: A **gerund** is a verb form which functions as a noun and ends in -ing (e.g. asking in do you mind my asking you?). A **gerund phrase** will begin with a **gerund**, an ing word, and might include other modifiers and/or objects.

Gerund ...

http://wiki.answers.com/Q/What_are_gerund

What is a gerund phrase?

gerund phrases: A **gerund** is a verb form which functions as a noun and ends in -ing (e.g. asking in do you mind my asking you?). A **gerund phrase** will begin with a **gerund**, an ing word, and might include other modifiers and/or objects.

Hard feeling d
Von Bredo
p 167.

me, I developed a lot more confidence. The odds against me were dropping, I thought. She was now in my neighborhood. I would at least get to see her. Maybe she would learn to appreciate me. A year after that, in seventh grade, I joined the bus patrol, which was the reason Richard Linwood spat on me at the beach. Coming home one day, Melissa, in a wild mood, threw some girl's math book out the window. So I had to give her a summons, I *had* to. I wrote her name down on the paper. My hand was jittery. When we all got off the bus, I just held it out to her. She furiously grabbed it and stomped off. Right after I got home she phoned me up. She was crying, begging me not to make her go to student court. She'd never throw anything again. I felt awful. I mean, what could I say but OK, let's just forget it. She said thank you, thank you, thank you. Afterwards I tried to hate myself for being a marshmallow, but in fact I was glad I could do Melissa a favor. It was like I was saving the damsel in distress, and I didn't care if I had to be the dragon and the handsome prince both at once. That was the only time I ever talked on the phone with her. Last summer she invited me a couple times to swim off the raft her father anchored out in front of their beach, but the thing was her big brother was always out there diving and showing off. He lifted weights and had these amazing muscles everywhere. I felt very inferior, though I admit I'm no ninety-pound weakling. Now her boyfriend is Skip Conlon, a basketball and football star, as you might figure. She is a cheerleader and as beautiful as ever. I don't see her that much, she isn't in any of my classes.

So I strolled on past Baycrest Nest through the brown, curving beach grass to the seawall, and I sat there thinking how Melissa and everybody else were all slumped down in their classroom chairs, learning all about the fascinating world of gerunds or the Belgian Congo. And there stretching away long and empty on both sides of me was the same old yellow beach, with the green water lapping softly up and melting back like a person in deep sleep. It was all just gorgeous, you know, delicious-looking. I took off my sneakers and socks to feel the water. It's May, and you can't really swim until halfway into June, not without freezing your pecker away. Still, with the water so clear, and the sun warm on me the way it was, I almost let myself go and jump in for the pure shock of it. Seagulls were gliding around, hardly flapping at all, like they owned everything, and under the glittery water a couple of horseshoe crabs scrabbled along, looking like frying pans, a big one and a small one. They were stuck together, you know, like the steam engine and the coal car, and so I figured they were doing it, the I.I., playing their basic roles in nature, but unawares, like all the other pea-brained creatures of the universe. It made me think of Zeke again, how he got caught putting the meat to Beauty, the time my mother threw water on them, all hysterical. I quickly switched my thoughts to how, years ago, Arnold Tolley and I used to fish horseshoe crabs out of the water by their tails. We'd carry them around, dripping, with their crisp little legs writhing in the air, and then we'd bash them into pieces on the rock jetties and bury their wrecked shells in the sand in rows with their tails sticking out. A few, the female ones, had hundreds of tiny jelly eggs in them, pale blue, like beads. I know how awful that sounds, but we were kids, and we hated horseshoe crabs. We were scared of their spiky tails, and also, while I was remembering all that cruelty, sitting there in the sand, I realized we used to think they were shaped like Nazi helmets, the height of evil, you know, so we killed them. Then, *that* reminded me of Richard and all of his Nazi crap. I even think he has a helmet. Well, that goes to show you. If something is really bothering you, you're not going to get away from it, even on a beautiful day. You're just not, I'm sorry to say.

At the moment, I'm in honor study hall, not my usual one, however. I'm over in the science wing with four or five seniors who are physics wizards. They're in one corner doing some complicated experiment. One is Jerry Luben, who won the Bausch and Lomb science prize last year. He limps. He also has these very distinct blackheads that are, you know, pop-able. I mean, he could get rid of them, but he doesn't, so they stay right there in his cheeks and ears like little insects burrowed in for good. Lee this summer got this tool in the mail that's a small metal stick with a ring on each end. You just slip a ring of the right size over your pimple, press, and as Lee says, so long zit. After he had it a week or two, Lee decided we should chip in for more tools that we could send to Jerry Luben and others like him, people we look at every day, who have, as the ad says, complexion woes. But I told Lee, hell, Jerry Luben is a genius. He *knows* he has complexion woes, but he doesn't give a shit. Sure, his social life is a fucking desert, but he probably wants it that way. After all, he's a genius. You have to give the guy a break. But nobody wants to be ugly, Lee says, *nobody*. Well, go ahead, I told him, buy the man a tool, see what happens. He never did though. He needed my support.

You get to go to honor study hall if you're responsible and worthy with good grades and shit like that. The faculty votes to give you an honor pass, and with it you can go wherever you want on your free periods—like to honor study halls, which don't have teachers in them and which are a big joke if you ask me. You get the wise-ass jerk-off types in there who always fool around and never get caught because they're too smart. They throw chalk and shoot spitballs and unhook girls' bras and all, and you really can't study, but who cares? If you're in honor study hall you can get the grades without studying anyway. It's just social hour. Unless of course you throw yourself in with guys like Jerry Luben, who can be very serious and boring, even when they're trying to be funny. Then I guess you have to study or just sit draped over your chair like me, in a stew.

Even though, Lord knows I've got a true shitload of work to make up (French quizzes, history paper, Chem lab and Chem test, some panel discussion garbage for English, etcetera, etcetera), I did not plop myself down in this quiet corner of the school to play Joe Earnest and get busy. In actual fact I'm here hiding from my so-called friends who prowl the halls of this jolly hole ready to jump out and ridicule me for my unstable nature, not to mention my shiner, which is now all faded yellow and tan, like a ripe banana. It's because I am the attendance record holder, for one thing. Until last week I hadn't missed one single day of school since the sixth grade, and at the awards assembly there were only two of us who were supposed to get the perfect attendance award. Mr. Devoe read off my name, and I had to get out of my seat in the back of the auditorium and walk dignified all the way to the stage, where I was supposed to sit with the other award winners for things like the Dalton Poetry Prize and the Betty Crocker Homemaker of Tomorrow Certificate. He handed me an envelope and then had me stand next to the podium while he called off the other winner, Lynn von Holt. Only she wasn't there. She never came up. It was all pretty funny. So until last week I was continually pushing up the record. In a way I'm sad about that, because, hell, I never get sick. I could have graduated with six years' perfect attendance, and nobody has ever done that before. What a shame.

First thing this morning as I was going down the stairs into gym, Rusty Forzano said to me, "Well, looks like you're really human like the rest of us. You're not a walking, talking robot Mr. Machine." It was sort of a mean thing to say, and

I don't even know for sure why he said it or what he was trying to communicate to me. "I think you watch too many
movies," I said, just to say something. "Huh," he coughed
out, "look who's talkin'." I went walking down past him
wondering why he didn't want to act plain friendly like he
very easily could. He's an all-right person.

Also, before homeroom, when I went to Coach Nicely's
room just to show him I was back and could play, he said,
"No, Bernie, you're not playing," and I felt suddenly awful.
Then he said, "Not until Monday at least. I want you to
practice these days ahead so you can have a chance to remember what game we're talking about here. Tennis, right?"
I said, "Yeah, tennis." And so my punishment is to practice
with the J.V. while the team plays a match that they could
very well use me in, though I know they will win without me.
The old peckerhead realizes Monday against West Islip will
be the tough match. He won't keep me out of that one. Hell,
he'd play himself if he thought he could keep the streak going. Except, he sucks as a tennis player. The whole J.V. can
beat him, though that's no big surprise, he's sixty years old
and he always wears a green suit, the same one day in day
out. You never see him in anything else, even on the courts.
He's a bachelor. He goes to Italy every summer to look at the
ruins.

Well, because I had to report to the buzzard this morning,
I didn't get the opportunity of scouting up Barbara, not
that I had planned to breathlessly comb the halls for her.
She wouldn't want that. Around her you have to act cool and
adult, not totally passionate all the time, even if you feel
totally passionate, at least not in public. For example, I did
not call her up last night to announce my triumphant return
to her life. I'm sure she would have enjoyed a call like that,
sort of, but when I thought about doing it, standing right
there next to the phone with my heart beating like a cowboy

chase, I decided we had so much to talk about we wouldn't be able to talk about anything, if you know what I mean.

So instead I called up Lee. "I'll be right over," he said. We strolled around for a while going nowhere until we ended up at the Mercers' place. They're very rich and never home. We usually climb up on the garage roof, which has nicely slanted wood shingles right up under the spruce branches. You lie on your back so when the wind brushes the branches the stars blink through like they're trying to untangle themselves.

I very dramatically related the story of my adventure to him, slipping in extra added details about the fight I was in, and making out with a wild Negro, which makes me feel guilty when I think of how he lapped it up. I mean why didn't I crank out an exciting version of the pure events and leave it? I don't know. But, well, there's how history is made, I guess, like the story of Paul Revere, "one if by land, two if by sea," and that bullshit. Because you know that's not how it really happened. Nobody cares how it really happened.

He was full of questions about how many licks I got in on the guys before I was leveled and how big Winona's lips were, and did I get tit and all. And I made it seem quite juicy. I even revealed that she gave me a hand job, which of course I have never experienced from anybody, especially not bare skin, but if you have a vivid imagination you can invent a slew of convincing details. "And she was only fourteen," I told him, though, come to think of it, I don't know her age at all, or her middle name. That got him. He flopped on his back and groaned and said, "No *shit*."

Then after a while he said to me, "You know, speaking of all the trouble your warty old pickle gets you into" (I told him the fight was because of Winnie), "I have a news flash concerning your old honey, hot Leslie. You ready? She now goes to all the tennis matches. And she roots for, guess who, Ollie Griggs."

"*Ollie?*"

"Yeah, and you know what else she's doing for him, too." I knew, but he said anyway, "She's spreadin' 'em, that's what."

It was hard to accept. That Ollie Griggs, all-star athlete and brain, senior class president, and New York State singles champion, who could obviously have any girl in the damn school, and who already *has* Cindy O'Halloran, a freshman in college and a prom queen ten times over, is in fact putting the wood to plain old Leslie. But from the way Lee described it, it had to be true. Lee even saw Leslie carrying his goddamn tennis rackets. He has three.

"Well, why should *you* care?" said Lee. "Shit, it's a compliment to you. First you, Hot-Nuts Hergruter, and then the Big Ace. I mean, you paved the way for him. Just think— *Trailblazer!*"

Hell, I don't know why I care. But I do, a little anyway. Only I told Lee I didn't care. He knew I would care, though. That's why he brought it up.

When we finally got around to the subject of Richard, Lee immediately said he was sorry Zeke was dead, and I told him he didn't have to be. It was dark, you know, and I had my eyes closed, and suddenly it seemed somehow like Zekey had been dead for months or like it was all just part of a story I once read, I don't know why. I mean, leaving for school this morning I stopped by his pen and sort of gazed in at the narrow path he wore from his house to the door in the fence where he ate and drank from his metal water dish and all, and I felt this wave of inner pain and tragedy, so you see, I really haven't gotten over it. In fact then and there I swore revenge on Richard Linwood, no matter how I had to get it. But last night, when Lee asked me what I had decided to *do* about Rick the Prick, all I said was, "I guess I'll just have to let bygones be bygones." The whole day I was feeling that way. The death of Zeke was not my problem at all. It was just another unchangeable fact.

"Are you *serious?*" he said. "Shit, if you think you can do that, you have your head up your ass. And in case you don't realize it, the way some people are talking, some people I won't name, that prick *could* and maybe even *did* kill your dog. Your good old dog."

"Sure I realize it," I said. "So what? He's probably better off anyway. Everything has to die. It's a free country."

Then Lee became disgusted with me. "Oh, yeah," he said. "Well, I *beg* your hard-on." You can't blame him, the way I was acting. I don't know. It was the still darkness all around me and the endless stars flickering sharp and close-down like the Hayden Planetarium, and me right on the round edge of the earth, like I was just a thing spinning in the universe on and on, as hopeless as the spruce tree and without any emotions, because who needed emotions. What difference did it make? They could've dropped the old H-bomb about then, and I would've grinned at it coming down.

Lee told me I was in bad shape and probably had pussy on the brain—slick, colored pussy at that. And he said Richard's suspension would end Monday, if I was interested. Then I wasn't interested, but I am now, and I admit, worried as ever. My life sucked me back down into worry this morning, like the undertow, so what did I do, standing there in front of Zekey's pen? I swore revenge. *Revenge.* Ha. Big deal, the great me, getting my harsh revenge, like I am actually dangerous and cruel. Jesus. What I am is a pansy. It's as simple as that.

A girl in green kneesocks just passed by in the empty hall crying her heart out, sobbing and sobbing, with her hands over her bent face and her loafer heels clacking underneath her. It was terrible. What would tear her up like that? I'll never know. Also, I'll never know who she is. I only noticed her socks.

I'm supposed to be right now at my appointment with Mr. Granger, my guidance counselor. That's another reason I skipped out on my regular study hall, so he couldn't uncover me. The old fart is concerned about me. He's always concerned about me, that's his job. I had a note delivered to me in homeroom; "Please see me as soon as you can. You have third period free. That will be fine. P. E. Granger." On the back I wrote, "I can never see you. I will be much too busy for the rest of my life. Regrets, B. A. Hergruter," and I ripped it up. Actually, he's not bad, but whenever he gets me in there, it's like he's my psychiatrist. He asks me these deep questions about my family problems and my goals, which is pathetic because he tries so hard. I feel a little sorry for him, and the whole time he leans back and pats his mustache with his stubby fingers, and his lips are pressed together, and the air whistles in his nose, like he wants me to see he's really wracking his whole brain for a way to improve me and get me on the right track. You can never satisfy a guy like Granger. For a while after freshman year I was a candidate for valedictorian. I had straight A's and all. Then, wham-o, a couple C's in French, a D in geometry, and it was all over, not that I gave a shit, but when the grades came through, you should have seen Granger. He was sweating, and he kept tapping my file with his pencil and saying, "It makes no *sense*," like he was the detective working-over the stone-hearted criminal. He's too dramatic, a real blowhard, and so I'm avoiding him something fierce. Too bad avoiding Richard can't be so easy.

One good thing happened today, and that was first thing in history I got back the spring exam which had been returned to everybody else while I was gone, and Mr. Fitch announced that I had the highest grade, 99. I could hardly remember the damn test, though, until I had it in my hands to inspect, and then it became familiar. Everybody was staring at me, and I was looking at what it said on top of my paper, a neat red word, *Excellent,* and then I looked around at everybody. Usually it's somebody else who gets the high grades in there. It's a very smart class.

I got to English a bit late because during lunch today I decided to stop being reserved toward everybody and start acting lively and joyful, and if they wanted to stay nervous about me like I was on the lam from the insane asylum, that was their business, but I wasn't going to crawl into a shell over it. I mean, so you run away from home. So you blow your attendance record. Big deal.

Things actually were not a lot different after I took on this palsy-walsy attitude, but at least I felt better. I was going through the halls like an ice-breaker, tossing out how-de-do's to guys who were making like they hadn't noticed me. I got to talking with a couple people, it was all right. Then, in the crowds on the way to English, who did I spot sauntering toward me doing the let's-ignore-Bernie routine, but, you guessed it, Leslie. I glanced quickly around to make sure she wasn't hot on big Ollie's trail, and then I said as our shoulders got about even in the traffic, "Hey, *Les*lie."

She went right on by without even the flash of an eyeball, saying, "Hey, *Ber*nie."

I spun around and caught up to her. "Leslie," I said. "How's the old girl doing?"

"Who wants to know?"

Suddenly, seeing her there in her pink shirt, and seeing how her bare throat went down beyond the first buttons, down to her jugs, and looking at her eyes again, I felt *close* to Leslie, intimate you know, and I really did want to hear how she was and what happened with her mother and the Hendrickses and all that. I felt soft. "Just me," I said. "I haven't seen you for a while."

She said, "Hunh. That's not my fault, is it?" She's always looking for somebody to blame for things.

"No, it's my fault. I ran away from home for the sake of raw adventure. Want to hear about it?"

"Thanks, but no thanks. You're making me late for driver's ed."

"Gee," I said. "Sure wouldn't want to be late for anything." It was the wrong comment to make.

"That's right," she said sharp. "So you can stop dragging after me."

So I did. I stopped short, and somebody walked into me from behind. You can't just stand there like a rock in a stream, it makes everybody upset. "Well, how about if I call you up then?" I yelled after her.

She twisted around to eye me, walking backwards with her books up against her pink chest, and she shouted, "Why don't you drop dead? Do yourself a favor."

Usually, when a girl tells you to drop dead, there aren't too many ways you can take it, but there in the noisy hallway, I don't know why, I somehow figured Leslie said it because she still liked me. She was only trying to sort of punish me, which I could understand. Of course I also know Ollie Griggs is definitely in the picture, and she definitely wants me out of the picture, and I can understand that, too, except for how Ollie himself sees things—not that I much care, but he sure has balls, that guy.

Anyway, that scene made me late for English. Everybody was still scrabbling with their books and papers when I came in, so it didn't matter. But what I'm getting at is how tense I quickly became entering that room knowing I was about to glimpse Barbara for the first time in days, and how, in spite of my newly adopted bold attitude of joy, I could not look at her in the face. I can't explain it. I strolled by her desk toward mine, looking downward like I was preoccupied with something, my shoelaces, I don't know, and it really got me, what she did then. She let two of her fingers trail out from under her desk and brush my knee, and she said, "Hi, baby," in a low voice. My eyes went up to her there in all her gold-red hair.

"Same to you," I said for no reason, and she really smiled at me.

After that, all through class I couldn't concentrate on much except how beautiful she looked, even from behind, and how straight her teeth were in the middle of that wet smile, and how, to be frank, I just wanted to *do* it, you know, stick the old wang right in there, which is an awful way to be thinking I of course realize, but shit, how can you help it? It's so basic.

And now, lo and behold, as if that wasn't enough to clue you in, where else am I right now but on Barbara's screened-in side porch, stretched out on the chaise with my pants full of one hot, pulsing rod. She's in the bathroom, taking a leak. Her mother and little brother are shopping, and her father is still at work. Outside there are rumbles of thunder far off, and it's sprinkling.

When English ended and we were out in the hall together, the first thing she said was why didn't I call her last night. "Well," I said, "you could've called me too, you know."

"I wrote you a *letter*," she said, which sent a pang through me. You should always reply to letters.

"I know. I know you did. I had a hard time in Cleveland. I mean, it wasn't easy to do things there, like read or write."

"So I heard," she said. "That's no reason not to send a postcard—or just call."

"It *is*," I said. "Because now I can talk in person to you. What I wanted to do was talk in person. I want to, you know, look at you when I explain things. It's important to look at a person."

All around us (we were just standing there) locker doors were jangling and clashing shut, and loud people were stooping down for books and ramming into each other, the end of the day. Barbara's eyes went over my face like she was deeply concerned. And I tried to look very sincere. "OK," she softly said. I barely heard her. Then she invited me to her house for dinner tonight, and she let me know we would be alone here, the way we now are. I felt my blood heat up on the spot. She had to show up for a short rehearsal for *Cyrano*, the spring play, which I would be in, too, if it wasn't for tennis, and I had to make some appearance at the J.V. practice for my punishment, even though the J.V. guys wouldn't give a shit if I skipped out, and of course Coach Nicely was over in Brentwood with the team, pacing over the grass looking nervous and calling out encouraging phrases once in a while like he does if he sees you play a good point, not that those Brentwood guys are any threat. They have to keep asking their coach which end of the racket to hold.

So we took the late bus, the activities bus, into town and walked to her house from there holding hands. All the while it was thundering. She asked me first about my eye, and I handed her the story about the brutal fight I was in, which by now I have polished pretty well. What fascinated Barbara, though, was not how I got slammed in the head, but how I actually had the nerve to date a Negro girl I hardly knew *and* take her to a wild, all-Negro party, where, holy God, it would have been only common sense to expect trouble. "Don't you *know*," she said, with her forehead wrinkled up like she was amazed at my dumbness, "don't you *know* how protective all Negroes are of their women, especially around *whites*? You didn't stand a chance. You're lucky they didn't stomp on you."

"Shit, you make them sound like animals. They're not so different."

"Oh, *boy*," she said.

"Really. Jesus, *I* protect women," I said. "In fact, I think that's what I thought I was doing. I admit I was a bit drunk."

"I don't doubt *that*," she said.

We walked on toward her house. Colorful things were coming out in the flowerbeds, daffodils and some I don't know. Finally she asked, "Well, what did she look like?" And I described Winona in detail, things like her smooth, strong legs, her neck, and even her just-right boobs, keeping it simple, like she was a statue. That is, I wasn't including any emotions—though, who knows, I could even love Winnie. At least I think I'm starting to love what I remember about her, things she said, the way she runs.

"*All* right," I suddenly hear, "what kind of trance are you in now?" It's Barbara in the doorway between the living-room and the porch. I don't know how long she's been watching me.

"Nothing," I say. "Just listening to it thunder."

"You're a moody person, aren't you?" she says, coming over to me. I'm sort of sitting up now. My bone is just about gone. We had no chance when we got here to discuss the whole Leslie problem or the whole Richard problem because our time is so limited. We had a glass of apple juice and zipped on out to the porch here, the perfect place, since any car coming in you can see way before anybody can make it to the house, even on the run. And for the last half-hour we have been going at it with steamy passion, mostly just kissing and rubbing our bodies together. Her lips are now quite red and swelled a little, and her eyes have that glitter in them that means she is excited. She puts her fingers on my temple and slides them down my cheek and under my chin. I pull her down by the arm. Here we go again. I'm on my back, and what she does is she lets one of her legs slip in between mine so her hipbone is on my pelvic region. And, Jesus, she still has her school skirt on, with nothing but bare leg under it. Her socks are off. I have kissed many girls, say ten, and Barbara is the best. Her lips press and slide and nip you like little creatures, right into your mouth, all over your face, everywhere, and also she squirms gently against you with her chest and arms. She's very loving and hot, you know, but not grabby and insanely eager like old Leslie. I bite her neck and I can smell the remnants of the perfume she put on this morning. She's making soft sounds in her throat that vibrate on my lips. My rod has sprung back and is straining up toward my belt. And now her hipbone hurts me, the way she's grinding down on it, but I don't want to stop her, I don't want her to roll off me. My hands are going over her back, over her shirt and bra straps, up to her neck and down. Finally I have to move her. She's killing my bone. I get her waist in my hands, but instead of slipping her off me, I ease her more onto me, and holy Jesus, she like widens out her legs so that she's straddling me, like a sex position, with her whole pubic mound right on my bone. Amazing. I arch into her. She lets out this low moan that makes my spine tingle. My hands are moving down just to where her ass starts to swell out, but I don't dare go any further, because, well, with your girlfriend you don't take chances, you just don't.

So my hands glide back up to her shoulders, from where I can sort of shove her jugs into me from behind, but I can't tell them apart, it's just softness.

"Oh, Bernie," she says into my mouth. We're kissing beyond control. Then, in a hot kiss against my ear she comes out with, "*Feel* me," or that's what it sounds like, and Christ, I don't believe it. I have never felt her. Of course, I have never got her so aroused either. She's *really* aroused. But now I'm thinking maybe she means *don't* feel me. Maybe she's afraid because she knows I'm experienced. At least I think she knows. So anyway, all I do is let my forearm sort of rub the squashed-out side of her jug. Her pubic mound is still slowly mashing my giant bone, too, which I have been trying to ignore, but now my nuts have somehow scrunched themselves up there, and I can't take it. By the shoulders I ease her over onto her side. She rolls her eyes open, wet and blue, and they go across my face back and forth. Then she starts kissing my eyes, and I think this is really serious. Below her eyes and through her cheeks her skin is flushed red, glowing behind her freckles. She's so carried-away and beautiful-looking. My hand goes down to her round hip. Her fingers are there, too, and she twists them into my fingers. She holds the back of my hand tight against her, and slowly slides it hard up the middle of her beating stomach right to her jug. *Amazing.* Right *on top* of her jug. I press down on it, and she lets go and I turn my hand around and squeeze it like a grapefruit and she goes, "Oh, oh, oh," and snuggles her hips against me.

"Not too hard," she breathes out. So I rub it for a minute and then glide up over it to the skin of her throat where I can see her pulse going. She sucks in air. I slip my fingers inside the collar of her shirt down to the swelling of flesh coming over her bra. She sucks in again, and, I swear, they *move*, they rise up. And now suddenly I'm aware of all the weird thoughts running through me, like how Lee's marriage manual says you should, if you're a man, think of as many unconnected things as you can so you don't get premature ejaculation, things like Ted Williams's batting average or what you ate for breakfast. But it says if you're a woman, don't worry, you'll just abandon all thoughts anyway, and it doesn't matter *when* your orgasm comes. It's the man that worries. But, luckily, for now my bone is, you might say, under control. I'm also thinking how now it's pretty obvious Barbara truly loves me, like her letter hinted, and that makes me suddenly wonder if Leslie loves Ollie Griggs, which I doubt, but even in the middle of these thoughts I can still passionately make out. I'm not distracted is what I mean, just thoughtful.

Now she's on her back on top of my other hand that's trying to get her bra clasp apart by pinching it through her shirt. But it's too tight, I can't get it. So I just wriggle my fingers in from the front to her nipple, and she's so aroused her breath rasps, you know, like a person dying. "Oh, God. Oh, God," she says. It's thundering louder outside.

Suddenly I feel her hands go down onto my actual ass, pulling at it, pulling me into her crotch. "Yes, yes," I whisper, but I sound funny saying it. It's not me.

"Bernie, Bernie," she says. "Anything, oh God, *anything*." She's clawing my nates, and I'm rocking with my bone on her thigh, feeling like I want to shoot and like I don't want to shoot. I stop, and she says, "Don't stop, don't stop." Her hips are wildly bouncing. When I look down, I see her legs spread out and bent like a frog's, and her skirt's up almost to her underpants. I let go of her jug and skim my fingers down over her side to her bare leg, madly kissing her and biting her lips all the time, and I start going up the inside of her thigh to her snatch.

Her snatch is all I can think about because it's red. It has to be. For years I've been meditating about it. Red snatch. Jesus, it's like wanting a special thing for Christmas so much you can hardly stand to think about it, but you *have* to think about it because you have uncontrollable desire. So I glide just the backs of my knuckles up that soft skin, up almost to the panties and then down, up then down, like I'm not anxious, and she's got that raspy breath in her throat and sweat on her forehead and everything. Hell, I'm sweating, too. Then, in a fever, I just go for it. My palm flattens smack onto it, like on a cushion, and I moan. I mean, I even feel like moaning. It's amazing. She's *wet*, she's wet even through the fabric, the cotton. And her face suddenly looks all distorted, with small eyes and sharp, flushed cheekbones, and she's going, "Oh, God, God, God, God, God," and she's clawing my back through my shirt, plain fiercely *clawing* it, except she has these short nails. I've got my face against her throat, kissing her there, and watching down along my arm to her bush, but I can't see past her bunched-up skirt. I wriggle my fingers by the elastic, and, God, I slip them in, three fingers, into all this juice. Christ, Christ. She's saying, "Unh, unh, unh," and then "Bernie-Bernie-Bernie-Bernie-Bernie-Bernie-Bernie-Bernie-Bernie" like she's some wild actress. My dong is massaging against her leg, and my fingers are going up in there, feeling all the things in there, I mean, *furrows*, it's not a plain tube, and Jesus God, I know she'll let me do it. I could *do* it. But I'm afraid to. Shit, I'm about to hose out just thinking of what I could do, what she *wants* me to do. She *does*.

Then—*shit fuck suck*—her father's Volkswagen, the chugging sound of it. I can't believe it. *Again*. She sits up like a spring, and I pop my hand out. "It's OK, it's OK," she whispers. "Don't, don't, uh . . . oh, goddamn it. Christ Almighty." She is looking out through the screen. Her hair in back is all tangled. Rain is coming down steady. The Volkswagen stops on the other side of the bushes. We hop up. She smoothes her skirt. I try to straighten my bone out. It's never been huger. I'll never hide it. I pull out my shirt-tail, but I suddenly see it has a big wet spot on it, and not even from shooting, but only from getting greased to shoot.

I shove my shirt back in again around my bone. Mr. Holland goes trotting by us, holding his briefcase over his head. We skip into the livingroom, where we have this checker game all set up to look half-finished, and we quickly take our positions, me in the rocker, and Barbara on the couch. Her father is stomping off water on the porch in front. I try to hunch over my bone with my elbow on my knee, and I realize I have her smell on my fingers, like tuna. Barbara leans back, looking straight at me. The door opens in the hall. Barbara stares at me, and her lips knit together, and she sends a kiss at me. I look at the checkerboard.

"Who's here?" shouts Mr. Holland.

"Me and Bernie, Daddy," says Barbara.

"Oh. Wandering Bernie, eh?" he says.

She rolls up her eyes. "Daddy, no. Adventurous."

He comes walking into the room, and I say, "Hi, Mr. Holland."

"Hello, Bernie," he says. "Stay seated, stay seated. Hey, we didn't know when we'd set eyes on you again."

"I know. I didn't either," I say. I'm trying to look back down at the board, like I'm absorbed, and he comes walking over to give me advice. He's amazing with these games, chess, checkers, go, anything—a real wizard.

But just as my eyes get to the board, *wham*, it slaps shut, and the pieces fly out at me. My head jerks back. Barbara yells, "I give *up*. That's *it*. I can't beat him. I can't *do* it."

"Barbie," he says, shaking his long head at her. "You have to play out even hopeless positions. You know that."

I start picking up the pieces. "Yeah, Barb," I say. "But she did play out all the others, Mr. Holland. It was just no use."

He says, "All the same—"

"Hell, Daddy," says Barbara, "hopeless is hopeless."

"All the same, there is the matter of courtesy." He looks

over to me and back to her. His hair is wet. His shoulders are speckled with rain.

"Very true," I say.

"Where's Glenda?" he asks. Her mother.

"Shopping with Georgie."

He looks thoughtfully down at the coffee table, and he unknots his yellow tie and lets it hang slung through his collar. He puts his hands on his hips. "Cats and dogs out there," he says. "Cats and dogs." We can all hear the rain drumming.

I'm on my knees reaching after the ones under the couch, when I suddenly realize there's this new sort of pain in my crotch that's building up from just an ache into something savage, like a mean cramp. I pull up straight, leaning on the arm of the couch. My hard-on is half-gone. But Jesus, it's like King Kong or some other monster has quickly got ahold of my nuts with a mind to crush them like jelly beans. I crawl back to the rocker with my head bent like a sick horse. Jesus *Christ*. I glance up. Barbara smiles at me. She thinks I'm being funny. Her father is over by the piano, going through the mail. I pull up into the chair. I feel like choking or coughing. It's terrible. I have to get to the bathroom. "I'll be back in a minute," I say to Barbara. I stand and start walking off as straight as I can, like the gunfighter hero who can't let his sidekick know he's been shot. But it's serious. It throbs. Is her father watching me?

In the bathroom it's worse. I pull down my pants and flip up the toilet lid, bang, and sit down doubled over. I can piss, but only a dribble. Then I try coughing. God, but it's like my balls are thawing out the way my fingers had to years ago when I froze them ice skating at Hidden Pond. My face is hung out over the white floor tiles, stop-sign-shaped, and I'm breathing deep. *Rap rap rap*, the door is suddenly knocking. I flinch. Did I lock it? "I'm in here," I say.

"Are you OK?" says Barbara through the door.

"Yeah, I'm fine. Be out in a minute."

She pauses, then she whispers, "You're not sick or anything, are you?"

"No, no, no."

"OK," she says. "I'm going to make cocoa."

"Great."

She goes off toward the kitchen. Her father is talking to her. "Oh, Daddy," she says. He lets out a laugh.

I sit up a bit for a look at my dong. It's like I'm stricken by disease, some beneath-the-surface disease, because it all *looks* regular down there, business as usual, except my nutbag is pulled tight from the aching.

I try to shit some, but nothing's ready to come out. Whew. Well, either I'm getting used to it, or it's slowly easing up. Sex, it has to be sex that crippled me like this, I know. Because my giant bone experienced only frustrated desire, and that's no good. You can't go against your biology. I mean, your instincts and, like, your basic urges have more say-so in your daily life than you mentally realize. I mean, shit, if you think your brain is in control, you're wrong, it isn't. So when your dick wants to shoot, you have to let it. It's like holding in a sneeze is bad for your eardrums. And that reminds me of how my mother first described sex to me. I was in the sixth grade. In the cafeteria that day I had heard Suki Beard say, "scumbag," which was new to me, though of course I knew it was dirty. So that evening when I was in my room at my desk spinning my ruler on a pencil and my mother was also in there doing some duty like folding sheets, I asked her what a scumbag was. It startled her. She looked at me. She knew it was dirty, but she didn't know what it was either. She had to go ask my father, who was downstairs at *his* desk, and then she came back and explained it was a sheath, you know, a rubber.

But that wasn't the end of it. She steamed right on ahead through the whole works, how babies are made, with the woman opening her vagina and the man slipping it to her. I don't know, she must've figured I was ripe for it, growing up and all. But, see, then when I asked her what it *felt* like, she said, well, you had this orgasm, and it was very pleasant, a little like a sneeze. And I thought, shit, a *sneeze*. I have never enjoyed sneezes. But anyway, it's not healthy to hold either one of them back, your sneeze or your sperm.

My balls still ache, but not so bad I can't disguise it. I stand, pull up my pants, and flush the toilet. There I am in the mirror. I'm a good guy, all right. My black eye is still obvious to me, but it's toning down to a kind of sick yellow. I crank on the faucets to wash my hands, but then I realize I shouldn't erase Barbara's smell, so I turn them off again, and I check my hands to see how they look. And there, stuck under the corner of my thumbnail, is a hair, a short, twisty, golden hair. It's from her *snatch*. It's almost white at the tip and orange along the middle, getting darker toward the other end. Jesus. I wrap it up in a piece of toilet paper and put it in my pocket. When Lee sees *this*, he will drop his drawers. Except maybe I won't expose it to him. It *is* quite personal. And even though I know that's what you have friends for, to share personal stuff with, well, it seems like you have to draw the line somewhere, like when you come to your girlfriend you do. I don't know why. It's just a feeling, like loyalty. I mean, then what if Lee asked me to get one for him? Sure, I know I wouldn't have to, but I'd be on the spot. No, some things you really have to keep totally to yourself. That's sort of a shame when you think about it.

Dinner was OK. Curried chicken, rice with raisins cooked in it, carrot and celery sticks, and raw cauliflower buds that you could dip into a blue cheese dressing that tasted awful. Barbara sat across from me, going on in her breezy way about her part in the play, Roxane, and how much fun it will be and everything, and she had her shoes off still, and her feet were up inside my pants legs, against my shins. It was sexy, in a strange way. Then after I politely asked about Ben, her older brother up at M.I.T., the conversation got around to my travels. And once again, I don't know why, but what I related was mostly a bunch of crap. I told how I got one ride in Pennsylvania with a weird, smily, bald man, who after I was in there a while slipped his hand into this rhinoceros puppet he kept on the dashboard, a pink rubber puppet, and how he talked to it about me, using two voices, for the whole ride, miles and miles. Barbara asked what he said about me, and I told her he mostly discussed how I was a mystery, because I hadn't explained to the guy why I was going to Cleveland or what I was planning to do there. Then I hit them with the horse story I made up during the long bus-ride back, about me coming around a bend on foot and seeing a dead or dying horse stretched out in the road with its eyes rolling and sides heaving. It had just gotten clobbered by a five-axle truck that kept right on going, and the owner was standing over it, a farmer in overalls, and he looked straight at me instead of at the horse. I almost got sick, I said, changing that detail from how it originally was with me actually throwing up. What I was thinking then was so what if this didn't truly happen. It *could* have happened, so it didn't make any difference if it didn't. I'm just not interested any more, I guess, in what I had for factual experiences, and I hate remembering how I left my snaketail in the car of the homo.

After dessert, walnut ice cream, we went back into the den, which is what we usually do, for a little TV. Her parents know this is in reality our excuse, but they are luckily openminded. They don't even care when Barbara kicks out Georgie. She says, "Georgie, go watch the upstairs TV. We want to be in private." "Oh, *God*," he usually groans. We don't close the door, and her mother's always clanking around outside in the kitchen, so we can't get real serious in there, but we can make out, and tonight I gently got my hand around her jug again, from the outside, and it was looser hanging off her, because she was sitting up. It felt very good holding it and all, but the odd thing was, it was also disappointing. I realized that what I had there in my hand was just her jug. I mean, it was her *jug*, sure, but that's all. Like her foot is her foot. It didn't get me all sensuous. But what really did arouse me was when Barbara pressed her forearm right down along my boner, and then slid her wrist and her palm from the tip of it on down, like she was petting a cat. Into my neck she whispered, "It gets big, doesn't it?"

All I said was, "Mmmm hmmm." I was starting to worry about getting those nut pains back, not that I wasn't very excited, of course. I was, but well, that's a whole new problem to me, those nut pains. They're sheer agony. You don't mess around with sheer agony.

Sometimes when we're in sight of her parents Barbara and I will hold hands, and they ignore it, sort of. I mean, they notice it, you can see them briefly noticing it, but they stay relaxed about it. Anyway, they try. It's hard to hold hands in Mr. Holland's Volkswagen, where we are now, because one of us of course has to sit in the back seat while he drives, and it's usually me. Barbara can trail her hand back between the seats so our fingers can weave together, but tonight she doesn't, and I remember last time she did, a couple weeks ago (which seems like a couple *years* ago), her father frowned down toward her arm, and she let go. So

I'm just leaning back here, with my own two hands in my lap holding each other, while they converse on and on about whether James Bond movies are any good or not, and the windshield wipers go flick-flick, flick-flick behind their voices. Then, as we're climbing the last hill toward my street, Mr. Holland asks me how's my tennis and did I offend Coach Nicely by cutting out the way I did. I tell him, yes, I offended the buzzard all right, and I explain my punishment, though to be honest I don't think the buzzard was really offended, it was just that he had to act like it for the sake of athletic discipline and the rest of the team. Tennis is one area where I know Mr. Holland respects me. He appreciates the game, and he gets around the court pretty well himself. His form is horrible, but at least he can get the ball back, which is more than you can say for a lot of people who own tennis rackets. Also, you have to realize he's old. But after tennis, in his eyes, I don't have any other wonderful qualities. Mostly when he throws a remark at me, he's attempting to playfully give me a hard time and, like, question me as a person. For example, he's always saying my eyes are too close together and asking whether my eyes grew any closer to each other since he saw me last. He asks me that all the time, like he's afraid I'm turning into a Cyclops. Close-together eyes means you're untrustworthy. That's what he's getting at.

Our porch light is on, just a bare, yellow bulb. Barbara slips out so I can push her seat forward. I say, "Well, thanks a lot for the ride, Mr. Holland." Then we're both there hunched in the rain. I'm looking at just the part of Barbara's cheek and chin that's lit by the little light inside the car.

"It's getting wet in here, boys and girls," says her father.

"OK, well, I'll see you tomorrow, Barb," I say.

"OK," she says. "Goodnight."

"Goodnight," I say, and I reach out and clunk her arm with the back of my hand.

Inside I know by his snoring that my father is sound asleep already. Down in the basement I can hear a man bellowing, "I guarantee it, Mr. Twitchell," on the TV. It's only ten o'clock. I pick some cucumber slices off a plate on the kitchen counter and go back out to the livingroom to look at the Long Island *Daily Press*, which has twenty-six comic strips in it that I have followed for years, except I blew it going to Cleveland. Now in ones like "The Phantom," "The Jackson Twins," "Mary Worth," and "Mark Trail," I can't figure out what's going on, but I read them anyway. I know the characters pretty well. Then in the sports I find a headline, "Hobbes High Netmen Take 82nd Straight." The story says, "Taking advantage of his opponent's weak serve game, team captain Ollie Griggs led Hobbes High Coach Vincent Nicely's netmen past Amityville to Number 82 in a row on their windswept home courts yesterday. The score was 5–0." It goes on to give the individual match-up results, and stuck at the end is a comment from the Amityville coach, "They just played a different brand of tennis." That's for sure. If we played their brand, we'd suck, too. And below is a picture of Ollie serving, only it's from last year when he wore that knee bandage. Then I realize Lee has so far not said one word to me about Eddie Burns, who is for the time being replacing me as his doubles partner. Eddie is fat, and he sort of rolls around the court like a beach ball, but he has very quick reflexes. Lee and Eddie are not exactly close. Sometimes Lee would waddle behind him, following him around, you know, until last year when Eddie hit him in the head with a tennis ball.

I put down the paper and look at the wet sneaker outlines I made across the floor coming in. Of course I know I really should be doing school work, my U.N. report, my French assignments, God, *some*thing. But tonight it's hopeless. If I can get through tomorrow, I'll have the whole weekend to concentrate on that garbage. Someone climbs the stairs. It's Claudia. She glances at me and goes into the bathroom. She closes the door and then she opens it and sticks her head out. "You missed orange sherbet," she says.

"So what?"

"We saved some for you."

"Well, thank you," I say. "I had walnut ice cream."

"Yuk," she says. "A letter came for you from Lakewood." She shuts the door again.

"Where is it?" I say loud. My father's snoring catches and stops.

"Somewhere," says Claudia.

I find the letter on the mantel propped against a color picture of me in my Cub Scout uniform with this cheerful expression on my face. What I was thinking about back then I have no idea. It's a long envelope with my address printed on, tight and scraggly, in dull pencil. It's from Winona. My armpits prickle. I open it and unfold the piece of paper, notebook paper.

> *Dear B,*
>
> I'm putting my name and address on this envelop so you will know the place to send a letter. It is number 2520½ Brookes Ave. Do you remember our house? Four houses down last night was a fire. The place was scorched hollow. There was firemen and noise and switching lights out front the whole night.
>
> I am going to quit the library because it gets so boring.
>
> How do you like school again? Do you miss Lakewood? Ha Ha You went back there right when we got to know

you. But thats allright. Latham says to say "relax and take it easy" Well I got to get my "Beauty sleep" so I hope you will send me a letter.

Goodbye Now,
Winnie

God. Don't ask me why, but this letter somehow depresses me, her handwriting and all. Also, it's embarrassing because the girl likes me. What I mean is, now it's obvious. Not that I don't like her, too, but having it come out at you like that makes you kind of recoil. And Lakewood, shit, that dead burg, all I want to do is forget it. I don't want to forget Winnie, but the thing is now I have Barbara and Leslie to worry about (not to mention everything else), and that's plenty. Also, now that I think back on it, what Winnie has that's wonderful, that makes you like her, or even love her, is her flashy eyes and teeth, her loose neck and shoulders, her skin, and how she just moves around, so easy and confident. But all that's on this paper is gray, crooked pencil marks. It's like getting back a photo of a fabulous sunset that you tried to take in black and white. So I slip it back in the envelope, and I scan the bookcase under the mantel until I come to *The Wandering Jew*, which I tried to read once, but only managed about two pages. It's very long. I jam the letter into the middle of Volume 3 of *The Wandering Jew*, and I slide the book back into place. I can't stand to even look at it. Once, as a kid, what I wanted for Christmas more than anything was a Remco Rocket Cannon. On Christmas Eve that year, I just lay stretched out on the couch with my face feeling all hot, the entire surface of my skin. My ears were sizzling, and my hands were sweating. I knew I was getting a Remco Rocket Cannon. The next day I would have it, and I was crazed because it was so close. It was hidden somewhere in the house, I knew. I could only control myself by lying down. The TV ads were what sucked me into it, and also I had seen the thing displayed in the stores. It was a whole battle station, with launching planes and colored missiles and a microphone so you could say, "Fire one, fire two," and all that. And, well, on Christmas I got it, this big long black and red and yellow plastic toy. It was horrible. The missiles just blooped out and rattled on the floor. The planes didn't fly, they sort of spun, and the microphone was plain stupid. When I talked into it, it made me sound like I was trying to fool myself about how great the Remco Rocket Cannon was. So I tried to ignore it. After a while it got stowed away in the attic, all brand new, in its box with a picture on it of a wild-eyed boy shooting off the rockets and going bananas with joy. For years after that, whenever I went into the attic, I couldn't stand to see the thing. I threw an old sheet over it.

I listen to the water gurgle down the sink drain. My father is snoring fiercely again. Claudia comes out, and at first she doesn't see me because I'm still over by the bookcase.

"Boo," I say.

Her head swings around toward me. "What are you doing in here?" she says.

"Looking for my mail."

"It's in your room," she says. She has her pajamas on.

"What's the big attraction downstairs?"

"I don't know. Some old movie with Edward G. Robinson."

All at once Edward G. Robinson reminds me of gangsters and guns and Latham and good old Richard Linwood, and I feel like the sun just went behind a cloud.

"Well, nighty-night," Claudia says. "I'm going to bed."

"OK. Don't let the bedbugs bite."

She gives me her unamused stare and goes off into her

room. Her hair is all brushed straight.

I plop down on the couch. I'm tired. I think I could go into the bathroom now and jerk off, beat the old meat so that I would feel better, you know, but I haven't got the energy. I realize I'm looking over at the corner of the room where we always put our Christmas tree. I can't figure out why I have Christmas on the brain, but I do. It's May. Outside everything is warm and soggy. I feel like now my mind is going on by itself, like when a wheel comes off your wagon and keeps rolling alone on down the hill.

CHAPTER 7

OK. I ADMIT I'm only up here trying in vain to escape from my life and all the mysterious troubles and pains that come along with it. But so what? This attitude of suffering appeals to me, I can of course see that. In a half-assed way, it shapes me into a manly and tragic figure, me in our slant-roofed, junk-filled attic, drinking slowly my second beer of the evening (which is also the eighth or ninth beer of my sixteen years on this earth), staring out the dusty window down onto our weedy front lawn and over at the Masons' garage across the street, where some dopey little kids are shooting baskets in the fading light, yelling and calling each other niggers. But shit, tragic or not tragic, my life still sucks the hairy one, there's no getting around it, I'm sorry. What I should be doing, I know, is putting my time to good use (as my mother says), though there are lots of ways you could look at a saying like that. Like, what's good use?

She doesn't know I'm up here. I had to sneak cubes of ice out of the freezer, and then I had to sneak up the stairs, which is not easy because of all the crap piled on them— the Electrolux vacuum cleaner that reminds me of a torpedo, a bunch of rubber boots, a sledge hammer, a crate of Barbie doll clothes, brooms and mops and my broken Daisy air rifle—that you have to step silently over. Yesterday morning, Sunday, while they were all out for a drive and to buy the Sunday *Times*, I hid nine cans of Budweiser here inside my father's old mildewed canvas navy suitcase. It still has in the zippered compartments two snapboxes of gold-colored uniform buttons with the eagle on them and also his New Zealand driver's license.

How we got ahold of all this beer, Lee and I, is quite interesting. We stole it. The mood for a night raid just swept over me because of how the whole day went on Friday, horrible—about as horrible as today, as a matter of fact. I guess one thing just leads to another. After I had dinner Friday night at the Moose Club with my father, I called up Lee, and we both put on the dark-hooded sweatshirts that we got with our caddy money, and we headed for the beach. But, to begin with, that entire day, as I said, was a horrible day. First thing, I finally got cornered by Mr. P. E. Granger, my guidance counselor (a wood sign on his desk has these gold letters on it, P. E. Granger), and he really gave it to me about my responsibilities, my potential, my future, and that garbage. And he asked me, "Do you have anything to say about any family difficulties you may be experiencing?"

I said, "No, I really don't," trying to be polite.

He said he was disappointed that I seemed to feel I could not confide in him. Then he said he thought my grades were secondary to my personal well-being.

"Boy, I agree with you there," I said.

"Nevertheless, they remain very important," he said. "Your

work here in school—your studies—are the key to your successes in the future, and frankly Bernie, that's what's on the line here, your future. I think you're aware of that."

I told him, yeah, I was aware of it, all right, and I told him not to worry. "Really I'm quite OK," I said, but I don't think he felt good when I left. He kept his mustache slanting sadly down.

Well anyway, that was a depressing way to start the day, especially since by the time he set me free I had no chance to catch Barbara before homeroom. They were already into the Pledge of Allegiance, which Ollie Griggs leads every morning over the loudspeaker. It was strange, squeaking along through the empty halls with Ollie and everybody else droning the Pledge like they were hypnotized by Martians and only I escaped. Then in homeroom there was a note for me from Coach Nicely: "See me. Urgent."

It turned out that at Thursday's match in Brentwood, which was canceled halfway through because of the rain (they only have two courts), Barry Rosen, who plays Number 2 behind Ollie, fainted on the court. He didn't hurt himself, but it was a sign of extreme fatigue because of what he has, which today we found out is mononucleosis. He can't play at all.

"I have no choice but to tap you for that slot, Bernie," the old peckerhead said. "How do you feel about that?"

I was standing there thinking what a jerk he is. "Fine," I said.

"Good, good. This afternoon I want you to give Ollie a battle. For the heck of it. What do you think of that?"

"Fine by me," I said.

Lee saw Barry keel over in Brentwood, and he said it looked like a big act. Lee is just mad, though, because now he has to go through the whole season with Eddie Beachball Burns as his partner. "That candyass wiseguy, Barry

Rosen, now that he's all accepted at Princeton, he thinks he can just forget school and fart around home for a couple months," Lee said. He didn't mean that, he was only complaining. He likes Barry. Barry is very good, solid as a backboard. He's a little guy, but he's smart and fast, and he doesn't miss anything. You have to beat him, he won't give it to you—which only somebody like Ollie can do. You have to be able to force him with your serve, and you have to have a lot of confidence in your overhead because Barry likes to just float the ball to the baseline if you try to force him into a corner and grab the net. He's tough. He gives Ollie fits. Their matches can last hours. My only match with Ollie (the only time before Friday that I was ever really on the court with just him) lasted about ten minutes. So, as you would expect, I had that to stew about all day, not that I was working up strategy, or anything. Shit, I'm no Barry Rosen. All I can do is hit the ball back to him and watch him smash it into one corner or the other, and I knew how embarrassing that was going to be, especially with Coach Nicely, and God, maybe even Leslie for spectators. But as it turned out it actually wasn't that bad. Ollie and I just worked on strokes, and I got something out of that besides plain discouragement. Leslie didn't show up either, which was a relief. Still, it was weird to be out there with Ollie, seeing him lope along from one side of the court to the other, flowing and intense like he is, with him not really saying much except every now and then, "Good," or "You're too close" (which I appreciate), and all the while I'm wondering is he thinking about me and Leslie or him and Leslie or him and Cindy O'Halloran and Leslie or what? Because all that was rolling around in my brain, and I was still able to whack the tennis ball. I don't know, though. Ollie, when you talk to him, is quite dull, not dumb at all, but like he doesn't have any deep thoughts. I can't explain where I get that idea. It's not like I expect him to constantly reveal deep thoughts to me or anything. All we ever talk about is tennis and maybe swimming or cars (he has a Porsche, his father is an orthodontist). But, you know, back in junior high when I used to get into those long after-school talks with Moon, the Negro guy, even though all we discussed was families and teachers in a joking way, I *knew* old Moon had very deep thoughts inside him. It was obvious. But with Ollie you can only wonder. It's odd.

Also on Friday I had to take shit from Mr. Fitch about how late my U.N. report was going to be. I told him I would have it Monday. (That's today, of course, only he didn't get it today, either.) On Friday I really believed I would grind it out over the weekend, but over the weekend I didn't do beans. When he asked me today if I had it, I said no, and he said nothing for a second. Then he asked, "How's your feud with Richard Linwood? His suspension's ended, you know. He's back in school today."

I said, "Yeah, well, I'm keeping out of sight."

He said he thought that was a good idea. I asked him if Richard really had to give up his knife, and he said he did. I felt good about that until I realized Richard won't have any trouble figuring out who cost him his Italian switchblade, and he probably won't have any trouble getting his hands (well, *hand*) on another one either. When I told Mr. Fitch that, he said just to report even the smallest problem to Mr. Devoe, which later in the day (before my lowly, rotten, miserable West Islip match) I almost did.

But going back to Friday, the whole day what I was wanting to do was just see Barbara and maybe sound her out about the significant new love developments we experienced Thursday night. Lee's marriage manual says you shouldn't be afraid to approach the issue of sex directly in words, not that I was going to give *that* a try (I mean, you know, like, *what* words?), but I did want us to have a chance to say in private what we were maybe thinking. In English only once she turned back to me with a heavy, blue-eyed look from under her drawn-down eyebrows and with a bit of a smile hidden in it somewhere, but that was all. After class, I nearly got to her, but Mr. Parizzi wanted to consult with me about my "arrested rate of progress," and from the corner of my eye I watched her hanging around, chattering outside the door, but by the time Mr. Parizzi gave up on me she was gone. Lee sometimes shares my locker because his is so far from most of his classes. Two months ago on the inside of the metal door he hung up a color photo out of a magazine of Dan Lurie, this amazing stud muscle-builder, who's in this tippy-toe pose, all oiled-up and spotlighted like the relief map of a country, with nothing on but a jock to cover his dong. When I got to my locker, I furiously ripped out Dan Lurie and tore him into confetti. Right away I felt bad about doing it, because Lee only stuck him there for chuckles. "That Dan Lurie," Lee said, "he's a pitiful asshole." But it was too late. I left the pieces there for the janitor.

After hitting with Ollie I wanted to hang out in back of the auditorium to watch the *Cyrano* rehearsal, but my only ride home was with Lee's father, and he was waiting with the engine running outside the gym. Lee and his father have the same name, Wesley Sand Bridgman, only Lee is Lee and his father is Wes. They don't get along very well. Mr. Bridgman is an important sales representative for a big company that gives him a new car every year, and most of the time it seems like he is either out of town or getting ready to go. Last summer he bought a beautiful old blue Thistle that Lee and I sailed all the time because he wasn't around much. We sometimes raced it in fact, but we never were a hot boat. The bay has a huge class of Thistles, maybe thirty.

They are mostly owned by doctors.

So in the car Lee's father talked tennis with us, saying we had his sympathies because we had to split as a team. He meant it. He liked talking with us, but you could see he was in a hurry. He drove fast and kept honking at people.

When we got to the driveway, before he turned off the key, Mr. Bridgman pulled this aluminum disk out of his pocket and gave it to Lee, and he said, "What's *that?*"

"I don't know," Lee said.

"Well, guess," Mr. Bridgman said.

Lee was turning it with his fingers. It was some bigger than a silver dollar. "I *can't* guess."

"Ah, c'mon. How about you, Bernie?"

"It's aluminum," I said.

"It's a future beer or pop can," Lee's father said. "That amount of aluminum is exactly what's needed to make one can, and cans someday will be stamped by machine out of pieces exactly like it."

I thought of that, I guess, because of my own red, white, and blue beer can, which is just about four inches straight in front of my nose sitting against the screen on the window sill. There are dead flies along the window sill, too, so dry they jiggle when I breathe on them. I'm not drinking my beer out of the can, though. I'm drinking it out of a cup, on the rocks. Warm beer would make me throw up.

Friday night at the Moose Club my father drank beers with shots of Johnny Walker, that's what he drinks there, it's his *usual*. And I had tomato juice with lemon, which is my usual because that's what he always orders for me. It's good, though. I never drink tomato juice except at the Moose Club. My father was taking me out for the Moose Club's fabulous thick steak, which he knows I love, to celebrate my surprise promotion on the team. Before dinner we sat at the end of the long bar on these red stools watching Pete the bartender whip together very complicated drinks in silver shakers for all the other Mooses who were yukking it up and getting loaded down the long bar, which sort of seemed like a highway with glasses on it and shiny little puddles. Six dusty mooseheads bent down over us from the wall, dull-eyed like they were bored stiff but listening anyway because that's all there was to do. Pete's hands were quite skillful the way they flipped around the bottles, pouring without looking while he joked and laughed.

"So how's the young tennis champ?" he asked me when he came down with my second juice. Of course that's his job, making friendly talk, and even though he means comments like that for my father mostly, I can tell he likes me. He calls me "Number One Son."

"OK," I said. I was thinking about how Ollie ran my ass off the whole afternoon without trying, and how if I could only be as good as Ollie Griggs, or maybe even almost as good, I would be satisfied, I wouldn't want any more. Then immediately I thought of how Ollie acts in tough matches, not satisfied at all. If he plays the ball the wrong way or gets beat on a shot he thinks he should have had, he slaps his thigh hard with one hand. After matches like that, his thigh can be bright red.

My father said, "The coach just kicked him upstairs today. That's what we're here celebrating."

"Yeah?" Pete said, making his eyebrows go up. "How's that?"

My father nodded at me so I would explain.

"Well, the old backboard, otherwise known as Barry Rosen, came down with mono, and I got picked to fill his sneakers," I said.

"Ho! *Kissing* disease," Pete said.

"Yeah, he's got his work cut out for him now," my father said.

Pete said, "Hell, look at it this way. Coach wouldn'ta looked Bernie's way, unless he damn well knew Bernie could do it, right? Coach knows his personnel, right?"

I was thinking, shit, our coach doesn't even know when he's got on different color socks.

"Oh, hell," my father said, "he can do it. We all know he can do it. All I'm saying is he's got his work cut out for him, that's all."

Pete looked at me with a big frown and he said, "You mean some racket-whacker out there can beat you, Bernie? I don't believe it. Say it ain't so." Then his frown swung up into a smile.

"Oh, yeah," I said. "A few guys can whip me." That was when the first little fear shot through me about the match I blew today. It was like finally I sharply realized, like when you sit on a tack, that I would truly be playing some tough competitors, and I knew I would today come up against a guy even Barry had trouble with last year. I took a quick swallow of juice.

Pete was leaning back into the cash register. A man down the bar yelled, "Hey, Pete," and Pete stuck his palm out that direction like a traffic cop. "Well, Bernie," he said, "you gotta mix caution with courage," and then he laughed to my father, and leaned forward with his arms out and his fingers woven together, and he cracked his knuckles. "Am I right, Freddie?"

"You haven't been right in ten years I've known you," said my father.

"Well, if not, I guess I'm the only one *left*, hey? I'll be back."

Then to me my father said, "I'll tell you, confidence is the big thing. You got to maintain confidence in yourself. You're no good without it."

"That *sounds* easy," I said.

"I'm not saying it's easy," he said. "It's *not* easy."

Then a fat man in a madras jacket that was stretched wide across him like a bedspread edged his way between us, saying, "Hey, Freddie, this the growing boy?"

My father introduced us, but I never got his name. He started in a mile a minute about his daughter, Candy, who was a freshman but shy (he thought because of her braces or else her weight problem or maybe she was just shy, who knows) and how the high school was making a big mistake if it dropped the baccalaureate this June, a really big mistake. There *is* a place for religion in education and all that. Suddenly we were swept up into the whole God question, him and me, because one thing I hate is people always trying to hand you their faith crap to show you what you're missing out on, I don't care if they're Catholics, Protestants, or what. I told him I thought you could believe whatever you felt like believing in the privacy of your own home—and anywhere else, as long as you kept it inside your own twisted brain—but a school is the place for facts not faith. That's the title of the editorial I wrote last fall for the *Dolphin's Leap*, our school newspaper, before I got the ax for reading *Playboy* in the office. I was feature editor. Actually, what I was doing when Mr. Schultz, the mechanical drawing teacher (a wheezey old guy), happened to bust in there without even knocking was I was hanging up the Playmate along with some lettering that I cut out of our headline-maker taped under her two huge boobies: "plain" and "chocolate," like they have in the cafeteria. It was quite embarrassing, as you would suppose. I was putting it up so Miss Fitzwaller, our advisor, would discover it. She always liked us, me and Buzzie Cochran, the editor. In fact, Buzzie and I used to sneak out into the parking lot on our free periods when we knew Miss Fitzwaller had a class down in the other end of the building, and we would take her new Chevrolet Impala down to the shopping center, where we would buy *Playboy* if we had the money, and if the geezer would sell it to us, some days he would, some days he wouldn't. She always left the keys under the floormat. Of course, if she ever found out we were stealing her car, she would have shit bricks, but she was very nice to us in most areas is what I want to say. She would have really laughed at plain and chocolate, I know that much.

Anyway, for me religion is like the Yankees—once I get rolling on the subject, it's hard to slow me down. Besides, all my ideas and concepts about it are standing up clear in my head from writing that editorial. I wrote it because we ran this informative feature article by Maryann Klein, who is very smart in science, about the moon, what it was made of, how the Earth got it, and all that. We also threw in a bunch of drawings of the moon that some sixth graders did over one whole page. It was mostly Miss Fitzwaller's idea, but since I was feature editor I received the letter that came from this angry mother about how shameful it was that we tore right through the creation of the moon totally ignoring the role of God. And it went on about how when the prayer was taken from our school children, communism was given a toehold in our educational system, where God retreats the Devil advances, and so on. Three pages of this horse manure.

So in my editorial I said instead of thinking and wondering about the creation of the moon, people should actually focus their thoughts on the creation of God. Where did we get this God? I described a caveman shuffling out of his smelly hole in the cliff and seeing the sun go down, or hail, or lightning blasting a tree, all the things that were enormous mysteries to this caveman. He was afraid of all these things, petrified is more like it, because he couldn't explain them. Then he came up with a terrific idea, very logical when you think about it, of somebody like him himself, a *man* in other words, but powerful, being in control of, say, lightning, and causing it. So then nothing was a mystery any more—what a relief. You had a sun god zooming around in a gold chariot, you had a god of rain and thunder. You had a sea god, a hunting god, a love god, whatever you needed. After a while, some wiseguy figured it would be better if they just combined all the little gods into one super god, which made everything much less complicated because you then had one overall answer for everything, no matter what. You were safe and secure. Except, of course, then supergod himself was the mystery, but you would still be OK if you loved him. It's sort of like walking by a mean dog. If you go right up to him like you're not really about to drop your drawers he won't bite you. You have to have faith.

Well, anyway, with my father stuck on the stool there just listening in his irritated way (he says you get zero out of philosophical arguments) and drinking another boilermaker (my father went to Purdue, poo-poo-Purdue as he calls it, who are nicknamed the Boilermakers, and he played football there), I gave the fat man all the logical basics of my God editorial (which, I should mention, got Miss Fitzwaller into trouble because of my comments about communism, not that she cared she was in trouble, but I felt funny about it), and he kept grunting and groaning and interrupting me with questions like, "But, Bernie, all these ideas you have come from your brain. But who made your brain? Did you ever think of that?"

And I would say, "You mean there's a factory?"

I could see his ears getting redder and redder. "In a sense. In a sense, there is," he would say.

"Baloney," I would say. I guess what bothered the old tub-of-lard was I was just a kid, a smartaleck. That's what bothers my father anyway. He doesn't like to hear me acting like I know anything either, especially if it's something I didn't learn from him.

Later at the table my father lectured me about how to be sociable. He said, "You can have your own opinions. I'm not denying you your own opinions. And if somebody's interested, you can go and calmly express them. But you don't want to ruffle people's feathers, you know? Be friendly, that's all. Hell, you coulda given the gasbag a heart attack."

I said, "Yeah, yeah." I could have said plenty right then, but the feathers I mostly didn't want to ruffle were the old man's. After all, he was taking me out to dinner, just me, which was a rare event.

So through the rest of the meal I sat still while he got going hard on the subject of aggression in competition, how to have it and have it under control, which—he said—is another way of saying concentration. "If you got concentration, you have the Number One quality of all athletes. It isn't strength or fitness or any of that, it's concentration that makes a true, superior athlete." He was talking loud and all, but he was sincere, it was obvious, and I appreciated what he said. The thing is, though, I do know he's right about concentration, and I also know it's what Barry Rosen has and I don't, but what I *want* to know is how do you get it if you don't have it? Because, Jesus, I played a truly miserable match this afternoon, anybody would agree, including Leslie I'm sure, who was there watching behind the hurricane fence. She couldn't help it, since I was playing right alongside Ollie. I lost, 6–4, 6–4, to this scampery little thin guy that Barry has never lost to, and actually, what's worse is that I played pretty well, crisp, you know, until it was 4–5 with me serving. Just hold your serve like you have right along, I'd tell myself, and then I'd blow it, I'd go and fuck-ing *blow* it. Both sets that happened. He started serving the second, and we traded back and forth until I canned the whole match at 4–5 again. I double-faulted four times in those two games. No concentration, no nerve. And I *know* that, but where do you go to get it? I guess if you could make concentration pills, you would be a millionaire.

I don't know. I sit here with this beer, and now it's really dark, and the record player's jangling down there under the ceiling, and I think, what do I know, maybe when God retreats the Devil *does* advance. If you don't have your religious morals around you like a fence, maybe evil can come creeping in. I mean, here I am, a shadow in the attic doing a bad thing, which is drinking beer and not for the taste of it. And the beer is beer we stole, too. The people in one of those glass-front houses high on the bluffs down the beach toward Hidden Pond were giving this dance party, with colored lights and a horn combo. In our blue sweatshirts with the hoods up, we both climbed in the dark right up the steep bank of railroad ties that are holding the bluff together to see what was happening on their patio at a close angle. This is what we usually do on night raids. We look in people's windows and stuff, and if they see us, which they never do, we just take off. Nobody could catch us. But Friday night when Lee stuck his nose over the edge and just into the light, he was face-to-face with a whole case of Budweiser. He kept signaling to me, but I had got to a spot about twenty feet away along the bluff right near the combo, and I couldn't figure what he was communicating. I was up there like a spy, you know, trying to pick out one voice in all the noisy, crossing conversations to follow what it was saying, and he was crouched below the edge, jabbing up out of the shadows with his finger. I knew he didn't mean let's go over the top and invade, that would've been sheer insanity. Then he climbed down, and I climbed down too.

"There's a whole shitload of beer up there," Lee frantically whispered.

"Up where?"

"Right up *there*. Right up *front*."

"Yeah? Can we get it?"

"Jesus. I would bet my pecker and one nut."

We both looked up to the top of the wall where Lee had peeked over, and I looked down the beach, trying to somehow come up with a plan for the beer once we nabbed it. We would have to bury it. It would be like our treasure. The yellow light slanting down over us from the party faded fast over the dim water, just faintly streaking the little rolls of the waves in their long lines along the shore.

Lee said, "What we'll do is I'll go up and drop it to you, one six-pack at a time, and you have to catch it so we don't shake it up too much."

I said, "Well, so what if we shake it up?"

"God. You don't want to shake up beer and ruin it, that's why," he said.

I knew we couldn't ruin it, but didn't say anything. You can't object to what Lee insists on if he's excited, he'll just get furious at you. He snaked back up to the top and silently swung them out into the air, the four six-packs. His hand would slip into the light far above me, and he'd strain up reaching, and the hand would come slowly back with a box of cans that would shine for a second and then come plunging through the shadows. I caught them all with no trouble, but cans would jump out the ends if I didn't grab them right.

We trotted along the beach with the beer until we got to the long granite jetty that protects the point where the shore bends around in toward Centerport Harbor. It was low tide. We hopped out along the rocks, like on a bridge to nowhere, out to where they were too seaweedy for our feet. Then we sat there, out of breath and excited, just holding our beer in our arms.

"Je-*sus*," said Lee. "*Man*. I could see the legs of the ladies that were standing two feet *away*. I almost didn't do it."

"Shit," I said, because he always exaggerates. "They were all hotsie-totsie dancing around the combo."

"Hell they were. Or maybe when you were up there they were. Christ, those ladies were so close to me I was shaking like a bastard."

"Well, shit, who cares if they would've seen you anyway. They would've peed their pants, you look like such a god-damn maniac, creeping up out of the dark."

He laughed at that, which is why I said it, to get him relaxed.

It took quite a bit of rummaging around in the sand and rocks and scrubby beach trees, especially since the night was so black, until I finally found a board with a nail stuck through it that we could use as an opener. We took it back to the jetty, where we left the beer, and we banged a couple of cans open, getting beer spray all over ourselves, which we thought was funny, and then we drank them. We were quite thirsty.

Lee said, "This stuff is warm as piss."

And I said, "Yeah, it tastes a little like piss, too."

We laughed. I guess we were both a little nervous, knowing how late it was by then, probably midnight. It was after nine when I got back from the Moose Club. My father just dropped me off in the driveway, backed his Buick right out again, and headed back to the action. My mother was drinking wine and playing Scrabble with Claudia and Lizzie around the card table. They really wanted me to join in, and I was tempted because I almost always win, but I felt restless, and I had to get out. I said no thanks, I was heading for Lee's, and my mother said he called about a half-hour ago, so I called him back, and we decided the hell with Ping-Pong, which is mostly what we end up doing, let's go have a night raid, it was only nine thirty. I was thinking, well, this also means the hell with caddying, which we had planned to get up for on Saturday at six in the morning. But caddying is truly a suckass job, as I have already mentioned, and the thought of how I would miss a loop on the links didn't exactly enrage me.

Still, though, midnight was pretty late. All one of our mothers had to do was phone the other one to find out we were not at each other's house, which is what they unsuspectingly thought. But once we had a beer in us, out there on that one cool, flat hunk of granite with the black salt water lapping calmly against it and the jewely lights far out along Connecticut, we told each other, what the fuck, what could they do to us, our parents? We could say we went for a long walk and we're sorry. They couldn't do a thing to us. We're getting immune to them.

So we each broke out another beer from our supply. It felt wonderful having the can in my hand, the second can, and having all the rest of those cans just waiting, you know, like when it's freezing out and you have a fire blazing in the fireplace. Right then in a flash, while Lee was rattling on about how Helen Bundy had given him now four hand-jobs, five if you counted the one from outside his underpants, and I was smiling to myself feeling lucky to have a good friend, I suddenly remembered the time in Lee's tent two summers ago when we were showing each other our pubic hair and when we actually *kissed* each other's wang, just for experimental reasons. Jesus. Wang-kissing seems horrible and disgusting to me now, but then, I don't know, I guess we did it because our wangs were just hanging in the breeze there, ready for anything. Then later that summer we got Bobby Bostwick, this thin little seven-year-old squirt who idolized us, to do the kissing. Lee put his whole dick in Bobby's mouth and tried to get me to do it, but I thought, what if he bites into it like a Tootsie Roll? Then I'd really be in trouble. Also, we shaved off our pubic hair to make it come in faster, but we couldn't tell if it did or not. It seemed weird to realize we actually did oddball stuff like that, when now I can ponder it from the standpoint of having some sexual experience under my belt. I was going to remind Lee of those times, to like get his opinion, but he was all stirred up about Helen Bundy, and he wanted me to bet that next Friday he would not finally put the old meat to her, which I didn't feel like betting, not because I thought he would do it and I would lose a quarter, but because I honestly didn't give a shit.

"You can dick her or not dick her," I said. "I don't give a shit."

"Well, listen to you," said Lee. "Holy fuck, won't you listen to the man of experience."

I said, "No, really, I hope you *do* dick her. It's no big deal, that's all. I mean, you don't love her or anything."

"Jesus Christ, who said I loved her? That's got nothing to do with it. C'mon. Are you gonna tell me you were *in love* with Leslie Wolstein?"

"No," I said. "No, that's not what I'm saying—"

"You don't have to love a girl to pop their twat. And girls *know* that, for Christ's sake."

"I *know* girls know that. What I'm saying is then it's no big deal."

"Big *deal*? Shit, it's the I.I., Bernie, the big I.I." Lee was spreading his arms out wide like an election candidate.

Well, sure, I knew the I.I. was a big deal. It *is* a big deal, but I was remembering that night with Leslie on Hendricks's white bed and also in the boat locker, how if I really liked her like Pam Sokel wanted me to, maybe it would have been improved, you know, like friendlier and easier, who knows? Not that I expect the ideal I.I. from Barbara, who maybe I love, or who I in fact *do* love—and not that I wouldn't give old Leslie another try either, if she wanted to—but, well, when you love the person it's more exciting, or so it seems, because of all the deep feelings you're having.

Lee threw his can out onto the water, *plunk*, and even though I could hardly make it out, I threw my can out at it, and I hit it, *clink*. "Hoo-ee," I said. And Lee said we had to drink two more so he could have a shot at *my* can. So we opened them. Then when I tried to stand for a whiz my foot pushed off something slimy, and I sat back hard on my ass and stuck my whole leg into the water. Of course, to Lee that was so hilarious, he yipped and yukked and kept saying, "Way to *go*," until I splashed him and said, "Chief Shit-for-Brains."

Up to before I slipped I was getting ready to tell Lee about Thursday afternoon on Barbara's porch and what it was like in colorful detail, and I even for a second wondered if I had on my same shirt from that day, with the little gold hair in the pocket to maybe show him, except it wasn't the same shirt, and besides I knew I stuck the hair behind a shoebox of old medicines in the bathroom cupboard. But after that incident of cold-hearted ridicule, I didn't say a word. I wiggled my toes around inside my soggy sock. Lee sat there and spewed out a mouthful of beer like a statue on a fountain. He said he thought maybe another brand, Pabst Blue Ribbon, would taste better. I didn't say anything. Then to get us back on sort of an even keel, Lee asked me what my plans for Monday were, and I said, "Nothing. Just stand there and knock the ball back. That's all I can do."

He said, "Hell, I don't care about West Islip. I barely give a shit if we win or lose any more. That fuzzy ball bouncing back and forth, back and forth, who cares? I'm asking what's your hot, foolproof plan for when Rick the Prick comes back? Out for blood, you know? Are you scared?"

"No, not now I'm not," I said.

"Jesus, I *almost* believe that."

"So don't believe it. I don't give a shit if you believe what I feel is what I feel. If I get scared Monday, I'll be scared, but I'm not scared now."

"Fuck that," Lee said. "You just won't admit it."

In a way Lee was right, and it made me furious then to think so. I mean, my big, sweaty fear of Richard Linwood is something I carry around with me now even when I'm not aware of it, just like I always have the ability to, say, hit a backhand, even when I'm jerking off, or something. It's like that old belt-buckle in the pavement. I know it's there, but I don't think about it much. Lee was trying to push that big fear into the foreground again, and I just wanted to sip my beer on that peaceful rock, that's all, and not worry-worry. I hunched up my shoulders and kept my mouth shut. The beer was making my thoughts scatter like a bunch of chickens. For some unknown reason what sprang into my complicated brain was the image of the Owl and the Pussycat, you know, from a poem I knew by heart as a kid. Only all I could remember was that the Owl and the Pussycat went to sea, the huge, blue sea, in a very safe and comfortable pea-green boat. They were bound for thrills and exciting times, that was for sure, but they were secure in that pea-green boat.

Lee tapped me on the elbow with his can. "Shit," he said. "I know I'd be scared. Jesus, I'd be very scared."

"Thanks loads," I said.

"So, like, I would think my old buddy Bernie is smart, and he would have some plan ready, see? Some plan for what you can do when . . . you know, when Monday comes. See?"

"Yeah. Well, what would be *your* plan?"

"Jesus, I don't know," he said.

"Well, my plan is nothing, zero. Got it? I'm just not letting the peckerhead near me, that's all."

Lee looked at me for a second. "OK," he said. "But like, he could still *get* near you. What if he gets near you?"

"Well, so then he's near me. I don't know. How the fuck do I know? What is *he* gonna do? You tell me that."

"Say he hits you."

"Oh, shit. Say he hits *you*. What would *you* do?"

"Hey, don't ask me. You're the one who's supposed to have the plan."

Then I yelled at him that I did not *have* any plan, which is what I was saying all along. And he told me not to get riled. "So then we'll just make up a plan," he said. And I said if you plan for it, it's like it's a game, with rules and everything. But it wasn't a game. Something would happen, and nobody would know what until it happened. Lee said no, it was like the air raid drills in school when you know that if the bell clangs you scuttle out into the hall and put your head between your knees. If you can do that, you don't go running around in circles, crying, "Holy Christ, we're gonna be bombed to bloody bits."

"So what?" I said. "Either way you fry your goddamn ass."

Anyway, when I finally did come face-to-face with Richard today, no plan would have done me any good. All day I steered clear of the mad beast with success. In homeroom I checked the master attendance list when it came around to see if his name might be luckily still on it, but it wasn't. He was somewhere in the building. I even went into the guidance office and looked up his schedule in the student schedules file so I could know exactly where to hang out to keep my little buns out of trouble. If *that* was my plan, it sucked. I was on edge so much every goddamn minute that I could hardly concentrate when I at last got a chance to talk to Barbara in person. I did have her on the phone Saturday, but she had to get off after two minutes because her mother had to make social worker calls, so we didn't talk about what we had on our minds, and I was depressed about it, since I had waited all morning for everybody to clear away from our phone, and then I got a busy signal for a whole hour before she answered. I told her I'd call her back, but I don't know, telephones are weird. All you're doing is talking into that cruddy mouthpiece with all the holes in it breaking your voice up into spaghetti bits to feed it through the wire, and all you have to look at is your fingernails, when what you really want is the person, with gestures and eyes and everything, especially when what you want to talk about is love. Of course, we couldn't talk about that so easy in the rambunctious hallway either, with me keeping both eyes peeled for Richard's big, round, black-haired head. True, love is a topic of endless proportions, and you can most of the time get across your love feelings without being specific in actual words, but in that jumble of people this morning all I could get across was how tense I was and exposed, like somebody's pet bunny lost in the woods. I asked Barbara a couple questions about the essay we were supposed to be ready to write in English that afternoon on ambition, and she answered them, giving me all the while that soft look like she knew I didn't care beans about what she was saying. In fact, once I realized how oozy with sympathy she was, I became disgusted, not at her, at me—Jellyfishman.

Barbara said, "Well, I've got Chem, now. But I hope you call me tonight because I would like to talk to you, you know, if you know what I mean, if we could have a few moments to talk."

"Yeah," I said. "I know. See you in English."

"OK. 'Bye," she said. She touched my wrist with her two fingertips, and then off she went. I felt suddenly relieved and frustrated at the same time. She was wearing her sleeveless, yellow shell top, with her lizard pin, that was so thin I could see the bumpy texture of her bra underneath it, but I didn't even know I noticed it until her back was turned and she was just a gold head going off in the crowd, like an orange in the potato bin.

The whole morning was awful. I was a man of misery. Outside the building the sun was beaming down, and breezes were sailing in through the open windows. I wanted to be out, out and away from the brick and the chalk and the long, pale, fluorescent lights. I told myself the next time I ran away I'd know how to do it right. I'd have money, and I would change my name. I spent my study hall writing in my French notebook a list of reasonable-sounding names I could adopt when the time came, like Armand Murphy, Simon Flatwater, Charles W. Garrett. Then I tore it out and folded it and put it in my hip pocket. A couple minutes later I took it out and folded it over again into an airplane, which I threw across the room at two girls, Karen Robertson and her friend with the buck teeth. They ignored it. They are dumbheads, girls like that. If a paper airplane floats over to you and skims your desk or something, you *can't* ignore it. You have to reach down and read it or tear it up or throw it back or whatever you feel like, but if you pretend you didn't see it, you're dumb and exasperating. And nobody will like you, and you'll never go to the prom.

I laid eyes on Richard at lunch. All morning I was planning to skip it, since all they were throwing at us today were dry, old franks, watery beans, and sweet, purple cole slaw, but by eleven I was so hungry I was saying to myself, fuck it, you're not going to let your life get all bent around for being a chickenshit candyass pansy. Do you think you can hide from the pecker for the rest of your days? I suddenly wanted to be Latham, strolling full of nonchalance through that goddamn school with a gun strapped to me, maybe two guns, and with my calm, dark eyes glittering with savagery. If I could be like that, living on the edge of evil, what would I care? All he'd have to do would be touch me, the cocksucker, and I would whip out my blue steel cannon and slam a hunk of fire into his greasy gut. Hah.

Well, my fate was descending on me, no matter what, and because I knew that and because all I had for breakfast was this little bowl of the end remains of a box of Wheat Chex, and I knew I had to eat *some* crap if I expected to play any kind of tennis later, I could not skip lunch. In the cafeteria I saw him right away, near the head of the food line. I ducked around the corner by the firehose cabinet and red alarm box. I figured I'd let him get by the old cafeteria ladies with their metal tongs and plastic gloves so he'd be concentrating on his heap of food before I went in after mine. It worked. He had on a white shirt and he was bent over a table at one far corner of the room with one of his hoody friends. Then, standing there gripping my tray with its steamy smells rising up to me, and gazing out over the eaters, I had a crazy thought, which was why don't I just go have my lunch with Richard and have a conversation with jokes in it like he was my good pal, the way he in fact was years ago. Why not? I knew why not. Because it was very risky, and because he is not my pal. I hate the bastard, I'm glad I do.

What happened though was I was keeping such an intense eye on Richard, like a robin watching a cat lick itself, that I hardly noticed what spot I was meanwhile picking to eat at. I sat down at the empty table exactly across from Pam Sokel's Luncheon Hour Giggle and Gossip Society. Even before I forked in my first mouthful, Pam twisted around in her chair with one small arm hooked over the back of it. She said, "Well, hel-lo, snobby," and a couple of the others looked across at me, too. I just chewed my cole slaw and gazed back.

Then I cheerfully said, "*Hey*. Pam Sokel, the local yokel. Long time no see."

"You always have to act smart, don't you?" she said.

"Yeah," I said. "It's the only way I can tell myself apart from everybody else."

"Oh, God," she said. "And conceited, too. How disgusting."

Sharon Sadowsky then pulled out a chair to offer me at the opposite side of Pam's table, and she said, "He could sit right here, Pamela, unless he still wants to be antisocial."

"No thanks. You guys are finished anyway." Of course, I was mostly staying put so I could keep my eagle-eye on my pal, Richard, by half-standing every now and then for a peek his way.

"*Well*. You *are* antisocial," Sharon said.

"It must be halitosis," Pam said, "the fear of offending."

Another girl said, "Or else it's the burning itch of hemorrhoids."

I was about to drop some good insulting remark on them all, like "You girls combined have the brains of the back half of a dead cow," but what the hell, I'm used to that kind of witchy bullshit from my sisters, and besides, I would probably come out in better shape if I went and twirled an eggbeater in a beehive. Well, I'll tell you what they can do for all I care. They can take their little wise-ass sayings and they can shove them up the old wazoo. The fat old wazoo.

I have a candle lit here, down on the floor in a Sucrets tin. And in the light of it, all the million tiny bubbles on the surface of my beer look like a map of the galaxy, slowly swirling and shining like the million stars. When you stop to realize it really and truly *is* that way, with us on our dot of a piddly planet, cranking along year in year out around our little jerk-off sun, which is like a grain of sand at Jones Beach in with all the other suns, you think, what the fuck, what difference does anything make, why don't I go up to Richard and say, "Richard, hey, listen, we don't mean piss

21) Sucrets tin:
ucrets are throat lozenge
weets.

to anybody, this high school is nothing, Long Island is nothing, New York is nothing, the damn country is nothing, the Earth is nothing, the whole dippy solar system is nothing, so hell, let's just be happy. How about it, Richard? What do you say, kid? Let's be happy." I know what he'd say. He'd probably say it with his stump. Anyway, I don't think he would enjoy being happy.

Then when I finished my franks and looked for him he was gone, and a bolt of fear went through me. It was OK, though. He had just disappeared. I didn't see him again until three o'clock, the end of the day. It was terrible, Christ, even more terrible than losing that tennis match the way I did. After English I was walking down the corridor with Barbara, and she was wishing me good luck and also sweetly apologizing for having to rehearse instead of watching me play "like loyal Leslie Wolstein," and me jokingly trying to talk her into it anyway, and then we rounded the corner toward my locker and saw, Jesus, who else but Richard Linwood, right there, I mean *waiting* for me, leaning against the wall, with his whole arm sickeningly propping up his bent stump, and staring at us. Thoughts flashed through me—all I needed from my locker was my racket, but shit, I could borrow one of Ollie's, so why go to my locker, why force things, why put my ass on the line? If he wants to stand there, it's a free country, he can stand there.

Barbara said, "Bernie! That's Richard Linwood!"

I said, low, "Aw, you wouldn't kid me, would ya?"

She looked at me, and we went on walking to my locker. Richard straightened himself away from the wall. My blood was rushing around in me. I gave him a glance in the eyes, and then I reached out for my combination dial, and I started spinning it. Richard angled his head in to look at the numbers I was picking. I dropped my hand.

"What can I do for you?" I said.

"You really wanna know?" he said.

"No, not really," I said.

"I want you to come on out where we can have a talk."

I said, "Well, I'd love to, but I've got a tennis match to play in about five minutes."

"This time I'm just asking," he said.

"I appreciate it," I said.

"Because you and me have problems, cuntface, you know?" And he stuck his pink-brown stump against my forearm. I backed up.

"That's for sure," I said. My eyes slid over to Barbara. She was standing next to me, very calm, watching our faces.

"Yeah. You understand that. So you can see why you and me need time to talk. C'mon, let's go out back of the auto shop." Out back of the auto shop is this bricked-in area for the school trash bins. It's where last year little Ralphie White got four teeth beat out by Clarence Pom-Pom Pomeroy.

"No, no," I said. "I can't spare a minute. We've got to get going here." I started spinning my lock again, and Richard bent to watch me. "I don't want you to know my private combination," I said.

"Tough shit," Richard said.

I said, "Tough shit. Yeah, well, OK, have it your way. See y'around." I half-turned to Barbara, and then I quickly jumped to the side when I saw the stump lash out. He smashed it into my locker.

He yelled, "You know what you're gonna have for me here when I see you right here tomorrow morning?"

I didn't answer.

"*Huh?* I can't hear you, cuntface."

I still didn't answer.

"*Ten bucks.* You know why? Because that's the first payment for my eighty-dollar, foreign, antique knife. And if you forget it, you know what I'm gonna do?"

"You bastard windbag," said Barbara. "Go roll in the mud."

But he never looked at her. At me he twisted up his face and screamed, "I'm gonna rip your head off and shit in your neck."

Well, there is no reply to make to a threat like that, unless you want to say, "You just try it, prick," which you would only say to some jerk you knew *would*n't try it, so I kept my mouth shut. Then Richard lunged at me, and Barbara shouted, *"Bernie,"* and I jumped backwards. He stopped. He had his stump cocked back like he was going to clobber me with it, and he was smiling. Then he turned and walked off. Around me, the few people who were watching the big drama from the sidelines started sidling away, and I just stared at them, feeling the drops of sweat slide out of my armpits and down my sides. My audience all looked like assholes. I wanted to shout at them that they were assholes.

Barbara said, "God, he is grotesque. He wouldn't dare do a *thing* to you, Bernie. He is a blowhard turd, and if he *did*, you could kick him between his stubby legs."

"Yeah, wham-o," I said.

It took me three tries to get my locker open, I was so shaky. Then we headed down to Mr. Devoe's office to report my "incident," as he would have called it if he had the chance, but he was gone reffing some lacrosse game, which is his hobby. Barbara and I sat on the radiators outside the auditorium where inside her rehearsal was beginning. I was flipping my racket over and over, and she stared at it like she was hypnotized.

After a minute, I said, "Well, kid, I guess I'd better move on."

"Move on where?" She grabbed my hand to stop the racket from going around.

"Tennis," I said. "Where'd you think I was going?"

"I don't know. No place," she said. But I could tell she was worried I would take off again for parts unknown. It surprised me.

Right then, though, my poor brain was so jammed that I couldn't talk, much less consider going anywhere, not that that isn't still a possibility. You know, a remote possibility. It was one of the last suggestions Lee made as we walked up from the beach Friday night. All his other plans were about ways to fix Richard once and for all, like dig an African pit trap outside his backdoor with poisoned stakes in the bottom. Lee said he would help me, whatever I decided. We were bombed. I feel rotten to recall how I ran like one of Attila the Hun's most deranged followers through people's yards and how I snapped the antenna off Judge Cooke's Mercedes right there in his goddamn driveway so I would have a brutal weapon to beat Richard with, slash him to ribbons. Lee said, "And, hell, even if that fails or say even if you end up *killing* him or something, you can just go make your ass scarce again, you know? Like to California. Lay low. Pump gas, you know? Live like a hermit, so they would all be too scared to ask about your past. You could buy a horse and only ride your horse. And wear black all the time. It would be fucking *great*."

In my condition at the time, I could really see how it *would* be great. I had no worries. I was in control of my future. I kept whipping my antenna at the tops of bushes and decapitating the little flowers I could see. I then just kind of fell onto our front lawn, and Lee went on to his house singing, "Hey, Paula, nobody else could ever do." I rolled over. I was dizzy as shit, and when I sat up I silently puked the three beers into the grass.

Inside, they were all asleep. It was pitch-dark, but I didn't bump into anything. I didn't want to bother with my toothbrush because somebody might hear the water come on, so I just eased into my bedroom, took my clothes off, and slipped into bed. The springs jangled, and my father grunted from his bed and started swearing in his sleep in a very mean-sounding voice. I lay still hardly breathing until he stopped. That sometimes happens to him, I don't know why. I always wonder what he's imagining then in his troubled, unconscious brain.

Saturday morning my mother was a little upset. She told me she waited up until one, and then she called Lee's mother, who was also upset and very worried. She said she heard me sneak in at two thirty in the morning, and if it happened again, I could not go out at all after eight. I had no comments to make. I knew it was hot air and she'd forget about it in a few days. She wanted me to account for myself, she said, but if I chose not to, I had that prerogative. I explained that I went for a very long walk with Lee, we didn't know it was that late, and that's all there was to it. She told me she didn't want me jeopardizing my health or getting into any kind of trouble.

"Oh, Mom, you have nothing to worry about," I said. She felt better, I think, even though she knows she has plenty to worry about, from her vantage point. I can't do a thing about it, either. Of course, my father's worse. It's a good thing he didn't find out how late I dragged in. I would get the third degree.

The fan of his headlights just now swung across the lawn and into the driveway. I quick blow out my candle and hide my can and my cup (which is my mother's Pyrex measuring pitcher with red markings) back in the old suitcase. Then I realize I'll have to wait until he comes inside before I venture down there. I would never pick my way down the stairs in the dark, and he would see the attic window brighten if I pulled on the light. I don't know what I'm so worried about, though. I could say I just fell asleep up here, no law against that, except he might suspect I was up in the dark pulling pud.

The car door thunks shut, and it comes to me in a flash what he said to me this morning before he left for work. (He works out at MacArthur Air Field.) He gripped my shoulder from outside the covers so I would open my eyes. I was awake anyway. And he said, "Well, Bernie, good luck today. Give 'em hell for your old man, will ya?" He was bending down over me with his maroon tie looped out from where the Roman coin tieclip I gave him for his birthday stuck it to his shirt. I could smell after-shave.

"OK, Dad," I said. I tried to speak it, but my throat was clogged, and it came out a whisper.

Shit, I wish to Jesus I *could've* given 'em hell today, I really do. Fuck. I sock my fist into the floppy suitcase.

CHAPTER 8

NEEDLESSTOSAY, last Tuesday morning when I arrived at school I didn't have ten bucks for you-know-who. His wicked goddamn wop switchblade was probably worth only five anyway, and I wasn't going to give him piss for it. He would despise me more if I did, and I knew those ten-buck payments would no doubt stretch out like the dotted line on the highway—and besides, I would despise me, too.

On the bus on the way to school, Lee asked me, "Well, what are you gonna do, then, when the deformed pecker comes for his moola and you don't cough up?"

I said, "Christ, there you go again. I can't see into the future, you know."

"OK, OK," he said. "I only want to hear what you're thinking. Then I'll tell you what I'm thinking."

I said, "Well, fuck, who knows? I don't know, maybe he'll forget all about it."

Lee said, "Holy *God!* You jerk-off. I guess you *can't* see into the future. You—"

"*Hold it.* All right. That's what I'm saying. Who knows shit? I mean maybe I'll slam him in the nuts, OK? How's that? That's what Barbara thinks I should do."

"She *does?* That's neat. He'd *kill* you if you did that."

"Yeah. So what do *you* think, Mr. Einstein?"

"I think you should say you have deep sympathy for him and his rusty switchblade, but it was his fault he lost it, and you can't pay for it anyway, because you don't make enough money caddying."

"*Terriff*," I said. "I'll make that Plan Number A-One."

"Well, what do you want? You asked me what I would do. That's what I would do."

I said, "Yeah, you'd shit in your hat, too, if it wasn't on your head."

He said, "You dickbrain. It wasn't me that killed your dog."

At that, a pang of guilt shot through me and made me shiver. "Just fuck off, will ya? I can run my life without your suckass advice."

"Oh, yeah, dickbrain? You don't look like you're doing so hot to me."

I shouted out, "Ah, go sniff your mother's panties." It's something Lee told me he did once last summer. He got them out of her dirty clothes hamper.

Lee jabbed my books off my lap with the butt of his racket and kicked them under the seat in front of us. Then he got up and went to the back of the bus.

I tried to stare out the window at the scenery, but my eyes blurred over. I kept blinking. The girl in front of me handed me back my books, and I took them without saying anything. Then I did my ax exercise, which is a thing I've done since I was like in third grade. What I do is I imagine

I have this very long, very big, very sharp ax that extends from my bus window like an oar to the roadside. If I mentally grip it hard enough and angle it just right, the blade slices off everything as we go along, telephone poles, trees, signs, and they fly like bowling pins. But a lot of the time the ax twists in my hands and only knocks against things, clonk, clonk, clonk, without doing the job. I can put supports and wheels and weights under it, and it's no use, it won't cut for shit. It can be a strain just to cling to the handle.

I knew all along that when we got to school I would go straight to Mr. Devoe's office. I don't know why I didn't tell Lee that, except that he can sometimes be a royal pain with his dumb questions, like he's your parent.

Mr. Devoe looks like a crude version of John Wayne, with his heavy eyebrows, wide nose and cheeks, and dozens and dozens of teeth, and his level shoulders that bulge his jackets. He used to teach swimming. In fact, years ago he taught me. He would get us out there sun or drizzle, high tide or low tide, no matter how mucky the water might be that day, and he would make us stroke and kick for the entire hour while he walked along the sand in his swim suit and his Fordham jacket. I remember his long, hairy, muscle-y legs. If we complained at all, he would say things like, "Listen, you go on acting this way, and you'll be getting on the bad side of a mighty tough hombre." I believed it. In those days, he reminded me, the way he laughed and squinted his eyes at you, of Davy Crockett. He looked like he could choke a bear to death with one hand. When I was a freshman he got into trouble at a basketball game for cracking two Negro guys' heads together so hard one of them got a concussion. They were trying to rob the AFS cookie and cider sale at halftime. Before that, Mr. Devoe was more of a happy-go-lucky person, but he became sour because now he can never be principal, only assistant principal.

Mrs. Ludlow, the old bag office secretary (called Pudlow by some), stuck her head into his office and then told me it was OK to go in.

He said, "I'm going to have to ask you to make it short and sweet, Bernie, because I'm on my way out the door. What is it?" He was standing by his bookcase that has a Civil Defense helmet on top of it and also the pictures of his five kids in a slanted row like dominoes. He had on a trenchcoat.

Right then it seemed so strange that Mr. Devoe would be cutting out before school even started that I tried to humorously ask, "Well, where are you heading?" In a way, I guess I was only feeling him out, because in the old days of swimming lessons, we got along with jokes, even though I was a youngster. But I shouldn't have asked him. He was startled, and he said he had a dentist appointment. He looked like he was going to sell atomic secrets to the Russians.

Then he sighed. "OK, Bernie. Just sit down there and out with it. Is it Linwood?"

"Yeah," I said. I sat down and he sat down.

"He hates your guts doesn't he?"

"With a passion," I said.

"You know there's not much I can do about that, don't you?"

I wanted to say, "Well, you could crack his fat head for me," but that was of course touchy, so I said, "Well, you could try."

"How about some details. Was there an incident yesterday?"

"Yeah, he threatened to rip off my head if I don't start making payments on his knife that you took."

"Does that scare you?"

"Sure," I said. "I've gotten very attached to my head."

"That makes sense. OK. Let me say this much, Bernie. Mr. Linwood has only this far to go." He held up his fingers like you would if you were examining a cube of sugar. "All right? And once he goes that far he's out on his ass for a month. He knows that. I told him that. Now he'll always threaten and try to blackmail people, he's a bully, that's how he is. He'll get away with it if you let him, but stay out of his way, and he won't go through with anything. He knows he can't afford to."

"He doesn't have to do direct things to you, Mr. Devoe. He is very tricky."

"I've been around this place too long for tricks, Bernie. Oh, I know he can corner you out off school grounds somewhere, if that's what he really wants to do. And what can I do about it? Zippo. No, the only way I can help you now is to give you some advice. Stay out of Linwood's way. If you can't do that, and he wants to tangle, well, you'll tangle. That's it. Then, fight hard. If you're unlucky, you'll get busted up a little. If you're lucky, so will he, and that'll put an end to it."

"*Maybe,*" I said. I was thinking nobody but me knows how Christ-awful crazy Richard really is. The only way I'd be lucky tangling with that maniac is if I came out looking a shade healthier than hamburger.

"As I say, Bernie, Linwood knows damn well he has to toe the line here in school. But if he's feuding, if there's a bone to pick, there isn't much I can do, understand? But, regardless, I want you to keep me posted on this. He's on very thin ice, Mr. Linwood is. I've really got to vamoose, now, Bernie, all right?"

I told him thanks a lot, and we left his office together. He dashed out through all the office confusion and then stopped in the doorway to whisper something into Mr. Rudleigh's ear, one of the phys ed teachers, who always has dark, wet circles under the arms of his Hobbes T-shirts, like the openings of caves. Mr. Rudleigh barked out a laugh, punched Mr. Devoe's biceps, and said, "Ho, don't you *wish*."

I was thinking then that it's funny how teachers stand out in school, the men teachers anyway. They're a little bigger than everybody else usually, but it's mostly that they always wear very drab clothes, and the rest of us are all so colorful and lively. I think that's why I liked Mr. Lacolle, my French teacher with the hiccups. He wore just those two shirts, pink and blue, and he didn't bother with a tie. All the sacred school traditions bored him or else amused him. He thought Senior Bermuda Day was a riot. One day every spring if you're a senior you get to wear Bermuda shorts to school. It's one of the senior privileges the administration thought up when the faculty voted to take away the Senior Smoking Lounge. I guess Mr. Lacolle really cracked up that day when his French Four class all traipsed in with their plaid Bermudas. We had French One right after, and he could not stop shaking his head over those Bermudas. He said they looked ridiculous. He said if somebody told the seniors they could have the privilege of walking around school all day with one shoe off and one shoe on they would do it. We loved hearing that, even though we could all hardly wait three years for our own Bermuda Day.

Well, having Mr. Devoe assure me Richard Linwood would probably not try to rip off my head because if he did he would be slapped with a month's suspension did not pick me up very much. True, I realized Mr. Devoe could not do a lot about my feud, I don't know what I expected of him. But at least I knew if he found a headless body in the boiler room, he would not puzzle over who was responsible.

All that day I was nervous. I was very nervous because I figured the prick was eagerly hunting for me (you know, like with his fangs glinting in the shadows), and I didn't know how long I could keep my shifty-eyed face out of sight. I would've given my right arm for the Cloak of Invisibility. A question I often used to ask people when I was feeling philosophical is would you rather be able to fly or be able to be invisible. Your answer, I think, gives a real clue to the shape of your personality. I myself would pick flying always. Now that I'm leaning the other way, it's a sign that my life has taken a turn for the worse, toward having to feel sneaky and vulnerable. I *am* vulnerable, that's the trouble. That's why I was nervous. I also knew if we were going to tangle, no matter how much the thought of it turned my innards to ice, I would want it to be in school so I could maybe be rescued, like the last time in the cafeteria.

But we did not tangle. I never glimpsed his pukey puss the whole day. When I had to go to my locker, I got a pass out of the middle of Chem to do it, when the halls would be empty. And for lunch I went into the teachers' smoky lunch-room and bought those peanut butter cheese crackers out of a machine, which I ate with water. They suck, those crackers, and I told myself I would bring a lunch on Wednesday, something I have not done since first grade. In the morning when I wake up I'm very hungry, and all I want to do is eat a big breakfast, not pack a lunch, and after breakfast I'm not hungry any more, and I don't care piss about lunch. I mean, I can never think about sandwiches, so I can never get excited about bagging up a few to eat later.

Tuesday afternoon at tennis practice I felt so relieved because I escaped Richard for a whole day that I played very loose and hard, and Ollie before he left (he usually leaves early with Leslie) told me it looked like I was getting my game under control. Lee ignored me on the courts and in the locker room. I took a shower afterwards, but he didn't. He went by the shower room all dressed and looking straight ahead like he was in a hurry, and I figured he walked on into town, or hitched, because he was supposed to ride home with me when my father came to get us. Sometimes, though, my father does not show up until six thirty or even later, if he gets hung up at the Moose Club, and Lee is not a very patient person. He can really hold a grudge, however, I'll say that.

So I just stood there in the cool shower all slack and still for a long time with my eyes closed like I was this destitute Mexican peasant so poor I didn't even own clothes or even a sombrero, getting drenched in that tropical rain but enjoying it because so what if I didn't have anything, it didn't matter. I didn't need a damn thing.

Then I strolled down to the auditorium, creaked open a side door, and sat way in the back in the dark under the balcony to watch some of the *Cyrano* rehearsal. Mr. Van Husen was parading across the stage trying to show Tommy Bauer (the hotshot, wise-ass school actor, who is slim and loud and kind of a jerk-off in school, and who some people like Ollie Griggs really can't stand, and who naturally got the part of Cyrano) how to move with his cape, even though Tommy does not yet have a cape to wear. So Mr. V. then promised to get Tommy a cape, a heavy one. I could see Barbara and some others watching from the side of the stage. She had her rehearsal pants on, and she had her weight on one leg so her hip stuck out. It's a familiar stance to me, even from way back here. Last fall when Mr. V. was directing us in *The Lottery* in the Play Festival Competition, Barbara would often fall into that stance on the stage until two days before the performance in dress rehearsal late at night when Mr. V. bellowed at her, "Get out of that goddamn tooty pose!" She straightened right up, and alongside of her there I could see her face redden through her make-up. "What's 'tooty'?" I shouted out. I was trying to come to Barbara's rescue, don't ask me how. "Prosti-tooty," he said. That infuriated Barbara, though Mr. V. is a good friend of her family and is regarded around town as some kind of artist of the theater because he is so dedicated to amateur plays and is a summer stock actor himself and a free spirit, my mother once said. He has a round black beard with a triangle of white on the chin. Two summers ago, before he had the beard, my mother got involved on the local theater guild production of *Rhinoceros*, which was kind of a big deal. Mr. V. was the director and the star. My mother designed the program cover. We all except my father went opening night, and I enjoyed it pretty much, but it was quite weird, you know, because it was about this rhino that just happens to run through this quiet French village, a totally impossible thing. My mother the next day sat me down in the kitchen to explain to me the philosophical thoughts behind it. But what I'm getting at is there was a cast party when all the performances were over, which my mother went to. It was a Sunday night in August. She had her hair done for it and all. It was like four in the morning when she finally got home from it in Mr. V.'s sports car. Yelling and screaming woke me up. I slipped over to my desk so I could see through the window. The old man was there on the lawn in his bathrobe with his wrinkled pajama legs drooping down underneath to his bare feet, and he was yelling that my mother was a tramp and a slut and a gutter whore. My mother was yelling back that he was a drunken, stupid, masturbating slob. Mr. V. was saying, "Fred, now Fred," from over by his car. My father yelled that he was a shitass faggot, and dared him to walk my mother to the door like a man instead of an assfucking queer so he could shove his nose out the back of his head. It was pretty awful. I don't think my mother was dicking around with Mr. V. I mean, to me it didn't seem like it, they were friends is all, and Mr. V. isn't a faggot either, I don't think, because he's married and has three adopted kids and three regular kids. He has a big house around the corner from Barbara's. The old man was in a fury that night, though. When he came to bed, I lay back breathing heavy like I was asleep. He threw his robe down and stood a long time with his two hands on the dresser and his head bent, just leaning braced against it. I don't know what got into him, why he would act like he gives a shit, since my parents are not exactly blissfully in love any more. Besides, on the other hand, I think my *father* might dick around some, or else he might like to. The reason I have that thought is a few months ago when I was getting the flashlight out of the glove compartment to hold so my father could see to adjust the fanbelt, I flipped open the Band-aid box he keeps in there and inside was a fancy rubber in a blue plastic container. I was shocked, but I was also a bit glad in a way that's hard to explain. It's odd, I mean, it was like the old man's life maybe wasn't so drab and simple and frustrating like I thought—or like I realized then I had always thought. Maybe he had an exciting side to him, you know? Maybe he was a secret wildman. Maybe he was putting it to some ruby-lipped blond bombshell who like worked as a waitress at the bowling alley. But I have not peeked in the Band-aid box again for more clues. He keeps the glove compartment locked most of the time. I was hoping the rehearsal would end so I could go down and see Barbara and afterwards walk her to her locker downstairs, where we could make out in the vestibule of the orchestra practice room, but they just went on and on. Of course, nothing was stopping me from sauntering down the aisle and sitting in the front rows with the rest of the cast, who I mostly know, but I was not feeling social at all. I wanted to relax, and I would've had no chance to converse with Barbara down there anyway, because she is in just about every scene they were going over, and even when she's sitting back in the audience, she's quite involved with the action. She sits forward and says the lines of the other characters. You can't even hold her hand.

After a while, I left and sat on the radiator outside the auditorium, looking out the windows for my father's Buick. He was a little juiced when he arrived, but it didn't bother me. I was feeling good. I told him I had hit the ball as well as I figured I could hit it that afternoon because I was loose and because I really concentrated.

"That's the key. That's the key, all right," he said. "Only, it ain't so easy under fire, in the heat of the competition. You gotta *develop* your concentration powers. Like anything else. Like any other part of your game. See what I mean?"

Well, I saw what he meant, and for no reason it made me all of a sudden depressed. He was egging me on, my father, egging me on to greater heights the way he always does, to show me how I could get better and better. And that's OK, I guess. But then it seemed just endless. You could endlessly improve and never be good enough. How could you ever satisfy a person who constantly wanted you to develop? I mean, it's not like I don't want to develop and get better, but I also want to like appreciate all the developing as I go along. But maybe if you want to grow up to be Pancho Gonzales you can't do that. You can't be anywhere near lackadaisical.

I almost called Lee up after dinner that night to say hello and let's bury the hatchet, but he can be such a jackass about those conflicts we sometimes have, and I decided I would give him more time to simmer down. I knew the whole thing was in a way my fault, for not accepting the fact that Lee was just concerned about me in a sincere way, but of course

I was not about to admit that, because it was also Lee's fault for being so insensitive and stubborn and dumb.

Amazingly enough, I actually did some homework, a few French exercises to be exact, and I started poking through the pile of U.N. books that's been on my desk so long they're three weeks overdue at the school library. I was trying to think up a topic, because you can't write about just the U.N., you have to narrow it down. In one book about the origins of the U.N., I found a short comparison the guy threw in at the beginning about how different the U.N. was from the League of Nations, and why the League of Nations went by the boards. Perfect. All I did was copy the passage down very neatly and change the sentences a little, making them shorter. I spelled a few words wrong, too, for effect, because it was only history and Mr. Fitch doesn't take off for spelling like he would if it was an English essay. That's plagiarism, of course I know, and I did not feel so great doing it, but let's face it, my back was to the wall. The thing was that Wednesday, the next day, was informal reports day. What happens is your most concerned teachers can send home these triplicate forms that also go into your guidance office file, which outline in detailed wording why they feel very good or else very bad about you. You don't get an informal too often. Until Wednesday, I only had two in two years, both good ones from English teachers. But on Tuesday night I figured there were good odds I'd get nailed with at least one bad informal, in French probably, and maybe even history. So, to be honest, I was doing all that homework mainly so I would have some solid sign of my worthy, dedicated self to hand in to Mr. Fitch and Mr. Kirk, to like undercut their souring opinions of me. On Wednesday it was just as I suspected. I got the informals. They're a big joke, really. I mean, shit, if I deserve a goddamn informal, I should get it in Chem, which to me is just a huge, foggy, boring maze filled with symbols and test tubes and Erlenmeyer flasks and which really has no point as a required subject. Sure, if you're going to be a scientist, take Chem, but if you're just ordinary like me you don't need that bullshit. I'm in an accelerated chemistry class, too, for the smart kids, because Mr. P. E. Granger got me into it. I have a straight B in there, and the reason is one person, Ned Gill, my lab partner, who lets me copy everything, lab reports, experiments, tests, the works. He sits in front of me and slides his answer sheet to the edge of his desk between the side of his body and his arm so I can read it without anybody noticing. He writes clear and dark. Old Ned is all that keeps me from sinking like a brick into the dismal swamp of failure, and we both know it. But did I get an informal in Chem? No. As my mother says, there's no justice.

In French, I got, "Recently, Bernie has been doing failing work in French Three. His slackened efforts are most evident in the classroom. It is suggested that he take more time to prepare for class discussions and exercises in order that what occurs in the classroom will be of greater use to him on the examinations."

Mr. Fitch said, "Bernie has always been a pleasant, articulate, cooperative student in American History. However, his long absence this quarter and his declining interest in his studies have resulted in his missing or not completing many written and reading assignments. He must reapply his attentions to the work he has been neglecting if he is to succeed as he should in the state Regents examination this June."

These did not shake me up half as much as they shook up my father, partly because, when you get right down to it, besides your parents who really and truly cares how you perform in school? School is not your life. It's your overall personality that counts in life, not whether you broke your balls for hours-on-end memorizing foreign words or the results of the Dred Scott decision.

The other reason I was not as shook up by those pain-in-the-A warnings as you might think is Richard Linwood finally got the big banana from Mr. Devoe, and not because of me either—at least, not directly. That was very cheery news. Exactly what happened I don't know, but I found out he got a nasty informal from Mrs. Twitchell, a 120-year-old battle-ax English teacher who everybody calls The Twitch or The Twat. Last year she almost had heart failure because Cookie Zuckman on Valentine's Day put a box turtle in Mrs. Twitchell's desk drawer before class. It had Tampaxes taped to it, and across the shell in nail polish was printed, "For the Twat." The turtle clunked around in there for half the class before she heard the noises and found it. She was in a rage for a week after that, I know, I had her for a study hall. On Wednesday, all Richard did (so I heard from Miriam Worthington, who was there near him getting a good informal) was he called her an old douche bag. She blew up, though. She tried to lead him out of the room and down to the office holding his ear pinched between her fingers, but he knocked her arm away before they got into the hall. That was all it took, I guess. Just calling her an old douche bag would've been plenty, for a popular guy like Richard.

I did not learn the prick was canned until after our so-called tennis match Wednesday afternoon against North Babylon, which was a joke. They're more pathetic than Brentwood. It was Ollie that told us, Lee and I, while we rode home with him in his Porsche. He does not normally go our way, but since the match was over so quick—about forty-five minutes—he said he would have the time to buzz down by the water if we were interested in the offer. It was such a rare offer that we *were* interested, more like flattered, really, that he would think of it. It didn't take me too long, however, to figure out what was behind his fresh, surprising generosity. It wasn't like he wanted to be good buddies with us, or anything. I was down watching Lee and Eddie wipe up the first doubles and making little under-the-breath jokes with Lee through the fence when he would come back to fetch a ball (things between us were back to normal, though on the bus that morning the dope kept up his ornery act), and Ollie got up from the blanket where he was sitting with Leslie, and he drifted down to offer the lift. I said, "Sure, Ollie, that would be great." Right away getting irritated at myself for sounding like his wide-eyed kid brother.

"You gonna shower?" he asked me.

I said, "What, did I sweat?"

He gave me his little thin smile. "OK, in about five minutes, then, when Lee gets through." He bent and snapped off a long grass blade, which he fiddled with some, watching the doubles. Then he went back to Leslie. When I turned to the match again, Lee and Eddie were shaking hands. It was over. So I followed Ollie's path up the rain gutter behind the courts to tell him I'd be right out, I had to get my books and crap. To Leslie, Ollie was saying, "Well, Les, I promised them a *ride*, that's why."

"You promised *me* a sundae," she said.

"I know, Les. But that was yesterday. You can get a ride easy. The late bus hasn't even left. You can still catch it. Tomorrow I'll buy you a sundae, or else Friday after the match."

"Oh, yeah. *That* I've heard before."

"Well, if you want to come along with Lee and Bernie, that's OK with me. We can squeeze."

Then Leslie spotted me off to the side. "No, thanks anyway, Big Boy," she said, looking soft at him, for my sake, I figured. She reached out and touched his hand. "I'll just suffer along alone. Think I'll get a little phone call tonight?"

"It's possible, it's possible," Ollie said.

Ollie is a fast driver. His car has seat belts, which he makes you buckle before he'll go anywhere, like an airplane, but they don't make it any less scary to ride with him, the way he slides around corners.

Usually, you don't see Ollie Griggs expressing himself in an open manner. He keeps his moods in. But he seemed quite talky and happy in the car as we zoomed along. Then I thought it was because we won easy and it was a sunny afternoon. Lee was bragging loud from the backseat how he got one of his guys in the nuts with an overhead. It bounced up, bang. I didn't believe him, but just thinking about it made my own nuts scrunch up close. And Ollie related how he was in the office that afternoon when Richard got the big hook. Out for a month for hitting Mrs. Twitchell. *Jesus*, I thought. What I pictured was him ramming his stump through her false teeth. (Until I got the story from Miriam Worthington.) I was overjoyed. The informals I had just got faded out as a worry. Ollie said Richard left Mr. Devoe's office by kicking the wood door open. He roared his black-and-yellow Chevy doing fifty out of the parking lot. Lee slapped me on the shoulder. "Hey, Bernie-kid," he shouted. "What d'ya *say*, Bernie-kid."

Ollie dropped Lee off and then me at the top of the hill. When he kept going out toward Crescent Beach instead of turning around for town, it came to me—Cindy O'Halloran must've got home from college. She lives only a mile from me in a long, modern house that has a flat roof with chunks of pink granite on it. So Lee and I were Ollie's excuse to drive to this neighborhood, and what's worse, *I* added up to the reason he could shake Leslie. Poor old Leslie, I thought. That Ollie Griggs is quite a ruthless person.

Of course, Leslie is not dumb. I know she smells some

kind of trouble, but she has not yet seen the whole picture. I know this because last night (Thursday night) my dear friend Pam Sokel got me on the telephone just to ask a teeny favor.

"Yeah? What?" I said.

"Well, it's about Leslie."

"OK, so what?"

"About Leslie and Ollie Griggs."

"I'm on the edge of my chair."

Pam said, "Do you want to hear this, or not?"

I did, I admit. "How do I know till you tell it?"

She paused. I could hear her nose breathing. "Well, as you know if you know anything, there is a big night coming next Saturday night. Right?"

"Right," I said. It's the fancyass senior prom, which I don't care beans about.

"OK, I'll be honest with you. Leslie is very upset. Yesterday she was expecting your friend Ollie to ask her to the prom—even though—*even though* it is very late to ask a girl to the prom. But she knew he was going to ask her at Stu and Herman's when they were getting ice cream sundaes. But, as you know, Ollie didn't go to Stu and Herman's, and he didn't go to Stu and Herman's today, either—"

"Ollie is not my friend," I said.

"—and what Leslie might like to know is, is Ollie just going to ignore the senior prom this year? *Or* is he going with somebody else?"

"Tell her to ask the handsome devil herself," I said.

"It might surprise you to know that I *did*," said Pam. "But she can't."

"Well, then why should I? He's not even my friend."

"You play tennis with him every day."

"True, but that doesn't make him my friend."

She clunked the phone against something. "Well, God, it

wouldn't kill you to *ask* him."

"True again, but I am not asking him. I think it's his business. But if you want my opinion, he's going to the dumb prom, all right, but not with Leslie."

"So you won't ask him?"

"Nope."

She hung up. I was glad then that I didn't mention Cindy O'Halloran, as if Pam didn't have Ollie figured out already. There isn't much you can put past that little witch. From me all she wanted was more evidence, or else she had Leslie right there breathlessly listening on another phone. It wouldn't surprise me.

The two most annoying things about that phone call, besides Pam's natural rudeness, were first, I thought it would be Barbara, and second, it interrupted my activities in the basement. The thing is, since I got the informals, the old man has decreed I can't go out on school nights and also I cannot make any phone calls, not one. I can only take calls —*if* I keep them under three minutes. When Lizzie yelled down to me, "For you-oo, and it's a girl," I thought sure it was Barbara. She knows the big foot came down on my telephoning, and we have had hardly any chance to converse since Monday after the incident at my locker. I wanted to tell her about my pigeon, which is the reason for my activities in the basement. I was down there saving the life of this scraggly gray pigeon by feeding it milk and wheat germ from an eyedropper.

Yesterday, after practice, I thought I would drink one of my Budweisers, but the day was warm and breezy, and with Richard out of the way for a whole month, I was feeling like the safari explorer who gets to hop out of the cannibals' kettle at the last minute because there's an eclipse of the sun. So I stuck my can under my sweater to carry down to the beach. I considered digging up one of Lee's beers, which

I think are still buried three feet north of a special locust tree, but that would be too mean and disloyal, and he would know who took it besides.

When I got to Hidden Pond, I walked around to the reedy end of it, where we used to build forts as kids. The reeds are tan and dense and so high over your head that when you're in there sitting, you can hear the reed tops rustle and swish, but you can't feel the wind yourself. It's like you're an ant in the grass. I opened my beer with the opener I thoughtfully remembered to bring, and I squatted there on a log pretending to be an Indian on a tribal survival test, sipping fermented reed water. In a few minutes I realized every now and then I was hearing some kind of fluttery sound that wasn't the wind. I looked around behind me, expecting to discover a nest of little birds I could peek at, but it was a pigeon, hunched close to the ground, stretching his wings out and knocking them against the reed stalks and folding them in again. He looked like he forgot his first flying lesson. But he was in fact sick and dying, I could see, when I got over to him. His eyes would sometimes close. You never see birds with their eyelids down unless they're in bad shape. I said to him, "Hi, pigeon." He blinked at me. When I picked him up, around his ankle I found a metal ring that said Bronx Bird Club Number R-1363, and I knew I had to take him home because he was a bird that depended on people.

I carried him bundled loose in my sweater, which I opened up on the coffee table for Claudia and my father. He had shat on my sweater. Claudia said, "Oh, the poor, little starving thing." She was going to pat him, but I told her not to, he was scared enough. She went to get my mother out of the kitchen, and she yelled to Lizzie and Jane downstairs that they should "turn off that dopey television show and come see what Bernie found at the beach."

"This bird doesn't have a prayer," my father said. "How do you know he didn't contract some disease?" Everybody was standing or crouching around the table, where the pigeon was just slowly spreading his wings across the *Look* magazines.

"How do you know he did?" I said.

"Bernie, look at him," said my father. "He's a goner."

Claudia said, "I think he's just hungry."

My mother said, "He could be fed with an eyedropper."

"I know. That's what I'm going to do," I said.

"Don't get your hopes up," my father said.

The girls and I took him downstairs and set him in a shoebox on the Ping-Pong table. He *was* hungry, the little pecker. He ate right off the spoon I held out, and he also put his beak around the eyedropper to like suck the milk into his throat.

After dinner, I fed him off and on for over an hour until Pam called. Then my father told me from his chair in the livingroom that I had to quit playing nursemaid to a damn bird and start acting a little more dedicated to my studies.

"God, Dad," I said. "You act like I'm on the verge of flunking out of school. My history paper is done, I'm caught up in French, and I don't have any other work."

My father yelled back about how he wanted me there at my desk doing *some*thing, even if I had to pretend I was doing something. I could've refused, and he wouldn't have done anything to me, but I knew his hard slave-driver mood would blow over in a few days if I went easy on him like my mother urged me to do the night before when she signed my informals. Anyway, to be frank, I was actually supposed to be reading *Of Human Bondage* for an oral report. The damn book puts me to sleep. I picked it off the list because the title sounded good, and it was by an author I heard of, but Jesus, to put it in common language, it bites the bone. I'll never finish it.

It's Friday night, and for the past half hour I've been perched up here on the woodsy slope behind Lee's house watching the windows that are lit, two in the kitchen, one in Lee's bedroom, and one in his sister Nancy's. I'm too far back to see much. Besides, they all have curtains except Lee's, where I have spotted no action, not that I'm up here to spy on him, there's just nothing else to look at, no moon, no stars, only dull tree trunks, grainy and black in the dark.

I'm early. Lee said to be here after eight, when Nancy would cut out for a pajama party. Also, by that time, he said, his mom would be enough in the bag so the coast would be clear. We're going to steal her Valiant. "Operation Rollaway" he calls it. He knows how to drive—he's had his learner's permit for three months, just about as long as he's had Operation Rollaway on the brain.

A couple hours ago, when he phoned me, he was mad. He didn't have to explain why. Tonight is the night that all along he has been planning to put the meat to Helen Bundy. The Big I.I. and all that. But for four nights in a row now, Lee told me today after our match against Port Jefferson, whenever he calls, her sister says she's taking a bath or is out shopping or walking the dog or asleep. Last night he tried three times. I told him, "Shit, man, you better face the obvious. You been shafted. You are just plain not the dong of her dreams."

He said, "But, God, you should've seen her last time. You wouldn't believe it. She had *both hands* on it, on my nuts, too. Fuck, I should've hammered her right then, *that's* what's obvious."

"I guess so," I said. I was beginning to realize why this week Lee was in such a lousy mood. "You know, maybe she just gave up on you because your twanger is so tiny."

"Go fuck a rock," Lee said. He whacked my ass with his racket. "I'll bang the girl tonight if it kills me. I'll go over to her goddamn house if I have to. I'll drag her out in the goddamn pricker bushes. You can have seconds."

So on the phone Lee didn't have to tell me Helen was still out to lunch. I knew she would be anyway. I was sort of glad, too, I admit. Because, all right, even though Helen Bundy is no delicate specimen of the feminine type, she *is* sensitive and, you know, nice. But in Lee's condition of wild anxiety, he can't appreciate that. He wants to put virginity behind him, like it's a sickness and horny Helen's the medicine. Now, however, banging her is out of the question, and poor Lee is frustrated and also hurt. Today he referred to her as "dumb and pretty scuzzy," and maybe she is, but she's not downright pathetic like, say, Denise Block. On the phone he said, "OK. It's tonight. Operation Rollaway. The old lady's been hitting the sauce since I got home, so if Nancy ever gets her fat ass out of the way, we can *roll*."

"Gotcha," I said.

"You can come right in, it's OK," he said.

"Well, I'll just wait up in the woods. I'll see you come out," I said. Lee's mother is a fierce boozer, not like my mother, who basically is only a wino. Lee's mother on weekends, especially when his father is out of town, gets herself plastered on vodka. Vodka is very strong, but the damn Russians slurp it down like it was going out of style. It's made from potatoes. I hate going in there when she's been tanking up on that stuff because all she wants to do is argue about nothing. One muggy night last summer I was sleeping over Lee's house, and since it was high tide and a full moon his mother suggested we walk down for a midnight swim. She was looped. Lee wanted to keep her out of the water because he was scared she would deep-six herself like a soda bottle. She was falling on the sand and crying, it was awful. Then, walking home again, she referred over and over to my bowlegs, telling me I should go to a doctor, a leg specialist, and get shock treatments. Lee kept asking her to please shut up. I felt sorry for him.

Whoops, the kitchen door is opening. It's Lee. I stand up, but he can't see me. He goes to where the Valiant is parked, eases open the door, sits behind the wheel a second, and then heads back into the house.

I'm on the steps when he comes out again. I whisper, "What're you doing?"

"Getting the keys," he whispers back.

Lee's plan is we push the car with the lights off out of the driveway and down the road to the corner. Then we start the motor far enough from the house so his mother doesn't wise up. When we're over the driveway hump, Lee gets in to steer. Suddenly, right in front of my face, a brake light flares on, and I jump back with my heart beating.

Lee's saying, "Get in! Get in!"

He's moving before I can shut the door. "The *lights*," I say.

"OK, OK," he says. They flash on, like the start of a movie hitting the screen.

I say, "God*damn*, we're rollin'."

"Operation Rollaway!" Lee yells out. "Fuck a *duck!*"

"What's first stop? Helen Bundy's?"

Lee says, "Fuck, no. That cockteaser, I'm through with her, for *good*."

"Are you serious?"

"Does your asshole smell like shit? Yeah, I'm serious. We could cruise by there, though. Maybe she's home doing it to herself with a carrot."

Lee is nuts. I switch on the radio.

"But, hey," he says. "First we're meeting Rocky. He told me he got his brother's I.D., and he can buy beer with it."

Lesley Gore is singing, "It's My Party and I'll Cry If I Want To," and Lee sings along.

Rocky Busby went out for the wrestling team this winter with Lee, only he made it, and Lee didn't. He is second-string 145, a loudmouth friendly guy, who is from Tennessee, and who always tries to trip you in the hall or chop you in the kidney as a joke, the perfect wrestler. He's a kind of wild, active, laughy person that you would like no matter what he did, like he was a big, happy dog.

We turn up his street, and Lee spots him standing where he said he would, by a hydrant, but Rocky isn't sure it's us until we pull up next to him. He grins, and I open the door for him. When he moves to get in, Lee jumps the car forward a few feet, and then he leans across me to yell, "Hey, turdball, be quick."

I flip the seat up for him to climb in.

"You taintlappers," says Rocky. "I been waiting here a half-hour. Who's quick?"

Lee says, "I told you I couldn't leave until my dumb sister left."

"Excuses, excuses," says Rocky. "Hey, Hergruter, how's your hammer?"

"What's a taintlapper?" I say. I haven't heard that one.

"What? Somebody that laps taint, what else?"

"OK, what's taint?"

"Your taint's your taint. You all got one. Taint your balls and taint your ass. It's your taint. It stinks, too." Rocky suddenly leans forward, grabs the muscles at the tops of my shoulders with his fingers, and squeezes. "Relax, relax," he says, and then he laughs. "You gotta be brave to ride shotgun with that numbnuts at the controls."

"You get Morton's I.D. like you said?" Lee asks.

"OK, Rock, let go," I say. He's squeezing harder.

"Let go? Jesus, Hergruter, I'm helping you pop the biggest zit I seen in my whole life, and it's covered with hair." He lets go. "What I.D.?"

"Shit, Busby, go ahead. Tell me you forgot Morton's I.D.," says Lee, turning to glance at him.

The radio's going, "Money talks, nobody walks." It's this weird ad for a warehouse of clothes that's open all night in New Jersey somewhere.

"I forgot Morton's I.D.," says Rocky.

Lee hits the steering wheel. "Way to go, shithead."

I care that he forgot it, too, but not that much, because I don't have any money. "All we have to do is take him back to get it," I say.

Rocky says, "Aw, you jerk-offs. You guys would lay down and hold your breath if somebody said the world was over. I said I'd get the fuckin' I.D., and I got the fuckin' I.D. You wanna buy beer? OK. I thought we're goin' to scare the juice out of Helen Bundy, like *you* said. What *are* we doing, that's what I want to know."

"We *are* doing that," Lee says. "But we need beer first, don't we?"

"Fine with me, man," says Rocky. "How 'bout you, Herg?"

"Fine with me," I say. "I don't have any money."

"Shit, I'll lend you a couple bucks, boy," says Rocky. "We goin' in style tonight."

This Helen Bundy raid is new to me. Cruising by her house, like Lee mentioned earlier, that's one thing. But scaring the juice out of her, I don't know about that. I like Helen, she's nice, as I said.

"OK, then," Rocky's saying, "stop by the Dock Deli."

"They *know* me in there," Lee says.

"Well, fuck, you ain't goin' in," says Rocky. "Just me. I'm buyin' Colt .45. The only way to go."

I say, "Hey, what's all this about scaring Helen Bundy? I never heard a word about this little project until now."

"It ain't my idea," says Lee.

Rocky says, "Fuck *you*, man. Who's got cunt-fever? Not me, man. Who's the one comin' to me all last week with fish-finger?"

Lee says, "Can I help it if her cunt stinks?"

"Shit, no," says Rocky. "Her cunt stinks so bad seagulls follow her down the street."

Lee laughs.

"Well, so what's the big plan?" I say, looking over at him.

"There's no plan," Lee says. "We're just going over there, is all. What're you worried about?"

Of course, I'm not worried, at least not like you would be worried about a lot of other things. It's just that I know I would get no satisfaction out of offending Helen Bundy— especially if she somehow found out it was me that was offending her. Because, for one thing, I suspect she secretly likes me, and for another thing, she doesn't deserve it.

Rocky's comment about seagulls reminds me immediately of L.R., my pigeon (L.R. standing for the Lone Ranger, which is like what he was, the last survivor of the platoon). When he was missing from his shoebox this morning before school, I knew that was it. He would be just a stiff lump of gray feathers over behind the furnace. Upstairs, my father was finishing his eggs, getting ready to leave. Everybody else was still in bed. He called down, "Well, how is he?"

"He disappeared," I said, trying to make it sound like a hopeful thing to say.

Clomp, clomp, clomp, clomp, my father came down in

his big, brown, shiny shoes. I was afraid to look around any, so I was standing by the Ping-Pong table in my bare feet, thinking why couldn't I have just left the stupid bird there in the reeds to conk off on his own without involving me and my family and all our emotions.

My father stopped on the bottom step, so he seemed a lot taller than usual. "Did you look under everything? The bed?"

Then we heard "Coogle, coogle, coogle" from over by the ironing board. I went and pulled the light cord and what do you know, there he was waddling around on the cracked linoleum by our old cardboard puppet theater, and bending his head sideways to see me. My father was right behind. "Look at that," he said.

"Hey, what do you think you're doing in here?" I said, and I picked him up. It was amazing, he was so much better overnight. He didn't fly at all, but when I put him down again, he walked fast right in back of my heels wherever I went, like a string was tied to him. And this evening my father brought back from the pet shop this five-pound sack of pigeon feed, which old L.R. loved. He pecked at it and scattered it around, flicking his beak like he was digging for something, for his favorite flavor of seed. Now he hops around the concrete floor, onto the linoleum, too, shitting all over, and cooing like he's happy. This weekend, though, or whenever he can fly again, we'll have to send him home to the Bronx Bird Club to all his good buddies who figure he was lost in action. Maybe I will write a long letter to the Bronx Bird Club president and he will send me a reward.

Here comes Rocky out of the Dock Deli with a bag that doesn't look like it has any Colt .45 in it. Sliding by me into the back, he drops it in my lap. "Well, fuck that guy," Rocky says. "I look eighteen, and if you look eighteen, and your I.D. *says* you're fucking eighteen, then you can buy beer."

"Then where is it?" I say. In the bag is just pretzels.

"Fuck, ask *him*. I don't know. Let's try Mueller's."

Lee asks, "What did the guy say?"

"Well, shit, he asked me my brother's birthday, and I said September, but I didn't say a day, because I forgot the day. And I forgot the year, too, so he told me I could just get the pretzels."

"Jesus Christ," says Lee.

"But now I know, OK? It's September ninth, nineteen forty-four. So go to Mueller's. That guy in there was a prick anyway."

"Only because you're a moron," Lee says. "Anybody knows their goddamn birthday."

"Fuck you. Who cares? There's a million stores."

We cruise along to Mueller's while Rocky reveals it's his idea for us to go to Helen's and give her a box of chocolates, only they should be Ex-Lax. "She would shit out her brains," says Rocky. He says his brother at Cornell got chained together by his fraternity with two other guys who were trying out for the fraternity and with three girls who were trying out for some sorority, boy-girl-boy-girl-boy-girl. They had to push an oil drum ten miles through the countryside after they all ate a box of Ex-Lax. They kept having to run clanking into the fields so somebody could squirt out diarrhea. And his brother joined the fraternity anyway.

Rocky hops out at Mueller's, saying, "September ninth, nineteen-forty-four. I'll always remember. It was a very cloudy day." He holds both his hands in front of the windshield to show us his fingers are crossed.

When he comes out again, Lee says, "Hot *damn*, he's got it." He moves fast through the parked cars, holding a big bag in his arms. I slide over to let him in front this time, and off we go with Lee squinting ahead into the traffic.

"Hoo, hoo, hoo-ee," yells Rocky. "Hey, gimme the fuckin' Medal of Honor, will ya? Man oh man."

"Did he ask your birthday?" I say.

"Naw, shit. He didn't give a shit. He was watching TV." Rocky's already prying open one of the cans, which he hands to me, saying, "Here you go. Pass it to dead-dick over there. That'll put lead in your pencil, boy."

Lee says, "God, let me at least get to a side street."

In a few minutes we're all laughing and singing and gurgling down this stuff, which it turns out is malt liquor instead of beer, and which tastes like rhino piss, Lee says, and I realize we're passing by the park toward Barbara's neighborhood, as I know Lee must be aware, but he's not saying anything.

Barb and her family are leaving very early tomorrow for some kind of family reunion picnic on the banks of the Hudson River, otherwise I would be tempted to have these two rabble-rousers drop me right here so I could pay the girl a nighttime visit, something I have not done since the fall. The procedure is I toss pebbles up to her window, and she comes down and meets me in the garage, and we make out in the station wagon. But she said today after English that I could phone before nine, if I felt like it, because she was hitting the hay early to get up at four.

"*Four*," I said.

"Yes, four," she said. "You know Daddy. He loves to get going before the sun does."

Well, I didn't know that, though it figured. I told her, OK, I would call around eight, but at eight I was in Lee's woods, and anyway I knew when I said I'd call that I wouldn't. I had nothing to say, except the usual crap, which amounts to us trading boring little complaints about the rotten things in our lives, like I would explain how lousy I played this afternoon, giving away eight games to this dipshit Catholic who crossed his neck-chains before every goddamn serve, and she would groan about how she really did *not* want to sit for hours in their car so she could eat cold fried chicken and play croquet with old ladies. You can't get serious with her is what I want to say—not that all that crap isn't serious. It is serious, but it's not basic, you know, it's not our true inner feelings. You might wonder why the hell would I want to discuss our true inner feelings. You got me there. Maybe I actually don't. But the other crap seems like a waste of time. I would rather just make out with her.

By the time Lee and I are into our second Colt .45's, Rocky's finishing his third. He has the window rolled down so he can yodel at anybody on the sidewalk. We're taking a sort of roundabout route to Helen Bundy's, through the older intown neighborhoods that have tall elm trees and two-story houses with wrap-around porches.

It's garbage night. Every now and then, if no cars are coming, Lee jumps the Valiant over the curb, going about twenty, and clobbers our bumper into the trash cans. The lids fly off, and they roll all over, spewing out junk like guts. To Rocky and Lee, this is hilarious, and I guess it is to me, too. We're all laughing our heads off.

Rocky's now kneeling on the seat, sticking his head and shoulders out the window and yelling, "Was it you who did the pushin', put the stains upon the cushion, footprints on the dashboard upside down?"

The houses are mostly dark. Lee yells, "Hey, Rock, shut the fuck up. I can't hear the engine."

Rocky's going, "Was it you who took your pecker, got into

my girl Rebecca, if it was you better get outta town."

I keep laughing, and Lee shouts, "You're gonna get us fucking *arrested*."

Rocky pulls his head in. "Shit, no law against singin', is there?"

I say, "There's laws against everything, you dumb hick fart."

"I swear you guys are prudes. You guys are fucking *prudes*," says Rocky. He's pretending to strangle me.

Suddenly, we swing around the corner onto Helen's street. I know her room, so I'm looking to see if her light's on, what for I don't know. We go slow.

Then Lee hisses, "Sweet fucking Jesus," and a hot fear grabs my heart. It's Richard Linwood's yellow-and-black Chevy, parked on the corner.

Rocky takes the can from his mouth, looks around, and says, "What?" We cruise quietly by. "*What*?" he says again.

"*That*," I say, as we pass. It's a dull black monster, with a yellow hood. In the back the thing's raised up like it's about to jump on something.

"Son of a cocksucking bitch," says Lee.

Rocky says, "Oh, *that* scumbag. Hell, it's just his old Chev."

"What a fucking *whore*," Lee viciously says. "I would never suspect it in a million *years*."

"You think he's up there with *her*?" says Rocky. "Little Helen Bundy and that one-arm jerk-off?"

I say, "Lee, he's not with her. He's at the Lanes." Helen lives right behind the Huntington Bowl-mor Lanes, which is the big greaser hang-out of the area, and which at the moment is all lit up on the left of us. The red outlines of three huge neon bowling pins flash in sequence like they're falling down, over and over. "Look," I say. "The whole parking lot's full of cars. They're parked every place. Shit, old Helen wouldn't touch that prick with a ten-foot pubic hair." The image of Barbara's twisty gold one zips through my brain.

"How the fuck do *you* know?" Lee spits out. I think he realizes I'm probably right, but he's enjoying his mood of raw fury.

Rocky says, "Well, let's go by again. Let's peek through her fucking windows and find out."

I say, "You can't peek through her fucking windows because she lives on the second floor."

"So get a ladder," says Rocky. "Fuck, you know, I think that scumbag is up there with her. Know why?"

"Why?" says Lee.

"Because she would love him. He's the only guy in this fucking town that could stick his hand up her twat all the way to the elbow."

"Je-*sus*," says Lee.

We're all laughing so hard he has to turn in behind Henley One-Day Cleaners and stop. Rocky opens the door and falls out onto the asphalt. I step down on his stomach. He grabs at my foot, but I hop away. I go around the cleaners to piss away from the glaring streetlights, and Lee and Rocky follow behind me.

"Shit," says Rocky. "This stuff goes through you like corn through the old mare."

Lee hawks up a clam. "*Hey*," he says. "I *got* it. Why don't we just call her up and say can we please speak to Richard?"

"What for?" I say.

"What do you mean? That's how we find out, shithead."

"Jesus, take my word for it. She hates him."

Rocky says, "Who are you? Dear Abby?"

"Hey, I don't give a fuck. If you guys want to call her, go ahead. I'm not stopping you."

Lee says he can't call because she would recognize his voice.

"Just put your dick over the mouthpiece," says Rocky.

"Shit," I say, "she'd recognize that, too."

Back in the car, Rocky opens three more Colt .45's. Lee drives down the road a mile to the marina, where there's a phone booth by the launching ramps.

Lee is saying, "Hello, hello, hello, hello," in deep voices and high voices.

"What're you gonna say if the fucker is there?" says Rocky.

I say, "Shit, you know she hasn't answered the phone all week. What makes you think she'll answer it now?"

But Lee ignores us. He shuts off the engine and guzzles from his can. Out in the harbor, the sailboat masts sway like they're alive, only it's the water that's really alive, full of fish and plants and little bitsy stupid animals, eating each other right and left. Last summer for a week at the highway department, I was on the road-kill crew, which was the truck that went around picking up raccoons and things that would just rot there if nobody buried them or carted them away. On my last day we got a call to go to a vacant lot that somebody said there was a big animal in. It was a four-foot heap of white maggots. You couldn't get near it unless you held your nose. They just swarmed and wriggled all together like somebody barely moving under a blanket. We ran up with shovels full of lime to throw on it. That was all we could do. They madly peeled away from the lime in agony. Packages and packages of old chicken is what it turned out to be, wrapped in cellophane. Sometimes that's what I think our whole goddamn planet is, one sick ball of rot that once, ages and ages ago before dinosaurs, was pure and perfect, but is now a hopeless heap of writhing creatures like that chicken, just waiting for the good old H-bomb to sterilize it all again like in the days of yore.

"OK," says Rocky. "Gimme a dime then." He leaves the

phone booth door open. We're outside, holding our cans and bending our heads in sideways to listen. Lee tells him the number, which I realize I know, too, like when somebody gives you the answer to a test question that you already knew but forgot. He dials.

"Hello," says Rocky. "Could I speak to Richard, please?" Rocky looks at us. "Richard Linwood." He pauses. "Oh, well, anyway—is this Helen? Well, anyway, I have a message for Helen. Yup. From her buddy, Lee Bridgman. He says he—" Lee dives in for the phone hook, while Rocky tries to shove him backwards. "He says—wait, he says—"

Lee is shouting, "Hang up, you prick bastard!"

"He says he wants to suck on her cunt till her head caves in!" Rocky drops the receiver and lets Lee drag him limp by the arm out of the phone booth. Rocky's laughing and laughing.

Lee throws him down, yelling, "You cocksucking shit-brain hick!"

Rocky's coughing, he's laughing so hard. "She hung *up*," he says. "She hung *up*."

Lee tries to drag him down the ramp and throw him in the harbor, but Rocky tears free.

"Take it easy, take it easy, you animal," says Rocky. Lee's throwing wet sand at him. "I fucking *swear* she hung up when I said your fucking *name*."

Lee flips his last handful of sand into the water. "You asshole maniac," Lee says. "I wouldn't trust you with a penny for bubble gum."

Because Lee and Rocky lost their beers fighting, they pop open two more before we hit the road again.

"OK, where to now?" I ask, trying to liven things up a little. Lee's on his dead ass beside me, staring out over the steering wheel at the water. It glitters in places. The air smells like tar and oil and seaweed. Rocky on the other side of me is sort of chuckling into his can and drumming with his fingers on the outside of the door.

"How 'bout Albuquerque?" says Lee. He starts up the car.

"Yeah," say Rocky. "The fucking desert, man. *Lizards*."

"Hey, Rock," I say. "How much of this shit can you gargle before you puke your guts out?"

"Me? Fuck. Six cans? I puked once after six cans."

Lee says, "You puke in here, asshole, and you'll lick up every goddamn drop."

"Aw, fuck you," says Rocky.

Stubborn Lee backs the car around, and even though both Rocky and me tell him to be reasonable and forget Helen and her slimy pussy at least for tonight, he insists he's going back to somehow get a glimpse of her. That's all he wants, a glimpse. Don't ask me why. We call him a jackass and a pathetic twat-hound.

"I'm driving," says Lee. "If you wanna get out, get out."

Richard's car is gone this time, and a light is on in her bedroom. Lee slips around back through the thick bushes. He's out of sight. Rocky and I wait in the car. Rocky's talking about how he would really honestly like to fuck Mrs. Crajow, the art teacher, who weighs about three hundred pounds.

"Shit, you'd never find the hole," I say.

Rocky laughs. "I know, but so what? In all that blubber you could make your own fucking hole. What's the difference?"

All at once, all this talk about pussy and fucking seems crazy to me. What's the point? Jesus. Out of the blue, I ask Rocky, "Hey, did you ever like actually dick a girl?"

"Hunh? What do you mean?"

"You know, with feelings of love and everything."

Rocky takes a glug from his can. "Fuck, you think I'm the kinda guy that would kiss and tell?"

"Shit, yeah," I say, and I laugh to get him feeling easy. I'm dizzy behind the eyes. "But forget it. You don't have to tell me. I was just wondering."

Lee comes ripping through the bushes, across the yard, and into the car. The engine roars. "What happened?" I yell. We're off.

Lee starts laughing. "Shit," he says, out of breath. "She had these goddamn curtains, you know? So I was climbing up there." He takes a breath. "And I was at the top, and the whole fucking vine-holder cracked apart. I grabbed the gutter, and the fucking gutter came off, and I busted my ass on the porch. The gutter got me in the head, and I'm fucking *bleeding*."

Rocky says, "Oh, Jesus Christ save us. Where we going? The doctor?"

It turns out when Lee finally pulls over that he has this little cut on his forehead. He keeps dabbing the back of his hand on it and licking off the blood. We're in the dead-end street of a housing development. I get out and piss against a tire. In the houses some lights are on, but you can't see anybody moving around. One house has unlit colored Christmas lights outlining all the front windows. My piss is still squirting out, endless like a waterfall. Lee and Rocky are joking loud in the car. Why do those people still have Christmas lights up? It's a nice house, a big house. Maybe somebody died in the family and they're all too depressed to do anything. Maybe they're just lazy and stupid in that house. I'm out of piss, but I let my dick hang out dripping.

Lee pulls half his body outside the window on his side of the Valiant, and he yells across the roof of the car, "Hey, dipshit!"

"What?" I look down at my white little dick.

"Hey, I'm thinking—"

"Congratulations."

"No, I'm thinking, you know, shit, we got to *practice*. Bay Shore is next Friday. You know that? Bay Shore. They're good. They were good last year when we had Gordie Millspaugh and Barry. I don't think they lost since we beat 'em last year."

"So, big deal. I thought you didn't give a shit whether we won any more."

"Yeah. Well, fuck, I hate to lose. I don't want to *lose*."

I don't say anything. I'm wondering what would happen if I didn't tuck my dick away, if I just let it dangle out my fly for no reason, for no occasion, you know, like those Christmas lights. They'd send me to Bellevue, that's what. Jesus, Bellevue. Beautiful view. I probably wouldn't even have a window.

Lee says, "So let's get out and hit tomorrow, OK? Forget suckass caddying. You wanna?"

"Sure, I don't care," I say.

Then, *BLONK*, the horn goes. Lee kicks at Rocky inside the car. "You dumbass shithead!"

Rocky screams out, "WAKE UP, ALL YOU CRAZY COON TAINTLAPPERS!"

"*Get in!*" Lee yells to me.

"I quick shove my old dick in safe and reach for the door handle. Rocky's holding it shut from inside. The engine's running again.

"WAKE THE FUCK UP!" screams Rocky.

I fill my lungs and scream out, "MERRY CHRISTMAS AND HAPPY NEW BEER." It feels great. I yank the door open.

Lee yells, "Jesus *Christ*, you crazy fucking moron shitheads." Our tires screech. We whip off down the empty street.

"Open some cans, Rock!" I say.

Rocky lunges across my legs for the window. "Happy

Easter!" he yells. Then he's puking.

"Holy shit," I say. I scramble over toward Lee to give him room.

"Goddamn it," says Lee, but he's laughing. "Keep it out the window, Busby, will ya?"

"Where's the fucking opener?" I shout. Joy has suddenly pumped into me from somewhere like a wind fattening a sail. "OK, goddamn it," I say to Lee. "Let's practice." I grip his knee hard in my fingers. "Let's fucking practice so we can beat the cocks off of any asshole around. Ollie Asshole Griggs or anybody. Ten hours a day. Shit, let's go down there right now."

"Now you're *talkin'*," says Lee. "Tomorrow. Tomorrow at eight. Or, fuck, seven o'clock."

"OK. Seven o'clock. You better be there."

Well, you might not think two wildass drunks like Lee and me would actually be able to keep a pact like the one we made zooming down the road Friday night with old Rocky blowing lunch all over the side of the car, but when we got home we shook hands on it, and lo and behold, come Saturday we were both up, not exactly at seven, of course (it was more like nine), but we went down there, and we practiced. We practiced eight hours yesterday, and so far today, Sunday, even though it's pretty breezy, we've been practicing four hours, since noon. The balls we started with are down to skin, which is the only reason we're quitting. Baldies fly all over in a little wind.

We're slapping along the boardwalk of the beach club, heading for the spindly, cruddy old water fountain to see if they turned on the water yet for the summer. But they haven't, so we sit on the warm planks with our feet in the sand.

I say, "God, I'm so thirsty I could drink a Colt .45." Yesterday, after tennis, we buried what we had left of that rhino piss with Lee's Budweiser down by the jetty.

Lee says, "Yeah, me too, but I'm not walking all the way down there. Tonight you want to?"

"No, I can't. I got a French quiz."

"Yeah, OK." Lee digs his rubber sneaker toe in the sand. "You know, shit, I wish I had a pigeon, too. I wish we both had pigeons."

"Hell, who's stopping you? You could get a pigeon." Lee came up to my backyard this morning for the big send-off farewell to L.R. Yesterday he was so healthy he was flying around the basement. The dumb bird knocked down all my father's old mildewy, rolled-up blueprints left over from back when he helped build the Brookhaven atom-smasher. They're top secret. So today was going to be what my mother called Back to the Bronx Day. She made apple-spice cupcakes and got my sisters to invite their friends over for the show. She even got out some onionskin typing paper, and she typed a tiny note for me that said,

To Whom It May Concern:

I am home again at last because of my friend, Bernard A. Hergruter, of 14 Bay Lane, Huntington, L.I., who found me near death on a lonely beach and who cared for me and returned me to good health.

We rolled it up like a scroll and stuck it in between his legband and his leg. Everybody was outside standing on both sides of the door like the people that throw rice at a wedding. I marched up the stairs, holding L.R. in my hands in front of me like a girl runs with a football. My father pulled the screen door open, and I stepped out onto the stoop.

I said, "Well, so long, L.R., and be careful."

"Goodbye, pigeon," everybody started to say, a lot of girls' voices. They all had cups of juice.

I tossed him up, and he flew about ten feet and landed on the clothesline. He swayed there on the line for about a minute, with his wings spread. Then he bent his head down to pull out my mother's note with his beak, and then he flew off a little further, over to the garage roof, so we all walked over there. He gurgled and cooed and sat perched on the shingles. That was as far as he got.

At the moment, my father's up in our attic knocking together a coop for L.R. so he can come and go when he wants through the window. He can have a home with us as long as he feels like hanging around. Everybody I think was glad L.R. decided to stay. Watching him soar away to the crummy city would have been like when you let a circus balloon go the day after the circus. It goes up and up until it's a yellow dot that you can see and can't see, and then it's gone, and you wish you never let it go.

Lee stands up. "My ass hurts from landing on it Friday night. I can't sit on hard things."

"Serves you right. You acted like such a dip, going back there like you did. Why'd you go back there?"

"Shit, I don't know," he says. "Hey, you wanna just hit these away?"

That's what we usually do when the balls get so worn down, we whale them out into the water. It's funny. As kids, we used to rummage through the hedge behind the courts hunting for the scuzziest dead old balls that somebody lost in there years ago, and we'd play with them. Now, hell, we belt away practically brand-new balls. I say, "No, let's hit some serves. My shoulder feels tight."

"Really? Now?"

"Yeah, five minutes' worth."

"I thought you were thirsty."

"Yeah, and I thought you wanted to practice."

"Shit, I don't care," says Lee. "Let's go."

The thing is, I am thirsty, but since Friday, when I couldn't ignore it any longer thanks to Lee, the big Bay Shore match has become one more black shadow looming over my life. Lee's right. They are very good. Of course, I knew that before he said anything. (Shit, I played third singles against them last year. I lost, too.) But, I don't know, it's weird. Your brain is always full of everything you know—I sure as hell didn't forget we had Bay Shore coming down on us— but sometimes it's like you have a stage in your brain with a spotlight you mostly train on only one thought at a time, and you keep all your unwanted thoughts skulking in the wings, the way a campfire at night in the forest keeps away a ring of eyes. Friday night Lee broke the spell, I guess. He scared me. God, I hate playing like some rabbity choke-artist, which all spring is what I've been—whether I won or not. I mean, shit fuck, I get out there feeling good, feeling warmed up, even with these turds in sneakers on the other side of the net, and I end up dubbing around like somebody's grand-mother. I *suck*. I love tennis, and I suck at it. Christ, it's not easy, either, playing on the Number 2 court all the time next to Big Ace, where all you hear is *pok pok pok*, and his fans clapping and oooing up on the grass bank, and Ollie going, "Hey, nice get," or "Good hustle," to the hopeless jerk-off that Ollie's got falling out of his jock after every screaming ball. So, what do you expect, I'm practicing. Don't ask me if I think it'll help. Practice makes perfect, right? Well, maybe it won't make me a hot competitor, but I'll sure as hell be a terrific practicer.

I've got foot fatigue. I can feel it in my arches as we cross to the courts over the dirt-packed parking lot. We walk slow. Lee bends over for a stone, which he tosses up and hits, *pling*, high over the road. He has powdery salt-marks under his sideburns from dried sweat, and they make me think of how thirsty I am and of our refrigerator, which has that big jug of pineapple juice sitting in it cold.

I flip my racket cover onto the grass at the edge of the court.

Lee says, "OK, Pancho, go wild." He throws all three balls at me at once, because he is annoyed, but he doesn't want to just say, "Hey, piss on this, let's quit."

I wait a few seconds for the wind to ease off. Then I serve one slow into the corner. Lee doesn't swing. He's not even looking at me. I follow out to where he's aimed his stare. It's a hunched, growling, black shape, coming down my street, turning, gliding along the beach road toward the courts. All the grillwork is gone so what's left is a long, dark hole between the headlights like the car has some horrible disease that only makes it vicious instead of sick. Just the sound of it makes the hairs on my nutbag twitch.

"Looks like we got company," says Lee. It's exactly what those wagon-train guys always say when the redskins come whooping out of the brown hills. "You wanna leave?"

"Shit, where would we go? He sees us."

"Yeah, OK. I'm just askin'. It ain't my dick he's got in the ringer. Maybe he only wants to bat the ball around."

"That must be it," I say. Actually, years ago, I did play tennis with Richard Linwood. We played a few times. He was OK. He could even toss the ball up to serve it by first putting it in the crook of his elbow behind his stump and then snapping it out straight so the ball would fly up.

The Chevy turns into the parking lot and rumbles up alongside our court. I don't look over. Richard kills the engine. Bonk, I slam a serve flat into the box. Lee stops it with his racket.

"That was *good*," he shouts. Good old Lee. He goes to the fence for the other two balls.

Richard's door creaks open. I look at him. I don't feel scared really, just nervous. He leans out. "Hey, cuntface," he says.

I train my eyes on him a little more, and then I look back at Lee. Lee serves. I knock it into the net.

"Hey, *cuntface*," yells Richard.

Lee serves another. I catch it on the hop. The Chevy door thuds shut. From the side of my eye, I can see Richard's big body coming closer. I serve one into the net. Richard stops at the edge of the court. He leans against a leg of the umpire's chair. I go pick up the balls. Across the net, Lee is watching me. He has no expression on his face. "OK," I say, "let's call it. Too much wind."

"Yeah, OK," he says. "Way too much wind."

I'm very alert and very calm, and I'm thinking all we have to do is zip on over to our racket covers and angle up the road home. And if he follows us, so what? What can he do? We are two speedy guys with two heavy warclub rackets. He can't do shit. Unless he wants to run us over. He could probably run us over. Jesus.

"*Cuntface*," Richard shouts when I turn my back to him. "I'm giving you five seconds to get your cheesy old hog over here or I'm gonna cut it off now and make you eat it."

I spin around, wind up big, and whale a ball far up over his head and into the giant fir trees on the other side of the parking lot. He flinched just barely, but I saw it, and it made a thrill of power surge up my backbone.

"You *c'mere*," yells Richard. He is furious. That scares me. Why does he get so furious?

"You talking to me?"

"C'MERE," yells Richard.

I turn to Lee and shrug. "He talking to me?"

"Shit, I don't know. Think he forgot your name?"

"Naw. Hey, you talking to me? Richard?" I don't know

whether I'm afraid of him any more or not. I feel tense and calm.

He takes two quick steps onto the court and stops. I don't budge. Is it because I have Lee with me?

Richard yells, "*Prick*. You make me come to you, prick, and it's gonna be fifty fuckin' times worse. You hear that, prick?"

"Why don't we keep like this. We hear pretty good like this."

Richard slashes his hand out from where it's been propping up his stump, and *clack*, a thin blade shoots out the end of it. My heart jumps. He moves it in circles, like he's turning a crank.

He's coming at me. My asshole ices up. I yell out, "Goddamn it, Richard, what do you want from me? I used to like you, remember? Shit, Richard."

Richard keeps coming. "I want my eighty bucks and one scummy inch of your hog."

"You listen, you goddamn maniac. I don't have any eighty bucks. I don't owe you any eighty bucks. And you come anywhere near me with that thing, and you're gonna be spittin' out my Jack Kramer along with teeth."

"*Listen*," he says. "Oh, cuntface, I'm listenin'. C'mon. Try it, cuntface prick. I want you to try it."

"Don't make me, Richard."

He's to the middle of the court, crouched and swirling that knife. I'm just standing in the doubles alley with both hands around my racket like a bat, shivering like mad. If he jumps at me, I'll run, I know I will. I can't help it. I glance back at Lee. He's clutching his racket, too, with his mouth hanging open.

"Lee!" I say. "Pick up those racket covers." He hops to the grass.

"Got 'em," he says.

Richard starts edging sideways like he wants to circle with me. I start backing up. I say, "OK, you dumb retard fuck, we're leaving. I don't want to bust your ugly bullet head into a million pieces. But you better fucking well face it, I will if you come after me. I'll fucking kill you, if you make me. Got that? But I don't hate you, so—"

"NOW, cuntface," screams Richard. He lunges one step, and I take off. Lee flashes on ahead of me, hauling his white ass across the parking lot. I stop. He's not after me. Lee's to the road already, still flying. Richard is back on the tennis court, on his knees. He's slicing our net into pieces. He's tearing at it.

I yell out, "Richard, you're crazy!"

"Come and stop me, cuntface!" he yells. He laughs, hacking away.

On the road a car goes by. I turn my head. The woman waves at me. I wave back. "Richard! You killed my *dog*, you cocksucking, fuckbrained cripple. You *killed* him, didn't you."

"Come kill me, Hergruter," he says. "*Kill me!*"

"I don't *feel* like it," I yell. I stand there shaking. He cuts and cuts. Jesus God, I *do* feel like it. *Fuck*, I want to smash him to flat mush like a horseshoe crab. I want to mangle him, kill him. A sound rises up into my throat, and then I'm making the sound, and my jaw clamps down over it, and it comes rushing through my teeth, peeling my lips back, bunching my tongue, twanging like metal in my neck. It stops. I run. My feet pound the roadway. The air swells and rushes like water. My ears fill. I can't see. Tears cross my face. I'm falling—no, running. I'm only running. Running.

CHAPTER 9

SOMETIMES, WHEN MY MOTHER can't stand it any longer, she just blows up. She goes into tirades about how my father is an ogre and a moron and how our house is a slum, the rotting slum of the neighborhood. He sits in his chair, and she stalks in and out of the kitchen, yelling out her speech of rage, and slapping at his newspaper with the dish towel. "A *slum*, a gutter slum. Your children *live* here. But does fat, drunken Fred care? No, fat, drunken Fred does not care. I wish I could tell you, Fred, how it embarrasses them to bring their friends here, to the craphole in the backyard, the swamp of the basement *playroom*, to the crumbling, stinking, mildewing bathroom where their father stumbles in to pee out his money on the floor" (she often will refer to the time he did piss on the floor), "but they *can't* tell you, so you must hear it from me. Oh, I know you hate to hear the truth from me, Fred, but it *is* the truth. They suffer here. Your children *suffer* here. Do they have a Moose Club to hide in like their father? Why doesn't their father ever invite his Moose pals to his lovely home? What would they think of you, Fred, if they saw the abysmal hell you have trapped your family into? What would they think of happy-time Freddie, back-slapping Freddie, always-good-for-another-drink Freddie?" Well, it can go on and on, generally about the house, our living conditions, how we're trapped, along with many other things that are awful to hear and think about. When my father has had enough of it, he mostly just gets up and slams out the door. The Buick roars alive, and off he goes. I'm always asleep when he comes back in, but usually I wake up. A couple times he pushed my mother, or yelled back things about her being a slut and a whore, and he has squeezed her arm very hard. She has thrown plates and that shit, too, like a TV comedy. Whatever my father does, she usually ends up crying and wailing, and so do the girls, and I go sit in my room, sort of frozen, hating how my parents can both be so wacko. But it was wonderful one time I remember, one gorgeous red-and-gold fall day when I was a kid. It was Halloween, only it was the afternoon hours before we were going to get our costumes on for the night's rush house-to-house filling our candy bags. I was playing in the woods and swinging all day on Bert Shupa's rope vine, that his father made for him far away from any house in a giant tree. It had a leather seat. And below in the neighborhoods leaves were burning, the smell of fires swept the air. When I got home, my mother and father were both wearing checked aprons, and they were making hot doughnuts together by the stove. Powdered sugar was covering the counter tops. The speckled doughnuts were heaped on plates all over the table, and they were still dropping unfried ones into the kettle of fat on the burner, laughing and kissing each other. That was the old days, however. Now if they get along at all, it's because they keep in different rooms.

Anyway, what I am getting at is the point of slums, which, if you compare our crummy little house with the ones normal for our neighborhood, our house *is*, you could say. But, shit, our house is the Taj Mahal compared to where I got myself to at this moment, namely the middle of the most horrible, depressing bathroom you have ever witnessed. I am peeing into this black, cracked, turd-streaked toilet, which has these two boards for a seat. The thing doesn't even have water in it. You have to fill this bucket at the sink to pour down over whatever you released into the pot. And the bugs are amazing. It's like the Russian army, they're all over the place and fast as hell, like a bead of mercury on a plate. And this bathroom isn't just for Winnie's apartment, it's for the whole damn floor, *four* apartments. It's actually Winnie's grandparents' apartment, but on the other hand it isn't, because they both died last week. I don't know how they died. I asked Winnie twice, and she hasn't told me yet. We're smack in the middle of Harlem. A few hours ago, when I got out of school, I took the train here, because Winnie asked me to come. She called me last night (Wednesday night) on the phone. She called Tuesday night, too, but I was down at Lee's.

I was out on the back stoop with a glass of lemonade just after it got dark. I was feeling lousy, too lousy to even want a beer, because of my lousy tennis match that day. I hit bottom, and it felt like mud, and I didn't think I'd ever bounce back. Like, there were balls I didn't even run for, lobs that went in, because I was doing everything else so terrible when the damn ball came right *to* me that I thought why run after the damn thing, what's the difference?

The phone rang ten feet away, inside the screen door, but I didn't get up. It kept ringing until my mother picked it up.

She said to me, a bit angry, leaning to talk through the window over the sink, "It's for you. It's the same person who called yesterday." Until she said that, I completely forgot I *had* any call yesterday, I guess because I gave up trying to figure who it would be, calling me from New York City, collect.

I took the receiver out to the stoop. "Hello?"

"Bernie Hergruter?" said this official voice.

"Yeah, this is Bernie."

"Go ahead please."

"Hey, Bernie! B, this is Winona Lockhart."

"Winnie!" I was amazed.

"I'm in New York."

"I know you are. How come?"

"Well, see, it was my grandparents' funeral today."

"It was?"

"Yeah, they died last week, and we took the bus here yesterday. I called you last night, too."

"I know. I wasn't here, and I couldn't for beans figure out who was calling *me* from the city. But it was you."

"Yeah. Hey, I thought you could like get in here some way. So like Latham, my brother Latham and me, we could see you, or at least get together tomorrow night, you know?"

"You mean, in the city?"

"You don' like that idea?"

"No, I like it. I just don't know how I'd get in there. I'm quarantined now because of my school attitude. I can't go anywhere."

"Not even the city?"

"What do you mean, 'not even'?"

"Well, shit, B. I mean, forgive me, but here he is, introducin' Big-Time B, the wanderin' boy, on the loose on his way to . . . let's say *Alaska*. Shit, and you tellin' me you can't get a couple hours for yourself in New York City? Well, forgive me."

I knew what she was getting at, but I was thinking, hell, the old man would never let me out of the house—especially the night before the big Bay Shore match—to go visit somebody in the city alone. I would have to cut out, and my parents would really hate me if I did that routine again. I don't know what they'd do.

I explained all that to Winnie, and she went, "Mmm hmmmm, mmm hmmmm, mmm hmmmm." Then she said, "Well, how would it be if I got on some old train out to your house?"

"Well, I don't know. I don't know about here. We could meet downtown, maybe, except I couldn't even get out for that, I know." I was thinking how it would be just impossible if she came to my house. God, with my father there and all, sitting and talking in the living room. It would be insane. Even Barbara hardly ever comes to my house. My parents don't react to my girlfriends so well, and I always work it to go to Barbara's house, say, or some neutral place, like Nathan Hale Rock.

"Yeah, OK. I couldn't get there anyhow. Forget it, that's all. See, I know how it is. You said you would send me a letter and you never did, and I sent you one."

I felt bad when she said that, thinking of her very friendly letter stuck away in *The Wandering Jew*. Her voice was the same as I remembered, warm, low, and smooth like the way she acted, like her skin. Then I started appreciating the fact that that girl looked up my number and called me twice from New York because she wanted me to come see her. She wanted to be *with* me. And Latham, too, I could see Latham and talk to him some more. Shit, I knew I had to do it. My parents would drop their drawers, but so what. A couple hours in the city, and I could take the train out again and be home by my regular bedtime. I could leave right from school on the bus that goes by the train station, and I could phone home from the train station to say what was on my mind, like it or lump it, which today I did.

"OK, Winnie, I'll work it out to get in there. You give me the address, and I'll get there somehow by six o'clock. How's that?"

"Or I could meet you someplace, B. OK? It's a little wild around here."

"OK, meet me at Penn Station, Track Nineteen, at six o'clock."

"Say, how come you can come now when you could not come a minute ago?"

"How did they die, your grandparents? I'm just interested," I said. Then I added, "It's too bad." I was going to ask how was the funeral, but it seemed not very considerate. If you went to a funeral, and somebody asked you how it was, what could you say? Nothing.

"I can't talk right now," Winnie said. "So I be seein' you then, at six, Track Nineteen. I'm glad you made up you mind to come."

"Yeah, me, too. OK. I'm glad you called the way you did. You sound just the same."

"Yeah. So do you. Well, 'bye."

"OK, 'bye, Winnie," I said.

" 'Bye," she said again, and she hung up.

When I phoned my mother today from the railroad station, I could tell immediately that she was fearful, you know, or else why would I be calling?

"Mom, I just want to say I'm going to the city, but I'll be back home tonight on the ten twenty-two if Daddy wants to meet the train. Or I'll take a taxi."

"Where are you going?"

"The city."

"I *know.* I heard you the first time. Where in the city are you going, if I may ask."

"Well, I'm visiting that person who called me last night. He is someone I met in Lakewood, a nice guy."

"Can you give me a number where we can call you if we have to?"

"No, I can't, because he didn't tell me where his grand-parents' place is, where we're going. He's just meeting me at Penn Station, and we're taking it from there."

"Bernie, your father is not going to be happy about this *at all.*"

"I know, but, hell, really it's OK. I'm not doing bad in school, and I'll be home early. He's got nothing to worry about, tell him."

"I wish you would tell him. Did you know last night you'd be going in?"

"Well, not exactly. It was maybe, maybe not, you know, but I would like to see this guy, see."

"What's the guy's name?"

"Latham Lockhart."

"Oh. Who is Winnie?"

"Who?"

"Winnie. Last night when you answered the phone, I couldn't help but hear you say, 'Winnie!' "

"Oh yeah. Well, that's the guy's sister. She's my friend, too. She actually made the call, that's why."

My mother sighed. "All right, Bernie. I'm sorry you left it to me like this."

I told her I was sorry, too, even though I could not have mentioned my plans to the old man the night before. He was a bit juiced, and when he's juiced, he isn't exactly The Great Compromiser. He would've said, "I'll give you a two-word answer: *no* and *no.*" I would be shoving my ass in the fire if I went against those two words. This way he has to accept it. I'm in the city already. What can he do? It's tough beans.

Beans is what we're eating for supper, along with hot dogs, corn from a can, rolls, and this fat bottle of wine, Chianti, and lime Kool-Aid. There's just the four of us—me, Winnie, Latham, and their mom, who isn't really eating, she's so sad. She's tall and thin like Winnie, and she has on a black dress and hat with a veil so that you can hardly see her face behind it. You can tell she's sad, though, because of her voice. It cracks. She's in the bedroom, just sitting on a straight-backed chair next to the mattress with her plate of food on it, still as a crow in a tree. We're around the rickety metal table in the kitchen, trying to make like we're having a normal meal. They're glad I'm here. I'm glad, too, I guess, but I have to say that this place, Harlem, is gloomy and also quite scary. It's not like Lakewood or South Huntington or Rasmussen Junior High School, which you could say are familiar places to me, at least in my memory. Though they are crawling with Negroes, the Negroes in those places act toned-down. They don't do a lot of things you might expect deprived, poor Negroes to do, like indulge in crime and so on, because they live near mean whites who would get riled up if the Negroes got too ornery. But here in Harlem it's like the heart of darkest Africa. It's untamed, and I bet there isn't one pale face within miles of me. I'm like a marshmallow in a goddamn coal mine. Negroes here can do anything they feel like, and they can get away with it, too, since basically speaking, it's their territory and no one else's. When Winnie and I left the subway station, I could tell she was nervous. She warned me in advance not to say anything if anybody yelled cruel remarks at us, or, to be specific, at me. "You just let Winona handle it," she said. "I sho' nuff will," I said, and she laughed at me. She had the jitters, though. So did I, I admit. In the past, whenever I thought of Harlem, I thought of it as a part of New York City, like The Bronx or Staten Island, you know, with garbage and dogshit in the streets and dark buildings and dirty stores and noise and weirdos, and maybe with more crime than the rest of the ugly old city, but I always thought it would look about the same—plain miserable and big. However, it doesn't. Harlem is the pits, I swear. It is about ten times as depressing as any place I have ever seen or heard of, and I don't mean just the slum building I am now in, I mean the entire godawful mess, block after dismal block of it. Walking along the sidewalk from the subway, we did get some stares and also one harsh comment, which I couldn't understand, from a group of men lounging and squatting down at the mouth of an alley full of car wrecks, it looked like. Winnie said to them, "Leave be, you jokers." And once we had to detour to another street because some kids on a roof were dropping soda bottles that slammed down and sprayed all over the pavement. If I was a kid in Harlem, I figured I would throw bottles down into the street, too. What I can't figure is why there are any kids in Harlem at all. Why doesn't everybody just move out the way Latham and Winnie did so they could close up the whole place and forget it? I mean, there are plenty of locations where you would think ordinary Negroes would much rather be, and where they would be accepted, too, like Long Island or Ohio, or even California. Why would anybody who wasn't half-twisted want to call Harlem home? True, a lot of people here probably *are* half-twisted (which is terrifying to realize), but then again a lot of them are probably just normal Negroes with jobs and refrigerators and favorite TV shows exactly the same as white people, only for some reason which for the life of me I can't fathom, they are spending all their days in what has to be just about the most horrible hole this piddly-ass world has to offer. I could ask Winnie and

Latham for their views on this puzzling situation, but this is obviously not the time for it.

I'm joking with them about my tennis match tomorrow, how I'm purely dreading it, and they're smiling, but they're sort of quiet. The feelings in this apartment are in general like lead. I would like to get away somehow, go someplace, but where? This is the easiest place to be, and they're company for their sad mom, too, I know. So I keep talking. I bring up the fact that at my house we eat off of paper plates like these all the time, the same tan color, because my mother hates a lot of dishes every night.

Then Latham says, "Say, B, how's it goin' with that mean and cruel cat, Richard? You beat his ass?"

For some strange reason, I am surprised Latham remembers the name of my enemy, because I guess the idea I had was that wild, man-of-the-world Latham had so much to keep track of in his own life that he wouldn't let my puny problems clutter up his memory.

"Well, not yet," I say.

"Shit, man, he *still* comin' down on you?"

"Yeah, you could say that," I admit. The worst, besides Zekey, happened Tuesday night. I was peacefully asleep very late, and CRASH, the window over my bed exploded. Glass flew into my hair and on my face. I jerked up, with my eyes kept automatically shut. My heart was banging. My father yelled, "Stay *down*, stay *down*," but I couldn't lie back because of the splinters. I'm no Hindu. My father's navy flashlight beam passed red across my eyelids, and back. "Oh, *Christ*," he said. "Did it get you?"

"No, no, no. It's OK. I'm OK," I said. I felt dizzy.

"What *hap*pened?" yelled a scared voice from the hallway. Lizzie.

My father said, "Nothing, honey. We broke the window, that's all. A little glass. Go back to sleep."

"How?"

"It was an accident. It's OK, now, honey. Go to bed." To me, he said, "Don't move. You got it all over you."

"I'm not moving," I said. Where was that prick bastard Linwood? Giggling in the dark hulk of his car? Listening in the bushes?

My father's slippers crunched on the floor. He slid my old sneakers onto my feet and led me to the bathroom. He had me stand bent over in the tub so he could gently brush off my pajamas and run his hand across my crewcut. Glass pieces chinked in the tub. Then I peeled off my pajamas and took a shower in my sneakers. When I got out, my father had my Boy Scout sleeping bag unrolled on the couch. It has a red flannel lining with totem poles every which way all over it, and it smells like campfires. I lay zipped in, balled up and warm for an hour without dropping off. You might think I was locked into a state of anxiety and sheer dread, but strangely enough, I first was thinking only about my uncomfortable wet hair and then about being rained on, like a Mexican peasant again. How would it be if I could live in Mexico, or say Haiti, in just an old, wrecked bread truck with no wheels in the sand by the hot ocean, eating tomatoes and fried fish and rice and bananas? I guess it would suck, but you never know.

In the morning I found rammed into the side of my father's canvas laundry bag like a fist in a fat belly this rock big as a softball. It was *painted*—all black. Needlesstosay, that really upset the folks. My mother said not to tell the girls about it, because what she was figuring was that it was the neighborhood—some vigilante jerk-offs from the neighborhood—flat out telling us they were fed up and warning us to get wise. Well, my mother, she feels persecuted, so I understand her train of thought. But I was not about to drop the Richard Linwood bomb on her. She'd tell the police, which I need like another asshole. They came, the police, and they took the black rock. The last time the police showed up at my house, they took my father. This was about five years ago. My mother somehow got a judge to order my father to leave the house, and he refused and refused to go. Exactly how she did it I don't know, but she had this lawyer perform some maneuvers to get her a legal separation, except the old man wouldn't even open the lawyer's vanilla-colored envelopes. He would just drop them in the waste basket by his chair. So one night the cops came after supper, and he had to pack up and go to jail. He was gone only a couple nights, and when he got back, for a while, things were better, but of course then they gradually got worse again. Anyway, watching the officer clomp out to his cruiser with the black rock in one hand made me mad. It was my rock, and he sure as hell wasn't going to figure out anything by running his magnifying glass over it. What it took me back to was the summer I came home from Camp Baiting Hollow Boy Scout camp with King Tut, who I won by eating watermelon. He was a huge box turtle. What you had to do was in five minutes collect as many seeds as you can from the watermelon you ate. I gobbled and slurped, and I was the winner. Actually, I got a horrible plastic model of a Sherman tank, but I traded it for King Tut. He wasn't afraid of me, and he ate lettuce and greasy slugs. When I got home with him from camp, we had the MacLarens visiting us, friends of my parents from when we lived in Maryland years ago, and Jackie, their boy, who was a year younger than me and who I played with when I was four. The day they left turned out to be Jackie's birthday, and since he loved King Tut so much, my mother said I had to give him away as a present. I said no. But my mother *made* me, I will never know why. And King Tut was all drawn inside like a rock when Mr. Mac-Laren carried him out to the station wagon.

So after I explain the black rock episode and the awful tennis court episode, Latham just sits there with his cup of wine, rubbing his whiskers. He sighs. Winnie looks down at the table.

"Goddamn, B," he says, "but you a lame cat, you know?"

"I'm a jellyfish," I say.

Winnie raises her eyes and smiles wide at me, and I grin suddenly because she looks so nice.

"Fuck it, man. I am disgusted, you know? That's right. You doomed, I got to say it. Doomed."

Winnie says, "Shit, Latham, that's bullshit. He ain't *doomed*. He just waitin', see?"

"Yeah, waitin' to get his white ass kicked to the fuckin' moon. B, listen, man, when you head fills up with kill feelings like you had, you *use* 'em, man—that's why you got 'em. I ain't sayin' kill the motherfucker. Shit. Just *get* him, man. It's all there is to it."

"You make it sound pretty easy," I say.

"Shit, B, it *is* easy. You think what *you* doin' is easy?"

"Shit, I don't know. I guess I do. It's easi*er*."

Latham snorts. "Ho, fuck, man, all right. You will find out you self. Just don' you run, B. You keep runnin' and you a gone goose, dig?"

I just look at him.

He looks at Winnie. "Winona, now, I'm goin' out."

Her face tightens.

"Shit, Winona, I been through this. It's how it is."

"Yeah, you tell Mama," she says.

Latham stands up. He takes Winnie's hand and squeezes it. He has on this loose, shiny green shirt and tight black pants and black shoes, truly quite slick-looking. He glances at me once, and he just goes on out the door. We hear his feet go down the stairway.

"Where's he going?" I ask.

She props her face in her hands with her elbows on the table, scowling at me. "Gamble," she says. "Dice, cards. Chasin' money. Usual bullshit. He still got all kinds of friends in this town, and I mean *all* kinds."

I get up and start taking plates over to the trash can. I put the top on the mustard. Winnie gazes ahead at nothing. I would like to say something to her, but I can't think of what. Finally, I come out with, "Well, hell, you're not worried about him, are you? If anybody knows what he's doing, it's Latham, right?" I'm trying to ease up her mind somehow.

Winnie smiles. "Oh, yeah, you right, all right. No, shit, *I* ain't worried. See, but Mama, she said, 'Stay inside these nights, Latham, and do me that much kindness,' but Latham went last night, and he went tonight. Somethin' about Latham, his life is his own."

I say, "Yeah, nothin' you can do about it."

"Nope," says Winnie. "It's just the dog in him comin' out." She takes the wine jug by the neck out into the other room that has a bed and two big chairs in it, and that the bedroom where her mother is is off of, and we sit in the chairs, which are shoved right next to each other in front of the TV. She turns it on. It's the weather.

Winnie says, "B, you forgot you cup."

I say, "No, I just threw it away." I go into the kitchen for another one.

The man says it was beautiful today and got up to seventy-five, but tomorrow will be cool and cloudy with a good chance of showers tomorrow afternoon and evening. I am hoping for a rain-out. Or a hurricane, anything. Today before practice, Coach Nicely called a brief but very serious meeting to reveal his deep strategy for Bay Shore. He stood up there behind his desk in front of the blackboard with rows of weird Latin words on it (Latin is a little weird, you have to admit), giving us his low-browed, marine-sergeant stare, and saying how the streak was on the line tomorrow, but he knew he did not have to tell us boys that. We were sprawled out through the room, the seven of us, stretched over two desks apiece, with the twenty or so other desks empty and slid around crooked the way they always are in Coach's room, and outside you could hear the happy-go-lucky shouting and babbling of everybody going home floating in through the open windows: "But it's not due until *Monday*, I don't think," and "Yeah, you can blow me, Cooper, you mung-bean," and the bus blats and fumes. The old pecker-head went on about staying cool, playing each point one-by-one, concentrating only on your match and ignoring the one next to you, but I wasn't really listening. I wanted to just get the hell out, so I wouldn't miss the bus to the station. Then he announced his strategy, which he said was only an idea he was offering, not exactly strategy. It was that we could switch me with Paul Mannes, who plays Number 3 singles, and also Lee and Eddie with Cake Lawrence and Vic Loebel, the Number 2 doubles team. That way we would be almost sure of three out of the five points, since Ollie would win no matter what. But, as my father would say, it ain't kosher. You play team tennis head-to-head, and you don't juggle your line-up for points. Still, to me, it was an appealing idea, even though it was shady. Nobody said anything for a minute. Then Ollie spoke up. "Coach, I have to say you're nuts." (Ollie can afford to talk that way to the old peckerhead. Ollie could probably even call him the old peckerhead, and Coach wouldn't flinch.) "If you think Craig would take that, you're nuts. He follows box scores. He knows how we've played the whole season so far. If you moved people around before, it would be different, but we've played the same line-up for weeks. It would smell pretty bad."

Lee said, "Yeah, but what would Craig do? Nothing. He

doesn't know beans about our line-up, anyway. The papers don't mean anything." Craig is the Bay Shore coach. He is a very friendly, very smart, and very athletic guy, who is making that Bay Shore tennis team into top players. In the winter they play indoors.

Ollie said, "Do what you want. All I know is it isn't fair. If the streak ends at ninety-three matches, so what? It just means it won't end at ninety-eight or a hundred and twenty."

Coach said, "I appreciate your views, Ollie, but that's not the competitive attitude I like to see. That's not an inspiring attitude."

"All I know is juggling your people is not fair," said Ollie.

I said, "Hell, nothing's fair, anyway." I was thinking, shit, what does *fair* mean? It wasn't fair that I was playing so lousy. It wasn't fair that Barry Rosen caught mononucleosis. It wasn't fair that they had Craig and we had the old pecker-head.

Finally, we took a vote, and everybody voted against the strategy and for being fair in the eyes of Ollie Griggs, which Coach Nicely said he was pleased to see.

When we left the room, I told Ollie I couldn't make practice because I had a dentist appointment. He said, "Yeah, I got to leave early, too. Don't worry. A couple hours today won't make any difference tomorrow. Just get to bed early. That's about all you can do."

You can also pray for rain. Then they would postpone it for a few days, which would at least give you a little time. Who knows, by then maybe the Russians would have blown us all up, and you wouldn't have to worry about it.

We're watching this war movie, World War II in Italy and Africa, long lines of army vehicles straining over very muddy roads and soldiers slogging along like drunks, they're so exhausted. They make me exhausted, just looking at them.

I'm beginning to worry about catching my train because I know I will have to call a taxi, and there's no phone in this apartment, which is the reason Winnie called me collect. It was a pay phone.

"How far away is that phone booth?" I ask. Cannon barrels boom and ram themselves backwards again and again, shaking their camouflage nets. They belong to the Nazis. Winnie's arm crosses from her armrest to my armrest. She looks over. Half her face flares up and fades out with the explosions. We're just about on top of the damn tube.

"Down at the Rexall," she says. "How come?"

"I gotta get a train out again in a couple hours, so I gotta call a cab." Actually, I don't have to call a cab. That is, I *could* risk the wicked subway, but my instinct for safety tells me a move like that is begging for bad trouble. I mean, like, Richard Linwood I can take. He's one guy. But if I nonchalantly stroll down into that black, endless cave full of thundering trains at *night* in this evil burg, it's like I'm inviting some gang of crazed boons to carve my creamy nates into fishbait just for the five bucks I have in my pocket and my sneakers.

Winnie sets her lips together in a little smile, and then she sighs and turns back to the war. More cannons go off. I guess the phone booth is close by.

"Say, B," Winnie says, "you gonna go in the army?" She looks at me again.

"The army? I don't know. Maybe. Or else the navy."

"Yeah? Can you swim?"

"Sure I can swim."

She laughs.

I say, "The navy's better because you just ride ships instead of march all over creation like robots, sweating and everything."

"You gonna fight?"

"Fight? Jesus, fight who?"

"Whoever they say. Whoever comes out against us."

Well, that's it, I know, the whole problem with the army. And the navy. You *could* have to shoot at people, and of course, what's even more horrifying, they would definitely shoot at you. Sure, if you're a soldier or a sailor, you get to have exciting and valuable experiences, like traveling to Alaska or Siam or someplace while getting paid for it, and it's also romantic, because you have a uniform, and you train with guys who are your friends like you're on one big team called the army. It's something men have done right from the start of civilization. They had to protect their land and their families from brutal, greedy invaders who wanted what they had, like Attila the Hun or old Genghis Khan. In fact, history is filled with wars and armies, which is a wonderful, romantic thought, and on the other hand, a quite depressing thought, too. You would think from all that history people today would learn to get along better. But I think the thing is people just enjoy having armies and being soldiers, like out of basic instinct. So I suppose being a soldier is not really too bad an idea—except for the chance it could kill you. A few years ago, when we sent our marines for some reason to Lebanon, I can remember sitting in the hammock we had then on the porch and saying to Freddie Umphenour that we were going to have a war and if it went on long enough, *we* would have to fight in it. Right then it got me that I might not live to be an old, old man. Something could kill me, like a war, which I would *have* to go to. I felt very unsafe, like in a nightmare when there's no place to hide from the thing that's crashing after you. Now, though, what's happened is that because we have the A-bomb and the H-bomb, all the armies and the navies are out of fashion. So it's less dangerous. If we *did* have a new war, it would last about one day, and whether you were in the army or not wouldn't mean piss because everybody would be fried black anyway, unless you were in a submarine. We hardly need our army any more. If some country ever starts to mess around, like Russia, or say like Cuba in the Cuban missile crisis, we can just say, "Hey, look, fuck off or we'll blow the hair off your asses by tomorrow noon." For that reason, the army may not seem too bad. Still, you can never be sure. To me, the army still seems a little risky. To Winnie, I say, "Well, nobody would ever dare come out against us. They know we would pound their whole shitty country into one big radioactive pancake."

"Yeah. Latham ain't goin' in, though. He don't have time for the army, and they can't get him, 'cause Latham is the man of the house."

"Yeah, well I'll probably go to college instead of the army."

"What college?"

"I don't know. There's a lot of colleges. I don't apply till next fall."

"Winona?" It's her mother calling.

"What, Mama?"

"Come see me."

Winnie lightly pats the back of my hand once, and pushes out of her chair. In the doorway she is outlined like a paper doll by the light coming out of the room. It's dark in here, except for the TV. A commercial is on. "Be sociable. Have a Pepsi."

Winnie comes out again. "We got it too loud," she says. "Mama is about to sleep."

"I'm not watching it anyway," I say.

"OK," she says. She takes two long steps to the TV and twists the knob. Blackness flashes in over the picture, shrinking in down to a little, fading blip in the middle of the screen. Then her mother's light goes off. The room is just about dark except for the glow coming up from the street, through the window curtain.

"Say, we could watch out the window a while at the people," says Winnie. "Plenty goin' on."

"OK," I say. I ask her what time it is, and she says near eight, and I say in a half hour I'll have to call a taxi.

She says, "Damn, B, don't you know no taxi gonna come this far uptown at night? This ain't Lakewood, Ohio."

We're on our stomachs, stretched across the bed, with our heads up to the window and our feet dangling off the side. Winnie looped the curtains back and propped the window partly open with a soup can. This is the third floor. Below is mostly cars parked under the streetlights or else rumbling along, screeching and honking for miles around. All the people going by are Negroes. Some are looking down out of their windows, too, like us.

"I see taxis driving around," I say.

"Yeah, but you never get a taxi by callin' on the phone, you got to stop one that's here already. Only they don't stop that easy."

For a while there I forgot that in the city you don't phone cabs like you do anywhere else. You just go up to the curb and wave and one will quick swerve over to haul you where you want to go. It's faster than calling, I guess, but not as sure. "Hell," I say, "they'll stop for me. I look wholesome, don't I?"

"Shit, man, you go try stoppin' a cab here at night and *dumb* is how you gonna look, dumb and crazy."

"Well, Jesus, it isn't really all that bad around here, is it?"

"*Bad?* B, listen. This is One hundred and forty-sixth Street. Shit, at night the *man* don't even come in this damn neighborhood, even if there's two of 'em."

Of course, I am aware that Harlem is a high-crime area. Any jerk who reads the papers knows that. But, like, when I peer out this window down to the sidewalks, the people all look sort of regular to me, not dangerous or anything. True, a few are drunk and staggering around and a few are wildly dressed, but after all these are Negroes, every last one, and this place is like a foreign country with different behavior patterns you have to accept and blend in with. Hell, I must be nuts. I realize I'm just trying to talk myself out of being scared shitless, because, fuck me, I have to go down there, and you should have seen the way those black faces stared at me this afternoon. And I don't get it. I mean, all right, so I'm a stranger, a conspicuous stranger, but I'm *harmless*, I'm basically good and friendly and not prejudiced. I feel like I ought to wear one of those double-placard signs over my shoulders that describes all of my noble qualities so the criminal elements down there will think twice before they drag me into some stinking alley and beat me into tomato paste with lead pipes. Because, Jesus, even though from my secure perch in this apartment they all look like normal citizens, for all I know they are ax murderers and child-rapers. Drug addicts and savage gangsters. I feel like suddenly I'm in the Alamo. "OK," I say, turning to look Winnie in the eye. "How am I getting out of here, then?"

"Shit, B, you stuck here till you wither and die." She laughs. "No, look, you can leave like you came, the subway. The subway is easy."

"*Easy!* Jesus, Winnie, this subway at night is about as easy as swimming blind through a jungle swamp."

"It's easy if you can be cool, man. Jus' be cool is all. I'll walk you down. Shit, I'll ride you all the way back to Track Nineteen, OK? You be safe with me."

"Yeah? I'm glad *you* think so. I'd be a lot safer calling a taxi."

She gives me a look of disgust.

I say, "OK, then. So you go to the subway with me, to protect me from raw danger, right? But you tell me, young lady, what makes you so immune to deadly crime?"

"Ain't nobody I met yet can catch me," she says. "Young *man*."

"Nobody except me," I say, and I nudge her shoulder with my shoulder.

She nudges back harder. "Shit, if I don't *want* nobody to catch me, nobody can catch me, not even Latham."

"Oh, yeah, shit on that. Back in the park that day I caught up to your little churning buns without even breathing hard."

"You din't catch *nothin'*. I stopped."

"Bull*shit!*"

"Yeah, man, I stopped to see who that was, running me down like some damn devil."

"Winnie, Jesus. You'll never get me to believe that. That's a bald lie."

"Yeah, OK. Someday we got to have a little race then. Then you believe it."

"Fine with me," I say.

We look at each other, and slowly her lips spread into this soft, little smile, and she says again, "Someday."

I look down into the street. I don't know why, but my throat got swollen all of a sudden. It was the way she said that *someday*, like we really are warm friends, you know, like we can admit that we are warm friends who really like each other, and who would like to keep on liking each other. I take a long swallow out of my wine cup and set it back next to hers on the windowsill.

In a quiet, low voice, Winnie says, "What you thinkin' about, so serious?"

"You," I say, because it's what I want to say.

Her breath goes in once and out. "You never make me believe that," she whispers. "That's a bald-face lie."

I push away from the window and drop my cheek flat onto the fuzzy blanket, with my face pointed at her elbow.

She does the same thing so that we're face-to-face sideways on the bed, just seeing eyes. We don't smile. We just gaze. My heart is going like a rabbit. It's love, for Christ's sake, pure love like in a fairy tale. I don't even want to kiss her or anything. It fills up my skull like steam heat. My hairs prickle. I can hardly tell where my body goes. My feet are somewhere miles away. It's like I am a simple, happy snowman, just happily soaking up the sunbeams, and happily flowing off in all directions. Amazing. Her face is six inches away. It shines polished in the window light. Our eyes keep going into each other like trains going into tunnels. Her mouth gently opens with tiny, wet clickings. The edges of her teeth glow. Her soft breaths roll to me and back like waves. Love. I love her, my inside voice says. I *love* her. How *can* I? This is crazy. My eyelids droop shut, and behind them, with her hair glowing, is Barbara. God. Barbara saying, "Anything, Bernie, *any*thing." I love Barbara. Oh, Jesus. But I *do*. I open my eyes. She is there, the same—dark, silent, beautiful. A princess.

I whisper, "You are beautiful."

Her lips thin slowly into that soft smile. She whispers, "So are you."

What? "What? Who is—?" My arm. I jerk up.

"Hey, kittens," says a voice. "Easy."

I look at him. I blink. Everything is black. Where is this place? It's, fuck, it's New York City. "What *time* is it?"

"After two," says Latham.

"Jesus *Christ*."

"Shush," he says.

"*Latham*," says Winnie.

"I gotta get *out* of here," I say. "It's two in the morning."

Winnie sits up beside me. She says, "B, you can't go nowhere now. Go tomorrow."

Already, though, I am fumbling in my pocket for the train schedule. I unfold it, but Latham grabs it out of my fingers. He says, "You fuckin' crazy, man. You ain't goin' outa here tonight. You in Harlem, man." He's bending to the window to read the schedule. "Shit, ain't no train till four A.M. anyhow." He flips it back to me. I can just make out the numbers. He's right.

"Well, Jesus, this sucks."

"You jus' fell asleep," says Winnie. "Anybody can fall asleep."

"Yeah, B, you OK. The world is still turnin'," says Latham. "Shit, you a grown *man*. Livin' you life, see?"

"Sure, but I got other lives attached to it."

"I know you do, man, but you ain't to blame for that."

"Jesus, they probably think I'm in Kalamazoo or some shit. I got to call."

Winnie says, "Right now?"

"Yeah, right now. I mean, what if they got the police out hunting for me?"

"Shit, man, cops can't find the peehole in their pants."

"I know, but it's my parents. They'll stay up all night, worrying up a storm. Really, I got to call."

Winnie slides by me off the bed. "Yeah, I guess you do got to call. But the Rexall's closed, and I don't know where they got another phone in this damn neighborhood, one that ain't been busted by some junkie."

"Down to Honey's," says Latham. "We can go down to Honey's and call. She don' care. You got some wine left? B, see man, you just hand this jug to Honey, and then you can call on her phone. She don' care."

"I'm going down there alone?"

"Shit, no," says Winnie. "Latham, he ain't goin' into Honey's alone."

"C'mon, baby, you *know* I ain't lettin' him go down alone."

"Latham, *damn*. You high on somethin', Latham."

"Shit, Winona, don' come down on me now. I got seven hundred dollars in my pocket, and if I am high, that is why."

"Where'd you get seven hundred dollars?" I say.

"Game of cubes, man. Three lucky little rolls. Then I walked."

"Musta been some game," I say. I can't really imagine people playing around with big wads of money like hundreds, but I know gambling is a way of life for some. You can become addicted to it with no trouble. People exist who would drop their last quarter into the one-armed bandit. My parents were in Las Vegas for their honeymoon in 1947, and the four days they spent there made a big impression on my mother. She often mentions how pathetic gamblers are. Winning seven hundred isn't pathetic by a long shot, though. Losing is what's pathetic, and since you mostly lose, gambling is a bad habit to have. I only bet when I know I will win. Like once I bet my mother twenty dollars that the smallest planet was *not* Mercury, as she was so positive. It was Pluto. She brought out her source, an astronomy book, because she said we could settle the bet only by having a convincing source, and *her* source said she was right. I got together a bunch of sources that said I was right, and my mother angrily typed a long letter to the place that printed her book telling about the bet and all, and they sent a reply to apologize (because their book was published before they had the final facts on Pluto), but they did not send the twenty bucks like my mother requested. So she wrote me an I.O.U. and signed it. It's in my box where my savings bond was, but I know I will never stick her with it. She wouldn't have collected from me, either.

Latham and I walk quietly down the stairs so we don't wake anybody, and we shove open the first door into the vestibule, which is very dark, and then the second one into the street. I still feel very sleepy, but I'm full of anxiety about what I can say to my parents, who are chewing their fingernails down to the elbow by now. I will just say I fell asleep. It's the *truth*. I fell asleep, and I missed the last train out, and I'll be in on the, say, 8:31, and I'll take a cab right to school. I'll miss a little of first period, but that's all. And I'm getting plenty of rest here in New York. I've been asleep four or five hours already. I can take care of myself, too, so don't worry about me, for Christ's sake. Of course, that's like telling the wind not to blow, I realize.

If you have never been to Harlem, you might imagine that after 2:00 A.M. the street action here would tail off to nothing the way it does in that song, "My Time of Day," where the guy is strolling through the city like a smooth, contented, lone wolf, but in fact this is like some kind of rush hour for warped Negroes. They're all over the place, flicking their eyes at me like snake tongues. I'm sticking close to Latham so they can see I've been accepted here, you know, and Latham keeps ambling along, loose in the shoulders, not paying anybody any attention, but you can see he's taking in the details.

We pass by a few noisy guys lying across this old car with big booze bottles in their hands, and Latham nods at them. I look straight ahead like the sidewalk is a log over a stream. Needlesstosay, I am quite nervous. I wonder if Latham is inwardly nervous, too, though he doesn't act it. He is humming. I cannot fathom why these slum people find it intriguing to stay up so late, but it could be that this is another aspect of Negro life that would baffle any white person. Or maybe this is just a very busy street. It's Eighth Avenue. Cars zoom back and forth.

Now Latham is singing, "I'm the *Hoochie Coochie* man, everybody knows I am."

I say, "Latham?"

He glances at me. "What?"

"I was wondering, do you ever lose at gambling?"

"*Lose?* Yeah, man, I lose. Shit, I lost bad tonight. Lost somethin' near to sixty dollars, but don' you go tell Winona, or I will bust you shoebrush head."

I ask him then why does he gamble if he just loses money like that, and he says, well, some cats win, and besides, he likes it.

You can't say anything to that, so I ask him who is Honey, and it turns out like I suspected. Honey is a prostitute. "She's real nice," says Latham, "but she ain't friendly. The bitch is all business, 'cept if she is high, but we ain't goin' there to buy cunt anyhow."

We walk down the sidewalk. I see the traffic lights change all in unison down the long avenue, and it makes me think of technology, you know, and how far along it has brought the human race. Music is coming out of a bar that has Miller High Life signs in the windows. Its door is jammed open by a chair. I'm beginning to feel like turning back, and the hell with my parents. I mean, they'll be OK, they're at home, safe. Out here anything could happen to me, like what if some wild, slobbering drunks came howling out of that cave of a bar after me? How could Latham save my ass?

"How far is this phone?" I ask. We've gone about four blocks.

"Not far, man," says Latham. "Listen, B, now I'm thinkin', you know? I'm thinkin' shit, like you in some bad trouble with this mother named Richard, right? You in real deep now, right?"

"Right," I say. The truth is that before Latham brought it up, I just totally forgot Richard Linwood. My brain was concentrating on the city and on getting to the phone, and behind all that I have this huge image like a billboard of Winnie's perfect, plain face.

"Well, like, I can dig how you come to be so powerless before this cat. Because it's like you don' know what to expect from the cat, 'cause he is crazy. Shit, he is so crazy, you hope he gon' just forget you before he gets to where he *knows* he just got to kill you, right?"

"I see what you're saying."

"You in a *flood*, man. You in a flood, standin' on a hilltop. And that brown water been risin' outa that motherfuckin' river for days and days, and now, *damn* if it ain't crawlin' up past you titties, and there you is, doin' nothin' but prayin' for that river to stop at you neck. Well, fuck it, man, lemme tell you somethin', man, it ain't stoppin'. It is fuckin' *time*, B. You got to quit prayin' and start swimmin', see?"

"Yeah, I see," I say. "But, shit, if you think I can go get me a bedpost and mangle the fucker, you don't know me. I can't *do* shit like that. It's like then *I* would be crazy."

"Shit, man, you crazy right now. At leas' you ain't straight, I know that. An' shit, you ain't a man, either, B. You a damn puppy dog. You dig what I'm sayin'?"

"Yeah. What you're saying is I'm scared shitless of the goddamn maniac, and I have to agree with you there. But this being-a-man shit is bullshit, Latham, because I can only be the way I am, see? That's all I can do. If the fucker fights me, then I'll fight him. If he gets lucky, he'll bust my shoe-brush head. If I get lucky, I'll bust his."

"Fuck luck, man. Only luck I see you needin' right now is luck to keep you breathin', dig? You need meanness, man, meanness like a tiger. That fucker got to believe you can waste him, same as he can waste you, dig? Shit, B, where you gon' get meanness like that, man? Huh? How you gon' make the cat *believe* he don' stop fuckin' with you, he gon' *die?*"

We're just stopped together on a street corner here, and Latham's low, forceful voice is hanging in the air among all the city noises. After a few seconds, I look up from the grainy sidewalk, and I say, "Well, shit, it seems to me the only way I can make *him* believe that is if *I* believe that, and goddamn it, I don't believe that. Shit, I mean, what do you want? Maybe I should take meanness lessons. Maybe that's what getting lucky is—getting *mean*." Then it hits me that Latham is like Lee, wanting me to have some foolproof plan like some actual knowledge of what will happen, so I can be without fear, because I will just *know—he will die* if he fucks with me, he will be obliterated. And hell, now it even makes sense. I mean, that's what bravery is, isn't it? It's knowing you have the power, *feeling* the power. You are so brave you can kill. You can do whatever it takes. You can perform. Except, fuck me, I am just too thoughtful to be jam-packed with bravery or even meanness. Because, like, what's bravery anyway? It isn't any Superman suit. Brave guys bite the dust like everybody else. I say, "Latham, shit. All my whole life all I have had is luck. I never get sick or in trouble or anything. I never had one broken bone, only a black eye. I got to stick with my luck until it runs out. Then I'll try being mean or brave or crazy or whatever it takes, see? But I don't know yet what it will take. The thing is, I guess you never know what it will take. Shit, *anything* can happen. Can you dig that?"

Latham shakes his head like he's giving up on me. He takes out a cigarette and lights it. "B, man, fuck it. I got no more to tell you. You know, shit, last time you an' me talked this way, I said you got to be cool, just cool. Now I think you got some cool—a little bit. I don' understan' you,

B, but like, I dig you smart, see? What you sayin' now, well, it must be somethin' to it. Shit, you got me hopin' it's somethin' to it, anyhow." Smoke jets out his nose.

I say, "Latham, I really do have to make a phone call."

"I know you do, man." He starts walking fast and I follow down just two doors from the corner, up some steps, and into a hallway that smells like old smoke. I ask him if this is Honey's, and he says, yeah, it's Honey's. All I have to do is ring the Number 2 bell two times and we can go on up there.

"Hey, but I forgot the wine jug," I say.

"Yeah, it don' matter," says Latham. "She don' care. You lemme talk to the bitch. You don' say nothin'. She got the phone right there by the door. I talk to the bitch. You dial numbers, dig?"

"What if there's somebody in there? Somebody else?"

"Ain't nobody in there. Go on, ring the bell."

I point my finger into the black button. It buzzes more than rings, and the sound carries to us down the stairway.

All along, from when Latham first mentioned her name, I was picturing Honey as this fat old Negro, sort of like Milly, Arnold Tolley's cleaning lady, but she turned out to be just the opposite, thin and quite young, say twenty, and she had on a blond wig. She was amazing-looking. She also had tight pants with high heels and a tight, creamy blouse that showed her belly-button. Somebody else *was* there, too, only it was not her client for the night like you might think. It was another prostitute, who was fatter and had on the same kind of clothes. Their pants came down over their legs like silk and stopped a little past their knees like bull-fighters' pants you see in the movies.

I was staring at Honey, and she was staring back at me, shaking her head and squawking a mile a minute at Latham, "What kinda jive trick you draggin' in now, you dogface nigger? You got nerve. Man, you do got nerve. You *know* this two-dollar gray boy thing ain't Honey's thing. You got me *insulted* now, you triflin', no-good, jive-ass nigger. Whyn't you get on back to Ohio, nigger, if you gon' insult Honey like I got to knock off any short-pants punk you can hustle up here? Go on, now, get out. Get out, now, hear?" All Latham said was this was no trick, we were just going to use the phone because it was an emergency. Then Honey started prancing around and complaining quite loud about how it was her phone, and she didn't like Latham and some punk coming in interrupting her night, no matter what kind of emergency we thought it was. He called her a crazy-acting bitch whore that gave away more cunt than she got paid for. I thought she would kick us right out then, but she only laughed at him. When it got quieter, I called home, not bothering about collect, and my parents were just like I expected—very upset. My mother answered. "Oh, Bernie," she said, and her hand went over the mouthpiece. My father then got on yelling about where was my concern and consideration and when the hell was I going to grow up and how did I think he was supposed to teach me anything. He said I was lucky I got in at that moment because if I hadn't called right when the 1:32 out of the city pulled into Huntington he was going to phone the police.

So then I had to break the news that I was not at the train station, I was still in the city because I missed all the trains. I told him, "Really, I'm sorry, Dad, but I fell asleep watching TV," which I figured would arouse his sympathies because that is his common problem with the TV. His blood was boiling, though, and he said we'd discuss it tomorrow after he had the chance to come up with some drastic punishment for me. That didn't worry me too much. What could he do? He couldn't lock me in the house forever, and I know he wouldn't hit me or anything like that. Besides,

I really do not deserve any kind of punishment, drastic or otherwise, because it was not my fault for falling asleep. But I have to admit the old man's heavy hand is not the big thing on my mind right now. The big thing on my mind is what's sitting beside me on this vibrating train seat. I'm not looking at it. I'm looking out the window at the green-brown potato fields with sunlight streaming down over them and the white buildings far off. And of course the sunlight means something else, which is no rain, no sign of any either, and that means tennis for sure. Weathermen are jerks. It's very hard to learn not to rely on them, though, they're so confident and scientific.

For the whole damn train ride, I have been trying to work up some determination to at least play good, all-out, ballsy, smart tennis when the moment comes, because if you're an athlete, you know it truly helps to be mentally prepared for competition. You can have physical talent coming out your ass, but if you don't have that mental grip on things, forget it. But it's hopeless, my brain is out of control. Making it focus on one type of thought is easy as making a trapped bumblebee stay still in the jar. The main trouble is I feel like shit. I have this headache that's like John Henry pounding a spike into the back of my neck, and I am tired and sad, and I would love to take a shower.

Also, as I mentioned, there's this thing on the seat beside me—my good-luck piece. When we left Honey's, Latham seemed a bit sour. He was smoking, walking on fast, and not talking. After a couple minutes of that, I came out and asked what was eating him. I was just curious. Was it Honey or me or losing that sixty dollars or what?

"I'm *thinkin'*," he said.

"What about?" I said. He gave me this stare so I shut up. We kept on walking in silence until we got outside his grandparents' slum building. Then Latham straddled his legs over the stoop rail and sat on it. "What's you name, man?" he suddenly asked me. I was stopped on the sidewalk, looking up at the windows trying to pick out the one Winnie and I were gazing out of before. I was hoping to see her face looking down at me, but they were all dark and blank.

"Who, me?" I couldn't figure out why he was joking with me.

"Yeah, you," he said.

"My name is Mean Bernie," I said.

"Yeah? You the cat they call B?"

"Sometimes," I said.

"Shit, man, then you the cat they all talk about. You the cat ridin' a streak o' luck, right? Ain't you?"

"Well, maybe," I said. "You never know for sure. So far, anyway."

Then in a disgusted tone Latham said, "B, you dumb, crazy, simple-actin' mule. Like, I tell you fuck luck, and you ain't never gon' do that, I know that. So you gon' be lucky, man. I am gon' hand you a good-luck piece, see, and you gon' keep it, dig?"

"What is it?" I said.

"Good-luck piece, man. Ain't you listenin'?"

"Yeah, I'm listening," I said. "What good-luck piece?" I somehow knew it was going to be something more impressive than like a rabbit's foot, but I did not in a million years expect it to be what it was—a gun. It is in a brown paper bag beside me, looking like my lunch. But if you opened the bag, you would see a plain, small, silvery .22. It's just resting in there, like naked. He didn't wrap it or cover it with a piece of bread or anything.

I stood in the dark kitchen, trying to make out whether Winnie was asleep on the bed in the other room. Latham was rustling paper out from under the sink. He handed me the bag. I opened it, but I couldn't see anything. "What is it, a lucky rock?"

"You got eyes, man," he said.

I tilted the bag to the window light. "Jesus *Christ*," I whispered. It was a shock, like those puppies in the soup carton. "Is it real?" I knew it was real. "I mean, is it loaded?"

"Yeah," he said. "Five shots. That's all you got, dig? Five."

I said, "Well, Jesus. I don't need *any* shots. I mean, holy fuck, I can't—"

He suddenly grabbed me by the arm. Fiercely, he whispered, "You hear me, now. I don' want you shootin' the fucker with that piece, see? I don' want you shootin' nobody. But the fucker means to come at you with a blade, man, you know it. Shit, you only got to shoot the street one time. Then you stick it at his fuckin' face. Not his gut, see? You make him look down the fuckin' hole. Then you tell him *loud* if he don' turn and run his white ass to Washington, D.C., you gon' push his fuckin' brains halfway there, anyhow, see?"

"Yeah. Oh, Jesus, but what if he still tries to stab me?"

"Shit, man, I don' *care*, man. If the motherfucker is that mean an' crazy, you do what you want. But don' mess up his head. Shoot his gut, dig? Don' you go wastin' the mother on account o' me."

"Don't worry," I said.

Well, I knew I had to accept the gun. Shit, what gets me is I even wanted to accept the gun. I mean, Christ, I must've been nuts. There we were, having a regular conversation about me killing somebody or not killing somebody, and I was imagining aiming it, shooting it, hearing it bang, seeing the spurting blood, watching the prick writhe and shudder on the ground, and me standing over him with the silver instrument of death smoking in my numb hand.

All I did then was thank him in a quiet voice and fold the

bag shut. I carried it into the other room. Winnie wasn't on the bed. I plopped down on a mattress in the far corner instead of the bed because I didn't know if the bed was claimed by anybody, but Latham said to me go ahead and take the bed, so I did, and he stretched out on the mattress in his underwear. I set my good-luck piece on the floor, and I curled right up in my clothes because I would've felt funny in the nude, even under the blanket. I shut my eyes, and it was like stars and planets whirling behind my eyelids, the universe gone wild. The city sounds swarmed in over me for a long time. Latham snored. Just after I sank to sleep, I tensed awake all of a sudden because I felt the bed sag down behind me. It was Winnie.

"Hi," I whispered. She had a nightgown on. "Where do you sleep?"

"Right here," she whispered.

"*Here?*"

She went, "Shhh," and she lay next to me, smiling in the dark. I put my head down, looking into her eyes just like before, only she slid her face closer so we almost touched noses and I couldn't focus. I'm going to kiss her, I was thinking. There wasn't anything else to do but that. I tilted my head slowly back until our lips just came together like pillows. That's all of us that was touching. I could feel my heart in my ears. Just those two warm strips of us together, softly pushing, until her tongue came out between. Suddenly, I got a hard-on. Our tongues pressed into each other, and then she pulled back her head, looking wide and glowing at me, and just like that, she turned her back to me. I put my arm around her. We slept that way, snuggled to each other. My boner was pressing into her small ass half the night, and I shot finally in my sleep, I don't know when, dreaming that Winnie and I were lying just the same way only in the daytime, with our bathing suits off, in the sunshine, on the wooden ribs of the bottom of Lee's Thistle, and with my bone way inside of her like almost stuck, and I shot. I don't know if Winnie knew I did or not.

Her mother woke us up about seven in the morning, making noises in the kitchen. I sat up fast. I knew then I wasn't getting to school until after ten. I hated thinking how much it's going to upset Coach Nicely and the whole team when my name appears on the absent list. But what can you do? They'll be glad as hell when I show up. Latham kept on snoring while I waited for Winnie to get dressed to walk me to the subway. The sun was coming up low and bright. I told her I'd be OK on the train without her if she would just explain again about where I had to change for Penn Station. She never did ask me about my paper bag, so I figure she was listening to us last night. All she said was, while we were walking down the subway stairs, "Well, B, I think when you said that about how you just want to be careful and wait, well, you right about that, you know? 'Cause shit, like, anybody can be hurt, you know? Anybody can end up in some damn jail, or worse, if they ain't careful —you, me, Latham, *any*body."

"Yeah, but you can't worry about it. That gets you nowhere," I said, and right when I said it I was thinking how stupid a thing it was to say. I mean, God, I was worrying like a bastard. So was Latham, and Lee, and Barbara. And besides, if she didn't worry it would mean she didn't give two shits about me going to meet danger and fate and all that.

My subway train came roaring in then, before I had a chance to sort of improve the conversation we had gotten into. I don't know what I would've said, though. I went banging into the turnstile without first putting in my little token. I was holding it up pinched in my fingers like an idiot. Quickly, I fit it in the slot and pushed through. I backed up, looking at her and waving. "I'll write to you," I yelled out.

"You better," she shouted. " 'Bye! Take care!"

Boy, now I just can't stop remembering that amazing, very stimulating dream of us doing it in the Thistle, how clear the sky was, how you could feel the boat rock. It was full of details, that dream. Most dreams your mind comes up with hardly have any details, and you can forget the whole thing in ten minutes. But last night was like we really were doing it tight together that way in the sun. Maybe what's so real is that I really did shoot, which gives the thing a little life.

Anyway, thinking back on that amazing dream reminds me of Barbara because of the many fantasies I have had about putting it to Barbara outside somewhere, like in the tall grass or in the water. Barbara. Jesus, it's weird, but at this moment I feel so distant from Barbara, not like I don't love her or anything, but like, I mean, how can I ever talk to her about the latest events in my life? How can I even seriously discuss them with Lee? I can't. Of course, I know you don't go around feeding everybody your life story, even if they want to swallow it hook, line, and sinker, but, on the other hand, if you get a lot of things happening in your life that you can't disclose in a comfortable way to your friends, you feel like you don't really have any friends, if you know what I mean. You become isolated.

I last talked with Barbara on Tuesday, when I called her from Lee's house. She was in quite a happy mood because of the jolly, relaxing weekend she had at the family reunion. In a strange way it made me mad to hear that, because of how last Friday she was nothing but sad complaints about her weekend future of croquet with her old-bag aunts, how she would miss me, and how she would be so bored she would read *Seventeen* magazine all day under a tree. She hates *Seventeen* magazine. My weekend was a joy, too, I said, and I explained that Lee and Rocky and I drove around beer-drinking Friday night, knocking over garbage cans, and that we made a pact, Lee and I, to practice as hard as we could for Bay Shore, and that Richard showed up and flicked out his fucking new switchblade and said he wanted to cut an inch off my dick. Of course, that horrified her, which is what I wanted, but I could tell she liked hearing me talk that way to her, no holds barred, you know. I think she thinks it means we have kind of a mature relationship. In a way we do. I could never talk that way to any other girl, except Winnie. But Winnie isn't fazed by it. She talks that way herself. Barbara told me I was a dope for not calling the cops right after he sliced the net. "Are you kidding?" I said. "The cops wouldn't do anything. They would go to him and say, 'We have a report you cut the Bay Hills tennis court net,' and he would say, 'Oh yeah? Well, then somebody's a damn liar. I didn't do a thing all day.' And the cops would go away, and I'll give you three guesses where Rick the Prick would go." On the phone with her that night, I sort of shrugged off the incident by saying it really didn't upset me. I told her I had the feeling I could take care of myself if I had to. "I'll beat his brains out with my Jack Kramer, if that's what he wants. I could've done that on Sunday. I was tempted. Next time I just might give in to temptation," I said.

I stayed puffed up on that bullshit until the black rock smashed through my window that night and reminded me that Richard Linwood is a goddamn maniac, not just an ordinary, scary bully. And in school Wednesday I somehow couldn't get myself to relate the rock incident to Barbara. It wasn't like I didn't want to. Hell, on the bus to school it's all I thought about, what her deep sympathetic, wide-eyed reaction would be. I found her before homeroom, hanging out by her locker, but tall, dramatic Tommy Bauer was hanging out there, too, joking with her, and I realized I was mad at Barbara all over again for spending time with that flaming asshole when I had life-and-death concerns to discuss. I was about to just turn and walk the other way when she spotted me. "Well, good morning to you," she said in a happy voice.

And Tommy said, "Oh, Lord, here's another one who looks like he just rolled out of bed."

I said, "Up yours, gimp," and I went by them not even looking at Barbara.

"OK, sourpuss," she said. "I hope to catch you later. I *think*."

Without glancing back, I gave her a short wave with my tennis racket. Shit, I don't know. You would think that if you loved somebody, or if you just thought you loved somebody, you would always be able to show it. But I guess that's not how people work. Your emotions get pretty complicated sometimes, and you can't do a thing about it. For example this morning I *know* I could've pulled Winnie hard into my arms there in the goddamn subway tunnel, like a romantic movie love scene, and she would've let me. Probably, I even wanted to do it, but the thing is you hardly ever see anybody do passionate stuff like that in real life, and when you do it's just embarrassing, not romantic, which I guess is one reason the movies are so popular.

We just pulled into Syosset, and a man leaving the train brushed the side of my seat carrying his jacket, and this orange ballpoint popped out of his pocket onto my thigh, like it was a gift. I get up to chase after him with it, but when I go two steps I realize, Jesus, I'm leaving the bag alone on the damn seat where anybody could peek inside it, so I go back and sit down. I need a pen anyway. To see if it works, I prop my foot up on my knee and write, "BARBARA," in fancy, curling letters on the smooth, rubber bottom of my sneaker. Then I prop up my other foot, and I write, "WINONA," in bigger letters on the bottom of the other sneaker. Then I write "Ho Ho," and "Hobbes High," and "GO, Dolphins, GO," just to keep the two names from seeming too symbolic there on my opposite feet, and also the pen feels good skating on the worn rubber.

I'm the first one out at the station. I have my bag clamped under my arm. Since I'm about out of money, I have to walk to school, but it's only a mile through the projects. Little Negro kids are running all over the street like chipmunks. Pigeons hop and swoop here and there. This whole week poor L.R. has been diving out of his new attic coop down into the yard to poke around for the right-size twigs. It's spring, and the dumb bird is throwing some kind of nest together, I guess, only all he's got so far is this collection of sticks in there where he dumps them in the corner, not woven or anything. The encyclopedia says pigeons build nests with their mates, and they take turns sitting on the eggs and all. Maybe old L.R. thinks it's his wife's job to weave all the sticks into a neat little bed. You know, he's the only living thing in my whole existence that I can think about now without getting nervous or depressed. Well, all I can say is I would feel better if I could get rid of this headache. Luckily, Miss Spong, the school nurse, happens to like me (we once had a long talk about nutrition in which we both eagerly condemned the miserable school lunches), and even though she is very stingy with her aspirin, she will give me a couple. You have to count your blessings where you find them.

"*Are you all right?*" Coach Nicely asks me again in a hoarse whisper. Everybody's peering at me through the fence.

"*Yes*," I hiss back. I'm at the service line just looking across the net at Jeff Something, the Bay Shore guy, my opponent, who is a heavy-set asshole. He has not said one word to me the whole damn match, not even changing sides. He is waiting with his racket on his shoulder for Ollie to fetch one of our balls that Jeff just whacked over into the middle of one of Ollie's points.

"Are you *sure* you're all right?" says Coach Nicely.

"*Yes*, goddamn it," I yell. People's eyes turn towards me from the other side of the courts up by the road. I glance down. I have to admit it looks terrible. My right sweatsock is soaking in blood. Even my sneaker is red all down one side to the toe. Blood shakes out onto the court when I run. I breathe deep in and out and then walk back to the line. I bounce the ball a few times. I toss. My serve slices to his backhand. He floats it high to my backhand. I chop it back short. He comes in. I know what to look for, that chip he likes down the line. But he nets it. God, 40–5. I have to have this. *One point*. I have to have it. Now this ball is blood-speckled, too, dark red in the white fuzz. I serve a looper into the backhand again, and he floats it to my backhand again. Go up, I tell myself. I push it to his forehand corner, and I come in slow behind it. Another high job. Blow long, yeah, blow long. "No," I shout. They clap loud behind me. I don't look up. Jesus, I've *got* it, goddamn it, 8–6. A split. We're even. OK, he's making mistakes now. He won the first, 6–2, but I played like shit that set, and now he's nervous. I got momentum. I can do it. I know I can beat this peckerhead. Just keep doing what you been doing. Put it in the court. Keep it up, keep it up.

"*Bernie*," Coach Nicely says behind me. "Get out here so we can look at that."

Jeff, who really is a jerky-looking clodhopper in his blue Bay Shore shirt, is outside the gate saying something loud and fast to Coach Craig. I lean my racket against a net pole, and I walk past them along the rain gutter, trying not to limp. It's finally beginning to hurt. I catch them both glancing down at my foot. Jeff says, "Hey, are you quitting, or what?"

"Shit, no," I say. "I got five minutes, and I'm taking five minutes."

When I flop onto the grass bank, everybody rushes in around me, Lee, Eddie Burns, Paul Mannes, Coach Nicely with his first aid box, and Leslie, too, and a bunch of other faces that I don't feel like looking around to identify. To Lee I say, "You guys won, didn't you?"

"Take off that shoe," says Coach Nicely.

Lee says, "Yeah, yeah, we killed 'em. But Paulie got wiped, and Lawrence and Loebel are out there playing like total robots in the third set. They're down, four–one."

I peel off my sock. Down the outside of my ankle I have this bleeding gash two inches long. I can hardly stand to look at it.

"My God, give me that gauze," Coach says. "How in the name of God did you *do* this?"

"You mean you missed it?" I say. What happened was after I finally tied the set at six, I decided I was feeling this surge of second wind. I decided, for Christ's sake, I'm going to win this damn set. The thing is this Jeff character is a nothing-ball player, a very good lobber. He just stands back there and pops every shot up into the air four feet over the net. I kept pressing the first set, and he would pass me at the net, or else he would lob over me, and I would run back and then try to run up again. I was getting exhausted, and I was belting my volley too hard and spraying balls all over. But finally, when I got down 3–1 in the second set, I began doing what he was doing. I laid back on the baseline and blooped it back at him, fucking moonball, but it worked. He actually hit the ball out now and then, and if I could slip a good one deep, I'd come up, and he'd lob short, and *bam*, I'd cream it. But I was tired. I was dizzy. My headache was back knifing me again. I stayed with it, though, getting more confident. The more points he lost, the more he got nervous, and he started getting too careful. He started under-hitting. I caught him at 6-all, and I was thinking, OK, you got him, don't let him off. Run down every goddamn ball. That game I darted up behind a deep return to surprise him, and he lofted a lob I thought I could smash, but the wind took it. It was over my head. I tore back after it, and I reached it on the bounce just before it reached the fence. I had no play, I was moving too fast. I skidded in a patch of sand out of control, and my right foot shot under the thick, meshed wire. Jerking it out again is what did it. Some sharp end dug in over my sock, and gouged out a fat piece of skin and hair that stayed wadded up on the end of the wire like a berry. The blood came fast. I rolled down my sock and sat there looking into my gash like it was a canyon. It had little walls. Blood was oozing into my sneaker. Because as usual, the other fans were oooing at Big Ollie, Lee and Eddie were the only ones who saw me slam into the fence. They were too far back, though, to right away get a load of the gruesome results. I was thinking, well, my sock is like a bandage, that's all I need. I never considered default-ing until Lee came up to the fence after I won that game and whispered, "Are you fucking *nuts*? You're bleeding like fucking Niagara Falls."

I said, "I know, but it doesn't hurt that much. I'm OK."

"Jesus Christ, you're fucking nuts. You're gonna pass out."

"I'm OK." I hopped up and down to show him. Then, when we passed changing sides, jerky Jeff looked me hard in the face. I looked at the hairs coming out the neck of his shirt. It obviously was getting to him, though, the way he played that last game. He couldn't keep the ball in the court. A few people caught on to the real drama and hurried to my match in a bunch.

The cut really isn't too bad, now that I'm making myself inspect it. The gobs of blood is what makes it look so grim. It's deep, though. Leslie got one glimpse and backed off to ogle Big Ollie. I cannot for the life of me figure out why she's here. Beautiful Cindy O'Halloran is clinging like a delicate, blond spider to the fencing behind Ollie's court, clapping and saying bright little phrases to him when he goes back after a ball. He grins at her.

"What's taking Ollie so long?" I ask Lee. He's holding down this thick patch of gauze while Coach passes the adhesive tape round and round my ankle.

"I don't know. That Randall's pretty good, I guess. Better than last year."

A voice says, "Ollie's up in the second. It's almost over."

Coach says, "Somebody run and get Bernie another sweatsock. Somebody must have another sweatsock. How does that feel, now?"

"Good," I say. "Is there any water?"

"Here's an orange." Eddie hands me one cut-up. It's delicious.

A storm of clapping bursts out around us. Ollie took him. Craning my neck to see through the swarm of fans, I get a picture of him shaking hands with Randall. They smile at each other. Cindy's the first one to him, throwing her arms around his neck from the side. I scan the crowd for Leslie, but she must've left. I feel awful for her, though God, what did she expect? I found out today at lunch that she's going to the prom after all—with Bingo Wright, who is the crazy-ass best friend of Rodney Lippett, Pam Sokel's boyfriend, and you could figure out who set that one up if you had an I.Q. of 2. Of course, by now she knows all about Cindy, so why she parked her sweet can up here all afternoon is a mystery to me. As Lee would say, the girl has toys in her attic.

Nicely's down there patting Ollie on the shoulder—the one Cindy's not draped over—and Ollie's laughing loud at whatever Randall just said to him. He must be an OK guy, that Randall.

Lee went to get me another orange before they're all gone, and now here comes Paulie Mannes with a bunch of socks. He's out of breath. "*Here*," he says. They rain down. "I got plenty in case you need to change 'em again."

"Thanks, Paulie. Hope your mother doesn't care if I bleed all over 'em." Already the red is seeping through my pure white bandage.

"Oh, God," he says. "Don't worry about that. You just have to win, that's all. Look, it's up to you now, the whole match, everything. Lee and Eddie won. Ollie won. But I choked bad, and now Vic and Cake are biting the radish down there, they look so nervous. God, I was nervous. So now you got to win, Bernie, or, you know."

"Or I lose," I say. "If I don't win, I lose. Big fucking deal." I know it's up to me now, for Christ's sake, and I can't stand frantic little Paulie dropping it on me like it's either win or get burned at the stake. I pull on the socks and start tying my sneakers.

Paulie stands there with his mouth slightly open. "Here comes Ollie and those guys," he says, but I've already caught the shadows sliding to me over the grass. I glance up. Against the sun, their faces are blurred and dark like a bunch of coconuts. Old Jeff is already out there bouncing a ball with his racket. I get to my feet.

"Whoa," says Ollie, "I want to see this famous ankle."

"Too late. All wrapped up. Do not open until Christmas."

Paulie says, "He got it stuck under the fence."

I say, "See ya later." Actually, I don't want to see any of them at all. I want to get out there, finish off that tub of lard, and go home. I don't want to talk to anybody or even look anybody in the face, I don't care who. Not Barbara, not anybody. Ollie holds his rackets out in front of me like that turnstile in the subway.

"Hey, hey, hold it a minute," he says. "That ape's not going anywhere. You been hurt. You got injury time coming." I stop. I think, holy shit, where's my racket? Then I remember I left it on the court. Ollie says, "You know, I once heard of a guy playing golf in Georgia that went into the swamp hunting a ball and got bit by an alligator. And you know, Christ, that's what sprang into my head soon as I heard all this gasping, and I looked over at your gory foot, and I said, Jesus God, where's the alligator?"

Everybody laughs except me. Cindy hugs his arm. It's the most words I have ever heard Ollie Griggs speak all at once that aren't part of some ceremonial speech.

I say, "Yeah, well I'm good as new now." It aches. It's like I have on one high workshoe laced too tight.

Ollie says, "Christ, I hope not. From what I could see, soon as you got hurt you were a wildman out there, a true wildman."

I'm thinking, well, you didn't see much then, asshole. I started whipping that pecker way before I hit the fence. It's insane, what you have to go through to get a little attention. Wait, why am I so riled? Everybody is a dumb jerk but me, that's why. Coach Nicely reaches around to put his hand on the back of my neck. I shake it off. "I'm going, I'm going," I say.

"We're all with you, Bernie," he says. "Keep forcing him. Keep thinking."

"Stick him, Bernie," somebody growls out.

Ollie says, "Man, you're doin' great. Don't let up on him for one damn point, or I'll come out there, and I swear I'll cut your other ankle."

"You try it, and I'll put a bullet through your alligator

gut," I say. Everybody laughs. They break apart to let me through. Lee trots down behind me. "Where have *you* been?"

"Getting oranges, what do you think? I went down to the cafeteria. But they're all gone."

"Yeah? So what good *are* you, then?"

"Well, fuck. They're gone. What do you want from me? Blood?"

"OK, get some water in a can, then. Get something. Use that noodle." That's my father's expression from years ago, "Use that noodle."

"Oh, aye-*aye*, sir," he says.

I step onto the court. Jeff is eyeing me from the other side. He's angry. Good. Craig is positioned behind the fence in his blue windbreaker.

"Hey," says Lee. I turn to him. "Listen, you pound that big turdball, OK?"

"OK," I say. The spectators are clustering all around for the big finale. Well, shit, there she is, Leslie. I can tell her at a glance by her permanent, though it's not as perky as it was when she first got it. Maybe what happened is she changed from an Ollie fan to a tennis fan. Or maybe her heart is shattered, and she's planning to go nuts on Cindy at the first golden opportunity, tear her hair out. Rip out her blue eyeballs.

"Starting right in," Jeff calls out.

What else is new? I nod to him, the go-ahead. He spins a serve soft to my forehand, a new tactic. I returned it high and hard over the middle, and I stand there watching it sail. Jesus, it must've just caught the line because he plays it. It arcs back into the far corner. I get there late, thinking, lob, lob, but I try slicing it down the line instead. Three feet wide. Idiot. What did you try that shit for? Easy, easy—boy, am I keyed up.

The next serve curves to my backhand. I slice it into the net. Jesus. The same stupid, fucking shot. Get it *up*.

He serves into my forehand again. Christ, trying to keep me wide, trying to move me around on my bad ankle, the prick. I bang it to his backhand and come in. I look for the cute little lob, but he tries passing across. One step, boom, I volley hard, out of reach. Loud clapping. Damn, that's *it*. You got to move.

I try to follow in the next return, but it hits the top of the net and rolls back to my feet. I kick it. The ball skitters off to the empty nearby court.

"Got two," Jeff sings out. He's rushing me, the bastard, and talking now, too.

"Score?" I say.

"Forty–fifteen," he says.

OK. Two points, that's all. Play easy. Put it back. Don't be so anxious. Don't get overaggressive. Backhand this time. I try to float it, but it's way long. *Stupid*. Four shitty backhands. The Bay Shore guys clap. I suck, that's the answer. I suck. But hell, so what if I lose his serve? Christ, I just gotta stop thinking and start playing.

Changing sides, I hear some guy yell, "Come on, Bernie." I glance at the crowd, and God, a mass of red hair. I look again. It's some girl from field hockey team practice. She has those shin guards on. The way her red head's cocked she gives a sort of sassy impression like Barbara a little, but shit, fat chance old Roxane would show her face out here, especially in the shape it's in right now. I ambled down to the auditorium after school to see if somehow she might shake free to watch maybe just *some* of the big match if I promised her a slice of team orange, but they were having the first big dress rehearsal. I waited for five minutes outside the girls' dressing room, counting the perforations in the acoustical ceiling tiles before somebody told me she was over in the make-up room getting slapped with greasepaint. She looked awful. All her freckles were blotted out with thick pink powder like chalk, and her smooth lips glistened beet-red and waxy, and her faint, pretty lashes were like tarred over. I stood behind her, watching her face in the mirror for a minute before she noticed me. "Bernie! I thought you were playing tennis. How do I look?"

"Like a clown," I said.

"Oh. Well, how sweet of you to say so."

"I'm sure it's perfect for the stage," I said. "But close-up it sort of bowls you over. I mean, you look like it's not you."

"Well, it *isn't* me," she said. "It's lovely Roxane, can't you tell?"

"Oh, yeah. *Roxie!* Hey, long time no see."

"Ages," she said.

Obviously, I couldn't really talk to her, so when she started giving more directions to the make-up girl, Audrey Nash, about what to smear on next, I just sidled out. I was late as it was. Now I'm thinking, hell, what do I care who's behind the fence, gawking, cheering, groaning, watching me transform myself into the hero or the goat? The damn balls either go in or out. What difference does it make? Win some, lose some, right? I mean, you can stick Barbara out there, or Winnie and Latham, or my mother and father, or Fidel Castro and J.F.K., and then ask me if I give a luke-warm shit. Go on, ask me.

I'm up 30–love. The first serve I just belted, and he muffed it off the end of his racket. The next he knocked back to my forehand, and we looped it back and forth maybe ten times before I came up and he sent it long, trying to hit through me.

Clapping. Lee yells, "Way to *go!*" My foot throbs, but that's all. How weird. I hit it. He hits it. I hit it. My body's covering ground like a dumb rabbit, flowing, stretching, hopping, but now it's like I'm somehow sitting inside at the rabbit controls, all breathless and sweating, a part of me anyway. And another part of me is above it all, drifting like a buzzard or the full moon, sailing on a fast, invisible stream of thoughts, waiting for the outcome—win, lose, anything—who cares?

It makes hardly any bang at all, a *poomf*, and the beer can spins in the sand.

Lee says, "Look! The damn thing didn't even put a hole in it. Just a dent."

"Well, what do you expect? Shit, it's no Colt .45."

"Yeah, but you don't need any Colt .45 to shoot a hole in a fucking tin can." That's what we're drinking, the remains of Rocky's Colt .45. Lee tosses me the can.

There's a bright metal scar along the seam. "Well, Jesus, I just creased it, that's why. You gotta hit it head-on if you want to ventilate it."

Lee takes a big guzzle. He coughs. "Yeah, well—" He coughs again. "Well, you just better hope you don't just crease *him*, or he's gonna ventilate *you* real good with that old wop toothpick."

I put the little gun back in the cigar box. Dutch Masters. "You don't listen, do you? He gave me this just so I could scare the prick with it, if I have to. I'm not supposed to shoot anybody, and I'm not gonna shoot anybody."

"Oh, yeah? Then take the bullets out. If you're not gonna blast him, you don't need bullets."

"I need bullets to scare him, asshole. The thing isn't gonna scare him if it goes *click click*."

Lee sighs and sits down on the rock. He mumbles something. I look at his face.

"What?" I say.

"I said, it scares *me*."

That's a surprise. Lee rarely admits anything actually scares him. "What?"

"This whole gun bullshit. I mean, sure, I think somehow you got to get the cocksucker off your back, but shit, a twenty-two, I don't know. Why can't you get him with a slingshot?"

I drink from my can. "Bridgman, your head's up your ass, and you know it. Tell me I'm gonna scare him with a slingshot. How about a squirt gun?"

Lee spits. "It's dangerous. That's all I'm saying."

"Shit, I know what I'm doing. I told you, I'm not shooting anybody. Jesus Christ, you're the man that kept asking, 'What are you gonna do? What are you gonna do?' and now when I tell you what the fuck I'm gonna do, you say, 'Gee, I don't know. It sounds dangerous.' Of course it's dangerous. Getting black rocks thrown through your window is dangerous, too. Everything is dangerous. I'm trying to fight danger with danger, see? And now you want me to sit back some more, pissing in my drawers."

"No, I just want you to be able to piss in your drawers, OK? Listen, tell me this. Let's say you do get the crazy prick down here, OK? I don't know how, but let's say you get him here, and you pull out the gun, and you tell him to fuck off, right? And he just laughs at you, and he's got his fucking knife out. You blast the sand, but he still comes at you. He wants that inch of pecker, and he doesn't care what's in the way. Now what, Big Bernie?"

"I shoot him, that's what." Just saying it sends like a surge of power through me. I take a deep breath.

"*What?*"

"I shoot his foot. You think I should let him slice my pecker?"

"His *foot?* You can't hit a fucking tin can two feet away."

"All right, so I lay it in his fat stomach, how's that?"

"Crazy. You're a crazy fucking moron. You lose, no matter what. Say he does back off. Say he doesn't come at you. You really think it's all over? No, jerk-off. If he comes here, you'll just have to shoot him. And when you get out of jail, he'll kill you."

"Nope, you're wrong. Soon as I show him he can't fuck with me any more it's over. *Over*, get it? And I won't have to shoot the fucking gun. I just gotta act like I will. Don't worry. It'll work."

Lee throws his empty toward the water. We're sitting above the high-tide line out of the moonlight in a group of locust trees. Nobody comes here even in the daytime because the beach is rocky, and the water drops off deep into the boat channel.

"Boy," Lee says after a while. "I just wish I knew where you all of a sudden got the balls to make up plans like this. It must've been your courageous tennis match or some shit, I don't know. I think you're nuts, though. I'll tell you that." He straightens up and walks over to take a leak against a tree trunk.

It makes me smile to watch him and hear him act so concerned, my best friend. I also smile because, shit, how do I really know what I'm going to do? I'm talking through my hat, as my father says. I mean, in a horrible way, it's bold and inspiring to say you really mean to plug some bastard with hot lead. So what if you secretly think you could never do it without being off your rocker? Of course, you have to wonder about soldiers. If you were a soldier, you would riddle some screaming, yellow Jap without thinking twice. I don't know. I guess in the right circumstances I probably would shoot Richard. So would Lee or anybody else. It makes me feel manly to think this way, like Matt Dillon, you know, with his back to the wall. What's left then but—*blam*? Justice is done. So hell, not even Richard would gamble I was too chicken to pull the trigger. At least I don't think he would.

Lee's right about one thing. It was the tennis match this afternoon that gave me this attitude of bravery. Being the hero was just about the most wonderful feeling I have ever experienced. They carried me on their shoulders and sprayed Coke on me and threw me in the shower. Coach Craig even walked down into the locker room to congratulate me afterwards. "That was smart tennis you played out there," he said. I suppose he's right, but really I never did decide, OK, now I'm going to play smart tennis. I just stayed in control, knocking the ball back to him until he would blow it. He was quite nervous, and halfway through the third set, after he flipped a lob way out, when I heard his racket clatter across the court, I knew I had him. He was upset. Before every point I would look down at my bloody sock, and it was like there was the reason I was going to win—because, if you know what I mean, it was also the perfect excuse for losing. It meant I didn't have to worry about losing like I always do in every other goddamn match I play. If I lost, what the hell, they would all know why. Usually, when I get a little behind, I start thinking, Christ, I'm blowing it, I'm choking. And then I say to myself, don't think that way, you shithead. Concentrate. If you concentrate, you *won't* lose. But then I can't concentrate. It's like when you're reading a book, if you think, I am reading this book, then you're *not* reading the book. The applause and yelling helped, too, of course. And, sure, jerky Jeff did choke, the poor turdball, but I was great. I can't deny it, I was great.

Though to me my cut didn't look that bad (it's only real deep in one small part of it, where I really got jabbed), Coach Nicely insisted I had to see a doctor, so we drove into town in his car, Lee, the old peckerhead, and I, and we went to this German doctor with a long name that he knew in the medical center. And, what do you know, I got three stitches with this curved needle and this real thread, and it hurt like a bastard. It still hurts. Somehow, I never thought you got stitches that way, I don't know why. It was just like sewing. They tug the damn needle right through your skin. Whew, I shudder just thinking about it. So I have a thick bandage on my ankle, and I'm not supposed to walk much or bend it much, but hell, we *had* to celebrate the big victory, which is what we're doing. And I really did want to show Lee the gun, not that he was all that impressed. I thought he would want to shoot it too.

Another thing good about being a hero was that my parents really couldn't blow up at me for falling asleep in the city last night. They were proud of me in my moment of glory, and also they were quite sympathetic about my ankle. When I told my mother I was sleeping over at Lee's tonight, she smilingly shook her head at me like she knows it's no use to stand in my way. I'll do what I want anyway.

Lee has been walking slowly along the edge of the lapping water with his hands in his pockets, and now he comes back into the trees where we have all the beer dug up out of our hole. He opens another one and sits down. He says, "Let me see that thing again."

I hand him the cigar box.

He slips the rubber band and lifts up the lid. "Too bad you don't have a holster, you know, like a shoulder holster. You can't carry this dumb box around until the prick makes his move."

I say, "Shit, I'm not that crazy. I already told you I'm leaving it here. I'm gonna bury it in the hole, and if I ever need it, I'll come dig it up, and *blam blam*, that'll be one less mean, ugly cripple on God's green earth."

Lee forces a laugh. "Jesus, you'll never use this thing. It's just a good-luck piece like you said. I can just see you when the prick comes by the courts again in his Chevy, and you say, 'Oh, wait a minute. I have to go get my cigar box.'"

"No, no," I say. "See, that's where you come in. I'll be waiting right here for him. And you go tell Richard where I am, see? You tell him I want to see him about a little problem we been having."

"Fuck *that*, man. Fuck that. That is where I *don't* come in. I don't come in *at all*. Not with guns and that shit. Fuck that."

I say, "Yeah, I knew you'd squirm out somehow."

"Well, fuck you. I'm not squirming out of anything because I was never *in* anything to begin with, OK? And I'm not getting in, either."

Well, shit. Of course I know he *was* in it, but obviously, for reasons of personal safety, he does not feel like remembering. Back when the prick was sort of harmlessly just chucking rocks at us, Lee was all hot on some plan of revenge. But what's the use of reminding him of that? "OK, OK, you pansy. I don't care. That was my plan. But forget it. He would never come down here anyway."

"Yeah, well maybe you can play clutch tennis, but you can also sure come up with some shitbrain ideas, that's all I can say. All you're gonna end up doing with this fucking pop-gun is blasting cans."

I say, "I hope so," and I like how it sounds, so I say it again in a lower tone, "I hope so."

We bury the cigar box and the four cans of beer we have left and this time we mark the spot with a piece of red plastic from some kid's broken sand bucket. We've got to get back to Lee's before his mother calls my mother to see where we are. Lee points up at a set of tiny red-and-white lights angling in between the stars—a silent plane.

"Where do you think it's going?" he asks me.

"I don't know. London. The polar route. Stockholm.

Where do you think?"

"Spain," he says.

I look back up at it. When you think about it, it's weird that up there's that like metal tube with wings and windows and seats and the people inside eating and reading, high high up in the black atmosphere, all alone and zooming, with everybody worrying if the damn thing'll make it all the way to London or Spain or else conk out and whistle down like a bomb into the ocean. "Why Spain?" I say.

"Why not? They got a lot of beautiful ladies in Spain, those flamingo dancers. Really, it's some country. I'm going there when I get out of school." Lee takes Spanish.

We trudge along in the sand. I limp a bit. I can hardly believe I played a whole set of tennis with my wound, the way it aches now. I was a demon out there. I wonder if Barbara heard about it yet, but probably she hasn't. Not knowing how our tennis matches come out doesn't exactly throw her into a frenzy of anxiety. Sure, she cares. She cares because I care, but to her, like she once said, "Tennis is just a sport, something you do for fun. It is not creative," which I suppose meant it is not art. She gets all cranked up over art. So, although I did seriously consider calling her up with the news of triumph, you can see why I thought, well, the hell with her. If she wants the news, she can call me for it. The phone rang twice during dinner, and God, I was hoping it was her. The first time it was for Claudia, and the second time it was Lee. Now I think what am I doing with Barbara for my girlfriend anyway? Why don't I have somebody like Cindy O'Halloran? Barbara is so wrapped up in her life she pays attention to me only when I somehow squeeze myself into it. And the thing is, I care about *her* deep passions. For example, take acting. I love plays. For many years I would always get the big parts in whatever my elementary school class was putting on, like Hansel in *Hansel and Gretel*. I started way back in the first grade when we had a fruits and vegetables review, which was about why it's important to eat the right foods. It was all in rhyme, and everybody was some kind of fruit or vegetable. I was Calvin Carrot and also the narrator, with a microphone backstage so I could introduce the foods. When all the parents were out sitting in the folding chairs watching the performance, I remember how poor little Donna Stevenson, who had crossed eyes, was so nervous. She was Lily Lemon. I introduced her twice, but she just shivered there next to my microphone in her yellow cardboard lemon suit like it was winter. She wouldn't budge. Finally, a couple of the vegetables shoved her out there past the curtains, and what she did then was pee. She peed down her leg. Boy, we thought that was hilarious. For three years afterwards, you could make Donna Stevenson cry by just mentioning Lily Lemon juice.

We're on the road going slowly up hill past the quiet houses. The moon's gone behind a pack of inky clouds. Barbara and I were supposed to hit the ball around tomorrow, but that's rain coming for sure, subtle as an anvil. I can't play anyway, not for at least a week, the doctor said, so I'm thinking we'll maybe find some place to make out. Besides, tennis is mostly just a good reason for us to get together. Even if you have a mature relationship with a girl, you can't just come out and say, "Well, how about if we go to the park tomorrow and make out?"

"The moon's disappeared," I say.

"Yeah. So's that plane."

"That was no plane," I say. "That was a flying saucer."

"Oh, God," he says.

"You can't deny it's a possibility," I say.

"I can deny whatever the fuck I feel like," he says.

I don't know why I brought up flying saucers. It's our old argument. Lee says flying saucers are a lot of bullshit, and he hates it when I say he's just being ignorant and stubborn and narrow-minded. I believe in flying saucers something fierce, but I have not yet seen one that I know of. Still, I often wish a flying saucer would drop down humming and take me for a little buzz around the solar system. What an adventure.

"Well," I say, "I guess you're right about that gun. You can have it, in fact. I'm never gonna use it for anything."

Lee stops walking. "How come?"

"Because I think that flying saucer is turning around and coming to get me. I'm going away for a few years."

"Shove it, will ya?" He heads on up the road.

"Really. So, you can have the gun. Old Richard's probably gonna switch over onto you, anyway, soon as I take off."

Lee says, "You're a real asshole, Hergruter, you know that?"

I laugh and swipe him across the back of his hair with my fingertips.

CHAPTER

GODDAMN, IF IT ISN'T prom night, the big jerk-off event of the whole high school social year. Thanks to Operation Rollaway, Lee and I are hunched down in his mother's Valiant in the huge parking lot of Aliperti's Gas House, where the prom is coming to life like this sadly joking imitation of those fairytale marble-room palace balls. Lee has binoculars, but you can't see much, except under the drive-in archway, which has blazing yellow lights trained down into it like Hollywood. It's quite funny. What happens is, say old Joe Blow, that you have always known as this dipshit who carries a Winston behind his ear all day and farts in the library, cruises in between those pillars in his father's Pontiac that's a million feet long, and he gets out with this egg-white prom jacket on and black pants and a colored waistband and a bowtie, and he goes around to yank open the door for old Sally Twotits, the oily-skinned, friendly clunk of a girl that you know because she sells ice cream bars on the lunch line and because her main claim to fame is a set of ba-zooms like blimps, which she hangs down over the freezer while she bends in for your Heath Bar and which you try to glimpse through her collar, but you can't see anything because they go on forever into a frazzly white bra, and she has on this shining, pale pink dress down to the ground and a sort of short cape and long white gloves. They parade into Aliperti's along this gold carpet that's lined with blue, flaming lanterns, and they turn the corner into the lobby, where you can make out other couples milling around like a herd of some weird pastel-colored animals. And a Negro guy hops into their Pontiac and zooms it out into the dark parking lot.

Well, this jazz has been going on for about twenty minutes now and still Rodney Lippett's Falcon and Bingo Wright's dad's bomb, whatever it is, have both not shown up, though a while ago Ollie and Cindy tooled in, snuggled together in his Porsche like she had just been giving him a hand job, according to Lee. I said, "Boy, I wouldn't put it past her."

Lee said, "Shit, I'd put it right in her little pink fingers." That Lee, he's more sex-minded than I am.

Cindy's bright red gown matched Ollie's bowtie and ruffled waistband so that they looked like some kind of team. Actually, it was nice to see a couple in love being thoughtful like that, but it was also a little ridiculous.

Ridiculous is Barbara's word for the prom in general. Today in the park I asked her if she would somewhere deep inside her someday maybe truly want to go to some prom, you know, in fancy duds and with a flower pinned on and all that.

She said, "You *must* be kidding."

"C'mon," I said. "Really. Say if next year I asked you to the goddamn prom, and I was going to wear one of those jackets and that crap, what would you say?"

"I'd say stick it in your ear."

"Really? You would?" Even though of course I did not actually ask her to any prom, it hurt me a little that she would say to stick it in my ear.

"Yes, cutie, but you wouldn't ask me because you would be aware that I think proms are boring and a ridiculous waste of time and money."

"You *could* change your mind," I said. "Like out of curiosity. Besides, proms are a fact of life. They are something everybody should experience, just like a football game or a play."

"They're *phony*," said Barbara. "And when you are aware of what's phony, you don't change your mind."

We were sitting way up the long slope in the tall, soft grass, with our backs against the brick wall of the Old First Church basement. Down below there were wisps of steam rising off the park courts into the sun, and in the field was a firemen's softball team taking batting practice. Last night it rained like mad for hours, and at midnight when it suddenly opened up, I pictured my father surging up out of bed to get the windows shut. We have these tall, swiveling windows that you have to slowly crank into the position you want, and it's a pain in the ass to get them shut in a storm, when you're half-asleep with the rain spraying in on your naked arms. Without me home, I know it must've taken the old man twice as long. Lee's windows slide smoothly down.

Today it was hot and beautiful, like summer. We had our rackets with us, but I knew the courts would be full of puddles like a slice of Swiss cheese, so I didn't have to back out because of my wound. I told Barbara and her mother and father the story of the great match while they were having coffee and bagels, which I didn't want, and they thought it was wonderful and that I was, as Mr. Holland said, "a man of real determination." Barbara shoved back her chair, hopped over to my side, said with a sigh, "My *hero*," and kissed my cheek. I said, "And don't you forget it." Mr. Holland said, "Bernie, are you telling me, with that gash you've got freshly stitched, you intend now to go run on it?" I smiled at Barbara. "Well, I guess I can hobble some," I said. But we went straight to our usual make-out place, the tall grass behind the church. If you lie down in it, nobody can see you, and you can hear anybody coming up the hill way before they could get close enough to gasp and gape. She was wearing her sleeveless white tennis top that gives brief shots of the sides of her jugs through the armholes and very short shorts that had me sneaking peeks for stray gold snatch hairs, which can often poke out around some girls' panties. I was aroused, and I wanted to move into the heavy action fast, but Barbara was being reserved, like she was saying, "Oh, we'll make out, I suppose, but only when I get good and ready." So I nonchalantly stretched out, giving her a good view of my fat boner, if she was interested. I was not about to get grabby. Of course, some girls respond very eagerly to grabbiness, but Barbara is not that type. She's the bide-your-time type. We discussed things, like how it was so hot you could probably almost swim, and how I hoped I'd be back in the line-up before we meet Bay Shore again, and schoolwork and so on, and it was obvious she had some more important subject she was holding back on. I wanted to say, "Come on, Barb, spit it out." But I knew she'd come back with, "Spit out what?" and clam right up. So I became a little argumentative, to liven things up, which is why we got into that prom business, because hell, it's not like her attitude about proms is some big secret. I didn't have to bring it up. "Phony," I said. "Well, I'm glad you told me. I guess the Thespian Society isn't phony."

"Give up, will you?" She threw me this look of pain.

"No, Barb, it's just that I honestly think you miss out if

you don't try everything. It doesn't have to be phony for everybody."

"Oh, God. Will you hand me a shovel? This is getting pretty deep."

"Well, then, I guess if I ever decided I *did* want to be a part of my once-in-a-lifetime senior prom, I would have to ask some other raving beauty, wouldn't I?"

"You're damn right, smartass. Like say, Leslie Wolstein?"

"What? She's going *this* year."

"Oh, you think I'm so naïve, don't you, you rotten two-timer. I bet you honestly thought I would never find out, didn't you? Hunh?"

"No. I mean, find out what? I mean, I thought you found out already, you know, from your letter when I was in Cleveland. You called her my faithful yak."

"Well, Christ, of course I *knew* she had that disgusting crush on you, and she used to drool after you in the halls, but I didn't find out all the ugly rest of it till yesterday."

"OK, so what did you find out?"

"Everything."

"What's 'everything'?"

"You make me retch."

"Great. Are you gonna throw up right now, or are you gonna tell me what you found out?"

"Why should I? You wouldn't tell *me*, you sneaky two-timer. I found out that you and that fat-ass cow made *love*."

I just shook my head. I said, "Well, if that's what you want to call it."

"*Did* you?"

"I guess so. Sort of. It wasn't Romeo and Juliet, I'll tell you that."

She jerked herself away from the brick and slammed her shoulders down into the grass. "*Ooooh*," she breathed out. "I swear to God you make me retch."

It seemed weird to me and also confusing to see Barbara ferociously squeezing shut her eyes, all worked up about that awful night at Hendricks's, when all along I figured she not only knew the sordid details but she was a bit tantalized by the whole episode. I could not have been more wrong. Then I realized that, in a way, it was flattering to me that she was so jealous—even if it was mostly an act, like I started thinking it was. I mean, to go from her kissing my cheek and calling me her *hero* an hour before to her all of a sudden getting ready to retch over my rottenness was a little suspicious, you have to admit. I'm not saying she shouldn't have been jealous, don't get me wrong. She's the jealous type, I have always known, but somehow that letter threw me off. Then I asked her, "Who'd you find out from?"

"Ho, *boy*," she cried. "You sound like you really believe I would tell you."

"Well, OK, why won't you?"

"It makes no damn difference, that's why. Half the lamebrain school could have told me how you left your *scumbag* in the Hendrickses' bed, and also how you—"

"That's *bull*! It was just the wrapper, the foil wrapper, and she was the last one out, not me."

"Just the *wrapper*! Christ! Oh, Christ, you are an idiot. It's just like a stupid idiot like you to blame your stupidity on someone else, too."

"Yeah, go ahead," I said. "You can go calling me an idiot. But I know the facts. The real idiot is whoever you got that story from, and it probably wouldn't take me too long to guess who it was either."

Barbara sat up, red in the face. "Well, then, idiot. How about you giving me the facts, then, if you're so knowledgeable?"

"I thought you already heard everything." Actually, I was quite startled that she would want to have me relate the facts to her. It didn't seem like the kind of story you tell your girlfriend on a beautiful, sunny day.

"Well, apparently, I missed a few things here and there. Why don't you fill me in?"

I knew what Lee would say to that, but I wasn't about to risk it. "They're not pretty," I said.

"Right now I can't think of anything about you I would call pretty. Except, you are pretty rotten."

"How generous of you," I said. I was sitting up with my chin on my knees, gazing at my sneakers. Then I had an idea. "OK, I'll give you the facts, but not until you look at this." I held my foot out to her. "See?"

"What? Your battle scar?"

"No. On the bottom. Read it."

She was quiet for a few seconds.

I said, "Well?"

She said, "OK, so my name is written on your shoe. So what?"

"So who wrote it there? Me. I was thinking about *you*, my girlfriend, while I was on the train yesterday, and I just wanted to see your name, so I wrote it."

"Well, what does that prove?"

"It proves I missed you. It proves I don't do much without thinking about you, even if I haven't seen you for days and days."

She sighed and turned over on her stomach.

"Well?" I said again.

"Well, that's nice," she said. "But it doesn't make you any less rotten. Now give me the facts. Nothing but the facts."

So I did. I related to Barbara the story of my first I.I. basically the same as I told it to Lee, only toned down a little when it came to the specific details about how excited I was, and I did not reveal that I shot in the rubber even before I stuck my rod into her box. In fact, I didn't mention shooting or anything like that. I made the whole event sound as ordinary as I could, which wasn't easy, seeing as how just thinking back on it made my hard-on swell under my shorts like a mole tunnel in the lawn. Also, while I talked on and on, I could not unglue my eyes from the two perfect domes of her nates, rising up right out of the middle of her flat body like fresh bakery goods. When I finally finished with the part concerning my thrilling escape, she rolled over onto her back again, faintly smiling, and before you could say Old First Presbyterian Church, we were feverishly making out. I mean we crashed together like cymbals. It was amazing. Immediately, my hand slipped under the back of her tennis shirt. I pinched her bra clasp together, and it sprang open just like that. We were kissing madly, eyes, ears, noses, the works. My one hand was rubbing up and down her backbone and the other I had against the side of her head to smooth her face where I wasn't kissing. Her hands were under my shirt going all over my back, up to my shoulders, down to my ass, squeezing hard and pressing. When I edged down to kiss her throat and her collar bone, she roughly began pulling my shirt off over my head. I had to get my arms free so she wouldn't tear the shirt. She threw it off in the grass. Then in a quick motion she peeled her flimsy shirt off, and Jesus God, her creamy jugs bounced out of her loose bra into the sun. I have never before been so aroused as I was then. Because of her nipples. She has these unbelievable, fantastic nipples, all rosy and bright and *big*, like round doorbells, with the middle part rising up like a fat little button. My mouth went right for one like a fish going after a bug, and I swirled my tongue around it and all, and that got her writhing and saying, "Bernie-Bernie-Bernie-Bernie," like that day on her porch. My bone was throbbing. Don't *shoot*, I kept telling myself. Think about coffee and bagels. I attempted to keep my very touchy boner off her bare thigh while she was at the same time pushing up into it and moaning. I concentrated hard on the faraway pain in my ankle, and I even thought about Winnie, how I hated leaving her so suddenly, how I might never see her again—but it was no use. And besides, doing that only took away from my intense activities of the moment—which, come to think of it, must be the whole idea, sort of like Novocaine. I held off pretty damn well, though, considering how long I was on the verge. What happened was, as soon as we got back to kissing and rubbing our chests across each other, I finally let my fingers trail down her legs, and then up inside her shorts to her thick and wet-smooth snatch, and she slipped *her* hand past the waistband of my shorts and gently gripped my hard-on, and finally I let fly. I was out of control. I heard myself let out this grunt like, and I shoved my crotch into her. I shot all over her wrist and arm, and she was saying, "Oh, *good*, Bernie, *good*," like it was this difficult thing I had been trying all day to do.

But what really got me is afterwards while we relaxed there in the grass, looking up at the happy fierce-blue sky, Barbara said, "Sometime, I would just like to spend a whole night with you, and sleep close together like this, and your hand would cradle my breast like now. It feels so safe." I just softly laughed, but Jesus, I knew that was exactly what I wanted to do, too, and then with a real jolt that made me shake my head, I realized that's almost exactly what I *did* do, two nights before, with Winnie—God, Winnie. I suddenly wished I could forget about Winnie. Then I thought I must be nuts for wishing that. Winnie is wonderful. I was confused. But I felt very good.

Bees and flies buzzed over us, performing their speedy,

brainless duties. We baked in the sun. My head was resting on her shoulder, and I could look down over her crumpled-up bra, focusing my eyes on her gumdrop nipples or the tiny beads of sweat like a village in between her jugs or down along the white line of little hairs to her belly-button, and it was all going slowly up and down from her lungs filling and emptying. It didn't take long for my old bone to wake up again, coming up in jumps like pumping an inner tube. When we started hard kissing again, though, after a few minutes Barbara pulled back her face and gave me a red little smile, and she said, "I do want you to be able to be inside me, Bernie. But we can't here."

Amazing. "Well, where?" I said.

She said, "Not now, but sometime." We kissed a little more, and then she sat up to pull down her bra, and she got dressed. I just picked up my shirt and carried it.

We walked over to the long, orange seesaws and did that for a while, and it reminded me of how mean kids used to hang you up in the air on those things for ten minutes and then drop you bang into the ground. They were mostly the bigger kids. In fact, when I got into the sixth grade, I had a gang that did the same mean playground tricks during recess. But my gang did mostly good things, like dig for fossils and run by the girls to show them how fast we could go.

You might think the only way I could possibly react to a girl saying she wanted me inside her would be by getting excited, but the truth is I was just dazed. All I cared about was "sometime" we were going to do it. On the way to her house I invited her to come by my place on her bicycle tomorrow and we could go to the beach and maybe swim if it stayed this hot. She smiled and said, "OK," and I'm now positive we'll do it tomorrow. I know this high, deep, very secluded field way past Hidden Pond where Lee and I camp summer nights and run around with our clothes off. It has pheasants in it and a lot of honeysuckle.

"That's *them*," Lee whispers. "What do you know, they doubled."

"Give me a look," I say, but even without the binoculars I can see a big Ford or something under the arches, and against the light as she gets out I can recognize Leslie's hairdo. There are four people, and she gets out the front, so it must be Bingo's father's shiny car. "C'mon, hog," I say. He shoves the binoculars at me. One of the Negro guys drives the car away, and they're all there in the spotlights, Pam, Rodney, Bingo, and Leslie, all laughing at something Bingo's doing with his arms. He's a real madman, old Bingo Wright. He's always talking to you in a different accent or quoting Shakespeare in a high voice when he's around a lot of people. Usually, he's sort of a nice guy, but he will also follow you along the sidewalk lighting matches and flinging them at you as a joke, so you never know about him. He's pretty smart in school, like Rodney Lippett, except Rodney's such a deadass. They start up the gold carpet, and Jesus, it figures, good old Bingo darts ahead to blow out the flaming lanterns, zigzagging from one side to the other. He looks like a pent-up dog finally let loose so he can sniff all the trees. "Jesus Christ," I say.

"Let me see," says Lee.

I give him back the binoculars.

"That shitbrain," Lee says.

Up front, near the arches five or six that he skipped are still flickering. The car-parker guys are lighting up the other ones again. A couple more cars pull in. Lee puts down the binoculars.

"I don't know," he says. "Proms could be OK. They could

be a fun thing if you had the right girl to take."

I say, "Yeah, well, I don't know if any girl that would want to go to the jerk-off prom would *be* the right girl."

Lee says, "Shit, ask me if I care what you think."

"Do you care what I think?"

"Give me a break, you hard-on," he says.

I'm wishing we could turn on the radio, but we have to keep very quiet because our voices could carry to the canopy, and those car-parkers might come kick us out. One goes by, and we have to duck so the headlights won't catch us. They sweep over the seat-top, outlining the bug splotches on the windshield. When they pass by, our eyes pop up to follow them down the row, so we know which way he's walking back. Suddenly, Lee says, "Fuck-ing *A!* Did you see that?"

"Shhh. What?"

"Rick the Prick's *car*, his fucking Chevy, at the end of that row by the fence. I swear it's his."

"Are you serious?"

"Damn straight I'm serious."

"Is he in it?"

"How the fuck do I know? It's his car."

"Well, shit, he wouldn't be going to the *prom.*"

Lee is training his binoculars down the row. I watch him focus.

I say, "You see anything?"

"Nah."

"You think maybe he lent his car to somebody?"

Lee says, "Huh, Richard? He wouldn't lend you a glob of snot."

"Well, Jesus," I say. "How the hell did he get in here? How'd he sneak by *us?*"

"Same way we did, only he got here first."

"Yeah. Shit, you think he knows we're here?"

"Don't ask me, asshole. All I saw was his fucking car. And

anyway, what difference does it make? We take off now and he will know we're here for sure."

"*If* he's in the car."

"Yeah, *if*. That's a big fucking if, you oughta know."

Lee's right, I realize. We can't just blast off right in front of him. He might want to follow us—whether he knows who we are or not. Then what would we do? We'd never lose him. I say, "So, what now? We just wait here until he makes a move?"

"That's my idea, hero, and I'm drivin'."

I don't say anything. In the *Press* today, I was termed a "hard-fighting hero," which I guess is what Lee's referring to. It was a nice article, but sort of short, I thought, and with no picture. The old peckerhead must've called in the story, as usual. You can bet it would've been made into a much bigger deal if Bay Shore had ended our seven-year winning streak instead of its just being Number 93 for the Dolphin netmen.

"Well, this sucks," I say. "This really sucks. We don't even have any beer."

"I tried asking Rocky to come with us, but he never answered his phone. Anyway, his brother came home and took back his I.D."

"He's half-retarded, anyway, that guy."

Lee snorts.

I say, "You know, Jesus, what if Richard took Helen Bundy to the prom, or something? We could end up beating meat here the whole night."

"Eat shit," says Lee. "I'll tell you what, you crawl over there and see if the prick's in there. If he isn't in there, we'll go, OK?"

"Sure, and what if he *is* in there?"

"I don't know. Shit, then it's your big chance. Shoot him."

I laugh.

"No, really," says Lee. "The prick'd never know what hit him. And they would all blame it on the fucking Mafia."

It is widely known that Aliperti's Gas House is owned by the Mafia. Lee and I have both heard that it is, and I don't doubt it. Lee thinks that if everybody knew that a place was owned by the Mafia, then the FBI would do something about it, but I told him, shit, everybody even knows who the Mafia guys are and where they live and all. On the highway crew this past summer, we often went by the Cozzis' huge new colonial mansion with stone deer on the lawn and white iron benches. Curtains are across all the windows, and you never see a car in there. The first time I saw it, we were cutting brush, and the driver we had for that job was a gray-haired geez named Mel Waller, who knew a lot of history about the town, where the trolley used to go and so on. All Mel would ever have for lunch was a quarter-pound of macaroni salad and four half-quarts of Schaefer. He had a round beer-belly. He pointed out the Cozzis' place to me as a Mafia mansion, and he also drove by a couple others the next day just to show us. Looking at those houses made me wonder, like Lee, how those big criminals stayed in business with ordinary people like Mel Waller knowing their addresses. But actually, if you read *Time* magazine, you see of course the Mafia guys commit crimes, *but* they mostly commit crimes legally. That's how smart they are, they hardly ever get caught.

"*Lights*," Lee whispers. We duck. Another prom car goes by. I stick my head up quick to see if it will light up Richard's car, and shit, that's his car all right, with him probably ducked down like us.

"Christ," I say, "this looks very bad. You know if he's in there, he saw us come in. And if he saw us come in, he knows we're here. And if he knows we're here, he's waiting to make some crazy kind of move. Shit, we can't go on sitting around like victims, can we?"

"Listen," Lee says. "You gotta figure he wouldn't recognize the Valiant. It's my mom's car, right? And he probably knows we don't have licenses, right? So even if he thinks somebody's over here, he doesn't know it's us. I think we gotta wait the prick out."

"Well, here's what I think," I say. "I think we should sneak right up to his Chevy to make sure he's really and truly in it, like you said before. If he is, OK, we wait. If he isn't, we take off."

"Shit, you wanna sneak up on that maniac, go ahead. Tell him for me it's past his bedtime."

"No, look," I say. "We don't even have to get that *close*. We only want to see the shape of his fat old bullet head."

"Yeah, well, what if he's keeping his fat bullet head out of sight?"

"He would only have to do that when the lights go by," I say, but I can tell already Lee's getting interested in my plan. "Look, all we do is first flick off the light inside the car so it doesn't come on when we open the door. Then, when a prom car goes by again, we swing out quick and run up there low between the cars so he can't see us."

Lee is quiet for a minute. A car passes and we duck. "OK," Lee whispers, "the next car that comes by, we roll out, only what we do is, we run *behind* him so Aliperti's prom lights will make him show up in the binoculars. I'm not getting any closer than I have to."

"OK. Fine with me." I know I will feel better outside this car anyway, if the prick *does* somehow know I'm here.

"Shit," says Lee.

"What?"

"Shit, I don't know which way to turn this fucking switch so the inside light doesn't flash on."

"Forget it, then. He'll never see it."

"Well, what if somebody else sees it?"

"So they see it. So what? Look, I'm sneaking out for a view of that Chevy, so you might as well come, too, because the light's gonna flash just as much for me as for both of us."

"*I* know," he says. "I'll unscrew the bulb. All you do is pry this fucking plastic thing off."

"Well, hurry up before another car comes."

Lee whips out the can-opener he now always carries, and he pops the light cover away into the back seat. "OK, got it."

We silently unlatch the doors. A car-parker cruises by behind us, and we both roll out of the front seat like depth charges. We scuttle to the row the Chevy's in and then over to the row behind it. The prom car stops close to Richard's Chevy. My ankle's suddenly hurting again. I almost forgot about it. We pant, watching the Negro guy walk back to Aliperti's arches. Lee steadies the binoculars on the trunk of the car in front of us.

I whisper, "Can you see from here?"

He's focusing. "Yeah. Just wait a minute, will ya?"

I'm peering through a couple sets of car windows. It's hard to tell from here which one's the Chevy.

"Holy *fuck*," says Lee. "He's *in* there. He's fucking *in* there."

"What's he doing?" I can't see a thing.

"Nothing," Lee whispers. He hands me the glasses.

I squat down by the side of the car so I can get almost a straight-on shot down toward the Chevy. There. Jesus. It's his head, that's all. The back of this black dome barely sticking up above the car seat like a helmet on a shelf. It doesn't move.

"See him?" says Lee.

"Yeah. Fuck a duck. What's he *do*ing in there?"

"I don't know. Pulling pud, I guess."

"No, seriously. You think he's just spying on the prom like us?"

"What do I look like, God? I don't know the reasons for everything."

I set the binoculars down on the asphalt. Lee can be a real pain when he's nervous. "Look, all I want is your professional opinion. Maybe he's just in there getting blown by Helen Bundy."

"Fuck you, Hergruter. Quit giving me shit about that skank, will ya?"

"Shhh."

"Listen, I don't give a fuck what he's doing. I think the prick maybe secretly wishes he was going to the prom, and this is all the closer he can get. Let's get our asses back to the car before somebody sees us out here."

"You go," I say. "I'm moving in for a better look."

Lee stares at me. "What are you, crazy?"

"I just want one good look at him, OK? Maybe it's not even him in there."

"You're fucking nuts," says Lee.

"C'mon, chickenshit. Nobody's gonna see us. We just go up three cars and then over behind there along the fence so we can get a good, close-up view. Even if the prick looked that way, he couldn't see anything. We gotta be quiet, that's all."

Lee spits a shiny clam onto the bumper of the car in front of us. It slides slowly along the sloping chrome. Just about everybody's arrived at the prom by now. No cars are winding through the parking lot.

"You coming?" I whisper.

"Yeah, I don't give a fuck."

I hang the binoculars over my shoulder, and we start crabbing along up the line of cars. The gravel crunches. Ten feet behind the Chevy we stop.

"Here?" Lee whispers.

I shake my head and point to the fence one car over on

our left. There I think we'll have an open view from the side, so we can see his ugly face. A stab of pain shoots up my leg every time I put my weight on my bad ankle. You just can't limp in a crouched position. And I'm trying to step flat so I don't slide my sneakers in the grit. When I get there, I lean up gently against the mesh of the fence and stretch out my legs until I'm sitting. My ankle's throbbing. I hope I'm not hurting the stitches.

Lee crawls up. Very soft, he whispers, "Gimme those things." I hand him the binoculars. He sticks his head up over the fender of this big white car and then quickly ducks back down again. He whispers, "Fuck, we are right *on top* of him. The prick sees us, and it's all over."

I get on my knees and slowly raise my head up beside the side-view mirror of this white car so I can look at him through the door window and the windshield. He's in the next car over, sitting with his head back against the seat, gazing straight ahead through his steering wheel at Aliperti's arches. His hair comes down low on his forehead. He's not moving a muscle. I duck down. I motion Lee to let me have the binoculars.

"*Why*?" he softly whispers.

I motion again, and he gives them over. I rise with the glasses in position like a periscope. I hold my breath. Jesus Christ. I can see his eyes blink. His mouth is open. Lee's tugging my shirt front. I drop down. "*What?*" I whisper.

He pokes the air sideways with his thumb, meaning let's get the hell out of here. I nod, but I want another look. I hold up my finger for one minute. Lee is mad. But I know the prick can't see us. He looks like he's in a trance, like a zombie.

Lee takes the binoculars. I stick my head up and then quick pull it down again because he's bent forward into the steering wheel, leaning against it on his stump, and his head was moving a little. I point up for Lee to take a look. He shakes his head. I keep pointing up, and so he gradually sticks up his head. He looks for two seconds and comes down with his eyes wide open. He is terrified. He shapes words with his mouth.

"What?" I whisper. I am now scared.

Lee makes like he is aiming a rifle. His arms shake. "A *gun*," he whispers.

I have to look. I slide up my face along the car metal. My eyes come level with the glass, and—Holy Jesus God—the black barrel of some huge gun. It is thick and nobbed on the end, and he is holding it aimed up into the car roof like a fishing pole. Suddenly he drops it out of sight. I duck. I am fiercely shivering.

Then, *brrrOOOM*. Lee goes, "Aaah." It's the Chevy engine roaring. I have my hands over my head like it's a nuclear attack. My brain pounds. The Chevy screeches off, and we jump up. Lee runs for the Valiant, and I hop along like Chester in a frenzy. The blare of the Chevy fills the parking lot. I glance at his streaking lights down the rows of cars as I bounce up to the Valiant. I am wincing, whew, it hurts. Then it hits me—that *gun*, that gun is familiar to me, I know it. That gun is part of Richard's old Nazi collection, a German machine gun. I've seen it before. I've handled it. I jerk open the door and slide in. Lee starts up.

"Follow him," I yell.

"Suck my *dick*," says Lee.

"No, listen—"

"I'm getting the fuck *out* of here." He cranks the wheel and zooms toward the back exit. Under the arches, the Negro guys watch Richard roar out the front. His taillights tilt when he takes the corner.

"*Listen*," I say. "That gun's a Nazi antique. It doesn't work. The barrel is plugged. It can't shoot."

We move fast down the gravel drive behind Aliperti's, banging through the potholes. "How do *you* know?" yells Lee.

"Because he once *showed* it to me." I remember that day. It was hot and windy, and I was invited to go sailing with Arnold Tolley, but at the last minute we couldn't go because his father had business, so instead I went to Richard's to see his machine gun. For days, with this funny, secret look, he had been telling me to come see it, and I was tantalized, so I rode over there. Richard led me to his room and locked his door with two bolts—not that he ever allowed his mother in there anyway. Clumps of dust were all over, and his windowsill was covered with old beach rocks and soda bottles and cans of dried-up glue and spider webs. He had absolute privacy, which seemed pretty luxurious to me. The gun was in a wicker picnic basket under his bed, wrapped in a cut-off pants leg. It was amazing. It was all heavy and bulging black metal worn to gray silver along the handle parts and on the sides of the short, fat barrel, and it had etched-in German writing on it. I put it in my arms and eyed down through the sights at things. I could hardly hold it up. I was used to my little Daisy cork rifle that I would knock over dominoes with. Richard told me he wouldn't trade my whole coin collection for it. I told him fat chance I would want an old, broken-down machine gun, but in fact I loved it. It scared me, and I wanted one like it. I thought then if I had it, I would like have the final power over anything. But he laughed when I asked him where he found it or bought it, and he refused over and over to even give me a hint. For days afterward, I couldn't stop imagining how wonderful it would be to have a gun like that. I figured I could hide it out in the garage somewhere. I could put it under the greasy tarp that hung down over our 3½-horse Scott Atwater outboard that we had then in the garage. We never did get a boat (but once my father and I rented one to fish for flounder), so nobody would look there. Actually, I had no idea what I would do with it except have it to inspect and hold, and then after a while I forgot all about it—until just now. It took a minute to remember, too.

Lee says, "You tell me when he ever showed you that gun," like he thinks I'm lying.

"Years ago," I say. I know he really believes me. Then down on the main road I spot the Chevy pulling up for a light in a line of cars. He's heading north toward town. "Hey, there he is. Shit, we *got* to follow him."

Lee quick shakes his head. "Fuck *that*, shithead. The guy is psycho. You wanna get us shot? Who knows if that gun is even the same one you saw? Why the fuck would he have it in his damn car if it didn't work?"

"Listen, I'm positive it's the same gun, and it has this like metal plug in it because if it worked it would be against the law."

"So maybe he took *out* the plug," Lee says.

"C'mon," I say. "We're going that way anyway. If he keeps straight on Jericho, we can cut through the Robert Hall parking lot and come in behind him up by Sears. Let's just see where he goes."

"The crazy prick'll fucking kill us."

"He'll never even *see* us," I say. "Stay way behind him, OK? You're driving. You don't have to get close. He doesn't even know we're here." Sometimes Lee will make like he's more of a chickenshit than he really is, I can never figure out why. This time maybe he thinks Richard is my business, not his business, and so he's begging for trouble for nothing. The thing is, Lee is usually very daring, and us keeping a distant eye on the unsuspecting maniac prick does not honestly seem too dangerous, though of course you never know. "Listen," I say, "if it was you in the jungle against some monster wild boar, you would sure as hell want to be following him than have him following you."

But already Lee has swerved hard into Robert Hall's, so if we move it, we can cut off the Chevy on the other side of the shopping center. He says, "I got news for you. This is not the fucking jungle. And if we just went home, that moron cripple'd have no *chance* to see us."

"He's not gonna have a chance this way, either." We angle fast over the painted car-slots to the exit ramp. Below on the turnpike, the Chevy passes by in the slow traffic. We turn in after it maybe six cars behind.

Lee says, "Shit, he's probably just going home."

"Who knows?" I say. I am tense and sweaty all over. I lean up to the dash to keep those little pink-red taillights in view.

"Hey," says Lee. "You wouldn't wanna clue me in on why we're doing this, would ya?"

"Because we can't pass up this opportunity, that's why. Because we can now see him and his whacked-out habits in action."

Lee goes, "Hunh, I don't know who's more whacked-out, us or him."

"Fuck, he's turning, see?" The Chevy swings off the turn-pike onto Grover Road, the long way toward town, over the tracks, past the hospital, the boat works, and the road to the high school. "Jesus, he isn't heading for his house, that's for sure." We follow. Only one car is between us, but we stay far behind so we lose his lights for five or ten seconds on the curves.

Lee takes a deep breath. He says, "OK, I'm sticking with the pecker into town, but unless he goes straight through to the Bay, it's over. I'm going home. You got that? You can get out and hop along after him, if you want."

"Yeah, I hear you." I look over at him. We're not going

that fast, but he's hunched over the wheel like a getaway driver. His face brightens and dims as the street lights zip by. My ankle's thumping the way my eye did that night of the party in Lakewood, but I'm not letting myself pull up my pants for a gander because I'm afraid it's bleeding, and what would I do about it?

"*Hey*," Lee says. "Where'd he go?"

"Shit," I say. We slow up. The road's empty except for a truck passing in the other direction. A traffic light far ahead blinks green. "He turned again," I say. "He had to. He could never all of a sudden scream through that light and disappear, not even in his hot bomb."

Lee says, "Shit, well, that does it." He pulls up in front of a dark laundromat. We look at each other. He slowly smiles. "You wanna turn around, don't you?"

"Fuck, *yes*," I say. I slap the dashboard.

"Yeah, you crazy dip retard." He wheels around fast and we're off again. Good old Lee. "OK," he says, "it could only be up Elmwood or down into Kelly's Marine, unless we missed him way back at the all-night Shell, that turn there."

"No, I looked in there. It's Elmwood, gotta be. Because he could've lost us easy where it breaks off sharp there after the turn."

"Fucking Sherlock Holmes," says Lee.

"So he's going up by the high school, and then he's heading down toward the gravel pits or the harbor."

Lee swings onto Elmwood. "I think the prick's just cruising," he says.

"Go slow," I say. I'm checking out the houses along the road in case he stopped in at one for some unknown reason. It's mostly old people living along here. We wind uphill toward the back entrance to the high school.

"*There*," Lee says, and Jesus, it's the humped Chevy

again, stopped without lights at the peak of the hill. Lee quick swerves into some driveway and douses the lights. I can't tell if Richard's inside it or not. "What the fuck's he *doing?*" Lee whispers. He's parked just about opposite the steep back road down to the high school, the same road Buzzie Cochran and I took when we would steal Miss Fitzwaller's car. They lock a chain across it at night.

"Maybe he's taking a couple laps around the track," I say. Just over the hill is the football field with a cinder track running around it and the rows of banked stands to the side up by the road. From here you can make out the back of the scoreboard, sticking up black against the sky.

Suddenly, the porch light of the little house whose driveway this is and another kind of lantern on a pole nearby flash on together. Lee goes, "Oh-oh."

"*Look,*" I whisper. Up the hill it's Richard, walking fast across the road to his car. "He's taking *off.*"

Lee leans out the car window. "We're lost," he says loud.

A man is standing on the porch in his undershirt. "You can't park here," the man shouts out.

"OK," Lee says.

"*Wait,*" I whisper. "He's hanging a U-ie." Richard's already swung his Chevy broadside in the road. His lights are still off.

The man stalks out to the edge of his lawn. "You kids scram," he shouts.

Lee starts the motor.

"No, wait," I say. "We back out now, and he'll *see* us." But just then the Chevy veers out of sight down the high school drive.

Lee speeds backwards into the street, brakes hard, and pivots us up the hill. When we get to where we first saw the Chevy, we stop. Nothing's visible through the gate. The school is far down behind the trees. Lee's shaking his head.

"Jesus, this is crazy," he says. "How'd the prick get through there, anyway?"

"I don't know. Maybe he cut the chain." It curls over the pavement like a snake. "Don't go in after him. Just ease up there behind the football stands so we can look down at the building."

"I wasn't going in after him, asshole."

"And cut the lights." We move slowly up over the brow of the hill, and Lee pulls up onto the grass. Before the stands is a tall, wood-slat snow-fence that keeps people from walking in to watch the games without tickets. The way we're sitting low in the car we can't see down through the fence and the criss-crossed steel beams that hold up the seats into the building complex. "Shit," I say. "We gotta go right up to the fence for a view."

Lee says, "Yeah? Waddya mean *we*, white man?" It's a line from Lee's favorite joke that has the Lone Ranger and Tonto riding through a canyon when they suddenly hear whooping, and the Indians rush in. The Lone Ranger goes, "Jesus, Tonto, looks like we're surrounded," and Tonto says, "Waddya mean *we*, white man?" When Lee says that, he in a flash reminds me of old L.R., who today when I went up to see him in his coop to change his newspapers, had an *egg* in his nest, a little pink egg. So L.R. is a *she*. She's sitting on it, but it will never hatch.

"OK," I say. "Stay and keep it running. I want to see what he's doing down there. Give me the binoculars."

But Lee comes with me, letting the car idle by itself. I hop over to the fence. And the Chevy is down there, all right, with no lights, gliding slow like a shadow along the loop around the flagpole past where the principal and important visitors always park. The growl of it rolls up the hill.

Lee looks down through the binoculars. He says, "Shit, you know he's gonna come back the same way."

"Yeah, but we can cut out before he can make it up the hill."

Lee tries propping his arms on the squeaky fence. Richard rounds the end of the loop to pass in front of the main offices where the school buses pull in. Lee says, "He's coming back! I really think we gotta—"

BAOW - BAOW - BAOW - BAOW - BAOW - BAOW - BAOW, the *gun*, like a string of giant fire crackers. Glass crashes. I'm sitting on the ground. I *saw* it. It sparked. Lee is tearing ass for the Valiant. I hobble after him and dive into the front seat. The tires dig into the grass and then squeal on the pavement. Lee's flooring it.

I yell, "Take it *easy*, take it *easy*. He was just shooting at the *school*."

Lee keeps going. "That gun can't shoot, can it? Not *much*, you *shitbrain*."

I yell, "So how was I supposed to know he fixed it? The prick told me he *couldn't* fix it." He did tell me that. But even though I believed him, I remember now I told him you probably *could* get it fixed, just to like pretend I knew something, and Jesus, I was right. Now I am terrified. I almost want to cry. I sit up in the seat and take a couple deep breaths.

"*Christ*, you had us squatting right next to his fucking *car*," Lee shouts. "He coulda fucking blasted us to pieces."

The dark scenery rushes by behind his head. "Will you fucking slow down?" I yell.

"What if he's coming this way?"

"So then turn off the road and let the fucker go by."

Lee glances at me and brakes the car. We turn in behind a few short brick apartments. Lee steers us in a circle around behind a parked pick-up that's aimed down to Elmwood. We can see a section of the road between the tree trunks. He shuts off the engine. I can hear him breathing. I can hear me breathing. A dog yaps in a room somewhere. We wait. Then the black Chevy rumbles by, not fast, toward the harbor.

During the summer before eighth grade, I used to go to these dance group parties that they held in the Huntington Yacht Club every couple weeks. You had to go in a sport jacket and wear a tie and a tie tack and loafers and that crap, and the girls would have on gloves, which was weird. That spring, when my mother signed me up and sent in the money, I didn't grump around about it, like you might expect. A lot of my friends would be there, too, and also, I sort of knew the ropes of these gatherings from taking two years of dull dance lessons that this slick-haired Swedish guy and his wife held in the old firehouse. They taught us the cha cha, the waltz, the bossa nova, the box step, the lindy, and quite a few others. The classes were boring and stupid, but I went through it because I had friends that were enduring it along with me, and I also got to see and even touch girls like Melissa Powell. (This was before she moved to my neighborhood.) Everybody would look forward to when the guy's wife would put "Mack the Knife" on the record player because it was always the last song, and then we would march out in a line and shake their hands. Then we could go outside in the dark and talk while we waited for our rides. In those days, being out alone at night was a big deal. The Yacht Club dances were much better, though they did not thrill me either. But at least they had a real band and refreshments and streamers and nobody constantly going, "That's it, that's it. Hands up, hands up. Step right, step left, now slide, slide, slide," and on and on. They had chaperons.

What reminded me of the dance group partly was thinking back on the prom last night, but also I am down here in the basement, rummaging through this big box of junk, which I will sometimes do, not looking for any special thing, and what I pulled out first I *thought* was the brown, plastic base that goes to the only trophy I ever won besides Most Improved Player. But it was not a piece of the trophy, it was a cover to some box. The trophy was only a cheap gold plastic cup glued to the base that said Best Dancer. Nancy Shreck and I won it the night of the last dance group party when they had a lindy contest. Afterwards they called us up to the refreshments table to receive our trophies. People clapped. It was the end of the night, but there were still big bowls of leftover orange Chee-tos lining the tables, which usually would be gone by the second break (guys would stuff them in their pockets), but they got soggy from the heat, and nobody would touch them. I liked Nancy Shreck, but we somehow never got to know each other very well. One interesting fact is at those dances when you first came in you got little folding cards with little pencils attached to them by strings. And you had to get the signature of who you wanted to dance with on the line of that number dance on your card. It was senseless, but we did it. When you got home afterward, your mother would go over your card and ask you who was Nancy Shreck or who was Suzie Something. I remember my mother was quite interested in the identity of Wendy M., because she wrote her name a lot on my cards, and I never would say much about her. Of course, that was Wendy Morton, who I didn't really like at all, but she loved me with devotion. She was the one I was going to put it to in case the world was ending and I couldn't wait. Why I danced all those dances with her I don't know. Maybe I just enjoyed imagining how this was a girl I really could dick if I wanted to because she had once fervently said so. Shit, I should have, I know now, but I was too young.

I should be outside. It's gorgeous and hot, and all the birdies are twittering, but I feel nervous so I came down into the basement for a little peace and quiet. My father just left to get the *Times* and my sisters are gone with him. I don't know what my mother's doing, she's upstairs somewhere. I'd leave for the beach, but Barbara said yesterday she would either come here by eleven or call by eleven if she couldn't, so I'm waiting and absently pawing through this carton of clacking junk. It's cool down here. The sunlight barely makes it through the windows because they're small and on ground level and any rain keeps them spattered with dirt. Everything's silent, too, but I am still nervous, because of what I am obviously planning to do with Barbara today, if she comes, and also because, according to my father, my ankle may have to be sewn up all over again, even though I think it looks OK, but mostly because I just called the police about last night.

On the way home Lee and I got into a big argument about what we should do, like call the cops or not, or call Mr. Devoe or not. I told him we should drive straight to the Florida Gulf together and take jobs in a shipyard and live in a tent and fish and get tattoos and everything. That only made him more upset, so I told him I was in fact bored stiff with these decisions about what to do. Lee said now Richard was not only a maniac, but he was an obvious deadly danger to society, and Lee was in a fever to finger him for the cops. I said, shit, if we did that, then we'd have to go on the witness stand, and Richard would some day come back and open us up like watermelons, especially if they confiscated his beloved Nazi machine gun. And I pointed out also that if we went on the witness stand, Lee's parents would find out how he stole the Valiant and illegally drove it around. His old man would shit bricks. That shut Lee up for a minute, but he was still frantic. He was banging his fist against the steering wheel and spitting out the window. To myself I was thinking, piss on society. Nobody was in more deadly danger than me, and what could I do about it—besides sit and sweat bullets, as the saying goes?

We followed the back roads home, keeping our scared little eyes peeled for the crazed zombie. By the time we got to Lee's, I realized that since I couldn't do anything, I *had* to call the cops so at least somebody would do something. But Lee started saying, no, no, we can't call the cops, it's way too risky. I said, to me it was plenty goddamn risky sitting around waiting for him to come by my house, drilling the walls like Al Capone. He said we should wait a couple days and just see if the cops get him on their own. I said, how the fuck are they going to do that? He didn't answer. We snuck back in his driveway with the lights and motor off. He would've forgotten to put the inside light back together if I hadn't whispered to him that the plastic dome part was still in back somewhere. At first, I wasn't going to remind him about it, the jerk. He was in such a hurry to get home, he didn't even drive me up the hill to save me stumbling up through the woods.

When I woke up this morning, the first thing I saw was the long shadow across my bookcase and new green wall from the cardboard my father taped over the broken pane in my window. Right then I knew, Jesus God, I had to call the police. And I had a safe, brilliant idea. I got dressed and ate French toast with everybody, and then sat in the kitchen sipping pineapple juice until it cleared out. The police phone number is written right on the phone on this little sticker. I dialed, and the guy said, "Suffolk County Police. Sergeant Sammis."

I ducked down the basement stairs so nobody would hear me if they happened to come back into the kitchen. I made my voice deep, and I said slow, "Hello, sergeant. I know who shot up the high school last night with a Nazi machine gun. It was Richard Linwood. L-I-N-W-O-O-D."

"What's this about now?" he said. I started worrying he was going to trace the call. They can do that.

"Rick the Prick Linwood," I said. "He was expelled." And I hung up. Even though I forgot to say which high school, I know the sergeant won't have any trouble. These cops can figure things out pretty fast if they want to. The phone call has to work. But though I even know Lee will realize it was quite a shrewd phone call, I am still nervous because like, say the prick ditched the gun somewhere, and they come to him saying, "OK, Linwood, where's this Nazi machine gun?" and he'll say, "I don't know what the hell you're talking about," and he would fucking well *know* that I had to tell the cops about it, because who else is there that knows about that gun who would rat to the cops about it? If that happens, he'll steamroller after me. Of course, he's already after me, so there isn't too much difference.

Now I have this drumstick, just a wood rod with a blue-painted ball on the end for a xylophone or something. Lizzie once had a xylophone. A lot of family relics are in here. It's a little depressing. I can remember when this abacus was new, for example, before I accidentally sat on it and broke the bars the beads slide on. I never used the damn thing, but it was interesting to have around. It wasn't just a piece of crap. What I first started looking at down here was not this junk carton, but what's in the box above it—my wonderful Dinky Toy collection, which is this army that includes tanks and .55-millimeter cannons and jeeps and personnel carriers and ambulances and antiaircraft guns and so on. Dinky Toys are good because they're solid metal and a lot of thought went into them, they're so detailed, but now all that military hardware just reminds me of Richard's echoing gun, not that I can totally forget it anyway, so I closed the box.

Here is a bunch of jigsaw pieces to different puzzles. If

you find a puzzle piece under a chair somewhere, this carton is the place you put it so if anyone tries to do that puzzle again, some of the missing pieces can be located. There are some dominoes, too, wooden ones with a serpent on the back. Well, the hell with this garbage. I fold the flaps of the carton together and stick the Dinky Toy box on top again. My mother is calling my name upstairs. She thinks I'm in my bedroom.

"Yeah?" I say.

"Bernie?"

"What?"

"Where are you?"

"Down here." I hear her footsteps coming across the kitchen linoleum.

From the top of the stairs, she says, "You have a guest at the door."

"Already?" I say. My mother would only say, "You have a guest at the door," if it was Barbara, but it can't be much later than ten. I hop up the stairs. My mother smiles at me as I pass by the stove.

God, it's Barbara, all right, standing in the livingroom in her pale yellow shorts and this open red shirt with her suit top on under it.

"Good morning," she says.

I say, "Hi. You're pretty early."

"Well, sorry. You want me to go home and try later?"

I laugh. "No, I just thought you said eleven."

"I said *by* eleven." She grins at me. "It's so nice I couldn't wait."

"Well, that's wonderful," I say. "Let's go." We head for the door.

My mother calls out, "Don't swim, now, Bernie. You can't get sand or water inside that bandage."

As soon as we get far enough from the house, Barbara

grabs my arm and says, "Did you hear the *news?*"

We stop in the street. I say, "Shit, I *saw* the damn news." It surprises me a little that it would get around so fast. Maybe it was on the radio.

"You *saw* it?" She doesn't believe me. "How did you *see* it?"

"We were there, that's all. We had binoculars."

"You went to the *prom?*"

"Well, we just parked outside it for a while. Did something happen at the *prom?*"

She says, "I thought you knew already. What, did something else happen?"

"What happened at the prom?" I ask.

"Leslie Wolstein broke her neck. She's in the hospital, and she's paralyzed."

"She did?" I say. "How'd she break it?"

"A bunch of them were playing chicken, and she fell off Bingo Wright's shoulders and landed on the floor."

"Well, how is she? I mean, is she OK?"

"I *told* you, she's paralyzed."

"How long is she paralyzed for?"

"Who knows?" says Barbara. "Maybe forever."

All I can think is what a dickbrain that Bingo Wright is. Jesus. We start walking again. "That's horrible," I say.

Barbara is staring down the road. "I know it is," she says. "What's the news that you heard? Or *saw?*"

So I tell her how Richard Linwood riddled Hobbes High School with a machine gun. She widens her eyes, but when I start to relate from the beginning how we parked at Aliperti's and how we snuck up on him, she says in a scary voice, "You mean, that bastard has a *gun?*"

"You can say that again," I say.

"Well, God, you know what? He sort of followed me riding over here, not followed me really, but he passed me going real slow three times, and he said hello to me, but I told him to bug off."

"Are you serious?" I say. I know she is. I suddenly think it would be smart to go home and maybe call the police again and tell them the details so they would really get on it. Shit, they might stick him in with the loonies for good. Also, I can't stand knowing he's cruising around here like that. Maybe he never even went home.

Barbara says, "Bernie, you know we have to call the police."

"I did call the police, but I guess they didn't catch him yet. I think we should go back and call again."

"OK, good," she says.

We turn around, and she holds my hand. I look at her face, which is looking down at the road. Her sandals flap against her heels.

I say, "Well, anyway, it's certainly a beautiful day."

She smiles, and then we both hear it, and our heads jerk up. Far ahead, the Chevy rounds the bend beyond my house, and I stop dead in the road. I breathe in. I feel icy. It comes at us like a slow-motion bowling ball.

"*Barbara*," I say in a rush.

"*What?*"

"We got to get the hell out of here." Then I think, Jesus God, what if he's coming to blast my *house*? I'm frozen. I watch the flickering windshield, the sharp, yellow reflections shifting. I wait for the explosions. But the car rumbles on by our mailbox and comes into the shade of the maples up the road. The windshield darkens. I can see his big head. He sees me. The car leaps up, screeching.

Barbara screams, "*Bernie!*"

"*That way!*" I yell at her. I point into the woodlot up across the street, and then I vault the other way over a rail fence, and hop quick through the Nicholses' yard to get to where I can hide behind their tool shed. I don't want to try running until I have to. I look back. Barbara's red shirt is zigging up the bank among the little gray-green trees. The Chevy jumps the curb and digs in before it hits the fence. I duck behind the shed. The engine roars once, then gurgles low and dies. I hear the door creak open and slam shut. I peer around the corner. He's maybe twenty yards away over the grass, with his fat ass propped against the back fender and his stump sickeningly folded into the other elbow, just staring at me. He has on shorts. I don't think I've ever seen the prick in shorts. I'm bent to tie my sneakers, which I only just slipped on in my hurry out of the house.

His voice shouts, "Come outa there, cuntface."

I step around so he'll see me. I wonder where the gun is. "What do *you* want?" I say, like I have no patience. I'm thinking, act calm.

"Come *down* here," he yells.

"Go fuck yourself," I yell back.

He stares at me. "You say that again, now. C'mon *say* it."

I yell, "What are you, deaf?"

His arms drop. He straightens away from the car and suddenly flings himself sideways over the rail.

I'm off before he hits the ground. I expected this. My ankle pangs sharp. I half-run by the Nicholses' furrowed garden patch and up the short slope to their back fence. I stop. Jesus, it hurts going uphill. I glance back. Richard pounds past the tool shed. All at once I realize I've been thinking, just run home, run home—but that's crazy. He'll crash in right after me. Christ, then what? Try anyway. I hop the fence into the Gallaghers', and I swoop down along the side of their house toward the cut between the big bushes that will lead me uphill again through two backyards, up over the Roerles' wood pile and wire fence, by Zekey's pen, and home. I'll never make it. I round the corner, and the Gallagher twins stand in the driveway next to a plastic wading pool, filling it with a hose. The concrete's dark with water. I rush by. Their blond heads follow. I dart between the bushes, but *fuck*, I can't make it, not up that hill. My ankle jabs along my whole side every time I push off with it. Behind me, his hard shoes crack across the driveway. Why don't I stop? Why don't I just let the cocksucker come? I keep running. Nobody catches me, nobody. Not that fucking maniac. Christ, he's wearing *shoes*. So I pivot on my left foot, and I cut fast down the bank along the thick row of bushes to the road. It curves down by the old vine woods and then falls off steep toward the beach. I'm thinking if I can just open up some distance on him, I'll hide somewhere and sneak back home off the road. I glance back. I don't see him. I ease up on my ankle. My breath comes hard. *Jesus*. Suddenly, he tears through the bushes ten feet behind me holding his stump in front of his face. I fly on down the bank. Fucking *shit*, he means business. Going downhill, I can land full on my left foot and just sort of glide over touching down on my right toe without losing much speed. I hit the pavement and hook hard by the front of Gallaghers'. I'm like some teeny chipmunk, skittering wild over the road, but *moving*, really moving now, air whistling in my throat, jewely bits of sweat spraying down. My ankle stings. His shoes crack on the road like whips. Ahead, through far-off tree branches, I can bouncingly glimpse patches of blue water, the white dot of a boat. The trees rise. The road steepens. Jesus, wheezing, I'm *wheezing*. A man comes into sight around the curve, a bald man with a towel draped over his shoulders. I slow up, closing in on him. He looks at my face. *Stop him*, I try to say, but it comes out, "Sto-chh," and I'm choking. I look back. Richard's slowed to a trot. The bald man strides up the hill. I hobble off the pavement to the soft roadside. I keep looking back. *Jesus*. My lungs burn. He knows I'm hurt, the fucker. So he's not stopping, only resting. *Run,* goes my brain. I'm shuffling in the gravel. *Take off.* But I walk, my breath whooshing, my eyes squinting back at him. He's walking, tilted forward like some heavy animal. I hear him panting. I glance down at my bandage, and it's red, but no blood is leaking out. I flex my ankle. It just stings. What now? Either I stay on the road all the way to the water, or I throw myself down the embankment and sprint into the vine woods. The road flattens in a half a mile along the beach front, but the vine woods are a long, slow tumble to the bluffs, the only good-size piece of land nobody could stick houses on, it's so steep. I'm looking back at his lowered head, and he's still breathing hard and looking at me, walking and walking. Shit, *now* I should go. I'm just resting him. So in a flash I'm skidding on my side through the dirt and leaves like sliding down a ladder. Then I'm up and angling sharp down the slope, skidding and hopping. It surprised him. I glance back, and he's slipping fast down the embankment, holding his stump out for balance. I keep careening down, knocking against little branches. His crashing and stomping is farther behind. I could lose him maybe, but I'm running out of woods. Up ahead I know is the new chain-link fence that cuts the vine woods off from the property of the Bluffs Home Owners Association. Over the fence is just more woods until the bluffs and the thick lawns with sprinklers. I don't slow for the fence, I just launch up for the top, slam into it with my hands and legs, and then fly on over and crunch into the leaves and sticks. I jump up holding onto a tree.

"*Richard,*" I yell, through my heavy breath.

He crashes to his leg for brakes on the slope so he doesn't clobber himself on the fence. He stands up, bent forward and staring at me. He's sobbing and heaving for air.

"*Richard,*" I yell. I'm holding onto the tree. "If you don't fuck off and leave me the fuck alone, I'm going down behind here, and I have a gun buried down there in the sand, and I'm going down there, and I'll get it, and I swear I'll blow your fucking maniac brains out with it if you don't *fuck off*."

He keeps looking and panting.

"The police are coming, too, you prick. I called the police about last night. You and your fucking machine gun."

"Show me!" he yells out, and he jumps for the fence.

I push off and run again. Up ahead through the trees is sunny green lawn and a line of blue sky—the bluff. The drop is fifty feet, but like in steps. The sand is all banked up with wood ties that I can maneuver on. I have before. I pound down into the sun. Blood is in my sneaker now, I feel it. All I see is the bluff, the scratchy grasses. I dart along the edge to the shortest first leap and then sail out. I flop hard into the sand. I stand up slow. I shake. The rest I'll have to shimmy down, feet-first. The ties stick out here like the corner of a log cabin. You can slip down fast if you don't care about splinters. I hear Richard thumping on the grass. After I'm started down, I crane my neck, and he's watching me from the bluff top. He's not jumping. Is he quitting? I back slowly down the ties like going down a treehouse ladder. Halfway down I can't see him or the bluff top any more, and I suddenly know I'm in trouble. I now have to get the gun. It makes no difference if I shake him now. He'll just wait somewhere for me. Or he'll watch me from up there and follow along the bluff until I make a move for home or until he finds a way down. For a second I think, *swim*, but I would drown, I'm so exhausted. The flashy water stretches out calm to the harbor light and the buoys. I'm down. I hop slowly through the sand and stones toward where Lee and I buried everything, our treasure. I could never gallop in this stuff. My ankle aches and stings, and I realize it stings from the sweat rolling down into it. My sneaker squishes. I have sand stuck all over me like a sugar doughnut. I keep scanning the bluff and not seeing him. I'm shivering. Where *is* he? Ahead, along the bluff, the lawns stop and the trees start again, but the drop is way too sharp and high to jump, especially in shoes. Then I hear him. My head swivels. I see him coming fast on the hard sand by the water. How? I try to run. Ten yards up is the jetty, and just after that is the locusts and our hole. But I just can't push at all in this loose stone. I hear his high breath like a saw. *Here!* Stumbling down, I tear away at the sand. I won't make it. No time to dig. By instinct I dive for our can opener, the flat board with a nail stuck through the end, and I turn on him with it.

He stops six feet away. He is covered with sweat. His white heavy legs are bleeding and dirty. The air whines through him. From behind his back, his hand brings out the switchblade.

"Richard!" I scream. "Stay the fuck away from me."

He stares at me. His thumb's pushing the knife button, but it doesn't spring out. He looks at it.

I am like ice all through, and trembling beyond control.

His stump pins the knife to his chest. He pries out the long blade with his fingers. He jabs it at me. "OK?" he yells.

"I'll *kill* you," I scream out.

"Is this where?" he yells. He falls on his knees, staring at me, with his teeth clamped together, jabbing and jabbing. Then he drills his stump down into our beer hole. Everything looks pink to me. I can't move. I'm paralyzed. *Leslie,* I think, *Leslie.* His stump scrapes the cigar box. He looks down at it.

I scream and smash him with the board. I smash his neck. He slumps into the hole. I'm yelling. I hack and hack along his side. I jump and land on him. I kick his guts. I can't hear. My board is gone. I kick his head. I keep jumping on him until I fall off. I stand up and fall down. He is wailing, crying. No, *me*. I'm rocking around and crying. Then I stop. I hold my breath. Quiet. The boats buzz. He doesn't move. I bend to see his face, full of streaming blood. In the hole the box sticks up on end. I pull it out. I start to cry again because I know I want to bury him. I want to cover him with sand, and I can't stand up.

The window that my father built L.R.'s coop into has hinges at the top so what you do is you prop it open by a long stick that's attached to the bottom. The stick has a row of holes through it like a belt, so when you open the window, you pick a hole to fit over the little nail that's stuck in the sill for however far you want the window open. It's very simple. Now with L.R. living here, you can only open and shut the window by first unlatching the coop door and then reaching inside to adjust the prop stick, which I just did.

Out in the north, heat lightning is flaring and flickering through the heaps of smoky clouds. Ten minutes ago, we were on the porch with the newspaper, Claudia, my father, and I, and a quick shower blew over, fat raindrops thumping down. My father said, "Bernie, go shut that attic window, will ya?" I hopped up, and he suddenly remembered my ankle. "No, wait," he said. "You sit down there. I'll get it. Or Claudia—"

"I can get it," I said. "Jesus, I'm not incapacitated." That's the word my mother uses when she discovers I neglected something I was expected to do, like she'll say, "Well, Bernie, were you somehow incapacitated this morning?" and I'm supposed to figure out what duty I skipped out on.

"No, now I said sit down there," said my father, but I was already moving through the door.

"I gotta check on the bird, anyway," I said. Water was

spattering in on the cement porch floor and hitting the spread-out sections of newspaper with little clicks. I was through reading. All I ever look at in that monster paper is the sports and the magazine section. One Sunday last summer I was over at Barbara's reading their magazine section, and Benjamin came downstairs, her big brother who's at M.I.T., and he said to me, with her mother and father and Barbara and everybody else right there in the room quietly reading, "Hey, what are you looking at with your tongue hanging out, the *crotch ads?*" It was quite embarrassing, especially because there was this lady sprawled out in her undies on one whole page in color, and sure I looked at her, who wouldn't, but I was honestly reading some serious article. He's a bigmouth asshole, her brother, I don't care how smart he is.

Now the sun's back, spearing beams out all around. Still, it's pretty cloudy. I'd open the window again to let some cooler air flow through, but L.R. hates it when I go into her coop. She pecks and pecks at my hand, I think because of her egg. My mother says I've got to take it away from her, but that seems mean. It won't hatch, though. She might as well sit on a jelly bean. She keeps softly cooing. Maybe she's on edge because I'm sitting here or because of the weather, the pale lightning. Yesterday at breakfast when my father and I discussed my glorious tennis victory of Friday afternoon, I explained about how I didn't exactly know what came over me, but I had concentration and this ferocious determination, and I was just hitting every damn ball where I wanted to, and my father said, "Well, yeah. Once in a while you can catch lightning in a bottle." Now I think that's a weird expression. I guess what it means is you can on rare occasions capture some kind of power, like the mad power I bashed old Richard with this morning. Boy, I really creamed the bastard, and I hardly knew I was doing it. I figured they would at least need an ambulance, but they didn't. They took him in a cop car, no sirens or anything.

I ache all over, my knees in particular (where I hit the fence), and my back and hands, and my feet, and of course my ankle, which has new stitches in it, four this time. I had to ride to the hospital emergency room with my father and this young, chubby policeman, who asked me a bunch of questions about Richard and his Nazi gun and switchblade. I gave a slew of details concerning Richard's sick, lonely life, and I made the prick sound about as deranged and pure wacko as they come. On the way to the hospital, I became scared all over again, wondering if he'd be there, too, but luckily he wasn't. At least, I didn't see him. The cop said he was up in some room somewhere, probably with his mother, and I asked if they had him chained to the bed. The cop frowned at me for a minute and he said, "Hey, son, what are you worried for? The poor guy looks like he fell off a roof. He can't even *walk*." That got me, "the poor guy," like in the cop's mind he *was* a poor guy, a victim, and not a true, open-and-shut, bloodthirsty fiend. I wanted to say, "Hey, you dumb cop, that madman wanted to slice off the pink end of my dick" (which was the only detail I left out of my tale of terror), but the emergency room had other people in it, ladies and so on, and besides, what Richard wanted to do to me does not mean diddlyshit any more. It's all over. Before my stitches, when the cop was leaving, I asked him what was going to happen to Richard now that they had him behind bars. The cop said he didn't know, so I asked him what he *thought* would happen, and the cop still didn't know, but he did say it seemed like the guy was missing a few marbles. The way he said it made me laugh, but I was thinking, shit, that crazed pecker never had more than one marble to start with. After that, I didn't talk much. I felt slowed-down and limp in the brain. I still feel that way, like I could sit in this hot attic until tomorrow morning—or, hell, till next week, if I wanted. I mean, what's my hurry? What is there to do besides what you want to do? It makes no damn difference how you spend your thousands and thousands of days on this earth. Your life will turn out one way or another, then you die, and that's that. So why strain yourself? Relax. You know, maybe if I had the chance to explain this philosophy to Richard, he wouldn't have made me beat him senseless. But shit, I had the chance, I know. The thing is, I wanted to beat him senseless. And so my life has assumed true, heroic proportions because I had a dangerous villain to face, and now he is in the hospital, looking like he fell off a roof. Except, what if he had somehow stabbed me or shot me? Then it would be me in the hospital, and my life would have *tragic* proportions—which are just about as good as heroic proportions. I mean, it's like I said, what damn difference does it make?

Of course, I could tell the old man was astounded at all of the horrible details I was revealing there in the emergency room, but he didn't say anything until we were riding home, and then he really let loose about family togetherness, and how if I'd only *told* him who killed Zekey or who flung that rock through my window or who was terrorizing me with an illegal wop knife, something could've been done long before this.

I said, "C'mon, Dad, that's hogwash and you know it. Jesus, say I *did* tell you, OK? How was the family going to save me?"

"Nobody was gonna *save* you. That's not what I'm sayin'. Look, Bernie, you got your family to help you, see? You gather your family around you when you're in trouble."

He had the car radio pumping out loud old-style music. I turned it off. "OK, how were you gonna help me, then?"

"We coulda given you support. If you only opened up to us, you know? Christ, that son-of-a-bitch shoulda been locked up when he killed Zekey."

"Yeah, Dad, but who was gonna lock him up? You? How would you prove he did it? Hell, say he even admitted it, what do you think the cops would do? Zilch, that's what."

"Oh, Bernie, it's too late now. You ran away to Cleveland. I'll never know what made you do that. But, see, we shoulda faced the son-of-a-bitch at the beginning. What was the bastard's problem, you know? We coulda found out, and then we would have *acted*. Insteada sittin' on our asses. And this knife crap, this black-rock crap, woulda never happened. What you do is you talk to his parents, you talk to the school principal, you talk to the police, you talk to him. You let 'em all know about this bad blood between you, see, and then if anything else happens you have this background to refer to, that they all know about, and you got everybody on your side, the police, your family, and you're not all *alone* against him. You got support."

I just sat there beside him, shaking my head. Because I know the way I did it was the only way I could've done it. Even Latham took a long time to realize that. But the old man was very worked up on the subject, I guess because the day had been pretty tense for him, too. The way it went was poor old Barbara came bursting into the house in tears, yelling to my mother that Richard was chasing me down with a machine gun, and my mother just about keeled over. The cop cars were there when my father and my sisters got home, which must've been pretty impressive. They all calmed down somewhat when the cops found the machine gun in the old wicker basket on the seat of the Chevy, because then they knew all he could do was stab me. He was out of bullets anyway, it turned out.

For a long while I stumbled back along the beach, clutching that cigar box like a football until I realized, fuck me, am I nuts? I can't go strolling home with a loaded .22. I was going to just loft the gun out into the water and ditch the box, but I figured Latham would be disgusted with me if I did that, so I buried it again under a notch in the seawall. I'll have to dig it out, though, before a full moon comes around, or else the tide will catch it. The first people that got a load of me were these four water-skiers in the middle of dumping all of their equipment into the boat, gas cans, cushions, sodas, rope, beach bags, and that junk. They were amazed and concerned, and the older guy, a college guy, drove me home, and then the cops questioned him.

They all cried when they saw me, Barbara, my mother, my sisters, it was awful. My mother had made this lemonade for the police, and there was hardly any left for me, so I had pineapple juice. I could barely talk, I was so thirsty. Then my father made me go with him into the bathroom to get slightly washed up, and when he peeled off my bandage, he said, "You're going to the emergency room," and off we went. My father told Barbara he would drop her off on the way, and so she came, just leaving her bicycle here, which reminds me I will have to bring it in if it starts raining again. She said she would phone me tonight to see how I was feeling, and I said, OK, good, and before she got out, she leaned up from the back seat and hugged me hard around the shoulders. She had on Coppertone. When she slammed the door, I immediately thought of Leslie, who already was right where I was going, the hospital. I was imagining her in this all-white room, barricaded in by a bunch of machines with lights and screens of twitching, electric lines, and her eyes shut. I did ask the friendly nurse who led me to the stitching room if she knew Leslie. She said no, but maybe the doctor did, but the doctor didn't either. It's a big hospital. I suppose everybody will visit her whenever the hospital lets you go in, and maybe she'll be OK, too, you never know. You can hope.

"Oh, easy, easy, easy," I'm saying. She's pecking and nipping my arm. "I'm just giving you some fresh air." On days like this the heat in the attic is like cotton, and you have to have a little air, or you could pass out. It bakes you. L.R. walks around in there, ruffling and cooing. The breeze is wet through the window, and warm.

Oh, God, it's the *phone*, and feet running over the floor to get it. It's for Lizzie, which is a relief. I know Lee's bound to call all breathless for the exact, complete story, and I don't feel like blabbing about it, though in a way I sort of do feel like it, because he'll enjoy it so much, and I'll really be a hero then. But if he calls, maybe I'll just say I'll see him tomorrow. Whenever Lee and I go on and on with our phone calls, my mother always says, "Tell him you'll see him tomorrow," but I never have tried that because I always know I'll have other things to talk about tomorrow. Now that I think about it, I realize I've *got* to go to school tomorrow, even if it is against doctor's orders. Everybody will want to see me and talk to me. I will be a celebrity, and nobody will get on me for not doing my French or my *Of Human Bondage* report because I have a good excuse.

"You dumb bird," I say. She's trying to peck my hand through the screen. Her neck is shimmering like an oil slick, and she's cocking her head at me, jerking it back and forth and in and out like one of those Egyptian sideways dancers.

"Dinner!" my mother's singing out below. "Come to dinner!" It's pot roast, which I love, and potatoes and carrots and salad. I stretch up, and I can feel all my little pains, sort of like a sunburn, but deep in. In fact, I am sunburned. Also, I am barefoot because my tennis team sneakers are in my gym locker, and at the hospital I guess they took the bloody one of the old pair I usually wear, and so now I have only one sneaker, which I was just going to throw out because what can you do with one sneaker? I decided to keep it, though, because it's the one I wrote "WINONA" on, and "Ho Ho" and "Hobbes High" and "GO Dolphins GO." I thought maybe I would send it to Winnie in the mail, in a plain box, but that's probably a stupid idea. Besides, you can hardly read it any more.

"Dinner!" my mother keeps singing out. Somebody just put a record on.

"Coming," I say. Heading slow down the clogged stairway, I realize, God, now we're all going to sit and eat and talk and act like everything's normal. But hell, I guess actually that's fine with me. It's all pretty much normal now anyway.

DON BREDES *was born in New York City, and raised in the Long Island suburbs. A graduate of Syracuse University and the University of California, Irvine, he has taught high school English, and is now at Stanford University, writing a second novel with the aid of a Wallace Stegner Fellowship.*